By the Same Author

a novel by

Carl Djerassi

The University of Georgia Press

Athens & London

Published by the University of Georgia Press

Athens, Georgia 30602

© 1998 by Carl Djerassi

All rights reserved

Designed by Richard Hendel

Set in Bodoni Book by

G & S Typesetters, Inc.

Printed and bound by

Maple-Vail Book Manufacturing Group

The paper in this book meets the guidelines

for permanence and durability of the Committee on

Production Guidelines for Book Longevity of the

Council on Library Resources.

Printed in the United States of America

98 99 00 01 02 C 5 4 3 2 1

Library of Congress Cataloging in Publication Data

Djerassi, Carl.

NO : a novel / by Carl Djerassi.

p.   cm.

ISBN 0-8203-2032-3 (alk. paper)

I. Title.

PS3554.J47N63   1998

813′.54—dc21   98-6748

British Library Cataloging in Publication Data available

To

GEORGE ROSENKRANZ

and

ALEJANDRO ZAFFARONI

for a cumulative century of friendship

Preface

At first glance, most readers would pronounce and interpret the title of this novel as a negative expletive. But all-capitalized—each letter pronounced separately—NO is also the chemical formula of the simple, diatomic molecule nitric oxide, which in 1992 the multidisciplinary journal *Science* named Molecule of the Year under the cover title "Just say *NO*." As will become clear, both meanings are relevant to this fourth volume in my science-in-fiction tetralogy.

In contrast to science fiction, the much rarer genre of science-in-fiction is based in real, or at least plausible, science. Except for some minor predating in chronology (to fit my plot), no significant aspects of the newly discovered biological properties of NO are made up. Nor, for that matter, is the conduct of the various scientific protagonists, entrepreneurs, and lawyers. They may not exist, but their manners and practices are right on the mark.

As a chemist, I could not resist the temptation to consider in these days of rampant chemophobia the recent extraordinary discovery that nitric oxide (NO)—an industrial gas and environmental pollutant (the discovery of which was honored by the 1995 Nobel Prize in Chemistry)—does in fact fulfill a singularly complicated and sophisticated function in the human body, where (continuously generated) it serves as a biological messenger, indispensable in a staggering variety of processes, including penile erection. This, in turn, led me to use the therapeutic treatment of male functional impotence as the vehicle for illustrating the role of a biotech company in contemporary biomedical research.

Current investigations on erectile dysfunction center around a device called MUSE (an acronym for Medicated Urethral System for Erection), the invention of VIVUS, Inc., a California company of the 1990s. The originator of MUSE and founder/chairman of VIVUS, Dr. Virgil Place, has generously provided me with unpublished technical information on the treatment of male impotence, which I have woven into my plot. But *caveat lector:* my description of the fictional MUSA system (Medicated Unit for Sexual Arousal and also the name of the genus to which the banana plant belongs) and especially its incorporation of NONOates (the class of nitric oxide releasers recently described in a report published by the National Cancer Institute) should by no means be read as constituting an endorsement of any treatment for erectile dysfunction.

Since my own scientific contributions in reproductive biology have focused on women rather than men, I could not resist introducing a second biotech development involving ovulation prediction—a current focus of my teaching at Stanford University. The electrochemical approach and the fictitiously named Wizard of Ov described in this novel are based in part on very recent developments by Conception Technology, Inc., in Fort Collins, Colorado. But the same caveat applies here as well: I take no responsibility for any child's paternity or any failure in sex-predetermination based on the use of this novel's Wizard.

———

The research scientist's culture and mores are tribal. Like most such behavior, scientific tribalism is acquired by example, by apprenticeship via a mentor-disciple relationship, and by intellectual osmosis rather than through textbooks or lectures. Members of the scientific tribe rarely describe their cultural practices, not because they have signed a covenant of secrecy nor because one's own cultural routine is rarely articulated but because research scientists generally are uninterested in dialog with the lay public. In science, professional advancement and recognition depend solely on approbation by one's peers, not on communication with or approval by nonscientific outsiders.

As a long-term insider of this tribe, I am attempting to narrow the ever widening gulf between the scientific community and the other subcultures of contemporary society—the arts and humanities, the social sciences and, most strikingly, the culture at large—through the medium of science-in-fiction. Until now, my novels focused on the academic world, but here I have entered into the biomedical field, where a great deal of exciting science and idiosyncratic practices occur as well. In *NO*, I have moved to another subculture with which contemporary science exists in a sometimes uneasy relationship: industry—more specifically, the small, entrepreneurial, research-driven enterprises sometimes collectively referred to as biotech.

As a founder, former officer and director, and occasional gadfly of several such companies—as well as a university professor—I am intimately familiar with this setting. Furthermore, in contrast to "big" industry, biotech companies of the eighties and nineties are a uniquely American phenomenon born out of academia (much of it right in my own backyard—the San Francisco Bay area). Because of their intellectual origins in educational institutions, biotech ventures have generated a series of contentious problems, arising from the interaction of profit-driven enterprises with supposedly nonprofit institutions and (ideally) disinterested individual scientists. These have caused numerous legal, philosophical, and ethical debates that will continue to influence the conduct of science within the academy, as well as the ways it is disseminated into the economy and culture at large.

One other issue that I have chosen to highlight here is the scientist's overwhelmingly patriarchal clan culture in which my fictional, and at times not so fictional, characters move. In my fiction I invariably return to two gender issues: the historic marginalization of women in the male-dominated scientific universe and the attempts of modern women, as well as some men, to change this state of affairs. No wonder most of my female characters are "independent"—a pejorative term to some but the ultimate compliment in my own eyes.

A striking phenomenon of the contemporary science scene is the remarkable Asianization of the American academic research laboratory: Asians now represent in certain disciplines, such as chemistry or engineering, the majority of graduate students in many American universities. In many of these institutions, more than half the postdoctoral fellows (the most exploited but also most productive sector of the research establishment) have received the bulk of their college or university education in Asia. Initially overwhelmingly Indian and Japanese, since the 1970s they have become outnumbered by Chinese and occasionally Korean visiting scientists or immigrants.

Of particular interest to me are the challenges facing the women from India for whom Renu Krishnan, the main protagonist of *NO*, is meant to be prototypical. Since their academic language back home is English, they do not suffer most of the overt language problems encountered by Chinese or Japanese scientists working in the United States. Yet like all Asian women in contemporary American science, Indians remain triply marginalized: as women in a historically male-dominated field, as foreigners of color (even should they become naturalized citizens) and, finally, coming as they do from a culture in which a woman's role is clearly defined, by the process of eventually losing part of their native culture without gaining an acceptable new one. Renu Krishnan represents a distillation of the complicated conflicts faced by such women. As she attempts to negotiate the demands of a traditional Indian family, while shuttling between a thoroughly modern American research environment and a more ambiguously poised Israeli project, Renu confronts in a pressing personal form the problem of bridging gaps between widely divergent subcultures that has been the challenge facing all my characters—and especially me, the immigrant scientist turned fiction writer in his adopted language.

1

"'So what are you doing at Brandeis about getting stiff pricks?'" Felix Frankenthaler mimed in a high falsetto. "What a bummer of a day," he sighed an octave lower, sinking wearily into his favorite easy chair. "I never realized my job description included fawning. They call it 'fund-raising': catering to tactless, uncouth matrons is more like it. When I accepted a full professorship at Brandeis I thought they wanted me for my research brilliance, my insightful teaching, my thoughtful collegial spirit — "

"Stop it, Felix," interrupted Shelly, who had instinctively covered her mouth to hide her incipient laughter. "We both know your virtues. What's bugging you? What happened at the banquet? And who are you talking about?" she prodded him gently.

"'Stiff pricks,' she said! I was trying to educate my table partners about our current research — the nitric oxide work, you know. 'Make it snappy and exciting,' Art — that development honcho, the chubby one with the repp ties — told us all before letting us loose among the alumni deep pockets, and look what happened. I suppose that's what he gets for letting the research faculty do his job for him. He called us 'stars.' Can you imagine him thinking we could be bought off with — that? And then this woman!"

Frankenthaler halted with an indignant gasp, evidently out of air.

"What you need is your usual nightcap," his wife said on the way to the kitchen. "Then you can tell me all about it."

"Ah," Felix said, cautiously sipping the steamed milk, flavored with just the right amount of cinnamon and precisely three drops of vanilla extract — the combination that years of experience had shown Shelly Frankenthaler to be the most effective soporific for her husband. But when he looked up from the cup and shook his head his face still held the same irritated expression. "I still don't know where I went wrong. I didn't make the obvious mistake, at least. I could've told them that nitric oxide is an industrial pollutant on a global scale," his voice had taken on a parodic tone, veering from portentous lecturing to over-excited salesmanship, "but that, recently, hot shots, like yours truly, here at Brandeis's Rosenstiel Basic Medical Sciences Research Center discovered that our body's cells communicate with each other through exquisitely timed, minute puffs of NO. I could then have told them that NO can exist in three different redox forms — positively charged, negative, or neutral — "

"By which time you would have lost most of your audience," Shelly smiled good-naturedly at her husband.

"Precisely! So instead, I kept it simple. I just told them not to confuse ni*tric* oxide, NO, with ni*trous* oxide, N_2O, which is ordinary laughing gas. But I couldn't just leave it at that, could I?"

Shelly shook her head sympathetically.

"I suppose that's where I slipped. My instincts as a pedagogue took over. I told them that these tiny wafts of NO mediate an extraordinary range of biological properties ranging from the destruction of tumor cells to . . ." he slowed to a halt and gave a rueful smile. "I *could* have said 'to the control of blood pressure' and let it go at that. But instead, I said, 'to causing penile erection.' After all, our fund-raiser's advice was to make our research sound exciting, and penile erection certainly excites. But note: the words 'stiff pricks' never crossed my professorial lips!" Frankenthaler leaned back and took several swallows of his milk. "I was about to add a politically correct remark, namely that the work was being pursued by a woman postdoc, an *Indian* to boot, but the bitch — "

"Felix!"

"Sorry," he said, hiding contrition by emptying his mug, "but that loutish woman really irritated me. So I just clammed up. I figured this was Art's party, he could save it. Why should I tell them about Renu Krishnan? That I was about to send her for a few months to Jerusalem to work with Davidson at Hadassah?" He narrowed his eyes. "Do I perceive a touch of disapproval in my spouse's eyes?"

The hard edge behind the banter did not escape his wife. "Disapproval? Certainly not. Of course, you could've been a bit more diplomatic and not displayed your penile erection — "

"Shelly! Puh-leeze."

She raised her hand. "You're too impatient tonight. Just let me finish. I meant that instead of flashing your penile erection work without warning, you could've prepared your audience."

"Very clever." Frankenthaler made no attempt to hide his sarcasm. "In what zippered fashion would *you* have done it?"

"Oh," she waved her hand airily, "I would have started with mention of the *retractive* penis muscle of the bull. Frankly, the word 'retractive' is less aggressive — admittedly also less exciting — than what you exposed at dinner." She leaned over to pat her husband's hand. "I would have outlined Gillespie's work on nanc nerves and his interest in neural transmission, then mentioned that the only reason he picked the muscle in a bull's penis is that it is a particularly rich source of such nerves."

"I'll be damned," Frankenthaler exhaled. He meant it admiringly, and Shelly, who knew her husband's nuances, took it as a compliment. Frankenthaler was amazed that his wife — a confirmed nonscientist — had remembered what he had told her about the origin of his own interest in NO research. It had started with something he'd read about nanc nerves. Had she remembered because he had explained to her — but that had been ages ago! — that when Gillespie in Scotland pursued the unknown neurotransmitter in non-adrenergic, non-cholinergic (nanc) nerves — the nanc signal — it turned out to be the same unstable, mysterious substance discovered in the endothelial cells of blood vessels by Furchgott in New York? Furchgott had called his endothelial relaxing factor — a fundamental and hitherto undetected mediator in the body for controlling blood pressure — EDRF. Eventually, the causative factor for both phenomena was found to be the simple diatomic molecule nitric oxide. Which was where Frankenthaler came in: blood flow is also indispensable in penile erection, and there, too, NO happens to be the key. Discovering how NO is produced in the body and how it is delivered had become his Indian postdoc's assignment in the laboratory. Renu Krishnan's responsibility was to pave the way so that clinical applications could actually be implemented.

"Sure," he said, his pride in his wife having mollified his temper. "But if I had followed your gentle, diplomatic route, by the time I reached our work on penile erection, neither that odious woman nor anyone else at the banquet would have been paying much attention. Besides, my dear, I was there to raise money for Brandeis, not for someone in Glasgow or New York. But enough of that. I have a long day tomorrow and it's time to go to bed. Both of us."

2

Here I sit thinking, which usually means talking to myself. Of course there is nothing wrong with that. According to a famous Russian, most people take this approach. "Thought itself is nothing but inner speech or social conversations we have learned to perform in our heads," my roommate at Wellesley — who was fond of spouting Mikhail Bakhtin, among others — once quoted.

I may have had a liberal education, but I still feel like an idiot. Here I am, twenty-six years old, with a postdoc in chemistry at Brandeis, and by most accounts a mature adult, yet I can't repress giggles when my professor asks whether I want to spend a few months in Jerusalem.

How would I explain it? "Professor Frankenthaler, a few days ago I received a letter from Ashok." Blank stare. He would probably think that Ashok is a town in India. There is always so much to explain: "Ashok is my brother, a computer scientist in Bangalore." And I suppose I would have to add that Bangalore is India's Silicon Valley and that it was Ashok, when he was a graduate student at MIT, who convinced Mummy that I should go to college in America.

"Renu is barely seventeen!" our mother had cried, but Ashok knew that our wonderful but very Indian Mummy would say that. "You know father would have approved," he countered, in a tone implying that he had just returned from a consultation with Papaji. "She will go to Wellesley, an all-girl school" (of course, he used the words girl and school rather than woman and college) "that is practically next door to MIT, so I can keep an eye on her," he said. He never volunteered that he'd already slipped me the application forms, that I had returned them to Wellesley, and that I had gotten smashing TOEFL scores. That last part, of course, would not have surprised my mother, who felt — long before my father's death — that first-class English was an absolute prerequisite for the marriage she had in mind for her daughter.

If I had tried to tell all that to Professor Frankenthaler, he'd have interrupted me long before I got around to mentioning the arranged marriage. "Get to the point, Renu," he would have said, politely enough, because he is polite. But I would have stopped then and there. I wouldn't have told him the rest. Not that the Prof wouldn't have understood. He prides himself on his "ethnic sensitivity," which is particularly cultivated in a place like Brandeis. But I would have been totally embarrassed. Embarrassed not because I am Indian but because I have lived here for nine years. I don't feel like an Indian woman anymore. I'm not sure I know just what that feeling is anymore. Or how much more I would have to explain before the Prof could understand why the prospect of a trip to Jerusalem should make me giggle.

If it hadn't happened in the late sixties at Wellesley, graduate school at Stanford in the early seventies would have changed me anyway. My first roommate in Palo Alto certainly helped the process along. Megan Reed was an MBA student, a stylish one. In bars she ordered Kir, in restaurants, ceviche, filo-covered finger food, arugula — never lettuce. She knew how to dress (one of her idiosyncrasies was a preference for thigh-high stockings rather than panty-hose), and she attracted interesting men in such quantity that I couldn't help but become the beneficiary of the overflow. Thank God, Ashok had returned to India by then. My brother is modern but not that modern. Ashok would probably even have disapproved of my

Stanford Ph.D. supervisor — a man who rode a chopped Harley-Davidson to school.

I hear from Ashok every couple of weeks. His letters are full of news and photographs and all kinds of clippings. When he sent the page from the Indian Express with the heading "Match Makers," I laughed as I scanned the entries. I used to read that page daily back in India, when I was still an Indian Indian teenager, although even then I was amused. Little had changed. Here was a "Handsome, God-fearing, sober, simple and unfortunately an innocent divorcee youth seeking details from Malayalee Ladies of similar character status. Those unwilling to conceive again will be considered." And farther down the column, an "open-minded male partner" was sought, "preferably with profound interest in cosmology, metaphysics, philosophy and raja-yoga; with strong belief in good and virtue, and with an urge to perceive the secrets of the universe and life."

Only then did I notice the entry highlighted with yellow marking pencil: "Alliance invited from well-settled professional Brahmin boy, 28-33/180 or taller, U.S. connection or green card preferred, for U.S. educated girl 26/152, fair, attractive, science Ph.D. Reply with horoscope to Box 1501-C, Indian Express, Madras-2."

It is true that I am 152 centimeters tall, twenty-six years old, and "fair" — a polite code for "light-skinned" — but so must be many thousands of Indian "girls." (I hate that word. And "boys"? If I marry, I want a man, not a boy.) But with an American Ph.D. in science? India is a huge country, but the number of 152-centimeter Indian "girls" from Madras with such a qualification must be very small. Just how minute that number was I discovered when I read my brother's letter.

What Ashok wrote was a curious mixture of explanation, excuse, and expiation. He didn't ask directly, "when do you plan to get married?" Instead, he dealt with my marital status as if it were a business question to be decided between him and my widowed mother. According to him, our mother had started to fuss now that I was starting to approach thirty (approach? I have four more years to go!). I'm sure it would have been different with Papaji. I was barely fifteen when we had our first 'man-to-man talks,' he used to call them. And now — with me a Ph.D. from Stanford — they were *treating me like a girl. Mummy, of course, wanted to engage a tra-ditional matchmaker, a request that Ashok had cleverly (his descrip-tion, not mine) deflected. According to him, the "Grooms Wanted" section of the* Indian Express *was likely to throw a much wider net for suitable candidates — an argument that apparently won the day with our mother since it did not exclude the possible involve-ment of a real matchmaker in the winnowing process.*

Then the excuses started. An advert (isn't it curious, I thought, that Ashok, with a master's degree in computer sciences from MIT, still used the British term?) would not only produce more choices but it would also delay matters: it would give me more time (for what? I wanted to hoot). Furthermore, by adding the bit about the U.S. connection and green card, he'd managed to insert a desidera-tum (again his word, and how infuriatingly precious!) that might actually produce some candidates in America whom I might then wish to interview personally. The horoscope part was purely a con-cession to our mother. ("It can't hurt," he'd had the nerve to add.) He never thought to excuse his use of girl *and* boy, *of course, and somehow that was worst of all. My sensitivity shows how un-Indian I have become. Ashok and Mummy were simply following* Indian Ex-press *house style, where unmarried women below the age of thirty are referred to as girls. After that, the newspaper converts them into spinster girls or just plain spinsters.*

And finally the expiation, puny as it was: "Mother didn't want you to know about the advert," Ashok wrote. "You might think her old-fashioned. But I thought you had to know. You have to admit that by comparison to the others, ours is rather modern and factual." Modern? *I wanted to shake Ashok. With a horoscope? "Please," he finished, underlining the word, "don't tell anyone that you know about it."*

It took me a day or two to see the humor of it. After all, they couldn't force me to see anyone answering the ad. And they wouldn't even dream of making me accept their choice. And when the Prof came up with the idea of sending me to Jerusalem, I couldn't help but smile. Imagine the scene in Madras when my first letter from Israel arrives. My mother has no idea that Brandeis is a Jewish university. (Not that there aren't plenty of non-Jews, even Indian grad students

---

7

and postdocs, around. The chemistry department is full of them; in the Rosenstiel Center we have a Sengupta and a Pakrashi.) But Hadassah Medical School in Jerusalem? How are the prospective grooms bearing green cards going to make appointments?

That's why I started giggling when the Prof asked if I wanted to go to Jerusalem.

"Renu," Felix Frankenthaler said a few days later, "I just got a call from Yehuda Davidson in Jerusalem. He would be delighted to have you work in his lab. All I have to do now is to raise some cash — $25K ought to do it."

"I don't want to try the NIH." He leaned closer across his desk as if disclosing a trade secret. "They take too long. Besides, I don't want the competition to hear what we have up our sleeves. At least not yet. And $25K certainly does not justify displaying all your cards before some NIH Study Section full of. . . ." He raised his eyebrows without finishing.

"I called the REPCON Foundation. Their director, Melanie Laidlaw, is an old friend."

"Wouldn't that disqualify her?" asked Renu. "I mean," she added quickly as she noted Frankenthaler's frown, "won't she disqualify herself?"

He waved his hand dismissively. "We are asking for peanuts — $25K. No overhead, no equipment, just funds for some exploratory research in male reproduction with a clinician in Jerusalem. And for a woman! It's not for nothing that 'REPCON' stands for 'Reproduction and Contraception,' and they're always complaining about the paucity of women working in the field. How could a female director turn down funding another woman, especially" — he threw her a brief smile — "one as bright as you?"

He rose from his chair to indicate that the meeting was over. "By the way, I haven't been able to get hold of Melanie Laidlaw. She's supposed to be in Europe at some sort of Kirchberg Conference on Science and World Affairs. I don't even know where Kirchberg is. But we'll hear from her soon enough. Anyway, you won't be ready with your first NO-releasers until next March at the earliest, will you?"

3

Jerusalem, April 8, 1978

Dear Prof,

Shalom! I should have written earlier, but the first week in Jerusalem has been hectic.

The language problem is minimal. Virtually all the people I deal with at Hadassah speak English. They have put me up at a house on Ethiopia Street with the rather imposing name Hadassah Organization Living Accommodation — Number 6A for short. Like everything else here, it has a history: originally a private home owned by Armenians who lost it during the War of Independence, it was successively a school, a TB hospital, and then a Hadassah dormitory for summer students. At one time some physicians also stayed here because the rent was very cheap. (The story goes that they got it by using "Vitamin P." The P stands for *protektzia*. The English word is shorter: "pull" or, more politely, connections.) Now, Number 6A is a women's residence for Hadassah personnel.

Ethiopia Street is narrow — essentially one-lane, with high walls on both sides — and is named after the Ethiopian church next door. More or less across from us is the Swedish Mission, while the end of our street overlaps with the fringes of Me'a She'arim. Quite a combination for a couple of blocks: Ethiopian Monophysite Christians, Scandinavian Protestants, and then the Orthodox Hassidim. As the only Hindu in our neighborhood, I am fulfilling a broadening ecumenical function. For that, I wore a sari at an all-women party the other day.

The No. 27 bus goes directly to the Hadassah hospital on Mount Scopus. The bus stop is only a few minutes away, but the walk takes me through the lower part of Me'a She'arim, where I never get tired of people watching. Orthodox Jewish men refuse to look at women, which means that, for a change, I can look at men the way they usually examine women — namely with unfiltered curiosity. It's like looking at someone through a one-way mirror.

The commuting takes time, and so do daily errands and shopping for items I should have thought to bring, such as a 220-volt hair dryer that will fit the local plugs. And then there is the relatively primitive selection of cosmetics and female sundries available here — a deficiency I would not have expected in the year 1978. But mostly, I have been engaged in settling as quickly as possible at Hadassah. I had not realized that the main campus, containing the medical school and the big hospital, was several kilometers west of here in Ein Kerem. It lies beyond the city limits, past the Holocaust Memorial at Yad Vashem.

I was taken to the memorial on my second day. Now I know why: it immediately gives an outsider a perspective on Israel's preoccupation with survival. I'd never given it much thought before — rather amazing ignorance, I now realize, for somebody at Brandeis. After a few days here in Jerusalem, I can already see that the terms "Jew" and "Jewish" have many more connotations here than in America. I am grateful to you for giving me the opportunity to appreciate that difference.

Professor Davidson still has an office at Ein Kerem, because he still teaches there, but his research unit and patients are now at the original Hadassah Hospital on Mount Scopus, reoccupied after the Six Day War. There is a lot of reconstruction going on — and there are major plans for expansion — but I am beginning to realize that for my work I will need access to facilities currently not available at the Mount Scopus site.

Yet what the hospital lacks in scientific amenities, it makes up for in its spectacular location. Out the window of my small laboratory (in a building designed by Erich Mendelson), I look east along the Jerusalem watershed, beyond a nearby Arab village and the barren Judean Hills, all the way to the shimmering haze marking the Dead Sea. And the stones! There are rocks and stones everywhere. It seems as if the land around here gives birth to new ones the moment some are used for construction (which is going on all over the city). The overpowering impression is of the absence of the color green. Even the trees are dusty, but somehow everything fits in with the surroundings. Like the Jewish cemetery by the Mount of Olives: no flowers, not a blade of grass — from a distance even the headstones look like strewn rocks. I feel positively Biblical (a novel experience for a Hindu!) sitting by my desk, which I have turned around so that I face the view.

You made a marvelous choice in sending me to Professor Davidson. He has not only read but also truly absorbed all the material you sent him about the neurotransmitter functions of NO. And what he doesn't know about the penis is not worth knowing. Which reminds me: he thinks absorption of my synthetic NO-releasers may be more efficient through the urethral mucosa than by direct injection into the corpus cavernosum. This just may be the breakthrough we have been looking for. He thinks I should get in touch with a Dr. Jephtah Cohn, active in bioengineering at the new medical school in Beersheba, about possible delivery vehicles. Finally, Professor Davidson is contacting an acquaintance of his, a vice president of Ben-Gurion U named Menachem Dvir, to see whether he can help financially with our project. I'll keep you informed.

That's it so far. Tomorrow, Monday, there is going to be an award ceremony at the Knesset for the first group of Wolf Prizes in Science. I had never heard of these prizes before, but the *Jerusalem Post* is touting them (somewhat grandiosely) as Israel's Nobel Prizes. They include mathematics and agriculture — two disciplines not covered by the original Nobel — which seems to be the Wolf Foundation's attempt to upstage the Swedes. Apparently, the Wolf Prizes have been taking some flak from the Israeli scientific community, because each is accompanied by a cool $100,000. The feeling around here is that the money could have been spent more productively in support of research within Israel, rather than giving it to scientific bigwigs from abroad who, according to the locals, already have too much money. In any event, most pillars of the local scientific community decided to boycott the ceremony. And so has Professor Davidson, who gave me his invitation. He said I might as well go and admire the Chagall tapestries, since the ceremony is being held in the hall where they are hanging. But I'm also looking forward to seeing those foreign bigshots — this is probably the closest I'll ever get to Stockholm!

With warmest regards, Renu.

"Renu," a voice called through the closed door, followed by several knocks. "Telephone for you. From America."

The Hadassah residence on Ethiopia Street was homey and comfortable, with some pleasing touches: the high ceilings, the stained green window shutters — a vivid contrast to the cream color of the Jerusalem stone masonry — the oriental tiles in the hallways, and the disarming, hand-written sign on the front door with its aging latch bolt: *You are kindly asked to SLAM the door when you enter and leave the house!* But it also had its primitive aspects — such as the communal bathrooms and public telephones — that Renu hated. Privacy was not one of the strong points of the establishment.

"I called to find out how you are getting settled." Frankenthaler sounded concerned. "I haven't heard from you or Yehuda since you left Boston."

Renu gave a précis of the letter she had mailed the day before, adding a brief description of the Wolf Prize ceremony and of the disapproving response of the Israeli scientific community.

"Here you have the only country with a biochemist as president, yet Ephraim Katzir managed not to appear." Renu knew quite well that this was the kind of scuttlebutt the Prof throve on. "The prime minister, Menachem Begin, had to take his place. I was surprised at the intensity of the objection, but one of my younger colleagues at Hadassah explained it for me. She pointed out that the Wolf Foundation made one mistake. They should have had at least one Israeli among the first group of winners. She predicted that as soon as an Israeli scientist gets a Wolf Prize, and they think *they're* in line for $100,000, the locals will show up. But you should have seen — "

"You said $100K?" Frankenthaler interrupted. "The Wolf Prize? Never heard of it." Ordinarily, Frankenthaler would not have admitted to such ignorance. But the six-digit dollar figure his favorite postdoc had just dropped got the better of him. "What are those categories again? Who does the nominating? Who won?"

"Two men from the Midwest — I think Wisconsin and Illinois — in agriculture. And two in math — one from Russia, the other from Germany. I'm afraid I don't remember their names. And there were three in medicine who got it for their work on the histocompatibility antigens."

"Snell from Bar Harbor?" Frankenthaler interrupted.

"Yes. For his work in mice. Dausset from Paris and Van Rood from the Netherlands shared it for their work in humans."

"Who else?"

"Ah," exclaimed Renu. "For me, the most exciting was in physics: it went to Wu from Columbia. I always heard that she should have shared the Nobel Prize with Lee and Yang for her contributions to the discovery of nonconservation of parity. It was nice to see a woman win it. *Alone*," she emphasized.

"Is that all? I'm surprised they don't have a prize in chemistry."

"I nearly forgot," exclaimed Renu. "Chemistry had a single winner with a crazy spelling. . . . Djerassi, that's who got it."

"You mean Isaac Djerassi for his work on methotrexate treatment in leukemia? I met him last year in Pennsylvania. The Israelis ought to have been pleased by that choice — he's a Bulgarian Jew, who was trained at the Hebrew University before moving to the States. But I would have expected him to get it in medicine, not chemistry."

"Not *Isaac* Djerassi. *Carl*. From Stanford. He got it for the chemical synthesis of the Pill. I don't know why I didn't mention him first. I once went to a lecture of his on the future of birth control — dismal according to him — when I was a graduate student in biochemistry at Stanford. A good speaker, but a bit arrogant, I would say."

"Aren't we all?" Renu could hear his chuckle over the crackle of the telephone. "Now tell me what you've been doing in the lab so that *we* can win a Wolf Prize." He chuckled again, but louder. Just as the *we* registered as a slight blip on Renu's mental radar, the chuckle ended. The Prof was waiting for her answer.

Jerusalem, April 28, 1978
My dearest Ashok,

The envelope already told you I am in Jerusalem. What it doesn't say is that I have been here now close to a month. I didn't want to tell you or Mummy about it before I knew what it was like to work here. I didn't want either of you to be upset, I suppose, until I knew myself whether the trip was worth worrying you.

On the whole, I am glad I came. I seem to be the only Indian around — most certainly at the Hadassah Medical Center where I am doing my research — although I understand that there are some Cochin Indian immigrants in this country. And yet I do not feel scrutinized or subtly discriminated against, as I do so often in the States.

I can see your face, Ashok, with that severe frown line down the middle of your forehead. "I don't want to hear about the States, I want to know why you went to Israel," you are probably muttering. I came because Prof Frankenthaler thought it was an interesting opportunity. It's connected with the very hot NO project I wrote you about earlier, which is going very well, thank you. But I also came to put some distance between me and the marriage advert in the *Indian Express*. As you undoubtedly know, there are no diplomatic relations between Israel and India, nor air contacts. I would first have to fly west in order to go east if I were foolish enough to consider interviewing prospective candidates.

The advert bothered me more than I wanted to admit —
to you or to myself. I started to feel like a commodity, not
even an all too marketable one at age 26. But I think I'm
over it. I suppose that's the real reason I've put off writing
until now. Working here in unfamiliar surroundings and under
conditions that are more time-consuming but also more
"Indian" (for instance, there is no real supermarket around
my neighborhood) gives me little time for sulking or even
planning alternative strategies.

The absence of an American-style supermarket is likely
to be a pain, but for the time being I relish the more Indian
experience of going to the market. I am staying in a rather
charming hostel for women from Hadassah — mostly used by
nurses and single, female medical staff — on a wonderfully
quaint street close to the Ethiopian church, onto which I am
looking from my window. The dark, domed roof with the
complex Coptic cross dominates my view, but interspersed
among the pine and cedar trees, which are rather common
in this old neighborhood, I can see the ubiquitous rooftop
cylindrical water heaters with their umbilical connections to
the solar panels pointing south. (We ought to have more of
these in India.)

On my first week, I joined one of the nurses for grocery
shopping to learn the local ropes. At a fruit and vegetable
stall we walked into a seeming fight between the owner and
a housewife. When I asked what all the uproar was about,
my guide explained. "They aren't fighting. The woman
asked whether he had cucumbers and the man bellowed,
'Do I look like I don't have cucumbers? Do I look like I
don't eat breakfast?' 'I didn't ask about your breakfast,' the
woman yelled back." I laughed, and I was pleased that I
understood the allusion. In what other country do you get
cucumbers every day for breakfast? In our hostel they are
served with cottage cheese, tomatoes, white bread, and
some nondescript white cheese that I skip. But I find the
tomatoes and cucumbers a refreshing change to my cereal
and low-fat milk back in Waltham.

So much for local color. For the time being, I'm busy pushing forward with my research. My present grant allows me to stay here for three months before returning to Brandeis. So you and Mummy need not worry. I should be back in less than eight weeks, unless something happens. I don't know what. I'm not hinting. There is just so much going on right now (the work is pointing in so many promising directions), it's hard to rule anything out. I will let you know.

All my love to Mummy and you, Renu

P.S. A few days ago, I met an irritatingly intriguing man who persuaded me that if you want to find out something from a person you have just met, start most of your sentences with "w" words. We met in Beersheba, not Jerusalem, but more about that in my next letter.

I'd already been here long enough that I'd started calling everybody by their first names, the way the Israelis do.

"Shalom," he greeted me. "I'm Jephtah."

"Shalom," I replied. "I'm Renu."

"I know," he said. "Menachem Dvir told me all about you. You're the American woman who came to Israel to solve the problem of all men."

"I'm Indian," I corrected him, but he waved the correction away.

"So? You come from America."

It was our first encounter. I never dreamed that it would change my life.

Funny, I thought, this business of first names. It's another way of identifying a person's national origin. In Israel I'm "Renu." In America it would've been "I'm Renu Krishnan." In France or Germany I'm just "Krishnan." Maybe I'm generalizing too much. Yet like most generalizations, this is often true.

"Shalom," he repeated and shook my hand. I couldn't help but reflect on the ambivalence of a handshake. It's like a hyphen — simultaneously connecting and separating. Ultimately, the meaning of a handshake can only be interpreted by the pressure, just as the meaning of a hyphenated word can only be understood in mov-

ing from one component to the other since, by definition, the real import of the hyphenated word cannot reside in either moiety. And then, with the handshake not yet completed, he said an astonishing thing. "Your hand and wrist . . . they are so easy." There was a sense of wonder in the way he pronounced those words.

How often do you get a compliment you've never heard before? When you do, you're prepared to overlook all kinds of trivial faults — especially faults of the blunt, Israeli variety. As I found out during our first day together, his seeming brusqueness was a veil for an initial shyness with women, especially foreign professionals, that appealed to me.

"Have you been to Masada?" he asked. "To Elat? To the Dead Sea? To — "

Jephtah was one of those who compensated for shyness with an overflow of enthusiasm. I laughed. "I haven't been anywhere but Jerusalem. I came here to work and I have so little time."

"But you must," he insisted. "I will be your guide. I, Jephtah Cohn."

He said the name with a disingenuous pride that seemed somehow to go along with his shyness. "Jephtah," I mused. "I've never heard that name before. What does it mean?"

"'He will open.' Firstborn males sometimes get that name. And Cohn is just a compression of Cohen — the priests."

I didn't think of it until later, but as I traveled back to Jerusalem, checking my appointment book, I found myself musing on his name. The four letters of his family name might have been drawn from the periodic table: carbon, oxygen, hydrogen, and nitrogen — the four elements defining all life. Jephtah Cohn, I thought. "He will open life."

A silly thought. And yet it made me shiver.

4

While in Israel, Renu had spent little time worrying about what to wear. To the lab, she wore jeans, or occasionally pedal pushers or culottes, and blouses, of which she had an ample supply, anklets or knee-high socks on her legs, and espadrilles or sandals on her feet. She was there to work, after all. And, besides, she had the type of slender build on which anything looked good, even a lab coat. Her deep-dark chestnut eyes — *drownable* one of her more verbal American admirers had once called them — and her hair — long, burnished, ivory black — were the features on which she lavished most of her attention. In Israel, where the choice of cosmetics was limited, she could at least play with her hair; she did so with much more extravagance than she had ever back in Massachusetts. At times she sported a mango-sized chignon or a long, thick braid, or perhaps a French twist, a straight, seductive sweep flowing over her right shoulder, or even pigtails tied with grosgrain ribbons.

After her return to the States, Renu continued to expend more time and effort on her face than had been her habit before she went to Israel. And whenever she arranged her hair or fixed her eyes in front of a mirror, Renu thought of the marriage advert: "26/152, fair, attractive." Other than her age and height, what did it really tell prospective grooms? What about her eyebrows, which were straight rather than arched, as if they'd been drawn with a ruler? Or her hair, her unblemished skin, . . . the *easy* hands and wrists? Or her lips, for that matter? Lately, she had been paying particular attention every time she outlined the baseline of her full lower lip; her favorite color: rose de garance. It was Jephtah who had pointed out that, without lipstick, there is no real line. The bottom of the lip simply merges gradually with the skin until it vanishes. "Ask any portrait painter," he'd said on the same day he'd run his pinkie lightly down her nose. "Did you know that when they draw a face, painters always start with the nose? Yours is quite classic."

Today, back in Massachusetts, Renu was paying very much attention to her wardrobe, as well as her face. She was flying to New York with Professor Frankenthaler on the eight o'clock shuttle from Logan. The forecast was for a hot and muggy August day. Ordinarily, that would have meant bare legs, an airy sundress, sandals. But today they were going to the offices of the REPCON Foundation, and nobody had to tell Renu how important this meeting was.

"Renu," Frankenthaler had said after her return from Jerusalem, "you have convinced me. It's worth trying. But if you want to go back to Israel soon, NIH funding is out of the question. In fact, I don't know anyone who will consider a grant application that quickly. Even private foundations have their rules and bureaucracy. You are talking about a fair amount of money: between funding your stay for a year — "

"It may take longer than that," she interposed. "Better make it two."

Frankenthaler cocked an eyebrow. "That long? Even more expensive then. But even for the first year — between you, Hadassah, and the man at Ben-Gurion, you're talking at least $100K. And then there is our cut for the Rosenstiel here at Brandeis and travel. . . . Better think of close to $150K."

"So what do you suggest?"

"Let's go to New York," the Prof offered. "You and I. Melanie Laidlaw ought to meet you. She should hear from your mouth what you think could be done with your series of nitric oxide progenitors and why you need to do it in Israel. She wants to see more women active in reproductive biology, so let's demonstrate to her that her discretionary money was well spent. Now if she could give us $150K. . . ." His eyes rolled heavenward as if he were praying to some god of reproductive funding. "One can always dream," he laughed.

———

Renu took one last look at the yellow trapeze dress reflected in the shiny elevator door. My mother believes in horoscopes, she mused,

———

and I have a lucky color. The frock was sleeveless but otherwise primly conservative, as was the combination of flesh-colored panty hose and black pumps. Renu hated "frocks" — they were something she always associated with English women. Even in the States, Renu had a problem knowing how to dress formally without using a sari or picking a frock. She hated herself for capitulating to colonial fashion rather than wearing something more natural to her, like Indian pants — churidars or salwars — with a kameez on top. But today, Renu was capitulating. She wanted to blend into the REPCON executive suite, to let the science speak for itself. Her hair was cinched in the tightest chignon she could manage.

Felix Frankenthaler's innocent comment, "Renu, how elegant!" produced only a forced smile and an even tighter grip on the satchel bag containing her papers. She had dressed up for the occasion, but that didn't mean that she wanted the Prof to notice. Had she overdone it? she wondered.

The Prof had warned her not to talk down to Melanie Laidlaw — in fact not to simplify anything. "Remember, she's not only got a Ph.D. in biochemistry. She also looks at most of the REPCON applications, which means that she's seen a lot of unpublished stuff you and I know nothing about. Laidlaw is the sort of person who will ask you if she doesn't understand something. So just relax. Mazel tov."

Renu couldn't help but smile. It was the first time the Prof had used such a Jewish expression with her. Was this a tribute to her status as a temporary Israeli?

———

Renu was surprised by the thoroughness with which Dr. Laidlaw inspected her while shaking her hand. Just as she had concluded that the appraisal seemed remarkably male, almost military, she was disarmed by a smile. "It's good to see a woman working in andrology. Tell me what you have in mind if this grant should be approved and, more to the point, why you think you need to work in Israel."

"If you don't mind," Renu said, "I'd like to get to that later." Melanie Laidlaw's eyes narrowed slightly at this, but it was too late now for any backtracking. "How much time do I have?" she asked.

The incipient frown on Laidlaw's face relaxed. "You two came down from Boston to see me, which I appreciate. I'll let you know if you take too long."

"Thanks." Renu leaned forward to place a stack of pages on the coffee table with the writing facing her host. The Prof had once told her, "Renu, if you need to go over notes with someone facing you, try to follow them upside down. It'll show the person that you really know the material — especially when you deal with chemical structures." Renu had followed Frankenthaler's advice from time to time while reporting on research progress across the professor's desk, but today's performance involved much higher stakes.

"May I take it for granted that you are familiar with recent work on the cellular functions of NO?" Seeing Laidlaw's brief nod, Renu continued. "So let me summarize some background in just a couple of schemes." She pointed to the top of the upside-down page in front of her.

"I'll just review briefly how NO is made in the body. The natural substrate, of course, is not the gas itself. In mammals, at the cellular level, the key precursor is arginine," Renu pointed to the chemical structure of this naturally occurring amino acid on the upper-left corner of the sheet, "which gets oxidized to hydroxyarginine." This time, Renu's pencil tip focused on one of the terminal nitrogen atoms of the arginine structure to specify the point of attachment of the newly introduced oxygen. "A further oxidation step produces citrulline," her pencil moved to the second structure, "which for our purposes is now garbage — and nitric oxide." On her scheme, the chemical formula NO was written in large red capitals.

"Of course, this looks simple on paper, but the details of the cellular biosynthesis are quite complex. Several academic groups have worked on this topic: for instance, Michael Marletta at Michigan."

She glanced quickly at Frankenthaler, who seemed to be shaking his head. Was that her imagination or was he signaling her to stick to the facts? He knew the Marletta story and how it had gotten Renu interested in nitric oxide. Marletta, then a young assistant professor at MIT, had been Renu's first research mentor. She had worked in his lab while still an undergraduate at Wellesley. He had started on a seemingly innocuous line of research — into the production of nitrate and nitrite in the body — research that the promotion committee at MIT considered so unexciting that it denied him tenure. His move to the University of Michigan, where he was now one of the brightest stars in the field of nitric oxide research, had occurred in the year Renu graduated from Wellesley. Rather than joining Marletta during the hassle of setting up a new research lab, Renu had chosen Stanford University for her Ph.D. In the end, she had regretted that decision — not because a Stanford Ph.D. wasn't a marvelous union card but because she had missed out on the opportunity to be one of Marletta's team members on the work she was now describing to Laidlaw. But why tell that story, other than to point out that she had been present at the very beginning?

"There are other academic groups active in the field, like Snyder's at Hopkins, Stuehr's at the Cleveland Clinic and, of course, lots of pharmaceutical teams such as Paul Feldman's at Glaxo, Murad and Kerwin's at Abbott, and especially Moncada's at Wellcome in England," she continued.

"The key to the biosynthesis of NO is an enzyme, nitric oxide synthase," Renu's pencil tip moved to the red letters *NOS,* "but this itself is not sufficient. For activation, NOS needs to associate first with the calcium-binding protein calmodulin." The pencil tip moved to a big circle designating that complex.

"I'm starting with these details in order to explain at what stage I arrived on the scene." She indicated Frankenthaler, who had been listening quietly while leaning back in his corner of the sofa. "These NOS-promoted steps leading to the production of NO involve no fewer than five electron oxidations — very fancy redox biochemistry. That field, and especially the question of biological electron transfer, was the focus of my Ph.D. thesis at Stanford. So when the opportunity presented itself to join Professor Frankenthaler's group as a postdoc to work on some aspects of the biological *function* of nitric oxide, I jumped at the opportunity, because in one way or another electron transfers are involved in every step."

"Lucky for both of us," Frankenthaler smiled.

"But now back to the *biosynthesis* of nitric oxide before moving to its function, which in turn will bring me to my work in Israel. I won't take long. . . ."

She glanced up at Melanie Laidlaw, who waved her on. "Take your time."

"There are three nitric oxide synthase enzymes — not just one." Renu turned to the second sheet. "One NOS," the pencil tip touched the upside-down word *endothelial*, "deals with blood pressure regulation. And as you will see in a moment," Renu again looked up for emphasis, "this is my current focus.

"Another NOS." Renu's pencil touched the word *neuronal* part way down the sheet, "is involved in nerve signaling. Incidentally, these two forms of the NOS enzyme are constitutive — always present in the cell, always available to create small puffs of the gas itself. This is actually one of the amazing features of nitric oxide at the cellular level. In contrast to all other chemical signal transducers, which move from one site to another through very complex biochemical mechanisms, NO simply behaves as a typical gas. . . . Like in this room: it diffuses rapidly out of the cell and can do so for quite a distance — say perhaps forty microns in one second — which could encompass quite a number of adjacent cells. Professor Frankenthaler has called this the 'promiscuous nature' of nitric oxide. What we still don't know is how such diffusion out of the cell acquires any sort of directionality."

"How do you measure these minute quantities of your promiscuous gas?"

Renu was taken aback by Laidlaw's interruption. Is she testing me, or does she really want to know? She shuffled through a few pages, taking care to maintain their upside-down orientation, until she located the appropriate one.

"Here you have a list of the current methods." Her pencil tip danced down the page as she briefly summarized the first three techniques: chemiluminescence, electron-spin resonance, and spectrophotometry. "The fourth," she moved to the bottom of the page, "is accomplished by the electrochemical oxidation of nitric oxide to nitrate. When you do this, the amount of electric current generated is directly proportional to the quantity of NO present. That's the method I've been focusing on, because it allows me to measure the NO produced in any particular instance rather than just over time, which is the limitation of the other techniques."

"Okay?" she asked.

"Okay," replied Laidlaw. "You were talking about the different forms of NOS when I interrupted."

It took Renu a few moments to return to the original order of her schemes. "Here is the last NOS, an inducible form of the enzyme, which is pushed into action only by extracellular stimuli. It's basically a defense mechanism operating by . . . chemical warfare." The metaphor had just slipped out, but Renu was pleased by it; over her shoulder she heard Frankenthaler's low chuckle. "The gas may kill the invading cells outright or do it indirectly by inhibiting some metabolic pathway of the attacker."

She turned to the next page. "Let's move on to function, for which we need another common enzyme, guanylate cyclase." In her eagerness to emphasize this enzyme's role, Renu forgot her upside-down perspective. The pencil line above the words, however, rested there for only an instant before Renu corrected the move by circling the two words. "This enzyme is an exquisite sensor for nitric oxide. The moment it 'sees' the NO" — four of Renu's fingers drew the quotations marks in the air — "the enzyme starts to generate cyclic GMP." She didn't even bother with the full term — cyclic guanosine monophosphate — for this cellular messenger molecule. "And this, in turn, promotes increased blood flow through vasodilation. But cyclic GMP is gradually destroyed by the enzyme phosphodiesterase. So if one wants to maintain vasodilation, one has to provide more NO or look for other phosphodiesterase inhibitors." This was an area Renu knew little about. A quick transition to the next subject seemed to be the safest way to avoid embarrassing questions. The ploy worked.

"These days, everyone's trying to answer two burning questions: how does NO activate this enzyme — to which we have some answers — and how is the guanylate cyclase turned off — for which we do not yet have an explanation.

"Now let me jump to function and utility." Renu turned the

sheets on the coffee table in the same tempo as the conventional "next slide" commands in a lecture, the short pauses offering a few precious seconds for reflection.

"The potential importance of nitric oxide produced by this inducible NOS is vast — in immunology, and perhaps also against other noxious agents such as intracellular parasites. At the neuronal level, there is a lot of speculation whether NO acts pre- or post-synaptically, whether it represents a new method of 'broadcasting' synaptic messages" — Renu's fingers twitched quotes again — "and, most intriguingly, whether it is the putative retrograde messenger so crucial in memory."

"We could all use some help on that front." Frankenthaler's dry comment was his first interruption. Without intent, it momentarily derailed Renu's carefully organized sequence.

"Yes. . . ." she said, uncertain until she remembered another piece of professorial advice from her mentor: "When you get stuck in a presentation, bring up some promising utility — theoretically feasible but as yet totally unproved. They can't argue with you, which means that you are again in charge of the agenda."

"There are other promising potentials here," Renu began, speaking slowly as she struggled to come up with them. "NOS stimulation and NO production have been hypothesized as participants in the daily resetting of the biological clock. Who knows, maybe we can — "

"Say NO to jet lag!" exclaimed Laidlaw. "Sorry," she added quickly, "I couldn't resist. But seriously, I hadn't realized that NO is also involved in circadian rhythms."

"It *may* be," Renu said quickly, "at least according to some recent work at the University of Illinois. But at Brandeis we've been focusing on the endothelial form of NOS — which works basically on blood pressure. Which brings me to *my* work." Renu leaned back, relieved to have regained the initiative. "Nitric oxide has a very short half-life in the cell. It needs to be produced all the time. There are chemical NO-releasers. Nitroglycerin is one of them; its effectiveness in treating cardiovascular diseases is almost certainly due to its NO-releasing function but, so far, other releasers — known releasers, that is — are few and far between: nitroprusside and nitrosoacetylpenicillamine and a few others. To track down more, I set out to synthesize a novel series of compounds, quite unrelated to the natural precursor" — Renu quickly returned to the very first sheet to circle the relevant molecule with her pencil. "In vitro at least, using an isolated rabbit aorta, my compounds look very promising. These materials should permit relaxation of the smooth muscle of various organs — "

"Which takes you to the corpus cavernosum and penile erection," interrupted Laidlaw.

"Precisely," said Renu somewhat archly. She had not wanted to be rushed into a discussion of impotence, but she could see there was no putting it off. "Impotence — or more appropriately for our purpose, erectile dysfunction in men — has been treated in many different ways. Beyond mechanical means" — Renu had known nothing about surgically implanted or inflatable penile prostheses, vacuum constriction devices, and related contrivances until Jephtah Cohn back in Beersheba had given her a crash course — "some approaches have involved direct injection into the corpus cavernosum of agents such as papaverine or prostaglandins. But now," she raised her palm as Laidlaw seemed to be about to interrupt, "that we know nitric oxide to be the active messenger for dilating blood vessels throughout the crucial areas in the penis, which of course includes the corpus cavernosum, we wonder," Renu's head turned toward Frankenthaler to demonstrate that her *we* included *him*, "about possible clinical applications of synthetic NO-releasers."

"I appreciate that." The manner in which Laidlaw pronounced the words suggested that the interview was about to terminate. "You've made a good case and I wouldn't be surprised if our committee decided to act favorably on your application." Her gesture included Frankenthaler, who had started to straighten in his chair. "But why Israel? Why not work here in the States?"

Why indeed? That's what Jephtah had asked — after he had told me how my hand and wrist were "easy." "Why are you in Israel? When did you arrive in the country? Where did you — "

"Stop," I laughed. I had barely gotten off the bus. "Is this how

*you greet strangers?" I asked as we walked through the scorching
sun to his car, a dusty Volvo 121, its inside temperature high enough
to sterilize glassware.*

*"Wait," he commanded and spread a towel over the passenger
seat. "I don't want you to get burned." Only after we got moving,
with the hot, dry desert air rushing through the open windows cre-
ating a modicum of comfort and a maximum of noise, did he answer. "If you want to know something about a stranger, start your
sentences with 'w' words: why, where, when. . . ."*

*We spent the rest of the day and evening together, exchanging
information about each other's scientific work and answering each
other's whys, wheres, and whens. I couldn't help but be infected by
Jephtah's enthusiasm for the new university. And his tales of academic improvisation!*

*According to Jephtah, prior to the 1967 war, when access through
the West Bank was impossible, Beersheba had lots of hotels, because
tourists had to stay overnight on their way to Masada and the Dead
Sea. All that had changed after the Six Day War, when Beersheba
returned to its status as a sleepy provincial town with a single tourist attraction (the weekly Thursday Bedouin market) and one hotel
(the Desert Inn). The new university buildings had not yet been constructed. Lectures were given in converted storefronts, and the various departments were housed in whatever digs they could find. Some
of the chemists had settled in one of the bankrupt hotels, the Ein
Gedi, which explained why one professor's office had a bed and sink,
since he'd simply moved into one of the guest rooms, whereas the
chairman of the department had established himself in a converted
bathroom. Their most precious instrument, an X-ray diffractometer,
dependent as it was on a steady water supply, got the place of honor
in the former kitchen where the ancient plumbing, which lost pressure every time a toilet was flushed, made it an instant invalid. "But
the department survived, and it's now one of the best at Ben-Gurion,"
Jephtah concluded with a proud grin.*

*That night, under a sky that seemed so laden with stars that you
almost felt like ducking, he took me to the nearby settlement of Omer,
to a hill overlooking Beersheba, to the gigantic concrete monument
created by the Israeli sculptor, Dani Karavan, commemorating the*

Negev Palmach Brigade of the War of Independence. The trip there at night, the only illumination the Volvo headlights and the stars, was a fitting end to a memorable day: the tall tower, the sweeping concrete forms — like sinking ships in a sea of desert sand — the simulated bullet holes, the stark inscriptions in a language I could not yet read, and finally the huge cave-like tunnel into which we stepped, with the lights of Beersheba shimmering at us from the distal opening. . . .

It was here that Jephtah introduced still another "w" word, different from the whys and wheres. "Will you?" he started. "Will you come back?" "Will you let me show you the Negev?" "Will you — "

"Lama lo." The words just popped out, whereupon we both broke out laughing. It was one of the Hebrew expressions I had picked up, because nearly everyone back in Jerusalem had answered my requests with lama lo.

"Why not?"

Research scientists generally measure time by three non-synchronized clocks: a ticktock metronome for life outside the lab; a dawdling slowpoke — at least adagio, more often even largo — while waiting for the outcome of a grant application; and then the researcher's favorite — a peculiarly idiosyncratic chronometer, which can move prestissimo, even though, more often than not, it might stop or even retrogress.

It was this second clock that had taken Felix Frankenthaler by surprise this time. He had expected fast, indeed expedited, treatment following the personal presentation of the grant application in New York. As the months dawdled by, he became irritated, then annoyed, and finally pissed off by the tortoise pace with which their application crept through the supposedly greased bureaucracy of REPCON. A year had passed without any real news. "God," he had muttered to Renu, "we would have been better off with the NIH."

Yet, much as Felix enjoyed pestering his friends, he didn't feel comfortable badgering Melanie Laidlaw in her capacity as director of REPCON. The only progress report he had received consisted of one unsolicited phone call: "I'm having some problems with referees," she reported, "wondering why the work needs to be done in Israel, but I think it will go through." And go through it finally did, just before Thanksgiving.

Frankenthaler heard the news directly from Laidlaw during the intermission of *Aida* at the Met, shortly after the triumphal procession on the stage — the brassy fanfare rolling satisfyingly through his thoughts for the rest of the evening.

Still in a triumphant mood, he reported the splendid tidings the next morning to Yehuda Davidson in Jerusalem and to Menachem Dvir in Beersheba in two pithy telegrams: "Penile erection funded."

By 1979, international telegrams were already considered an inefficient as well as unfashionable means of communication. But Frankenthaler was in no hurry. Indeed, he wanted to document his pleasure in a few concise words that might also serve to embarrass a straight-laced clerk. Oral communication he reserved for his protégée, whom he telephoned from New York.

"Renu," his voice boomed into her ear. "Mazel tov." Frankenthaler barely stopped to take a breath. "Our application has at long last been approved — and without any cuts in the budget. You can count on two years of support." He chuckled. "You can buy yourself an apartment rather than move back to your Hadassah hostel."

"It isn't exactly a hostel." Renu felt that her Jerusalem abode merited some defense, "but I'm afraid we forgot to add the purchase of a flat to our budget. . . . I'll probably rent something more private — now that I can make some longer-term plans. You might as well have said '*birkhotai*' — congratulations." Her excitement got the better of her; the Hebrew phrase came out as a whoop of triumph.

"Good God," he exclaimed. "So we've reached the point where an Indian goy translates Hebrew for an American Jew!" He shushed Renu's attempt at apology. "But you know, Renu, now that we have some travel funds, I ought to fly over after Commencement and stay for a week or so. That will give you about six months at Hadassah — ample time to provide something to talk about. Also, I want to meet your colleague Cohn."

5

"Renu! Renu!"

It took her some moments to locate the voice in the milling crowd outside the customs control exit of Tel Aviv's Ben-Gurion Airport. The mob was so thick and unruly, it reminded Renu of the international arrival hall in Delhi. Each passenger seemed to be greeted by at least three generations of family. Jephtah Cohn's waving hand rose above the human wall. "Here, let me take the bags," he panted, putting them to use as battering rams. "You look wonderful," he gasped. "I was worried I'd miss you."

He dropped the two suitcases by his side. "Let me look at you," he grasped her at arm's length. "Shalom, Renu," he murmured, taking a step toward her. "It's been nearly a year and a half. Such a long time."

"Shalom, Jephtah," she whispered back and threw her arms around his neck.

In the car, Renu started to shiver. She had never been in Israel in December. "Don't you sabras believe in using the heater?"

"I do," Jephtah rubbed her arms to stimulate her circulation. "But my car doesn't." He grinned at her, his teeth a white flash in the passing lights.

They'd been driving for a while, the aging Volvo filling the night with a hoarse roar. The darkness, occasionally broken by the headlights of oncoming cars, and their eager conversation had caused Renu to disregard their route. Suddenly, passing through a section of highway illuminated by high street lamps, she saw a large green highway marker in Hebrew, English, and Arabic. One arrow, labeled "Ashqelon," pointed to the right, the other, pointing straight ahead, read "Beer-Sheva."

"This isn't the way to Jerusalem. Where are you taking me?"

"Where else but to the metropolis of the Negev," he chuckled. "Courtesy of the Jephtah Cohn private tourist service."

"But — "

"I know: 'Professor Davidson expects me in Jerusalem.' In fact, he does not. When I offered to pick you up at the airport, I suggested that I take you first to Beersheba to show you a surprise. It's connected with our project," he added quickly.

Renu vacillated between amusement and irritation. Generally, she did not like to be surprised.

To mollify the irritation, he explained, "It's already Friday morning. You need at least one day to get over your jet lag, and you can't do any work in Jerusalem on Shabbat. So why not spend it with me in Beersheba?"

"With you . . . ?"

Jephtah ignored the implied question. "I told Menachem Dvir that you were coming to Israel. He didn't seem surprised. He seemed to have heard about your REPCON grant before I even got your letter."

Jephtah was a fast but careful driver. He had not taken his eyes off the road as they talked, but now she sensed a quick turn of his head toward her.

"He asked whether you had met Dr. Laidlaw."

It was her turn to look at him. There was something in his tone that suggested things held back, but his face seemed innocent as ever. "I met her last year," she said neutrally. "The Prof and I went to the REPCON offices in New York to make our sales pitch. And I met her again last month, when she asked me to stop by before my departure for Israel. She apologized for the delay in our grant approval. According to her, funding work in Israel took some persuading."

Again she felt a sweep of his eyes. Renu turned halfway to inspect Jephtah's profile. In the low illumination from the dashboard lights she could see his sharp, Semitic nose — *Roman*, she had called it when she tweaked it once last summer during one of her first overt gestures of affection — and his curly hair running over the edge of his turtleneck.

"By the way, she just had a baby. It's nice to see a woman her age having a child without giving up her profession. I wonder how she's managing." Renu said.

"Maybe she has the right husband. What does Mr. Laidlaw do?"

"I don't know who her husband is, but it isn't a Mr. Laidlaw. Justin Laidlaw was a biochemist at Columbia. He died a few years ago. But your mentioning Dvir now reminds me of something odd."

"What?"

"I didn't think anything of it at the time, but she asked whether I had been in touch with Menachem Dvir recently."

Jephtah didn't seem impressed. "Had you?"

"Of course not. The Prof handled all the administrative details. But don't you think it's curious how both Dvir and Laidlaw asked about each other?"

He gave the question perhaps two seconds' consideration before adding eagerly. "I'm just glad Laidlaw came through with your grant."

Renu smiled in the darkness. "Don't we have Dvir to thank too? Do you think they've been talking about us?"

Jerusalem, December 28, 1979
Dear Ashok,

Let me state at the outset that I do not at all regret surprising you again with a letter from Israel. Judging from your recent brotherly missives, you expected a response from Massachusetts focusing on matters matrimonial. I had plenty of reason to return to Israel, but your last letter represented one additional nudge. I think it was the photographs you included more than anything else that did the trick — although *your* short list of prospective brothers-in-law helped.

But I would demean the motive behind this trip if I ascribed it primarily to my irritated rejection of the matchmaking attempts of my family back in Madras. The main objectives are twofold — one professional, the other personal.

You know (though probably Mummy doesn't) that my work is starting to take a fascinating and potentially practical turn by addressing the problem of erectile dysfunction —

otherwise known as male impotence. (I can just imagine the response of prospective grooms, if, instead of "U.S. educated," your advert had described my present professional expertise!) I'm here working with Dr. Jephtah Cohn, from Ben-Gurion University in Beersheba. During the past year, he has come up with a marvelously simple approach for self-administration of an essential neurotransmitter into a man's penis.

Jephtah (in Hebrew his name means "he will open") is also my personal reason. When I arrived in Israel about two weeks ago, I stayed the first two nights in his flat. Since he is a bachelor (two years older than I), I presume that this stay alone should disqualify me from further consideration by Messrs. Coomaraswami, Kurtha, and the others I have already erased from my memory — a prospect that does not displease me. Before you jump to any conclusions about carnal congress, dear brother, let me inform you that when we finally went to bed around 3 o'clock in the morning in his small two-room apartment (that's all a junior faculty member gets here in Beersheba) I slept in his bed and he on the sofa in the living room. Considering the condition of his sofa and Jephtah's height (195 cm), you can see that he is very much a gentleman.

I think you would like Jephtah. He is good-looking — in an Israeli sabra sort of way — very smart, very practical, truly unaffected, a good conversationalist who never consumes all of the conversational oxygen by himself, and a terrible dresser (but so are most young men here). Also, like so many locals, he wears a perpetual two- or three-day shadow around the lower part of his face, which, I learned quite soon, can scratch. (I am in the process of persuading him that he looks equally manly when clean-shaven.) I nearly forgot one of his most charming qualities. Although he claims to be rather gruff in Hebrew, his sense of humor flowers when he switches to English. The other day he described a local professor as sounding "like a Tyrolean yodeler in the midst of a colonoscopy." Perhaps "Tyrolean yodeler" cannot be translated into Hebrew.

I hope that you might visit me here one day, once you have reconciled yourself to the fact that I am not prepared to follow the (Indian) marital route. This does not mean that your sister is against marriage. Quite the opposite. But it will have to be on my terms.

Let me end with the beginning of a fairy tale: "In the country of Israel, there is a suburb by the name of Omer near a town named Beersheba. In Omer there is a small apartment house in which there is a bedroom, and in the bedroom there is a double bed, occupied by a naked couple, the female partner of which is awake — writing a letter."

Consider this an affectionate declaration of independence from your loving sister, Renu

———

Jerusalem, February 25, 1980
Dear Prof,

Shona tova! I have actually started to take Hebrew lessons at an *ulpan,* which means that I am already beyond the shalom stage. As you can see, I can wish you a very belated "Happy New Year" like the natives. I'm taking the course because I have been spending a fair amount of time in Beersheba. The social life down there is limited to the people at the university, their family members and the like — a polyglot crew, as you'd expect in Israel, but it is amazing how quickly they all revert to Hebrew as soon as they socialize. I was getting tired of always asking what everyone is laughing or shouting about. Frankly, I can hardly wait for the day when I will understand a joke without Dr. Cohn's assistance.

He is the main reason why I've been spending so much time in Beersheba. He has surprised everyone, including Prof. Davidson, with the functioning prototype of the delivery system we plan to use for the Phase I clinical trials in Jerusalem. These will start as soon as Prof. Davidson has decided which α-blocker to use as a test case. He feels that it would be safest all around if we first test Dr. Cohn's delivery device for erectile dysfunction with a known hypotensive agent, before examining the nitric oxide releasers I brought with me from Brandeis. Prof. Davidson is looking at α-blockers already in clinical use for standard antihypertensive therapy but focusing on agents that are particularly effective on corpus cavernosyl tissue and thus potentially useful in stimulating penile erection. His group has been working in this area for quite some time, so much of the groundwork has already been laid. Prof. Davidson believes that men with diabetes mellitus — over a quarter of whom suffer from erectile dysfunction — would be the first appropriate clinical population in which such a product would find widespread application.

Dr. Cohn felt right from the beginning that self-injection into the penis with a hypodermic needle was not the way to go. While this was the intuitive subjective objection of a man disliking the idea of sticking a needle into his penis, the observation from the Davidson laboratory that absorption of certain pharmacologically active substances from the urethra is remarkably effective proved to be the clincher. Dr. Cohn was immediately attracted (as was I) by the apparent contradiction that the urethra, an organ adapted for *excretion*, could also serve as an efficient avenue for *absorption*.

His plastic prototype is a molded unit, consisting of a barrel-shaped handle, about 1.5 cm in diameter to which is fused a 4 cm long, essentially unbreakable tube of a couple of millimeters diameter — substantially narrower than a standard catheter. The stem fits into a hard plastic sheath, which makes the whole unit look like a short, chubby swizzle stick. To use the device, a man first urinates, then shakes the penis to remove excess urine, unsheathes the protective cover of the device, inserts the open end of the stem into his urethra, and slowly pushes it in for the entire length before pressing the plunger to release the active ingredient, which is contained in a minute pellet. The device is then withdrawn and discarded. The expectation is that the active ingredient will dissolve in the small amount of urine remaining in the urethra and then be absorbed and transported into the corpus cavernosum. At least, that's the plan. Of course, we all agree that it would be far preferable if the man could just swallow a pill, but none of us has so far figured out how to incorporate NO-releasers into an orally active formulation. According to recent scuttlebut some Pfizer researchers are working on a pill containing phospodiesterase inhibitors. I think they'll call it Viagra. We'll see who gets there first.

The Beersheba group has already coined a name: MUSA. It is an acronym, which does not stand for "made in USA" but rather for "medicated unit for sexual arousal." Dr. Cohn has made about a dozen units. One MUSA is being mailed to you for your scrutiny under separate cover with an appropriate label for customs clearance.

As you well recognize, this is a very short progress report. The real action will only start when the tube is loaded with some active ingredient to be selected by Prof. Davidson. But I have seen a blank MUSA inserted, and the whole procedure seems quite simple and certainly painless. With a bit of practice, it should take no more than twenty seconds from beginning to end.

It is already past midnight, so I am concluding with a hearty *Liala-tov,* Renu

What would my mother, my brother — just a few weeks ago, even I — have thought if I admitted to corresponding with my professor about penile erection and urethral insertion? In fact, what would my professor's response be if he knew of my participation in the premier insertion of a blank MUSA into a real penis? In true heroic medical tradition, the first volunteer was the pioneer himself — Dr. Jephtah Cohn.

If our research proceeds at the rate it seems to be going, I will have to acquire the blushless skill of openly mouthing simple un-

ambiguous words in a candid manner: penis, erection, ejacula-tion. . . . I have already learned that sabra humor is an effective solvent, if not diluent, of Indian female reticence. Initially, it was an effort, but it's fast turning into a habit, if not yet an addiction.

Sexual intimacy with a professor or boss — in other words across professional caste boundaries and levels of power — is fraught with dangers, complications, improprieties, and worse. My experience at Stanford taught me that. But with one's collaborator? And espe-cially one in the field of penile erection? It offers a freedom of ex-pression, of behavior, indeed of laughter, in sexual matters that I never before imagined, let alone experienced.

The first night in Beersheba, I was too bushed to notice Jephtah's eagerness, and he was too considerate of my exhaustion to display it. He didn't wait too long the following day, though. At breakfast he showed me the MUSA prototype. In retrospect, I realize I was being set up. It worked.

As he showed me the unit, he gave the prototypical sales pitch as well. "The occasionally used treatment for impotence — self-injection of papaverine into the penis by means of a twelve-millimeter, thirty-gauge hypodermic needle — is, in my opinion, a nonstarter. At least on the scale on which I eventually visualize this product being used. . . . Sure, diabetics know how to inject themselves, but most men are too squeamish with any sort of needle around their penis." According to him, for most men, sticking a needle into the penis would be incompatible with the two big E's — Erection and Ejaculation. I pointed to his MUSA prototype on the breakfast table and asked how his two E's would be compatible with the insertion of anything, even the blunt end of a MUSA stem, into the urethra.

Someone listening to our conversation through a keyhole would so far have judged it professional enough, though a bit flip. The MUSA happened to be lying on the table near a couple of bananas and a cucumber. In Israel, I had them often enough for breakfast. Only later did my sly Jephtah volunteer that he had served them that morning for their symbolic function. In any event, he readily admitted my point about a man's likely reluctance to insert anything into his urethra. It was one he had considered from the outset. That's why he'd coined the MUSA name. In his mind, the "sexual arousal" component of the acronym would be the direct outcome of the rec-ommendation — planned to be included in the package insert di-rections of an eventual commercial product — that the woman part-ner be the actual inserter of the device.

By way of illustration, he proceeded (with a skill that suggested some prior practice) to sculpt a passable replica of a circumcised penis out of a peeled banana, all the while reminding me of a taxo-nomic nugget I had forgotten: that Musa just happens to be the botanical genus to which this most phallic of all fruit — the ba-nana — belongs. "Here," he said, handing me the banana and the MUSA. "See how easy it is to insert." I just took the banana and bit the tip off. I don't know what made me do it. It seemed a very un-Indian response. I wouldn't even attempt to guess how the hypotheti-cal listener on the other side of the keyhole would have interpreted the decibel level of our laughter.

I've heard it said that sexual fantasies are exciting because they are totally private and tailor-made for the fantasizer. But I've never read any description of the excitement associated with straightfor-ward scientific discourse of highly charged sexual topics. It occurred to me that the right term for that feeling is jouissance—*a word that was fashionable among undergraduates during my Wellesley days. Back then, I was never quite sure what it meant. But I felt it that morning and so, I'm sure, did Jephtah.*

Quite deftly, he turned the conversation from the male's two E's to the female's three I's. Without even asking what words I associ-ated with these letters, he named them: Insertion, Insemination, and Implantation. "They're crucial," he announced. "Some women dream about them, others are terrified of them."

From there, it was just a small jump to discussing contraception. What did I think of the Pill? he asked. Did I use it? I have been asked that question before (though, of course, never in India) as a preamble to sexual dalliance. But at breakfast? I could have said that it was none of his business, but having just bitten off the glans of his sculpted banana, I felt I owed him more civility than that. So I turned the question around, asking what Israelis used, especially

---

38

in the army, since both men and women had to go through obligatory military service. "The Pill," he said unequivocally. What about men? I asked. Did they use condoms?

"Candom?" he echoed in Hebrew and shook his head. One could buy them in drugstores — primarily Durex from England — but if a woman was not on the Pill, mostly partners relied on coitus interruptus. Venereal diseases, it seemed, were an American problem, not an Israeli concern. "Have you ever been on the Pill?" he asked again. None of the aspiring grooms busily answering my brother's Indian Express adverts, no Kurthas nor Coomaraswamis, would dream of asking such a question. Indeed, if they'd heard the answer I gave Jephtah, they would have fled, never to return.

"Yes, but not now" was meant to imply that I was not a virgin, though currently not sexually active. Jephtah's nod convinced me that he'd interpreted my answer precisely that way, although women with dysmenorrhea are also known to take the Pill. But then he changed the subject. A winter rainstorm — an unusual event — had been predicted by nightfall. "Let's be tourists before the onset of Shabbat," he announced, and off we went in his Volvo, our destination David Ben-Gurion's Kibbutz Sdeh-Boker, some thirty miles south of Beersheba. "You, as an Indian, must see it," he announced mysteriously.

———

He didn't take me by the most direct route. On the way out of town, we passed the main mosque, the railing around the minaret's tip resembling a circumcision scar; facing it was one of the frequent reminders of competing cultures — the slender transmission tower of the Israeli military headquarters studded with microwave disks. When we crossed the main bridge over the wadi at the town limits, I was struck by another contrast, this one ecological: the boneyard barrenness of the surrounding desert and distant mountains, broken occasionally by the tamarisk and eucalypti planted years ago in Israel's first decades and the chlorophyll-green of the corn and cotton cultivated by the new settlers.

Jephtah's reason for the roundabout approach to Sdeh-Boker was that he wanted to pass by Nevatim — a settlement of Indian Jews *from Cochin — and another new-immigrant town, Dimona. The only adornment of the tan or ochre brick-and-concrete apartment blocks was the colored laundry hanging from the windows — the Negev equivalent of the flower boxes in the Alpine villages of central Europe. Soon, we were back in virtual desolation, except for occasional Bedouin encampments and the phosphate mines at the foot of the distant mountains. "Now watch," Jephtah alerted me as the road turned right. He slowed the car to a crawl.*

It was quite startling: the straight metal fence, topped with barbed wire, isolating several square kilometers of flat desert, girdled by a four-meter-wide belt of clean sand to display the tracks of any intruder. Shimmering in the distance, I saw a large silver dome and adjacent tall tower, all surrounded by palm trees. Was this oasis a Mecca of the Negev, a guarded mosque and minaret? Jephtah made a U-turn on the empty highway. "The nuclear center," he said, and stepped on the gas.

Kibbutz Sdeh-Boker was a true oasis in the sense that so many kibbutzim are: miracles of a blooming desert created by European, shtetl-educated immigrants and their descendants. To me, the most stunning aspect was the straight line, as if drawn with a ruler, that often separated a leaf-green field from the sienna desert. Jephtah had turned into a bubbling Zionist. He could hardly wait to show me the Desert Research Institute, established a few years ago, and another kibbutz, Revivim — meaning "rainfall" — the oldest in this area. "But first," he almost turned reverential, "I've got to take you to Ben-Gurion's home, where he spent the last twenty years of his life."

The moment we entered the small, sparsely furnished bedroom of Ben-Gurion's home, a white frame bungalow with a corrugated tin roof, I understood Jephtah's veneration. Every Indian would behave that way in Gandhi's last home. Then I noticed the only picture on the otherwise bare walls: Mahatma Gandhi — there in Israel, in the middle of the Negev I have to admit that it brought me to tears. The room looked as if Ben-Gurion had just left it. Books were stacked on the night table, black slippers were set by the narrow cot, the tips pointed toward the room as if their owner had just stepped out of them to get dressed. In the adjacent study, filled to the ceiling with books that overflowed onto the small conference table, again there was only one photograph: not of wife, family, or friends but of his military aide, who had committed suicide.

—————

We made it back to Beersheba just before the threatening sky finally opened up with a biblical deluge. Jephtah had stopped at a drug store. "Do you want anything before they close for Shabbat?" he asked. I just shook my head: this time, I had come well stocked with toiletries and cosmetics.

Back in his flat, as the rain resounded against the windowpanes, Jephtah lit the Sabbath candles. "That's about as religious as I get," he laughed and put the small bag from the drugstore on the table.

Late that night, after we had made love for the first time using one of the condoms *he'd purchased at the pharmacy, I practiced my first MUSA insertion — albeit with a placebo. "Jews are not supposed to do any work on Shabbat, but we can ask a* shikse *to do it for us," he said, handing me his MUSA prototype.*

"I thought you weren't an observant Jew," I joked, but actually I was excited by the idea. Not just because we were naked and amorous but because in a sense it was research. *The procedure took much longer than the claimed twenty seconds — I was too cautious, and we both laughed too much.*

The torrential rain suddenly brought back another Indian image. In contrast to the usual macho trade names of American condoms — Sheik, Trojan, and the like — a popular Indian version is called monsoon. *The season when, I explained to Jephtah, couples stay indoors and have sex.*

"Let's call these 'revivim,'" he said, and pointed to the imported Japanese condoms he had bought. After that irreverent Sabbath, the Hebrew word for rainfall became our code for sexual coupling.

—————

Erectile function is exciting territory. I would be lying if I didn't admit that I enjoy traversing it. As a professional participant — the only female in our research team — I can do so quite openly. I particularly enjoy it when Jephtah is present. Dissecting the responses of some of our male colleagues has become part of our pillow talk on the nights we share a bed. For that, the Ethiopia Street establishment in Jerusalem is out of the question, and so Beersheba has become the geographic omphalos of my sexual fantasies and realities.

Yet I have grown to love Jerusalem. It's time for Jephtah to become the amorous commuter.

6

It was their first Sabbath evening in the studio flat on Horkanos Street, just south of Hanevi'im, the Street of the Prophets. Renu had moved out of the Hadassah residence after two months of apartment hunting. From now on it would be up to Jephtah to commute on weekends.

The table was barely large enough for the ecumenical meal Renu had planned: the Sabbath candles, kosher wine, and braided loaf of kosher challah, interspersed with the Indian dishes she had managed to concoct with the aid of the all-purpose garam masala mix she had brought from the States.

"Ten candles!" Jephtah exclaimed. "Aren't you overdoing it?"

"Not for the Sabbath meal I've prepared for my Jewish man." She jabbed him affectionately. "Listen to what it says here." She reached for the magenta-covered paperback perched precariously at one edge of the table. "'It is meritorious to light as many candles as possible in honor of the Sabbath. Some light ten candles, others seven. In no event should less than two candles be lit. The candles should be big enough to burn at least 'til after the meal, and one should endeavor to procure nice candles.' And look at these Havdalla ones," she pointed to the braided candles, "surely they qualify as 'nice.'"

"They *are* nice." Jephtah tried to hide his amusement. "But

Havdalla are meant for the end of Shabbat, not the beginning. Never mind, they're nice and that's what counts." He reached for the book. "Let me see what you're reading."

"One moment." She pushed him away. "'The Talmud states: The one who is accustomed to buying nice candles for the Sabbath will have children versed in the Torah. It is, therefore, proper for the woman, when lighting the candles, to pray that the Almighty grant her male children, bright in the study of the Torah.' Now you can have it."

He ignored the proffered book. "And have you been praying?" He took her face between his hands, but Renu quickly wriggled free.

"Hindus pray in private," she said quickly and changed the subject. "Here, take a look at the book while I bring the rest of the dishes to the table."

"I can't believe it," Jephtah burst out. "*Code of Jewish Law* by Rabbi Solomon Ganzfried. What made you get this book? Where did you find it?"

"In addition to working with Jews, I'm now sleeping with one." She ogled him from the stove. "I thought I should learn something about Jewish religion and practices. A woman clerk in a bookstore recommended this one."

"But it's so *Orthodox*," Jephtah blurted. "It's the last thing I would have recommended. I wish you'd asked me."

"I wanted to surprise you . . . like using ten candles." She started to light them. "Also, we've hardly ever talked about religion. . . ."

"How much have you read of this?" He waved dismissively toward the book.

"Mostly I skimmed it. But there were sections on women, on menses, on sex — mostly when not to have it — that I read in detail. I never realized Jews had to cope with so many prohibitions. It seems that according to Jewish law, what is not prohibited is restricted."

"*Orthodox* Jewish law." He picked up the book, but then slammed it down. "The *haredim*."

"Relax, Jephtah, and sit down." She led him to the chair. "What are the *haredim*?"

"'Those who tremble' — presumably with the fear of God — the ultra-Orthodox," he grumbled. "And you can see that I tremble — with irritation."

"Relax," she repeated. "I'm not turning Orthodox. But I couldn't help reading some of it because I actually found it . . ." she hesitated, "funny, or at least entertaining. But let's eat. This is the first Shabbat meal I've ever prepared — even if it is Judeo-Indian cooking."

Jephtah grinned. He never held grudges for long. "I see the Judeo part," he pointed to the kosher wine bottle and the challah, "so where is the Indian?"

"Coming up, my Beersheba nabob." She lifted the cover of the serving dish. "Chicken Korma," she announced, waving the cover to fan a whiff of cardamom in Jephtah's direction. "Marinated for twenty-four hours in yogurt with yours truly's special garam masala, containing cardamom seeds from *green* pods, and then cooked with finely chopped garlic and onions. Chicken, not pork. Hindus, like Jews," she gestured with her head toward Rabbi Ganzfried's tome, "don't touch pork." She didn't mention her distaste for culinarily undisguised veal or beef — the remnants of an Indian habit she had never completely kicked, although a tasty, well-done hamburger and even a spicy Polish sausage had penetrated the Brahmanic taste barrier at Wellesley. Nor did she volunteer that she had made up for the sausage digression with a vegetarian interval in California as a mild sort of dietary penance. By now, Renu considered herself liberated from dietary laws, and she was, at least by Israeli standards.

"Delicious," pronounced Jephtah, who had dipped his fork into the serving dish before Renu had even laid down the cover, "but the author of your book back there," he gestured with his thumb without even glancing at the magenta-colored volume, "would not have touched it. Chicken and *yogurt*." He shuddered in fake horror. "I can hardly think of a more serious violation of Jewish dietary laws."

"All right," Renu covered the plate. "No meat for you. But there is a lentil, spinach, and ginger dish that should pass through your kosher filter. And rice," she started to spoon some onto his plate. "The yellow color is saffron, which, I am sure, will not cause you to sin."

"You can't scare me," Jephtah laughed and uncovered the chicken. "I've been known to eat pork loin, baked ham, bacon and eggs — you name it. Though not in Beersheba," he added.

———

With the dishes piled up precariously in the small sink and the candles still flickering, Renu and Jephtah moved to the sofa, which seemed hardly wide enough to accommodate two adults and Rabbi Ganzfried's *Code of Jewish Law*. Renu picked up the book.

"I want to tell you why I found some of the sections amusing. I didn't mean this in a demeaning way — Hindus are broad-minded when it comes to other religions. But what would you call this?" She flipped some pages until she found chapter 150. Assuming a censorious tone, Renu proclaimed: "'A man should accustom himself to be in a mood of supreme holiness and to have pure thoughts, when having intercourse. The intercourse should be in the most modest possible manner. He underneath and she above him is considered an impudent act.' Jephtah," she giggled mournfully, "we have behaved impudently. Wait," she put her hand over Jephtah's mouth. "Just one more, from chapter 151, which applies to our research. I quote: 'One is forbidden to bring on erection or to think about women. A man should be extremely careful to avoid an erection. Therefore,'" Renu snickered, "'he should not sleep on his back with his face upward, or on his belly with his face downward, but sleep on his side, in order to avoid it.'"

She let out a final guffaw before turning to Jephtah. To her surprise, he was barely smiling. "What's the matter? Do you think a rabbinical interdiction will be issued against MUSA and nitric oxide?" She grinned conspiratorially. "Maybe it's lucky that the chemical symbol is NO."

Renu took Jephtah's chin into her right hand and turned him around until they were facing each other. "What's the matter?" she repeated. "I thought you'd be roaring with laughter."

"Of course, it's funny on one level, but not necessarily in Israel, and especially not in Jerusalem. If the *haredim* ran this country. . . ." He shook his head. "They may not control what we do in bed, but they certainly could and would affect our daily lives. Just read the chapters in your book dealing with the Sabbath laws. Someone wise once called them 'mountains suspended from a hair.' The Torah lists thirty-nine major classes of acts forbidden on that day." He reached over to take the book out of Renu's lap. "Let's look how applicable some of those prohibitions are to life in 1980." His finger ran down the table of contents. "Here we are: chapter 80, 'Some Labors Forbidden on the Sabbath.'"

Jephtah turned the pages at a speed that made even skimming difficult. "'It is forbidden to shake off snow or dust from a black garment, but it is permissible to remove feathers from it with the hand,'" he read, and then went on, turning page after page. "There are ninety-three of them! I never knew that." He slammed the book shut. "But forget about erections, pious thoughts at intercourse, and who lies on top of whom — "

"God forbid!" Renu interrupted with a typically Israeli intonation that caused even Jephtah to laugh.

"That's just what the *haredim* say He did," he grinned. "But let me finish my rant. Let's take two crucial issues, marriage and childbirth, to show how hypocritical and politicized our system has become — almost a theocracy. Suppose you wanted to marry an Israeli Jew. You couldn't. Not in Israel, because only religious marriages are recognized here, and you would have to be a Jew to partake in one."

"So? I could convert. Hindus can be very open-minded about that."

Jephtah stared at her. "You would?" he stuttered.

"I might — theoretically, that is."

"But . . ." he said.

"But what?" she laughed.

"But nothing, I guess," he said lamely. "You'd have to do it the Orthodox way," he pointed to the magenta volume that had fallen to the floor. "They don't recognize other conversions."

Renu's eyes followed his finger. "No," she shook her head. "Not Orthodox. But there must be some alternative."

"To conversion? Here in Israel, none."

"I meant in getting married. You don't have to marry in Israel."

"Ah yes," he nodded. "You can fly to Cyprus for a civil marriage. That's the closest place."

"And when I return with my husband?"

"Under Jewish law, your marriage would not be recognized, and your children would not be considered Jewish." Seeing her shock, he rushed on. "Let me tell you why I'm so irritated by all this hypocrisy. If your parents were Jewish — say they were Cochin Indians — and you never practiced any form of Jewish religion, never went to synagogue, never followed even minimal Sabbath rules, not even what you and I just did — you could still marry legally in Israel. But if you, a Hindu, underwent a Reform conversion — for instance at Brandeis in the States — and fully practiced Reform Judaism, you and any child you might have would still be goyim." He shook his head in disgust.

"At least, he wouldn't be a bastard," Renu said consolingly.

Jephtah threw his hands over his head. "Bastard? Let me tell you something about Orthodox bastardy, what we call *mamzerut.* To be fair, the concept of *mamzer* according to Jewish law is often more liberally understood than elsewhere: a child born out of wedlock to a Jewish mother or to two Jewish parents is not a bastard, provided the union can theoretically be legitimized. But — and this is a monumental 'but' — if the mother is already married — in other words committing adultery — that child is considered a *mamzer.*"

"Why just the mother? What if the father were married?"

"He can screw around as much as he wants to," Jephtah exclaimed bitterly. "Though," he raised a warning finger, "the Orthodox law can also be more cruel. A *mamzer* can never marry a Jew, meaning that such a person can never be legally married in Israel, and that *mamzer* stigma can never be erased. It is passed on to all future generations: according to the Orthodox, for all eternity a *mamzer* can only marry a *mamzer.*"

"Maybe there is a historical reason — "

"*Maybe?* Of course, there is. There always is with us Jews. In this instance, the historical reasons — say two thousand years ago — made sense. I can respect history without having to accept that all bible history is unalterably applicable today. But that is exactly the view of the *haredim.*"

"How do you know all this about *mamzers?*" Renu was trying to defuse Jephtah's anger, but she was also curious.

"Because I am one."

It's amazing how one thing leads to another. If it hadn't been for my desire to surprise Jephtah with some Jewish touches for the Sabbath, I would never have run into Rabbi Ganzfried's book. I would never have pressed Jephtah's button about the haredim. *Oh, I suppose we would have reached that topic eventually. But now, in one fell swoop, I know more about him than I might have learned in months.*

Because the fact of his mamzerut *led to more explanations, more history, he did open up. I wish I could have met Jephtah's mother. A Holocaust survivor from Vienna, she eventually made it to Israel; her young husband disappeared in the camps. She married again in Israel and had two children, Jephtah, and his sister Eva. A few years ago, while Jephtah fought in the Yom Kippur War, Esther Cohn discovered that her first husband had survived and was living with a wife and children in Canada. According to Orthodox law, Esther Cohn's children were the progeny of an adulterous relation that could never be atoned for. Jephtah and Eva are perpetual* mamzers. *Eva, whom I would love to meet, has solved her problem — if it was one for her — by marrying a Reform Jew in Seattle. Is it because Jephtah's second-class status was only uncovered after he'd risked his life for Israel that he feels so bitter? The mother wanted to fight for her children's legitimacy in the rabbinical court, but she died before their case even made it to the docket.*

"Now I ask you," Jephtah challenged her. "Could you consider living in such a country? I mean really settling down?"

Renu shrugged. "It depends."

"On what?"

"The man."

Jerusalem, May 17, 1980

Dear Ashok,

I beg you not to play the role of an Indian father any more. Papaji is dead, and I have been away too long to be treated that way. Act like a modern brother, and help me make our mother feel less unhappy.

Even though the man I met here in Israel has not yet formally proposed marriage (and I am still sufficiently conventional that I would like him to take the initiative), I am quite confident that he will raise the question in the near future. When he does, I will accept.

This should make Mummy and you happy, because the marriage I foresee is in many respects the kind of marriage you are promoting, with one essential difference: I am making the decision myself, based on my feelings and knowledge of my future life partner.

With that future in mind, I am learning various aspects of Jewish religion. One of the aspects of life in Israel, or perhaps I should say of Jewish life, is the emphasis on family structure and value. We respect that in India, and they (or should I say, we) do so here as well.

I am studying at an *ulpan*, a kind of school where I am taking Hebrew lessons. I am picking up bits of the language, like *ulpan* itself, or *mamzer*. *Mamzer* is too complicated a concept to explain in a letter. However, one day I shall tell you a touching tale of the rescue of a *mamzer* by a Hindu maiden.

I am learning also about Orthodox Jewish practices. Not deliberately so (don't worry--I have no intention of turning Orthodox), but it's another one of those things you just pick up in Israel.

Did you know that Coca-Cola has been declared kosher for Passover? Not recently, but several decades ago. The Coca-Cola company considers the ingredients of Coca-Cola top secret, but they allowed Rabbi Tobias Geffen, the former Orthodox rabbi of Atlanta to examine them. He discovered that one trace component (present in one part per thousand) is made from nonkosher animals. In principle, this should not have been a problem, because if a nonkosher component is *inadvertently* present in a ratio of not more than one part in sixty, food is still considered kosher. In the case of Coca-Cola, however, the trace component is added deliberately, which means that the halakic threshold of one in sixty does not apply. The precision of this gives you some idea of the complexity of Orthodox dietary laws.

The outcome of the story tells you something of their power, and the ingenuity with which the Orthodox live with them. Guess who gave in? Not Rabbi Geffen! He actually persuaded the almighty Coca-Cola Company to change the offending ingredient and replace it with a substitute made from cottonseed oil.

Somehow, I have a feeling that such a kosher transformation will also happen to my life.

An affectionate shalom,

Renu

7

"This morning, the place of honor is with the back to our magnificent view," Yehuda Davidson motioned Felix Frankenthaler to the only chair with armrests in the spartan seminar room. "The shades are down because Dr. Krishnan plans to use the epidiascope."

Renu, her back to the screen, was shuffling the transparencies she planned to use with the overhead projector by her side. *Epidiascope* was one of those formal words that Yehuda Davidson liked to try on for formal occasions — those, as well as titles and a tie.

With the exception of Jephtah, the other men were all from Hadassah. Aside from members of his department, Davidson had also invited some clinicians specializing in cardiovascular disease and diabetes, who he hoped would be willing to participate in the initial clinical trials. No one else was wearing a tie, not even the American visitor.

Davidson tapped the table with his pen. "First, let me formally welcome Professor Frankenthaler to this meeting. He was responsible for sending us Dr. Krishnan, who, as most of you know, has been playing a key role in this tripartite collaboration." He nodded briefly in the direction of Jephtah, who was busily cleaning his fingernails with a mutilated paper clip, before returning to Renu. "I have asked Dr. Krishnan to summarize the results to date. Later on, during Professor Frankenthaler's stay, we hope to agree on what it will take to bring some of the Brandeis biochemical work and the Ben-Gurion biomechanical wizardry to clinical fruition."

At the mention of Ben-Gurion, Jephtah leaned back in his chair until he achieved a precarious balance on the two rear legs. The homemade fingernail file dropped to the table.

"Renu, the floor is yours."

She cleared her throat. It was a nervous habit she could never shake, although at this moment she felt supremely confident. An interesting combination, she thought, as her eyes swept around the table: my lover, my mentor, my colleagues. When Davidson suggested that she summarize the work, Renu had accepted gratefully. She wanted to impress these eleven men in one single performance — not an easy task with an audience ranging from Felix Frankenthaler, who still behaved toward her as a benevolent father figure, to Jephtah, who had seen her naked just a few hours before. She decided to pitch her talk at two: Yehuda Davidson, whose influence on her career, if she were to stay on in Israel, was likely to be significant, and one of the physicians, the diabetes man. Neither one really knew much about chemistry. By emphasizing the fundamental importance of her chemical studies to the clinical treatment of erectile dysfunction and ending up explaining the project she was about to initiate — work she had only discussed with Jephtah — Renu thought that she would be covering most bases.

In a clear, well-modulated voice, she began. "Without penile erection, natural propagation among primates is impossible. Never mind the size of the penis — quite small, in gorillas, probably the size of a man's thumb," she said in as offhand a manner she could muster, "but quite huge, proportionally speaking, in man — it is the erection that makes all subsequent reproductive events possible."

Renu had practiced that opening statement. It seemed just right to her: startling in its bluntness, yet relevant and spiced with a piece of gorilla esoterica that most women would be unlikely to raise in all-male company. By doing so, she hoped to establish her credentials as a member of the club. If I can carry this off in front of an all-male audience, she thought, then everything after that will be downhill.

"It is estimated that at least ten to twenty — perhaps even thirty — million men in the United States suffer from erectile dysfunction. As you know better than I, such a condition is caused by an inadequate supply of blood reaching the penis." She looked at her audience as if searching for potential sufferers. "This, of course, is caused by either a failure in relaxation of the smooth muscle tissue of the penis or the inability of the penis to retain blood."

She shrugged modestly. "Old hat to you, of course. Now," she raised one finger in preparation for the only other sentence she had carefully rehearsed, "the holy grail of impotence therapy is a substance that would produce an erection of sufficient firmness and duration to allow for satisfactory intercourse — a drug with a minimum of undesirable side effects. Again, as you know better than I. . . ." Renu paused. She realized that she had used that phrase before. But why not? It will flatter, or at least disarm, a male audience being addressed by a woman about impotence.

"All kinds of attempts to overcome this problem have been made in the past, ranging from oral administration of apomorphine, which produced erections but also nausea, to direct injection of papaverine into the corpus cavernosum, which is effective but can lead to priapism — too much of a good thing," she added sotto voce, "and a subject to which I will return, um, shortly." Renu forced herself not to look at Jephtah. One glance, she thought, and I'm finished — unless gales of laughter are somehow helpful to a presenter in my situation.

She collected her thoughts. "What is needed is a rational approach to curing erectile dysfunction — in other words, a basic knowledge of the mechanism of *normal* erectile function. Which leads us to NO — the holy grail of erection."

With these words, she turned on the overhead projector.

"Because of the divergent disciplines represented here, I'm uncertain whether all of you are aware that yawning and penile erection are produced simultaneously by dopaminergic agonists, such as apomorphine. This is certainly true in male rats, where such symptomatology has been used for assay purposes to demonstrate the role of nitric oxide." Renu quickly glanced around the table, noting with amusement that both Davidson and one of the medicos were unsuccessfully stifling yawns.

"Combined yawning and erection does not seem to occur in humans, nor would it be particularly desirable." The resulting laughter sounded like a locker room. Renu hurriedly placed another transparency onto the projector.

"At Brandeis, we were particularly interested in synthesizing new NO-releasing molecules." Just as she had done with Melanie Laidlaw in New York, Renu emphasized the high chemical reactivity of NO in biological systems and its resulting short half-life. "That's why we and many competing laboratories have been trying to develop longer-lasting sources for NO. I have come up with a group of compounds in Professor Frankenthaler's lab that appear to be unique." Though careful to give credit to her mentor, Renu deliberately departed from the usual collaborative "we" of scientific presentations to underscore her role. She pointed to the screen. "We call these substances NONOates — "

"Let's not broadcast this generic name too widely," the diabetes specialist interjected, flashing a broad grin. "Men may derive some subliminal message. And we all," the all-encompassing sweep of his eyes included Renu, who didn't blink, "know how important psychogenic factors are in tumescence of the penis. But go on," he waved her on with a benedictory gesture of his hand.

"Right," she said curtly, but then stopped. I won't let him get away with this male sensitivity. "I am inclined to ignore your psychogenic problems for a moment — "

"Mine?" interrupted the man. The stifled snickers implied that the rest of the men were not certain whether he was joking or complaining.

"Not *yours* personally," Renu reddened. "I was referring to psychogenic factors in *men* in general."

"Forgiven," granted the man somewhat pompously. "But why ignore them?"

"Because nitric oxide will exert its effect whether a man suffers from organic or psychogenic dysfunction. Once the material is dispersed intraurethrally, it's taken up by the spongy tissue around the urethra — "

"The corpus spongiosum," Davidson interjected.

"Precisely," Renu nodded gratefully, "and from there it goes to the corpus cavernosum." Renu realized that this was old news to most of the audience, but she wanted to be sure that *everyone* knew that she knew it. "And if NO does the job," she rushed on so as not be interrupted again, "my NONOates ought to have the same effect." She glanced briefly at the diabetes man. "They're called that because they have two NO molecules connected in tandem to a nucleophile — in our case a secondary amine. The beauty of *my* system," she quickly looked at Felix Frankenthaler, whose encouraging nod indicated support rather than displeasure at the use of the singular possessive, "is that, on the one hand, the NONO grouping causes spontaneous release of NO in the aqueous environment of the cell. On the other hand, the nature of the secondary amine, to which the NONO function is attached, can be varied in such a way as to modify the rate at which NO continues to be released. Additionally, the chemical constitution of the amine handle will also affect in a predictable manner the lipophilicity of these molecules.

"Such fat-solubility is quite essential when combined with Jephtah's delivery vehicle." She pointed to the MUSA device with which Jephtah had been toying.

"Hellstrom's group at Tulane had already shown that direct injection of some primitive NO-releasers," Renu's use and intonation of the word *primitive* made clear her disdain, "such as sodium nitroprusside, directly into the corpus cavernosum of macaques produced erections that were comparable to those produced with papaverine.

"So, Mordecai here," she gestured toward the pharmacologist member of their group, "who has a few rhesus monkeys, has set up an assay in which he is examining my NONOates for intracavernosal blood pressure, erectile length of the penis, and duration of effect. He has picked two candidate compounds, code-named NONO-1 and NONO-2, shown on the next transparency." Some seconds passed while Renu contemplated the chemical structures with pride, turning to Frankenthaler to add magnanimously, "If they really work, you'll probably have to give them a catchier name.

"We come now to a key contribution from Hadassah: the observation — already alluded to — in Professor Davidson's laboratory, that for the purpose of producing a more prolonged erection, absorption of certain drugs through the urethra is more efficient than injection into the corpus cavernosum. That reminds me," she said, looking up from her notes. "Not so long ago, Solomon Snyder's team at Johns Hopkins reported that the concentration of nitric oxide synthase — the engine driving our own body's NO generation — is highest in the membranous urethra. Four times higher than in the penis.

"So there we are," concluded Renu. "To deliver my NONOates, we are depending on Jephtah's invention." She reached over to pick up the MUSA. Holding it up into the air, she slowly withdrew the applicator from its protective cover. "Like a perfume dispenser — "

"Bravo!" interrupted Jephtah. "I've been searching for a better description than calling it a 'stem' or a 'needle.' Let's call it a 'pheromone dispenser' — after all, when a woman inserts it slowly into a man's urethra it should be arousing. That's why MUSA also stands for 'medicated unit for sexual arousal.'"

"Let's not get carried away," warned Davidson. "It's charming, especially the way Renu is demonstrating it, but as a practicing urologist, let me say that we should not underestimate a man's reluctance to insert anything down there. In the end, it will have to be efficacy rather than clever acronyms that carry the argument."

"Hold it, gentlemen." Renu laughingly waved her hand. "The MUSA may be a perfume dispenser to some, a stiletto to others, but its real significance will only become evident when a micropellet of the drug is inserted into the delivery tube," she held up the unit by the barrel-shaped head of the plunger. "As far as I am aware, to date only blanks have actually been inserted into a penis." She avoided looking at Jephtah. Instead, she glanced at her watch. "I have taken more time than I had expected. I wanted to end by outlining briefly my ideas about synthesizing novel NO-antagonists — in other words, compounds having the opposite effect — but I'll leave that for some other time. Anyway, our present focus is on the production of nitric oxide and of erections, rather than how to turn them off.

"Now it's time for Professor Davidson to outline the clinical protocols." She picked up her transparencies and moved away from the screen.

———

"That was an impressive performance."

Frankenthaler and Renu were standing in the lobby of the King David Hotel.

"Most impressive," he repeated. "And not just your presentation. You've really changed during the past six months. You've. . . ."

"Matured?" She laughed, pleasure shining in her eyes.

He wagged his head. "More than that. I'd say your self-confidence really shows."

"And what do you think of the clinical plans?"

"I agree with Yehuda. Before loading a MUSA with one of your NONOates, we've got to demonstrate the feasibility of urethral delivery with a known agent. I agree that papaverine is not the right one — it's too much of a sledgehammer: it takes an injection of sixty *milligrams* to produce an effect. What if you end up with a ten-hour erection?" He laughed, but his laugh had more than a tinge of embarrassment.

Renu found his embarrassment oddly contagious. Her response

came perhaps a second too fast to sound casual. "So what do you think of Professor Davidson's proposal?"

Frankenthaler nodded reflectively. "I buy his idea that we first fill a MUSA with a naturally occurring blood vessel dilator. Prostaglandin E_1 makes sense. It's even metabolized right in the penis, unlike papaverine. And the dosage is small. Hans Hedlund in Sweden has already shown that direct injection of six *micro*grams — one ten-thousandth the dose of papaverine — will have an erectogenic effect."

"But what about establishing an effective dose in our delivery system? And his not wanting to try it first in normal men?"

"You don't mean 'normal' men, Renu," he corrected her. "Men with erection problems would hardly want to be considered 'abnormal.' You mean 'men with normal erectile responses.'"

I forgot how sensitive men can be, she thought. "Of course," she said meekly.

"And it really wouldn't prove anything if we did," he said firmly. "We shouldn't envisage this as a product for Casanovas. We must focus on men whose impotence is associated with functional disorders — vascular diseases, diabetes, prostate operations — conditions that are more common among the older population. And don't forget, in affluent countries that age group is increasing all the time. A point I'm sure the pharmaceutical companies won't overlook."

"So we start with subjects already under medical treatment?"

"Absolutely. I'm glad Yehuda invited those clinicians. They certainly paid attention to you — and I'm sure they're already thinking of potential candidates for tests. I bet we'll have some volunteers before I leave for the States — men who had normal erections in the past and have now lost that ability. If the MUSA delivery system is to deliver the goods, it will have to work in those men, within a few minutes of application, and without *Playboy* or *Penthouse*."

He headed for the elevator. "By the way," he paused, his outstretched finger not quite pressing the call button, "tomorrow I'm driving down to Beersheba."

"Oh?" This was news to her.

He pressed the button. "I want to meet with Menachem Dvir. He called me this morning."

—————

"Renu, you were terrific." Jephtah embraced her the moment the door slammed shut. "Speaking of erections — "

"Was I?"

"Maybe not now." He squeezed her again, tight enough so she could feel the bulge in his groin. "But I had one during most of your talk. It's amazing how even straightforward scientific discourse can turn one on. He led her toward the bed. "There you were, the only woman among all those men, telling them what you will do about raising their cocks. I wonder how many were fantasizing about what we're about to do. . . . I'm sure your NO is very powerful stuff, but don't underestimate the power of a well-stimulated brain."

—————

"What an afternoon," she murmured. The sunlight threw a zebra pattern on their naked bodies as it shone through the Venetian blinds. "Here I lie with one of my research collaborators, satisfied and content, instead of being in the lab. And all that because my professor suffers from jet lag and needs a nap." She tousled his hair. "I didn't know how good it feels to make love after a long lecture. And in this soft light where I can count every eyelash of yours. They're so long — like a woman's."

Jephtah turned halfway to take her into his arms, but she wiggled free. "One moment," she blurted out, "I just thought of something." She scampered barefoot to the small bookshelf by the window. "Here," she announced, waving the *Code of Jewish Law* in her hand, "I've got to read you something."

"Good God," he groaned. "You're still not done with that stuff?"

"Just one prohibition! I promise." She placed the open book on his belly and proceeded to riffle through it. "'It is forbidden,'" she intoned, simultaneously placing one of her hands over Jephtah's mouth, "'to have intercourse by a light, even if the light is shut out by means of a garment. It is also forbidden to have intercourse during the day, unless the room is darkened. At night, if the moon shines directly upon them, it is forbidden' — "

—————

Jephtah pushed her hand away. "I hope we have a moon tonight. This *mamzer* can hardly wait to sin again."

"I'm glad that we share a grant application," said Felix Frankenthaler as he settled himself in his chair.

"Unless your 'we' means our respective institutions, you're flattering me," Menachem Dvir replied. "I've got nothing to do with the science." He was rocking slowly back and forth in his beat-up desk chair, shirtsleeves rolled up above his elbows, hands linked behind his head, while the window air conditioner groaned under the summer heat of the Negev. "You know, I'm not a scientist — really more of an engineering type, and now simply an administrator. I couldn't even make it to your scientific review yesterday, which I regret. The executive committee of our board of governors is meeting this week, and I've got to be at their beck and call. I'd much rather have learned about the progress of the MUSA project." He smiled graciously.

"It's not just about MUSA, you know. It's really about nitric oxide." Frankenthaler's demurral was only millimeters deep, but Dvir's apologetic smile was centimeters wide.

"I know, I know. It's just that I'm mostly familiar with Jephtah Cohn's work. Quite a clever young man, isn't he?"

"I suppose so," replied Frankenthaler. "I've only met him yesterday for the first time. But the device is clever, no question about that."

For a moment, the two men faced each other in an awkward silence, conversation having run out.

"Let me show you around," offered Dvir. "We can't compare with Hadassah — not yet anyway — but it is exciting to see a new place. Something you should appreciate. After all, Brandeis is barely thirty years old, isn't it?"

"You know that?" Frankenthaler was surprised.

"We do our homework when we receive distinguished visitors."

During the first decade of its existence, Ben-Gurion University's physical plant — at least the buildings worth showing to a visitor — required less than an hour to tour. On this occasion it was also much too hot for wandering around. Instead, Dvir spent much of the tour in front of the map of the projected campus, weaving back and forth in his narrative between history and future plans.

Just when Frankenthaler assumed that his visit was winding to its end, Dvir said, "There is one other matter I wanted to discuss with you. At the advice of one of our governors, a compatriot of yours and a venture capitalist by profession as well as avocation — a rare combination, you'll have to admit — we've filed for a patent on the MUSA device. In the USA," he added.

"What?" sputtered Frankenthaler. "But you can't do that — "

"Of course we can. In fact, as our governor pointed out, we'd be derelict in our duty to the university not to do so very quickly before anything gets published."

"And REPCON? They're supporting your work! Don't you think they should be consulted first? In fact, they *have* to be consulted."

Dvir pulled at his jaw, eyeing Frankenthaler as he said slowly, "Yes and no. Now that they're supporting us, of course they should be consulted about possible patents. That's the 'yes' part of the answer, the one I wanted to discuss with you."

"And the 'no'?"

"Cohn's original design and the first few prototypes were all completed before we received a single shekel from any outside sources. Therefore, REPCON does not enter into that part of the equation. Our resources are very meager. My job is to look for new sources of funds. The patent application is one step in that direction — but there are others we'll have to take if it's to produce anything. That's where we need your agreement — and help. Let me explain."

Dvir's analysis was pithy and clear, his proposal by no means unreasonable. The Ben-Gurion MUSA application had to be filed quickly; for legal reasons it could not list the Brandeis or Hadassah groups, since they had not played any part as "inventors" in the formal sense of the word. But the device itself was of no use unless it could be loaded with an active ingredient — the Brandeis contribution — and shown to be efficacious, a job that the Hadassah clinical studies promised to demonstrate. But even if the studies did pan out, then the class of NONOates synthesized by

Renu Krishnan would have to be patented before that work was published or even openly discussed.

"I don't know what went on yesterday, but you were likely skating very close to public disclosure," Dvir warned. "And if you agree with my analysis, then you people at Brandeis better proceed quickly. If you need to talk to REPCON, please talk promptly."

"Actually, we don't," mused Frankenthaler. "The initial work on NONOates was done before we got their grant. I'll have to consult the appropriate people at Brandeis as soon as I get back."

The rest was simple. They agreed that the Ben-Gurion device patent would be coupled with the Brandeis product patent and a use patent, to be filed under the inventorship of the Hadassah group, and that a three-way meeting would be held in Jerusalem before Frankenthaler's departure. The principle of dividing eventual profits among the three institutions was immediately agreed upon; the apportionment of the actual size of the three slices would be left to the university administrators.

"That leaves us out, thank God," concluded Frankenthaler.

"You, maybe — but not me," said Dvir, flashing a very large grin. "You forget I'm an administrator."

———

Frankenthaler was standing to go when Dvir asked, "I gather you'll clear the question of future patent applications with the REPCON administration. How well do you know their director?"

"Melanie Laidlaw? Very well. I've known her socially for . . ." he seemed to be counting, "over half a dozen years. As a matter of fact, when she was still married to Justin. I knew him first."

"What was her husband like?"

Frankenthaler eyed him speculatively. "Justin? An outstanding scientist."

"That's all?"

"I'm not sure what you mean. He was also a very decent man . . . a real mensch. Why do you ask?"

Dvir shook his head. "Idle curiosity. By the way, how is Dr. Laidlaw?"

"Enjoying motherhood."

8

Jerusalem, December 24, 1980

Dear Prof,

It is amazing how fast one gets acclimated to local circumstances. Only as I started on this letter did I realize that your lab at Brandeis is closed for the Christmas holidays. Here in Jerusalem — at least in Jewish Jerusalem — today is just another Wednesday. Anyway, holiday or workday, this is a truly memorable day: MUSA *works!* The initial dose-ranging studies were performed in twelve volunteers ranging in age from 31 to 59 years: four diabetics, four with vascular diseases, and the rest impotent because of prostatectomies. With prostaglandin E_1, the effective dose — meaning good erections lasting thirty to sixty minutes — was between 250 and 500 micrograms (although the youngest man seemed to respond at 125 micrograms). As part of the protocol, we established a rather primitive scoring system for evaluating the quality of erections — a scale of 1 to 5; 5 being tops and 3 considered "stuffable." (Let me emphasize that the term was coined by a male urologist and not by me!) Jephtah Cohn is now assembling a device that may provide harder data. If it works, I shall describe it to you.

I understand (I was not present personally) that there was some initial reluctance on the part of every man to insert the stem of the MUSA into his urethra. But since the procedure is really very simple and quick, and the results overwhelmingly convincing (erections scoring 3 to 5 occurring within a few minutes), none seemed to have a problem the second time around.

Trials with higher doses of prostaglandin E_1 in the 500-

1000 microgram range are being considered, but with caution. The reason is that one "normal" volunteer (we both know what the quotation marks stand for) recklessly decided to try 750 micrograms. The resulting erection required rather heroic measures to reduce. This has convinced me that we should be extra cautious with dosages, just in case we overdo it on the erection front once we embark on clinical experiments with our NO-releasers.

For the moment, there is no purpose in my doing more chemical work on NONOates until we establish the efficacy of NONO-1 and NONO-2 in the MUSA system. Professor Davidson is willing to give the go-ahead for clinical trials as soon as the sub-acute toxicology is completed, which ought to be shortly after Purim. The acute LD_{50} toxicology in rats worked beautifully: they yawned and erected without any problems until absolutely huge doses were administered — at which point, Mordecai Rubin said, "they died smiling." Since the NONOates are new chemical entities — in contrast to prostaglandin E_1 about which a lot is known — Mordecai is performing sixty-day studies in rabbits. The MUSA stem does not fit into a rabbit's urethra, but he solved the problem by using ophthalmic tweezers to insert the micropellets containing our drugs. All one needs to do is to turn a rabbit on its back, whereupon it lies as if paralyzed, with its limbs spread. Even I could have done it with a little practice.

As soon as the human efficacy of NONO-1 and 2 is established, then the dawn of NO-releasers as erectogenic drugs will have risen (pun intended, I'm afraid — but I assure you it's nothing compared to what I hear bouncing around our lab these days).

It is clear to me from the recent experience of our single "normal" volunteer that we are going to need MUSA systems capable of delivering a detumescence-inducing agent. A MUSA containing an effective inhibitor of NO biosynthesis might do the job, but what about an NO-scavenger? That ought to be much more efficient than taking some conventional vasoconstrictor like Sudafed by mouth. At the outset, we might try some MUSAs loaded with phenylephrine to see whether the transurethral approach works for such compounds.

I am attaching a list of potential NOS inhibitors. You will note that I am taking my lead as to chemical structure from Paul Feldman's publications describing arginine analogs in that regard and also his recent model of the NOS active site. I have some hot ideas about NO-scavengers, but more about these in my next letter. I have approached Professor Raphael Mechoulam of the Department of Medicinal Chemistry in the School of Pharmacy here about access to some lab space. Mechoulam, who, I gather, is a candidate to become rector of Hebrew University and thus a person of some local influence, seemed very understanding. Please let me know what you think of my plans.

Shalom,

Renu

P.S. Professor Davidson is sufficiently optimistic about the eventual outcome of the Phase I clinical studies that he has authorized our pharmacologist to undertake two-year toxicology in rodents if the sixty-day rabbit studies turn out to be clean. The sub-acute toxicology in rabbits is fine for our initial studies in man, but if our erectogens are going to be used for prolonged periods in clinical practice, carcinogenicity (God forbid! as they say here) must be ruled out. You never know about nitroso compounds in biological systems. By starting these two-year oral feeding studies now, we should gain some time.

I wonder what the Prof would think if I told him the real story of Jephtah and his overloaded MUSA.

Jephtah may be a mamzer, *but in some respects he's also the typical macho sabra: like the way he boasted, not long after we first met, about his* profil 97. *I hadn't the foggiest idea what he was referring to — a shortcoming he was quick to remedy.*

It seems that shortly after his seventeenth birthday every Israeli is subjected to a battery of tests — physical and psychological — in preparation for his impending military service. The results are scored with a profil *number. Jephtah's, I gathered, had been a 97.*

"Not bad," I said, "but why aren't you a 100?"

"100?" He sounded testy. "There is no such profil. *The top score is 97."*

According to Jephtah, there is no 100 because no Jew is physically perfect, since he has been circumcised. If that is so, does it mean that the circumcision is supposed to teach a man that he isn't perfect? That he should exhibit a bit of humility? And what about the women going into the army? Do they get the extra three points?

I'll probably never find out. All our conversations recently have started to center around the commercial implications of our work — the outcome of some conversations he's had with Menachem Dvir. Dvir thinks all aspects of our approach — the MUSA device, the NONOates, the urethral application of erectogenic agents, even eventual NOS-inhibitors — should be patented. I'd never given it much thought, but Dvir's arguments carry some weight. What could the universe of potential MUSA users be? When I told Dvir the actual numbers — the millions of men suffering from functional erectile problems — I got the feeling that he's already planning several buildings on the Ben-Gurion campus to be funded with potential profits.

It was this conversation that convinced Jephtah we had to find out — and promptly — how normal men responded to the treatment. Might they not also be potential customers?

"What's 'normal'?" I asked my three-points-from-perfection man.

"All the way down to profil *21," he laughed, which is apparently the minimum score acceptable for military service.*

And so it came to pass that two weeks ago, at one of our revivim *Shabbats, Jephtah insisted on trying a prostaglandin-containing MUSA — the only one he could get his hands on: a 750 micrograms unit, left over from the first set of dose-ranging trials.*

He had taken one precaution: he'd asked me to insert it about half an hour after we'd had intercourse. We hadn't seen each other for a week, and he wanted the chemically induced erection to be distinct from his natural arousal. Jephtah's response reached its apex within minutes. We promptly started to have sex again.

At first, everything went normally. Better, in fact; I was excited by the power I could exert on a man with a MUSA in my hand, and Jephtah was scoring a 5 — at least. But then his groans took on a painful sound until, finally, he just rolled over on his side, moaning, knees drawn up as if he were trying to hide his rigid phallus.

I didn't know what to do, other than stroke his head and murmur pointless assurances that the pain and the erection were bound to recede. But Jephtah got up, pacing up and down for at least thirty minutes, biting his hand and trying to muffle his moans. I offered to call a doctor, but Jephtah just shook his head. Finally, I could bear it no longer. "Jephtah," I whispered, "I'll dial Yehuda Davidson. When he answers, I'll hand over the phone and you better talk. Tell him the truth, but don't tell him that I inserted the MUSA."

The rest was pretty straightforward. Davidson apparently showed little concern and even less sympathy. "Lie down flat on your back to minimize hydrostatic pressure. Under no circumstances stand up or walk. Don't even lie on your side. Put ice packs around the groin and upper thighs," he said, and he prescribed sixty milligrams of Sudafed. He didn't even inquire where Jephtah was calling from. "We better talk about this," was all he said as he rung off.

I packed Jephtah's socks with all the cubes my little fridge held, stuck them into plastic food bags, and then forced them between his drawn-up legs. It didn't seem enough, so I gave him a cold beer can to hold between his thighs. Once he calmed down, I went out to knock on the door of the only neighbors in our building I felt comfortable bothering on a Shabbat evening and asked them for more ice cubes. Thank God they're not Orthodox.

9

"Dr. Krishnan?" the tall American asked. "I'm Martin Gestler. I am on the board of governors. May I talk to you? And may I call you Renu?"

Lama lo? she nearly said, but instead Renu simply nodded. They were standing in the milling crowd following the groundbreaking ceremony of a new building on the Ben-Gurion University campus — one more model on Menachem Dvir's campus map turning into reality. Jephtah had invited her because his lab was expected to occupy some of the new space. The sun was blinding.

"Let's walk over there into the shade," Gestler motioned to some tamarisk, leaves gray from the construction dust, "and have something cold to drink. I have a proposition for you."

"I have a proposition for you." That's how Gestler had started. If you think about it, proposition can suggest the gamut from sexual to commercial. In this instance, it turned out to be startlingly commercial.

I had heard about Gestler from Jephtah and Menachem Dvir, the day they broached the patent question. At the time, they hadn't mentioned his name. They only referred to "the American," even though there are plenty of Americans on the Ben-Gurion board.

Israeli institutions — like Hebrew University, the Weizmann Institute, and Ben-Gurion itself — tend to have huge boards. Most of the positions on them are largely honorific, reserved for major donors who are expected not only to continue donating but to bring in new patrons, who, in turn, also join the board — a form of charitable metastasis these places are happy to cultivate. But among that teeming pool of philanthropists, socialites, do-gooders, and even a few free-loading collectors of board memberships, there are always some individuals who do the real work in small, executive sessions.

According to Dvir, "this American" fell into that special subgroup, and he, like many others in this class, fit a profile the administration valued highly. He was one of the Americans (on rare occasions, not even Jews) who had become Zionists decades after the establishment of the State of Israel. Impressed by success, by track records, and prepared to (as they say) "leverage" them, these are the new entrepreneurs. Instead of gazing romantically at the creation of Israel through historical kibbutzim-style spectacles, they wear the modern designer glasses of a typically American venture capitalist go-getter, who is interested in high-tech industry and high-value exports, not citrus or sweet Mount Carmel wines.

Only when he actually made his proposition did I realize that this Martin Gestler was Jephtah's and Dvir's "American." I hadn't visualized him as a strapping, athletic sort of man. He looked ten years younger than his chronological age. He wore his hair cut smartly short, and his face had none of the two-day stubble I've gotten accustomed to among the sabras. Above the slightly beaky nose were some very good eyes. I couldn't help but notice them: they fixed on mine and never let go.

As a preamble, he granted that the neurotransmitter aspects of NO were quite spectacular basic research. He told me that, though not a scientist — in fact, an MBA — he had been in the pharmaceutical industry long enough to appreciate good science. (At this point, of course, I had no way of knowing how much of an expert he really was. That only came later.) He granted that it was given that my NONOates — he bowed ever so slightly in acknowledgment of my role — would help (I liked that he didn't say "might") erectilely dysfunctional men (he even knew the right words!). But, he queried, leaning in close, had we really considered how glamorous penile erection would be from an investment standpoint?

"Frankly no," I said. It was reflex. I had been trained as an academic, pure and uncontaminated by thoughts of anything so vulgar as profit.

"Then, as a governor of this university, let me tell you something," he turned around and waved his hand toward the blinding sunshine. "Here is a real opportunity for this university — as well as Brandeis and Hadassah," he added in a lower tone, probably to

emphasize that they were of a lesser priority to him, "to create some real equity and income. Equity through stock ownership, which would eventually translate into endowment, and income through ongoing royalties."

Why tell me all this, I wondered.

He seemed to have read my mind. "The key to all this is the American market. You people here" — *again he waved into the sun* — "have not the slightest idea what it will take to get a drug such as your NONO — by the way, a marvelously catchy name (I *couldn't help but beam*) — past the FDA. And this is where you come in."

At which interesting point we were interrupted by the chairman of the board of governors, who had been frantically searching for Gestler. They bustled off into the brilliant glare.

"What's it like to be back?" Frankenthaler's question had a fatherly ring. "It's been . . . what? fifteen or sixteen months? I trust you missed us."

"Well . . ." hesitated Renu. For her plane reading, Jephtah had slipped her a thin book: a collection of Taoist yin and yang sayings by Lao-tzu. One kept sticking in her mind: "True words are not beautiful. Beautiful words are not true." She had wondered why Lao-tzu had been so absolute.

"I can't say I really did," she finally said. "I've hardly had time. I've been so busy on several fronts — "

"But you are so efficient."

Of course it was meant as a compliment, but then she recalled another Taoism: "Efficiency is not persuasive. Persuasion is not efficient." Again, so absolute! She demurred. "Efficiency isn't enough. Results have been pouring out so fast, it's like trying to drink from a fire hose." *As if this weren't even truer of my private life,* she added silently. "Still, it *is* nice to see the old labs, even if only for a day or so. By the way, I want to thank you for letting me be the speaker."

"You deserve it," he said benevolently. "Besides, it will do the urologists some good to listen to a woman."

"Are they mostly urologists?"

"Most likely. It's called 'International Society of Impotence Research,' so they ought to have representatives from other disciplines: psychology, psychiatry, endocrinology . . . certainly geriatrics . . . maybe even the odd person from epidemiology. Still, I'm sure it's mostly run by urologists, which means they're all men."

"I meant to ask," Renu sounded curious. "Why don't they call themselves 'International Society of Research on Erectile Dysfunction?'"

He shrugged. "Maybe it's for historical reasons. Or because urologists like to be blunt." He laughed. "I suppose we'll have to be equally blunt then, won't we? Let's go through your slides. I'd like to see how much you can cover in your thirty minutes."

"That's why I was curious about terminology." She opened her attaché case to remove a set of enlargements of her slides. She handed Frankenthaler the first sheet. "I plan to start off by making the point that 'impotence' — generally implying an inability to reach or maintain an erection sufficient for satisfactory intercourse — is not only too limited a term but that it also carries with it a lot of pejorative baggage." She read directly from the text: "'Desire, orgasmic capability, and ejaculatory capacity may all be intact or only somewhat impaired even in the presence of major erectile dysfunction. But the resulting sense of inadequate sexual function can lead to loss of self-confidence and depression.'"

"You sound like a sex therapist. Where did you pick up all that?"

Renu felt a rising blush. She hurried on. "Some of the clinicians at Ben-Gurion medical school, where they emphasize what they call 'the total patient,' are particularly interested in distinguishing between the organic and psychological aspects of male impotence. I didn't just want to stick to NO basic research. I wanted to know what our NONOates do to a man. Professor Davidson let me participate in most of the clinical discussions, even in some of the interviews with the first group of volunteers. Incidentally, most of those were physicians."

"Really? I'm impressed."

She turned to the enlargement. "In my talk I'll repeat the epidemiological stuff I mentioned last year in Jerusalem: that about ten to twenty million American men suffer from erectile dysfunction but that this estimate would have to be raised by another 50 percent if one also includes cases of partial erectile dysfunction. I'll then summarize the evidence that NO plays a key role in erection, and — "

"Be sure to say 'holy grail' of erection! When you used that expression in Jerusalem, I practically heard the overture to *Parsifal*."

My, my, thought Renu, so it really worked. "Okay," she nodded without looking up. "Then I'll tell them about our NONOates — just one slide, because there are unlikely to be any chemists in the audience — and then show this blown-up view of a MUSA. I want them to see where the micropellet is placed in the stem and how it is then pushed into the urethra. But the main emphasis will be on the most recent clinical data. They're covered in the last three slides."

"Three slides of numerical data might be a bit too much — at least for my taste."

"I went over these with Professor Davidson. He felt I should take my time with this information; it's certainly the most convincing part for an audience of clinicians. But don't worry: I have something to hold their attention. I'll start with this one." She slid over another transparency. "It's our scoring system for erectogenic efficacy."

Frankenthaler skimmed it quickly. The lowest score, 1, meant failure; 2 represented some engorgement, while 3 constituted full tumescence. With good lubrication, penile insertion into the vagina was just about possible with score 3, hence the urological expression "stuffable." Scores 4 and 5, of course, presented no problems for normal intercourse.

"You haven't seen the next slide: it's Jephtah's idea." She handed over the transparency and waited.

"What is this?" Frankenthaler asked suspiciously. "I mean this Rube Goldberg contraption — not the penis."

I couldn't tell the Prof the whole story with a straight face. It was Jephtah's idea. For him, a one-to-five scale was simply too crude.

"Too qualitative," he said, dismissing it. "Let me see whether I can come up with something better." And he did.

On one of our regular Friday evenings — by now without condoms, because I'd gone back on the Pill — my Jephtah faced me with a 4.5 or better erection. "Hold him in your left hand," he said. In private, between us, it was always him. *"Now press this cup against the tip." He produced a homemade gadget, consisting of a concave rubber cup connected via a spring-loaded rod to a dial measuring applied pressure. I pressed the cup gently against his glans. "Harder," he said. I started to make a joke about the scale ending at 1000, but he impatiently waved me to silence. "Push until he bends," he said. "That's the whole point." I pushed, harder, while Jephtah eyed the pressure scale. "620 grams," he exclaimed as his penis started to buckle. He looked at me triumphantly. "Don't you see? It's a quantitative measure of stiffness!"*

I squinted at the scale. "620?" I said, sounding disappointed.

"Give me that." He snatched the gadget away."

————

"The buckle weight," Jephtah called it. Studies conducted with a number of "normal" volunteers — ex-military contemporaries of his, who approached the tests more as a competition than scientific research — demonstrated that a buckle weight of 450 grams or higher was more than adequate for intercourse. Yehuda Davidson was amused but also interested. In the end, he asked that I use the 1 to 5 score in my New York talk but told me that I could intimate that future and more extensive studies would employ Jephtah's "penile buckle meter" for data analysis.

The results summarized in Renu's last slide, though still very preliminary, were impressive. A total of thirty-seven men had been tested in double-blind studies with placebo controls using varying doses of NONO-1 and NONO-2. Both substances produced erections in the 3 to 5 range in over 80 percent of the men — a spectacular result, given the history and variety of functional disorders responsible for erectile dysfunction in these volunteers. Since the number of erections scoring 4 or better was higher with NONO-2, this agent was selected for future work to determine the incidence, if any, of priapism and other side effects. For this study, priapism was defined as erections lasting in excess of three hours. Pain, of course, would have been considered a separate problem, but so far little of that had been encountered.

Frankenthaler was pleased — enthusiastic, in fact — and so his reaction was almost irritated when Renu told him about their struggles with Hadassah's Institutional Review Board.

"The IRB, which has to approve all clinical protocols, has become the rate-limiting step," Renu told Frankenthaler. "For these initial studies, they agreed that the rabbit toxicology was adequate, but now that we're interested in larger numbers and longer use, they're starting to raise questions. I admit that NONOates are new compounds and that one has to be careful, but it seems to me that we are dealing here with minute amounts — as you know the effective doses proved remarkably low — of a substance that will be administered for very short periods only a couple of times a week on average."

"So what does the IRB want?" Frankenthaler's tone indicated that, like Renu, he felt a proprietary interest in NONO-2.

"First, they have raised the question of potential carcinogenicity, especially now that we want to enlist some volunteers for longer-term studies and repeated use."

"Fair enough," conceded Frankenthaler. "We are dealing with nitroso compounds."

"We've started two-year feeding studies in rats. As soon as the first year is completed — which ought to be in another couple of months — they asked that some of the animals on the highest dose be sacrificed for pathological examination. Fortunately, Mordecai started with large enough groups to allow for that."

"Anything else?"

"Two more requests. The first, which I have underway, is a detailed study with isotopically labeled NONO-2 to identify all possible metabolites. The second, however, is something I wouldn't have anticipated. They asked that we consider possible effects of the NONOates on women."

"I don't get it," Frankenthaler said flatly. "No one is administering these compounds to women. And I don't recall anyone having raised that question during the first MUSA trials with prostaglandin E_1."

Renu was pleased to see that her professor had worn the same blinders as she. "In a way, we are administering the active ingredient to women — through the man's ejaculate. The objection didn't arise earlier because the prostaglandins are natural constituents of semen."

Frankenthaler clapped himself on the forehead. "How could I have forgotten that! Women are getting plenty of prostaglandins in ejaculates every day — well not every day, of course, but. . . ." His voice petered out.

"Exactly," continued Renu solemnly. "So the board raised the question of transmittal of NONOates via the ejaculate. 'What if the half-life of your agent is thirty minutes?' one of the medical members of the IRB asked."

"Well? We were actually shooting for that, weren't we?"

"'And what if you have men who have early and abundant ejaculations?'"

"Fat chance for that in most of these men," Frankenthaler muttered. "Most are probably in their fifties or older. Still, I suppose one has to answer that."

"Of course," said Renu. "Professor Davidson said we shouldn't even argue the point. He is now organizing a study on young, healthy, 'normal,' volunteers," Renu drew the quotation marks in the air, "mostly medical students, who are being asked to produce masturbation ejaculates at three, five, eight, twelve, fifteen, and twenty minutes after a single administration of NONO-2. They'll do it right in the urology clinic with someone holding a stopwatch, and I'll determine the NONO content of the fresh specimens."

"That's all?" the Prof asked, relieved.

"For now," Renu nodded. "The IRB will let us do a Phase II clinical study with 150 volunteers with various functional disorders — postsurgical, neurological, and drug-therapy-related erectile problems. They also want data on more extensive use, provided there is at least a forty-eight hour interval between MUSA insertions to avoid any possible carry-over effect of unmetabolized drug. But for real Phase III clinical trials, we must wait until the two-year rat feeding is completed and full pathology reports are available, meaning sometime in the second half of 1982." She leaned forward, eyes shining. "You know, I never understood how exciting it would be to be involved in the development of a therapeutic drug. Now, I want to learn what's required to take it all the way. . . ."

"All the way?"

"Through FDA approval. So far, the work has all been done in Israel. But if NONO-2 is to be commercialized, the States are the most important site."

"You *are* ambitious — "

"Yes," she said firmly, "and curious. That's why I'm going out to California for a couple of days after the conference before returning to Jerusalem."

"To do what?"

"I'm going to see a man named Martin Gestler. He used to be the CEO of ZALA Corporation. They are located in the Stanford Industrial Park in Palo Alto. I haven't been back to the Stanford area for over four years, but I remember ZALA from my graduate student days. It used to be called Zaffanori Laboratories, after Alfredo Zaffanori, the guru of new approaches to drug delivery. According to Gestler, they know everything there is to know about getting a new drug delivery vehicle, like MUSA, through the FDA. To give you just one trivial example: Gestler advised us never to use the word 'device' for the MUSA."

"What does he suggest? Gimmick? Thingamajig? Gizmo?" Frankenthaler was carried away by the apparent silliness of the advice.

Renu laughed. "Actually, he was serious. He said 'device' carries with it regulatory complications because at the FDA the term connotes things like pacemakers, IUDs, and the like. It's waving a red flag. He advised we refer to the MUSA as a 'platform' for a new delivery system of a drug; that way, they'll focus on the regulatory aspects — safety and efficacy — of NONO-2 alone." She laughed again, "We have time to decide whether it's a 'platform' or a 'contraption,' but Gestler has arranged for me to meet with some of the regulatory staff at ZALA to learn what we should expect from the

FDA. Even more important, I want to get a feel for how much money needs to be raised to carry out these studies. Our REPCON grant certainly hasn't covered the cost of the clinical studies at Hadassah. And these, apparently, are nothing compared to what it will cost to extend the work in the States."

Frankenthaler had started to pace up and down. He always did that when he wanted to change the subject. Now he stopped to look down at Renu.

"Tell me," he said slowly. "What are your plans after our REPCON grant expires? We could, of course, apply for a renewal, and I suspect we'd get it. But you shouldn't continue to work on soft money. You're too promising a scientist for that. What about starting to look for a tenure-track position back in the States? Have you asked yourself that?"

"As a matter of fact, I have."

And so has Jephtah.

"Could you consider living in such a country?"

He asked the same question several times, and I never said "no." But I didn't respond with an unequivocal "yes," either. I always had to qualify my answer with "it depends."

What it really boiled down to was whether we would stay together permanently.

It took me some time to realize how much his mamzerut *status bothered him. One might have thought that a secular Jew, whose religious observance is limited to lighting Sabbath candles and fasting on Yom Kippur, would have been more or less impervious to it. Yet I can see that Jephtah had taken it as a personal reflection on his status as a citizen of the State of Israel, as a veteran of the Yom Kippur War, in fact, on his standing as a Zionist Jew, who — like the majority of Israelis — happens not to be religious. And as a deep insult to his parents — decent, law-abiding citizens, who were judged, retrospectively, to have cohabited illegally for decades. I'd even wondered whether his bachelor status at age thirty — rather uncommon among his Israeli peers — was related to his concern that attempts to marry in Israel would advertise his* mamzerut.

In the end, it's not even clear who proposed to whom or who was

the first to say lama lo *to the question, "Shall we get married?"*
Formally, it was Jephtah who asked. But operationally? Who does
the proposing when all is said and done? The one who asks or the
one who answers? There's a Taoist puzzle.

"Mamzer or kosher," I said, not even knowing whether these two
words were antonyms, "who cares? If you marry a Hindu, it really
doesn't make any difference."

"But I thought you'd consider conversion," he reminded me.

That's when I realized that marrying a Jew was important to
Jephtah. "Yes, theoretically," I said, "but most certainly not to Or-
thodoxy." I had never told him that I'd actually paid a visit to the
rabbinut, where religious law was dispensed. One of Jephtah's Beer-
sheba friends took me there — an old Nissen hut from British mili-
tary times. The moment I walked through the door, I thought I'd
entered a nineteenth-century shtetl: thousands of files, tied together
with string, stood in stacks from floor to ceiling, and black-hatted
men in caftans with long sidelocks, some on ladders, were pulling
down files and blowing off the dust. I fled.

"Even if you convert, any children of mine will be mamzers,*"*
Jephtah reminded me. I asked him to be sensible. If any children of
ours married in their twenties, that would be around 2010. Lots of
things could change by then. There could even be peace in the
Middle East. That's when I got him to laugh. "Maybe my dream
will come true: another mammoth immigration to Israel from the
only untapped source — the Soviet Union — so full of non-kosher
Jews that the mamzers *would take over."*

But once I realized that the biggest affront in his eyes was the
seemingly irrevocable mamzerut *of any children he might have, I*
decided to perform some research of my own about this mamzer
business — simple research that paid off spectacularly. There it
was, right in the Encyclopedia Judaica: *"As the offspring of a union*
between a Jew and a gentile takes the status of the mother, a child
born of a mamzer and a gentile mother will be gentile and not a
mamzer; thus after proper conversion to Judaism, the child will ac-
quire the status of a legitimate proselyte and the fact that the father
was a mamzer will be totally irrelevant."

And then we started planning. Or was it daydreaming? What if the MUSA-NONO project really took off? Really became a widely accepted therapy for erectile dysfunction? In the States? And we both worked there — together?

"When shall we get married?" Jephtah asked after descending from cloud ten (if Dante had nine heavens, why couldn't we have one more?).

"Let's talk business when I return from California," I stalled. I hadn't told him yet what Gestler had proposed.

I never thought that the word business *would prove so apt.*

Frankenthaler sat down again. "And what was your answer?"

"It's complicated," she said. "First of all, I plan to get married."

"*Mazel tov*," he beamed. "And who is the fortunate man?"

"Jephtah Cohn."

"Oh," he said, half an octave lower. "Is he prepared to move to the States?"

"I haven't asked."

"You haven't?" Frankenthaler looked baffled.

"The real question is whether *I* want to move back to the States." She frowned. "I wonder why I said *back?* After all, I'm from India."

"Because you're Americanized by now."

"You really think so?" She gazed at him pensively. "I think the real answer is that I'm de-Indianized."

Palo Alto, California, June 3, 1981

Dearest Ashok,

I was happy to gather from your last letter that both you and Mummy are pleased at the prospect of my getting married, even if it won't be an Indian marriage. But the when and where? That's complicated. Let me explain.

As you can see, this letter is written from my old California stomping grounds. I've had a fabulous visit, which may actually provide an answer to your question. You are the first person — even before Jephtah — to hear of my plans.

My visit to Palo Alto was arranged and partly funded by

Martin Gestler, who used to be high up in the management of ZALA Corporation but lives now in Jerusalem (on Ethiopia Street, of all places, but hardly in a hostel!). The company's founder and board chairman, a Dr. Zaffanori, is one of the pioneers in the development of new drug delivery systems. When I told him about Jephtah's urethral delivery system and my NONOates, he became very interested. Originally, I visited ZALA to get some *free* advice about dealing with FDA regulations, but after meeting Zaffanori — who, incidentally is an extraordinarily charming man (and what a dresser!) — I had a brainstorm.

I had heard that ZALA has a few in-house postdoctoral fellowships, so I asked whether they would consider inviting Jephtah to spend a year there working on new approaches to drug delivery via the urethra (which would be a new area for ZALA) and having me as a part-time intern in their regulatory affairs department. If I worked only part-time, I could take some courses toward an MBA at the University of Santa Clara. Of course I'll need some supplementary income — a subject I plan to explore with Mr. Gestler.

And why do I want to get an MBA? I think I was born too early. The situation may well change in the next decade or two, but looking around the American chemistry departments that interest me, I see very few women on the tenure track. And Indian women — even hyphenated ones? Those can be counted on the fingers of one amputated hand. Do you understand why I have decided not to try for an academic career? By the way, you should have been at my talk last week at the biannual meeting of the International Society of Impotence Research. I caused quite a sensation: the only woman speaker, presenting findings on male impotence to boot. NONO, hurrah!

But I'm not rejecting the academy so much as I'm turning toward something that appeals to me more. The last two years have gotten me hooked on the drug development process, with its interdisciplinary approach and attention to ultimate practical utility. Getting some business training is bound to help, especially if a company is set up to market MUSA and NONO.

And what does that have to do with the when and where of my marriage? When I get back to Israel, I'll propose to Jephtah that we marry in the States, in Seattle, where his father and sister live. You and Mummy can travel to Seattle from Madras in either direction, because it's just about half way around the world. I can hardly wait to see all of you after so long a time. If only Papaji were still alive.

Shalom and much love,

Renu

10

I may be approaching sixty, but a diminished attention span has never been a problem with me. Yet here I am, Felix Frankenthaler — a long-tenured Brandeis professor — on top of Mount Scopus listening to my colleagues plan how to bring on erections in millions of unhappy American men, and I'm unable to concentrate. Am I the only one here who can't attend? Look at Gestler: from the way he's describing the staggering amount of work and money it will take to bring NONO-2 to market, you'd think he never had an off day in his life.

Of course, we're lucky he's interested in helping us. Not only is he not charging us, but he'll probably be the person who'll raise the first ten million we'll need to get the venture underway. I thought I was good at fund-raising, but now I see what pikers we academics are compared to these West Coast entrepreneurs. He makes me feel old and . . . envious. Envy is not one of my usual character faults. I certainly don't feel it about other people's money or positions. About the only time I find myself envious is when somebody beats me into print — but that's called ambition, not envy. So what's bugging me?

I should be glad he's taken Renu and Jephtah under his wing.

He's funding some of their expenses out of his own pocket so they can spend the coming year in the States. But it isn't about science anymore — at least not for Renu. It's about FDA requirements, U.S. clinical trials, manufacturing, marketing . . . *! Do I care about any of this? Renu and Jephtah seem to care. The speed with which Gestler arranged for their training appointments at ZALA Corporation and the alacrity with which the two accepted place my initial dips into the director's kitty at REPCON into a slow coach category.*

Renu seems to have picked up a lot from Gestler. When I think of all the balls she has in the air now, my head starts to spin: studying FDA registration at ZALA, business administration courses at Santa Clara in the evening . . . and her plans for a wedding on the last day of Hanukkah in Seattle. Was it Gestler who persuaded her not to try for an academic tenure-track slot? If so, how did he do that in one or two meetings? I bet she'll reconsider after a year in Palo Alto.

Martin Gestler, ex-CEO of ZALA — I can't figure him out. At best fifty, he looks like a man doing zillions of push-ups every morning. Why did he give up the top job in what I understand to be the most innovative American company working on new drug delivery methodology? I asked Dvir, who seems to be a buddy of his, whether he'd been fired — if he got the "golden handshake" — but Dvir just shook his head. "You must be kidding," he said. "Gestler could get a job anywhere. Besides, he's still on the board of ZALA. We're lucky at Ben-Gurion to have snared him for our board before the fat cats at Hadassah or Weizmann thought of it." I wanted to know what's so rare about him, whereupon Dvir turned surprisingly romantic. "Money is not everything to him. At least not just making money, unless it is for a useful purpose — and by 'useful', I mean useful to Israel," he laughed.

"Where does the man live?" I asked, but Dvir just shrugged. "Why don't you ask him yourself, if you're so curious." So I did.

"I still have my house in Atherton — the Gold Coast near Stanford — because real estate just goes up and up there, whatever happens in the rest of the world. But recently we restored a lovely old house in Jerusalem, on a small street right across from the Ethiopian church. So where do I live?" he grinned and shrugged. "I

spend so much time in the air, that all I can say is 'now I buy my plane tickets in Jerusalem.'"

Gestler says we'll need to study at least two thousand more volunteers in the States, in fifty different centers with a variety of dosage regimens. Satisfying those requirements, he warns, and all the other things he hasn't even mentioned, means we'll be in the middle or perhaps even late 1980s before we're past the FDA. Yet he doesn't seem fazed. "Par for the course," he calls it.

Menachem Dvir laps it all up. He got what he came for: everybody has already acceded to his request that the manufacturing plant — at least for the MUSA platform — be established in Beersheba. Having won that point, he's now arguing that the chemical pilot plant for NONO-2 should be set up next door and that all of it be built right from the start with FDA standards in mind. The Beersheba mayor, Tuviyahu, has already promised a free site. That should prove persuasive.

I keep looking at Menachem across the table. He doesn't have the foggiest idea what I'm going to spring on him tonight. All I can think about is what he'll say.

Say "yes," I'm pleading, while everyone else in this room is mouthing NONO.

"Shalom," Menachem greeted Frankenthaler. "This has been quite a day. Aren't we lucky to have Gestler involved?" He leaned back expansively and stroked his chin. "Amazing how much has happened since you visited me in Beersheba last year, isn't it? We really have to thank you for sending Renu to Israel. That's what started it all — Renu's little REPCON grant. And if the clinical studies here pan out, Gestler will raise ten million dollars from his venture capitalists!" He rolled his eyes.

Frankenthaler was barely listening. For a change, he wanted to move to a topic other than NO. "A lot more than that happened during the past year. . . ."

"You mean Osirak?"

For a moment, Frankenthaler looked blank. "Osirak? Oh, of course, that — your bombing of the Iraqi nuclear reactor."

"We've taken quite a beating in the world press," Menachem observed. "It's two months since we defanged Saddam Hussein and we're still being pilloried. Next week, I'm leaving for Canada, for the Kirchberg Conference in Lake Louise. You have no idea what official scolding or even crucifixion," he spat out the word as only a Jew can, "is in store for me." He looked sharply at Frankenthaler, all good humor dissipated in a cloud of irritation. "What hypocrisy, even among scientists who ought to be clear thinkers. Yet underneath all that condemnation, that pointless verbiage, there will be people who are glad that we did what we had to do. And if they aren't glad now, I guarantee you they will be some day."

"You still go to these conferences?" asked Frankenthaler. "What do you hope to accomplish there? And what does Osirak have to do with those Kirchberg discussions?"

Dvir leaned back, his dark mood lifting. "You'd be surprised," was all he said.

Frankenthaler was about to start on his real mission when Dvir continued. "By the way, Kirchberg reminds me of Melanie Laidlaw. I met her there once. Did you ever talk to her about the patent discussions we had last year?"

Frankenthaler was momentarily nonplused. Had Dvir known somehow what was on his mind? "Yes," he began cautiously. "In fact, I did talk to her about patents. To my surprise, she seemed rather relaxed about it. She felt that if the universities used any royalties for institutional support, REPCON would have no problem with the proposed arrangement. Their main concern is with birth control, anyway. They wouldn't want distribution of new contraceptives prejudiced by some exclusive marketing arrangement with a pharmaceutical company. 'Nitric oxide releasers for treating impotence?' she laughed. 'Public sector distribution seems rather unlikely.'"

"By the way, how is Melanie Laidlaw? What's her child's name?"

Frankenthaler fidgeted before replying. "Adam," he said brusquely. "That's why I wanted to meet with you. I have something for you to read."

New York, July 24, 1981

My dearest Menachem,

You may wonder why I asked Felix to take this envelope with him to Israel and to deliver it in person. First, I don't want to take the risk, however remote, that this letter might fall into someone else's hands. Second, the date of delivery is not crucial, since you will undoubtedly ask why I had not written this letter one or even two years ago. And finally, Felix has gradually guessed much of what I am now writing. Therefore, he is the only messenger I can trust.

I did not respond to your last letter because I was not ready then for a confession. Important confessions should be made in person. But even though this confession is the most important one of my life, I felt that *you* should not have to face *me* when you learn this: You are the father of my son.

I know there is much to explain here. I imagine you want to know more about the *how* right now than the *why*. But please (if I can ask you for any more forbearance) bear with me and let me tell you about the *why*. The *how* is far, far simpler to spell out.

As you know, I have never had a child before. While there were times during my marriage when I considered motherhood, circumstances, as well as Justin's own ambivalence, led me to postpone it until too late. It was only when I was a widow, and the choice seemed utterly irrevocable, that I came to appreciate what I had lost. And it was only then, by ways I never could have foreseen, that the lost choice came back to me — only after I thought I had put the possibility aside forever and buried myself in my work.

It was my new work that gave me back what I had lost. The REPCON directorship provided me with security — professional as well as financial — and perhaps most important, self-confidence and total independence. At the same time, my biological clock ticked louder and louder, and with it I became aware of an increasing desire to become a mother. I felt that in my present position I could achieve it functionally and that I could afford it emotionally, for myself and for my child. But as you know, I had no sexual partner after Justin's death until I met you. Yes, I had speculated about artificial insemination with an anonymous sperm donor, but the idea of my not knowing anything about the father of *my* child repelled me. I could not divorce myself from the importance of the biological identity of the father.

Suddenly, you, my Menachem, appeared out of nowhere, like a sexual angel from the sky. More than that: as the only proper choice for the father of my child. But I knew almost as immediately that any hope of living together with you would not be realistic. You are in Israel and I in New York; and while I am free, you are not.

By now, I can imagine you are wondering whether you are dealing with a romantic lunatic. How could you, "infertile" Menachem, impregnate me? Remember that first night in Kirchberg, when you told me that Solomon visited the Queen of Sheba only three times each month, but that it was quality rather than quantity that counted? One of the great advantages of my position with REPCON is that I am one of the first in the world to know about advances in reproductive biology, including those in the field of male infertility. Do you remember when you asked me in London what the Belgians were working on and I said "ICSI"? I didn't tell you then, but ICSI stands for "intracytoplasmic sperm injection," a procedure permitting fertilization of a woman's egg with *one single* normal sperm.

I gambled that my Solomon, Menachem Dvir, still had enough viable sperm to penetrate a woman's egg in a petri dish — an assumption that made me lie to you. This is my first confession and you must believe me when I tell you that it is the only deliberate falsehood I ever told you. There are times when I did not disclose the entire truth — just as you did not — but that was done invariably by omission of a fact rather than by deliberate commission of an untruth. Remember when I surprised you with a condom because of some supposed yeast infection? I know you could not have forgotten, because I can still see that hilarious expression on your face and the effect on your wonderful cock as you saw me apply the rubber band so that none of your precious seed might be spilled. What you may not remember is that immediately after you had come in me I ran to the bathroom, ostensibly to discard my condom with your priceless semen. But I did not discard it. Rather, I dropped it into a small Dewar, containing liquid nitrogen, and the rest you can imagine.

You did, indeed, have some normal spermatozoa; not sufficient to impregnate anyone on your own, but adequate for intracytoplasmic sperm injection of a healthy egg, which I provided. When Felix Frankenthaler told you, some months later, that I had gotten pregnant, I did not lie about the father. I just did not volunteer his identity to Felix. I thought that it was sufficient for me to know who the father was.

(There is, of course, the question of when and what Adam needs to know, but that will depend, in part, on your response to this letter.)

Now that I am opening up to you as if I were in a confessional (what a terrible simile for a new Jewess), I will admit that during my pregnancy and the first few months after Adam's birth I felt no guilt about having deprived you of that single sperm. Subsequently, on more than one occasion, at dinner parties or during one-on-one conversations, I brought up, as if it were a hypothetical case, what I had done. It was easy for me to bring up the subject. I just told people about ICSI, one of the hot new projects supported by my foundation, and then asked, "What if . . . ?"

I was flabbergasted by the depths of feeling my question generated. "But she *stole* his sperm!" was one of them — a comment I didn't just hear from men but also women. Initially I was very defensive, pretending I was speaking on behalf of the accused sperm thief. I kept insisting that the man couldn't do anything with this one sperm. "But neither could *she!*" one woman once yelled at me, as if she had actually known it was my egg your precious seed had fertilized. "*She* and *her* egg couldn't do it alone. She needed ICSI. And *that* does not belong to her!"

I still remember that exchange, because in the end it touched me so deeply. I almost wanted to explain that, in a way, ICSI *did* belong to me; that indirectly, I, through REPCON, had made possible its invention; and that the biological father, believing himself to be infertile, could not possibly have thought his semen of value. And if something is valueless, how can you steal it? Felix had a reply to that. "There is no difference between the goods stolen and the value of the goods."

Another question asked of me was what if the man did not believe in reproduction, convinced that too many people were already in this miserable world? I just shrugged, because in your last letter you had already presented me with prima facie evidence of your interest in procreation. Most Jewish men feel as you do. And how do I, your *shikse* lover as you have called me more than once in bed, know that? Because, as I hinted earlier in this letter, I am a new Jewess, having converted, though not to Orthodox Judaism — but that is almost beside the point. Although we never really spoke about religion, I felt that it would matter to you that any child of yours be borne by a Jewish mother. So you see, deep down I always thought of Adam also as *your* son.

I have told you of an overwhelming fact of life. I must end with a more theoretical fact — of death. When I had my last physical exam, it was discovered that I had a fibroid tumor. I am going to have a hysterectomy. Tens if not hundreds of thousands of women have hysterectomies annually. It's certainly not life threatening (other than that no future conception of life is possible — making Adam even more precious to me), but it did make me think. What if?

I am an only child whose parents are dead. I have no close relatives, although I do have friends. At least two of them, Felix and Shelly Frankenthaler, are close enough that they have agreed (shortly after Yom Kippur, of all days!) to act as parents for Adam if something happened to me and no one else was prepared to assume that legal role. But I felt that for Adam's sake and my own guilt you should know that you are his father. I do not wish to place a burden on you that you did not seek nor does anyone, except the Frankenthalers, know of your paternal connection. All you need to tell Felix is *yes* or *no* after you have read this letter. He promised not to try to persuade you in any form to assume legal guardianship of Adam in the event of my death.

Let me end on a mythological note related to Solomon and the Queen of Sheba — after all, that story brought us together. Did you know that there exists also an Ethiopian version? I only learned about it recently from Edward Ullendorff, a professor of Ethiopian Studies. According to him, the Kebra Nagast (to Ethiopians, in terms of importance, the equivalent of the Old Testament or the Koran) states that Solomon and the Queen of Sheba indeed had carnal relations, but it also implies that Solomon did not know that the Queen was pregnant when she returned to Ethiopia, where she gave birth to a son, Menelek — the founder of the Ethiopian imperial dynasty. What is so poignantly relevant to us two — hence the reason why I am citing my references to show that I have not made up any of it — is that, eventually, the queen sent the boy Menelek back to Jerusalem with the request that Solomon educate him. Attached is a photo of an Ethiopian representation of the entire legend, divided in the original into forty-four small pictures in cartoon-strip format, taken from one of Ullendorff's articles. Perhaps some day, you and I could look together at the original in the Ethiopian part of the Church of the Holy Sepulcher in Jerusalem, notably at number twenty-six, showing Solomon and the queen "sleeping" with each other; at number thirty-one, in which Menelek asks, "Tell me about my father"; and number

thirty-five, depicting father and son. We would ignore
number forty-three, the queen's deathbed confession.

You and I enjoyed in the deepest sense of the word a
Handel opera in Vienna. A couple of months ago, I heard
Handel's oratorio, *Solomon*, for the first time in my life. The
last duet by Solomon and the Queen of Sheba ends Handel's
piece; in its last line, the two sing of "Praise unbought by
price or fear." Adam's birth does indeed deserve praise.

Stay well, my Menachem and my Solomon,
Melanie

11

"Renu, this is *estupendous* news. Congratulations," Alfredo Zaffanori greeted her, his carefully combed, silvery hair quivering every so slightly with the pumping motion of his enthusiastic handshake. Yet the touch of his well-groomed hands and long fingers was gentle, his skin had a manly softness that one usually associates with pediatricians. Alfredo Zaffanori had not left his native Paraguay for the States until he was in his twenties; he still slipped into occasional Hispanicisms, of which the obligatory *e* before an *sp* or *st* was the most charming.

It was the spring of 1983. Renu was now in her second year at ZALA; she had been there long enough to have become accustomed to Alfredo Zaffanori's linguistic lapses. She was about to demur diplomatically, to say that the great news from Israel about the successful completion of the Phase II clinical trials with NONO-2 was the result of a team effort, when Zaffanori spoiled it all. "But tell me, Mrs. Cohn," he leaned down to whisper in a confidential tone, "what are your plans?"

"Calling me 'Mrs. Cohn' is *estupido*," she wanted to say, but she caught herself. Renu Krishnan was fiercely proud of her Indian

names. It wasn't because she had started to publish as Renu Krishnan — a common enough reason for a modern professional woman
not to change her name after marriage — but because she had a
streak of nationalistic pride, coupled with a sense of personal autonomy that required the uncontaminated, unhyphenated retention
of her birthname.

The reason for Zaffanori's query suddenly occurred to Renu. My
God, she thought, he *knows.* He isn't referring to NONO, he's talking about. . . . So Martin told him!

Martin Gestler had become an advisor, almost a confidante,
rather than a Papaji substitute to Renu. As early as their second
("call me Martin") meeting, he had convinced her that a change in
her professional life was worth considering. It had been his prag-
matism, the straightforward nonproselytizing manner of his proposition, that had made her say *"lama lo,"* even before checking with
Jephtah. She was sure her lover would agree because he had a
natural practical streak, whereas hers was just starting to develop.
It took Martin's tutelage to make it flower, and flower it did.

"I'm by no means suggesting that you drop an academic career,
nor do I want to propose that you turn away from science. Even if
ultimately you should decide to do one or both — "

"God forbid," she said, giving the words such a Jewish intonation that they both broke into laughter.

"God doesn't always forbid, although some Jews behave as if He
does. He also assists the prepared," Martin said, surprising her by
the earnestness of his tone. "It's amazing how many academics are
convinced they have chosen the ideal life without making even the
slightest effort to discover what else they could do in the outside
world. Furthermore, you're damn lucky to have participated in an
important discovery which may have *practical* applications." He
mimed the dismissive tone of the "pure" scientist. "And to have
done so while you're still young enough to learn some aspects of
the other side of the R and D coin. The D side," he added dryly,
"has its own excitement and rewards. In the drug field, only when
the D is completed is a drug a drug. Never before."

"But — "

"Wait with the 'but,'" he interrupted. "I'm almost finished.

Even if you should return to an academic career, you would do so knowingly, and it would make you a much better teacher, even a better researcher. You're still young enough to be able to afford to spend one or two years exploring some of the other options." He slowed down. "Now what's your 'but'?"

"But I agree," Renu burst out. "You're banging through open doors." She'd once heard the Prof use that expression and had decided to save it for the right occasion. Clearly, this was one.

"Oh," he exhaled, and laughed. "I knew you were smart," he added and poured out his "proposition" involving the exposure of Renu at ZALA Corporation in California to the tougher and "dirtier" aspects of drug development. It was in the process of elaborating on his professional plans for Renu that her marital prospects came up. When told the name of the intended groom, Martin smiled broadly. "You're even smarter than I thought."

———

Martin Gestler, one generation younger than Alfredo Zaffanori, had been the latter's protégé and one of the first employees when Zaffanori Laboratories was founded. By the time the company went public, the name had changed to ZALA Corporation and Gestler had become CEO. Even though he had resigned from the day-to-day management of ZALA two years ago, shifting to a Palo Alto–Jerusalem commuting schedule controlled by his current Zionist-prompted entrepreneurial and pro bono activities, his association with ZALA and Zaffanori was so close that he could take initiatives without consultation. In that regard, sending Renu and Jephtah to California had been a trivial step. More than a year had passed since that summer, and everything had gone well. In fact, too well. The time was ripe for complications.

———

"Martin," Renu approached him in a momentarily quiet corridor at the ZALA offices in April of 1983. Gestler was in Palo Alto to attend a ZALA board meeting. "I've got to talk to you," she said quietly. "I need your advice," she added. "I need an hour with you — alone."

When they met, she waved away the proffered coffee. "No caffeine for the next few months," she announced. "I'm pregnant."

"Congratulations. How wonderful," he said, though not with total conviction. "So what do you plan to do?"

"That's what I wanted to explore with you. I think we ought to return to Israel, where it's easier to raise a young child. Jephtah has family there — an uncle, an aunt, several cousins. . . ."

"That's not enough of a reason," Gestler said. "People have children in California. You have done fabulously well here. ZALA would love to keep you on — if you were interested in a full-time position."

"I'm not."

"I know," he said quickly. "I would have been disappointed if you'd said yes. I see a bigger future for you. But why drop out now? You'll have your MBA by the end of the year. I wouldn't throw that away if I were you."

"What do I need it for?"

"You don't, if you've decided on a university career."

She sighed pushing back her hair as she slumped in her chair. "I'm still undecided. Especially now."

Gestler moved his chair closer. "In that case, you need a crash course in venture capitalism. I know, I know," he said, waving her to silence. "You've heard enough about it in school to write a book, but I think right now you need to hear about it from both sides: the investor's and the entrepreneur's."

"Why?" she asked suspiciously.

"Shh." Gestler said. "Just listen."

———

Gestler's lecture, because that's what it soon turned into, almost made her forget her morning sickness. Initially, Gestler hunched over in his chair so as not to tower over Renu close by his side, but soon he started wandering up and down the lounge as he spoke.

"Why don't you sit down, Martin," Renu finally interrupted him. "I'm starting to become dizzy. I have enough trouble keeping breakfast down as is."

He had been in the middle of an explanation of why he had done nothing so far about raising funds for a NONO venture in the States. The reason, he said, had to do with the two basic ingredients that go into a high-tech start-up company in the biomedical field: "On the one hand, you have a researcher, the proponent of an idea or even an actual discovery, on the other, a venture capitalist, possessing not only money but also good judgment — "

"You make it sound as if good judgment resides mostly on one side," Renu observed wryly.

"For business judgment, it usually does," he replied, "and especially so when the one with the idea is an academic."

She laughed. "And where do the Martin Gestlers of this world get this monopoly on good judgment?"

"Ah," he exhaled triumphantly. "Good judgment comes from experience. And experience invariably comes from bad judgment."

"Oh," she said, seemingly chastened. "Go on."

Gestler's key point was that the man with the idea needed money to demonstrate its feasibility. The wilder and more interesting the idea, the bigger the gamble and the tougher the bargain struck by the venture capitalists; theirs is a statistical game, based on diversification of risk. The venture capitalist expects failures, Gestler emphasized, and therefore must benefit handsomely from occasional successes. So he drives a flinty bargain for his initial investment.

"Flinty?"

"Yes, 'flinty.'" Gestler leaned closer, as if the explanation required proximity. "Flint is hard, but it also produces sparks when struck. The hard component is the demand — usually successful — for a healthy portion of the initial stock in the new company. The sparks come later. If the venture doesn't go belly up, more money will be needed, frequently within a year or two when some preliminary feasibility of the man's idea has been established."

"Martin. I know I shouldn't keep making seemingly silly interruptions but, all the time, you keep talking about 'the man with the idea' — "

"I know what you're going to say," he cut her off. "And you're right. Henceforth, I'll use a word without gender — a person's idea — but the fact is, until now it virtually always is a man's idea. As you will see in a moment, I'm interested in changing that. Now don't interrupt any more or we'll never get done."

During that second or even third round of additional financing, according to Gestler, the original venture capitalists may put in more of their own money or, more commonly, bring in other investors at a higher stock price, thus diluting everyone's risk while, at the same time, generating a paper profit on their original shares. He raised a warning finger, while grinning conspiratorially. "This is pure paper profit, because there is no market for the stock. The game really starts to become interesting — the first sparks start to fly — when the biotech company has demonstrated the potential applicability of the original invention to humans *and*," his voice grew triumphantly louder, "*has managed to establish some sort of proprietary position*, usually in the form of issued patents or at least filed patent applications. Now a *real* financing becomes possible — usually through trying to go public. That's, of course, when stock is sold to the public through underwriters and that's when the value of the stock moves from fantasy paper to real paper, meaning dollar bills. With all of its accompanying baggage: greed, greed, and more greed. We can forget that problem for the moment, because we're still a very long way away from that stage with NONO, but we can't ignore a more important one."

Gestler had again started to pace. "While the applicability of a drug or device to humans may have been demonstrated in principle — a fact that may suffice for going public — that doesn't mean," he stopped, spun on one heel for a dramatic pause, "that it will be *accepted* by the market, meaning the medical profession."

"And what about the FDA?" interjected Renu.

"I've taken that monumental problem for granted because, after a year here, you know all about it. Which," he bowed for a moment in a curiously deferential fashion, "is one of the big differences between you and most, if not all, of your colleagues in the NONO venture." He caught himself. "'Venture?' A Freudian slip, because I am now using the word in both meanings. But to return to reality, which is to say the stock market: assume we now are a public company. Quite frankly, the value of our shares is still based on hype — *must* be based on hype — even if it's hype generated by the investor's, rather than the underwriter's or the management's self-deluding optimism. And when I say 'optimism' I am only using a code word for avarice, the desire for a free lunch. So you often find an absurdly high valuation for start-up companies, bearing no relation to actual value or to that of firmly established, operating, and *profitable* corporations."

Gestler's verbal underlining, the rise and fall of his voice, was a highly effective mannerism. Renu received and digested each emphasized nugget of information with the appetite of an MBA student rather than the disdain of an academic purist from the ivory tower.

"So by the time our new company has its new drug out on the market, the realities of the marketplace take over." Gestler's strong baritone voice suddenly turned a confidential pianissimo. "Suppose, for instance, that the company's initial losses are bigger than the self-deluding optimists had anticipated." He issued a low, bitter chuckle. "Or it turns out that the profits don't really grow exponentially. You'll understand that, Renu, now that you're going to business school."

Gestler started talking faster. "The insiders start with business plans based on the total number of sufferers of whatever disease they're trying to cure." Gestler's shift from *we* to *they* initially seemed bewildering, but Renu took it as his attempt to present the picture both from the insider's view and the outside critic's perspective. "They multiply that number by the estimated annual cost of their drug to the patient, thus coming up with an estimate — usually quite optimistic — of the product's total market potential. And *then*," Gestler's voice turned triumphant again, but this time he could not hide completely the note of disdain, "they assume initial *modest* market penetration, with supposedly *conservative* expectations of annual growth rates. But these words — *modest, conservative* — are totally subjective. Thus, they may predict an initial capture of 10 percent of the predicted total market — surely that's 'modest,'" he said dismissively, "and then insert annual growth rates of ten, twenty, thirty or whatever 'conservative' percentage they assume. If sales levels actually materialize within that range, then the stock retains its initial value — unless major perturbations occur in the overall stock market, which, admittedly, are completely outside their control. Or the company's predictions may truly have been 'modest' and 'conservative,' in which case share prices soar to everyone's satisfaction. But," he nodded with mock sadness, "more often than not, the initial market penetration may be 1 percent rather than 10 percent, and increasing one's market share may cost a real bundle, leading to huge losses which last much longer than the outside world — or even the inside management — anticipated. That's when the sparks *really* fly — and the stockholders' class-action suits follow."

"Tell me about those." Renu had heard about them in her MBA classes, especially when doing realistic case studies. She suspected the explanation she would hear from Gestler would be different.

But Gestler would not deviate. "Some other time. If I start on those, we'll never finish. All this is only a preamble to what I would now like to tell you." He sat next to her and briefly patted her arm. "The NONO venture is fundamentally different. That's what I want to discuss with you. That, and your possible role."

"My role?" Renu burst out. "But I'm pregnant. I haven't even figured out yet how to play the role of mother."

"Let me explain," said Gestler, and patted her arm again.

I wouldn't be surprised if April 3, 1983, turns out to be one of those key dates in my life, like my birthdate, the day I came to the States, the day I met Jephtah, the day I realized I was pregnant, and now the day I listened to Martin and his plans for SURYA. Of course the name SURYA came later; first came the plan. The way Martin described it, it was clear that he'd given it a lot of thought, based on plenty of past experience, some of it the very worst imaginable. Thus, he assured me, his present judgment was rapidly approaching impeccability.

SURYA, our NONO venture, would be different from virtually all of the biotech models he'd described to me that day. The key to the difference was timing, which, according to Martin, is the key to all success in life. If he had to choose between proper timing and good luck, he said, either as an investor or an entrepreneur, he'd always pick timing, and this time *he planned to enjoy both.*

By now, we had crossed several important hurdles: we had filed patent applications for the drug (my class of NONOates), we had filed a patent for the MUSA device, we'd even filed a use patent to cover intraurethral administration of any erectogenic drug, not just the NONOates.

We were in a unique proprietary position, since, so far, no interferences or substantial prior art had been cited by the patent examiner. In fact, our patent counsel in Washington — a firm picked by Martin — was struggling to keep our patent from being allowed too promptly. There was no reason to let the seventeen-year clock of an issued patent start prematurely. Why cannibalize patent exclusivity before the product is close to being marketed?

Even more important, we had not approached anyone about financing. By waiting, we had managed to get past most of the initial hurdles without having to consult any outsiders. We had not only demonstrated the clinical utility of NONO-2 but also of our mode of application in a couple of hundred Israeli patients. And at Martin's urging (I still see the triumphant glow in his eyes), we had held off the real search for capital until the two-year rodent carcinogenicity studies were completed and came out clean. Martin said he knew of no other biotech company that had reached such an advanced level of development without having had to raise a shekel — his word, not mine.

Of course, we had had to raise a fair amount of money (though only a fraction of what it would have cost to do the same work in the States, rather than Israel), but all of that was pre-SURYA dough: the Brandeis-initiated grant funds for all my chemical work, the two REPCON grants that made the Israeli connection possible (and, even more important, my marriage), and the Ben-Gurion and Hadassah institutional funds. According to Martin, the Hadassah-sponsored Phase II clinical studies of MUSAs loaded with NONO-2 alone would have cost a cool five million dollars or more if conducted in the States.

"And I haven't even talked yet — not even whispered," Martin added with his disarming grin, "about the glamour of the project. I don't care that you people insist on calling it 'erectile dysfunction.' You're dealing with the key to male sexual performance, a commodity

*for which men (and most venture capitalists are men) are prepared
to pay dearly. So you see what we've done, Renu? By waiting, we've
stacked the deck. When it comes time to strike a bargain with venture capitalists, the usual roles will be reversed: the flint will be on
our side." And then he proceeded to define the multiple meanings of
"our" and "we."*

*First, the entrepreneur: in "our" venture, there was no "man with
an idea" — not even a "person" — but rather three institutions:
Ben-Gurion, Brandeis, and Hadassah. I'd assumed that he had
listed them in that order for alphabetical rigor, but Martin soon
disabused me of that notion. He was on the board of governors of
Ben-Gurion, the university with the smallest endowment — in fact,
a piddling one — and with the greatest need for a real winner. It
could have been Zen-Gurion and he would still have listed it first.
But by having three nonprofit institutions as "Founder's Stock Owners" (a key term whose crucial importance became clear later) the
element of greed had become redefined in institutional rather than
personal terms — according to Martin an extraordinarily interesting difference.*

*But the "we" didn't mean only three universities. It also involved
Martin, who planned to put in some of his own cash as an investor
and to be the person "with good judgment" who would bring in
some of the other key investors. According to him, persuading Alfredo Zaffanori to participate would be an enormous coup. "More
about that later," he said, turning to the most relevant expansion of
"we" — namely me.*

*It was clever how he started: "And now, Renu, I'm removing my
pure investor's hat and am putting on the yarmulke of the prospective company executive, and that's where it will stay. This company
has such superb prospects that I've decided to do something that I
promised myself only two years ago never to do again: get involved
in corporate management. Just consider the challenge. You've got a
company with its operating components in Israel looking for capital
from American investors and needing to penetrate the American
market. The person running the company at the outset should be
able to operate in both places. With all due modesty, I concluded*

that I was the right candidate, one who also happens to have the best interests of one of the prospective founders at heart. I hardly need add that the appropriate Ben-Gurion people concurred."

"What about Brandeis and Hadassah?" I asked.

"They're lucky," he replied, waving my question away. "They're getting a free ride on my Ben-Gurion horse. If Ben-Gurion wins, so will they."

The rest was quite straightforward. He would serve as chairman of the board of the new company — so far nameless — to be incorporated in Delaware (with its liberal laws governing corporations) but headquartered in the San Francisco Bay area, the hotbed of American venture capitalism and entrepreneurship. "You've got everything here," he said in a tone brooking no contradiction, "aggressive venture capitalists galore, bright, technically trained people, unsurpassed climate, two great medical schools, and a first-class international airport." That's when he took a breath. "And an occasional earthquake or two. But you know all that: you're here now." He would also serve for the time being as CEO and president, but none of this would require his full-time involvement or giving up his desire to buy his plane tickets in Jerusalem.

"And how will I accomplish all that?" he asked innocently. "With you as the day-to-day manager," he said, pointing his extended index finger at me, a pistol made out of gold. "Of course, there would be a stock option in it for you — something to sweeten the deal." He grinned, and I could have sworn there were diamonds flashing from his back teeth.

"How sweet?" I stammered.

He named a figure that even now I cannot bring myself to repeat. At the time it only left me gasping faintly, "Why me?"

I had already anticipated the answer. Initially, the operating concentration would still be in Israel. Menachem Dvir had already pushed through the MUSA production facility and the NONO pilot plant. Most of the work in the States would be farmed out: the assembly of the FDA file and, most important, the huge clinical studies. The person to supervise the lean corporate staff in Palo Alto would have to be someone familiar with all aspects of the project, preferably a scientist, because ultimately — assuming successful entry into the American market — more research would have to be done to stay at the "cutting edge of the penile erection field."

Ouch, I thought, making a note to keep that phrase from appearing in our promotional literature.

"But I'm pregnant," I responded automatically, probably for the third time that morning.

"Don't you believe in working mothers?" he asked, without giving me a chance to respond. "I do. And if you don't, then don't complain to me about glass ceilings. I'm not suggesting you sacrifice motherhood at the altar of professional ambition — "

"So what are you suggesting?"

"For the job I'm describing, you don't even have to work in the lab. You'll have a good income — not superb, because we'll be a lean company, spending most of our money on getting to the market as quickly as possible — and with that stock option, if everything works out, you'll be financially independent for life. In the meantime, you'll have enough money for help, an au pair or whatever. There's a good infrastructure for infant care around Stanford — all kinds of graduate students with small children. And you have a husband. What about him? What about his role?"

My God, I thought. I've been listening to this without once thinking of Jephtah. What about his role? Not as a father — I know he'll do fine at that. But as . . . what?

12

"Which Hindu god deserves our prayers of thanks?" queried Jephtah as he brought some herbal tea to Renu. She was feeling squeamish again. "It's Shiva, isn't it?"

"*Mehra prem,*" she pinched his cheek playfully. Every once in a while, she used the Hindi words for "my love" both as a private expression of endearment and as her sign of revolt against the Indian custom of prohibiting wives from addressing their husbands in such affectionate terms. Among Indians, *mehra prem* was reserved for male voices. "Not Shiva. If we ever need a corporate logo, I suppose Shiva's lingam might be a suitable symbol. But I'm already pregnant, so the phallus is hardly relevant."

"A lingam-less marriage? God forbid," he exclaimed in mock horror.

"Relax, lingam-bearer. Right now, miserable as I feel, I need to pray to somebody concerned with my fertilized egg, not with any future fertility. God forbid. But let's not argue about gods." She was quiet a moment, one hand resting below her ribcage. "Still," she added thoughtfully, "what about his religion?"

"His?"

"Our son's."

"It will be a daughter," Jephtah's tone was categorical.

"How do you know that?"

"I can just feel it."

"All right — a daughter then. What shall we name her?"

"Naomi."

Renu looked nonplused. "Naomi? That's it? No other choices?"

"In Hebrew, it means 'beautiful, pleasant, delightful' and our daughter is bound to be all that. Just consider her parents."

"Flatterer." She gave him a playful slap. "And when did you reach that momentous decision?"

His impish grin disarmed her. "On March 16, 1983, at 6:05 P.M., five minutes after you'd told me you were pregnant."

Renu waved him toward her. "Come, *mehra prem*, give me a kiss. You are a darling, even if you are opinionated."

Jephtah sat next to her on the sofa, his arm around her shoulder. "Naomi Cohn," he mouthed the words gingerly. "Naomi Cohn sounds perfect. It's so short you can't maltreat either name. I hate nicknames: 'Sue' for Suzanne or 'Ev' for Everett." He shuddered in mock horror. "They're mutilations."

"My, my," Renu exclaimed, "I didn't know what button I was pressing. And who's Suzanne?"

"I never knew any Suzanne," Jephtah said quickly. "The name just occurred to me. But don't you agree that Naomi Cohn is ideal?"

"I'll have to think about it. We have nearly eight months to make up our minds — even if it does turn out to be a girl. But 'Naomi Cohn'?" A faint censorial touch had slipped into Renu's voice. "I think it's too short. What about Naomi Krishnan-Cohn?"

"Why not Cohn-Krishnan?"

"No reason. Let's throw that in the hopper as well." Until now, her tone had bordered on banter, but she suddenly turned serious. "But what about her religion?"

"Jewish," he said unequivocally.

"You'll take her to a synagogue? Other than at our wedding, you haven't been to one since we arrived in California."

"Well . . ." he hedged. "We have a few years to worry about that. I just meant she ought to *feel* Jewish . . . like me." He threw up his hands in a gesture that implied a fait accompli.

"Is this my *mamzer* speaking?" she asked softly.

"Why do you say that?" he said sharply, leaning backward as if he wanted to put some distance between them.

"Calm down, Jephtah darling," Renu stretched out her arms to draw him closer. "You know I'm on your side. And anyway, we know our child won't be a *mamzer*." When the Reform rabbi of the Seattle Temple Dehirsch Sinai had married them — in spite of the fact that Renu was still a *shikse* — he had automatically removed the *mamzer* stigma from any children of theirs. Correcting this injustice was the only reason why the rabbi would officiate at a marriage with a non-Jew.

"A lot of good that will do us in Israel," growled Jephtah.

"We don't have to return to Israel," Renu said quickly. "At least not in the near future. We could bring up Naomi here; when she's three or four years old, you could take her to a Reform synagogue and. . . ."

"And what?"

"Have her confirmed or converted or whatever term your local rabbi uses to make her a Jew."

"Stay here for three or four years?" he asked slowly. "I thought we'd go back to Beersheba," he added absently. For a moment he was silent, staring at the wall. Then he turned to his wife. "I got a phone call from Menachem Dvir today. He told me I could have a job running the MUSA facility in Beersheba, along with a research appointment back at Ben-Gurion University. It's a great combination for me — university and industry — and Beersheba *is* a good place for bringing up a small child," he said lamely, seeing Renu's changed expression.

"And what would *I* do in Beersheba?"

"Bring up Naomi and — "

"Jephtah! You can't be serious. We'll *both* bring up our child — or maybe even children — but I'll also work. I didn't go to Wellesley, and then to Stanford, and then to Brandeis, and then to Hadassah, and now to Santa Clara, just to take care of a little girl or boy in Beersheba. No," Renu sat up straight. "You got a phone call from Dvir? Let me tell you what Martin Gestler told *me* this morning."

He listened without a single interruption, but Renu could see his mood darkening. She thought she'd amuse him with the proposed name of the new venture.

"Syria?" Jephtah spat out the word. "You can't be serious."

"'Surya,'" she enunciated each letter carefully. "S U R Y A," she spelled it. "The Hindu sun god."

Jephtah gave a dismissive shrug. "If you and Gestler feel you've got to stick to Hindu mythology, why not Shiva Products? You are dealing with the penis, aren't you?"

"People also pray to Surya as a healer," she said soothingly. "And according to Hindu mythology, Surya has twelve different incarnations. Since nitric oxide plays so many different biological roles in the body — from penile erection to cancer and brain function — couldn't we think of NO as a cellular Surya?" Seeing his dubious expression, she added hastily, "Anyway, Martin liked it."

"What about me?" he asked. "Where do I fit in all this — other than as a father?"

"I'm sure there'll be a position in SURYA — or whatever the final name of the company will be," she added quickly.

"And when I ask for a raise, do I come to you?"

It was the first serious argument in our marriage. Do I know so little about my husband of three years? Or have I changed so much during that time? I guess it's both. Until now, I've never touched Jephtah's manhood except in the literal sense, and there our respective roles were not only clearly defined but mutually enjoyed.

I really got sick that night. I threw up until dawn — probably a combination of early pregnancy and deep unhappiness. Jephtah, who doesn't hold grudges, held me in his arms. "Let's not talk about Hindu gods for the time being," he whispered. "At least until we're out of your first trimester." But neither he nor I waited that long.

Jephtah was the first to return to the topic, not more than a couple of weeks after we had our first significant clash. "I spoke to Alfredo," he announced, "and I think we have a solution. At least an interim one."

"Alfredo?" I was about to ask, when I realized he was talking about Alfredo Zaffanori. So it's "Jephtah" and "Alfredo," while I cannot tear myself away from "Dr. Zaffanori" . . . who is so damn elegant, and so very kind. Yet there is an invisible moat around him — an air of authority, his awesome reputation that dampens contradiction. Or maybe it's our age difference. If I could go back thirty years, I'm sure I would find a tall, dashing Latin Romeo, with a thin black mustache — the hirsute underline of Latin male arrogance — so different from the unsubtle, black brushes Levantine men grow. If that man had said, "call me Alfredo," I would've said an instantaneous si como no, the Spanish equivalent of the Hebrew lama lo, which somehow has acquired such an all-purpose Esperanto affirmative meaning in my psyche. But Zaffanori's mustache is now silver, as is his hair; his demeanor is benevolently imperious, and the energy barrier to my calling him by his first name is insurmountable. So what did Dr. Zaffanori say to my Jephtah?

Of course, it's all second hand; I wish I had been a fly on "Alfredo's" wall. Did Jephtah really say to Dr. Zaffanori that he wanted "to drop the urethra?" That he found his research on trans-urethral drug delivery "too constricting?" At least that's what he claimed he'd said. I don't quite believe it. It's too brusque, almost impertinent, and so . . . unfair.

I keep thinking — and I know it sounds odd but I keep thinking — wasn't it the urethra that brought us together? Somehow, I have the feeling that there is a message here, husband to wife, a declaration of independence in which the urethra has turned into a pejorative synonym for SURYA.

In any event, he said he wanted to broaden his horizon, technically speaking, and that's where "Alfredo" made him an offer that I had to agree was indeed beyond refusal. If I hadn't been so tempted by Martin's proposition to try corporate management — a synonym for power, albeit of bantam class, considering the petite corporate fiefdom SURYA was likely to represent at the outset — I also might have accepted Dr. Zaffanori's invitation. Within minutes, I stopped worrying who had told what to whom, how it all had started, and what had motivated Jephtah to accept on the spot, without talking it over with me. (But then, what right do I have to even raise that question? I may not have signed on Martin's dotted line — after all SURYA doesn't yet exist — but I really had made my decision before broaching the subject to Jephtah.) But all that became academic as we started to talk about the science of Zaffanori's tempting offer — one scientist husband to his scientist wife.

"ZALA is setting up a new R and D venture — almost an independent company — called Electrotransport Therapeutic Systems — ETS for short," Jephtah started. "With his reputation and Midas touch, people are fighting to give Alfredo money. He's already raised funds for almost five years of off-balance-sheet financing. In other words, ETS's research expenditures won't penalize ZALA's bottom line. This is important, because as a public company ZALA must pay attention to its stock value. They are no fly-by-night start-up — they already have an operating income."

Renu stared at her husband. "Who's the MBA in the family?"

Jephtah shrugged dismissively. "It's important that the new ETS employees understand the rules of the game. Five years of R and D expenses will be paid up front, but at the end of that period we've got to deliver. I say 'we,' because Alfredo offered me a job as a group leader. ETS is like a new biotech enterprise, except that it's still within the corporate framework of ZALA — hence much more secure than some de novo venture." He eyed her speculatively. "Of course, I don't get a stock option like yours — "

"Jephtah, please! What's mine is yours. Besides, I haven't got it yet. Nothing has really been decided."

"Sure, but — "

"But what is ETS *doing?*" she interrupted. She was about to say that competitive posturing was not going to settle anything, but instead she kept mum. After all, she *was* interested.

"Ah yes," he said and put his feet on the coffee table. "You know almost better than I what a leader ZALA has become in *passive* transdermal drug delivery systems."

Renu nodded, somewhat impatiently. Having been trained in ZALA's regulatory affairs department, she knew most of the dossiers dealing with the novel skin patches the ZALA scientists had developed for delivery across the skin of such drugs as nitroglycerin in angina pectoris, estradiol in hormone replacement therapy, and clonidine for hypertension. Her latest assignment was to help in the assembly of a nicotine patch application to the FDA. "Go on," she said.

"So far, these systems have been limited to delivery of uncharged organic molecules. What ETS will solve," Jephtah announced vatically, "is the delivery across the skin of *charged* molecules — especially large ones, like peptides and proteins. You know the present situation: you can't administer them orally, because they get degraded in the gastrointestinal tract before reaching the intended target, so you're dependent on injections to maintain therapeutic levels. Wouldn't it be great if, in spite of their large size and affinity to water, we could get them across the skin?"

Renu made no attempt to hide her impatience. "Get to the point. You said ETS would solve the problem. How?"

"Iontophoresis," he declared, savoring all six syllables.

Renu knew what iontophoresis was — the movement of ions across a membrane under an externally applied electric current. "Fine," she said. "But how?"

He leaned forward, whatever resentment he may have been harboring giving way to enthusiasm — the Jephtah she had fallen in love with had suddenly reentered the room. "The principle was known a long time ago — in fact, too early to be of use. There is one experiment I even learned back in Israel, Leduc's, from around the turn of the century. He applied a constant current to two rabbits placed in series. Positively charged strychnine, in the form of its sulfate, was applied via the first rabbit's skin by means of an anode, whereas negatively charged cyanide ions were introduced through the cathode. Both animals died, one of strychnine, the other of cyanide poisoning. But," he waved her to silence, "when the two delivery electrodes were reversed, nothing happened, just as nothing happens if you apply strychnine or cyanide to the shaved skin in the absence of any current. And *that* was published in 1900! Think of what we have now at our disposal — especially here at ZALA — with all the in-house membrane technology developed during the past decade, and with Silicon Valley and all its electronic and miniaturization technology at our doorstep. We'll develop skin patches that incorporate the electrotransport system; we might try direct as well as pulsed current, so that we could produce steady or pulsatile drug delivery. . . ." He stopped to draw breath. "It's almost certain that drug delivery rates by electrotransport should be directly proportional to the electric current applied. Just as more liquid can be pushed through a small hole by increasing the pressure, so increasing the electric current ought to do the same thing or perhaps push bigger molecules through, *charged* ones, like proteins."

"Not bad," she said, her curiosity rising almost in pace with his excitement. "Just don't electrocute the patient. When do you plan to start?"

"Before you do," he said.

13

"It's about time to raise real cash, preferably a lot of it, so we don't have to go back to the well too often; each time we do, everyone's stock ownership gets diluted. I'd say ten million, just to be safe."

Martin Gestler was in one of his restless moods, pacing up and down in front of Renu's desk in the small office suite they had just rented in an office complex called Palo Alto Square. It stood on the corner of Page Mill Road and El Camino Real, diagonally across the street from the ZALA Corporation headquarters. It was a good address, Martin explained. "We've got law firms and CPAs right in the building; we can use the ZALA library across the street and, initially at least, lean on them for clerical support — for a fee."

He reached the far wall, whirled on one heel, and returned to his first subject. "Usually, the first round of financing is nerve-wracking for a start-up, but . . . we . . . are . . . different." He trod out the words in audibly separated strides.

"Just wait and see. It'll be a cinch. We'll push for four dollars per share, but I'll bet they'll still knock on our door, asking to be let in. Speaking of doors," he stopped and surveyed his surroundings as if for the first time. "This *is* a spartan suite." His gaze came to rest on Renu Krishnan sitting behind her rented desk. "Hardly the way Zaffanori would furnish a new office. He's got very expensive taste. Like his clothes." Martin looked down at his off-the-rack gray pants, at the accordion creases below his belt, before uttering a brief embarrassed laugh. "Not like me — but then I'm not a great believer in exterior appearance." He unbuttoned his collar button and loosened his tie. "If I have anything to say about it, that's the way we're going to operate — at least in the beginning. We ought to make it plain that the money we raise will go to launch the MUSA platform in the States, rather than on fancy offices."

"How did you come up with four dollars per share?" asked Renu.

"Art," he said and waited.

Renu did not disappoint him. "Art?" she echoed. "I don't get it."

"It's an art, not a science. How do you establish a value for a start-up? With no sales and usually no product, all you have to go on are art and — and of course hype, some of it even justified. But I'm talking about SURYA. As I keep saying — to the Ben-Gurion board, to you, to Alfredo Zaffanori (who, incidentally, agrees with me) — and as I will soon say to investors, we *are* different. We have a product, we know it works, and we have a proprietary position."

"But?"

He nodded. "As I've said before, Renu, you're smart. There *is* a big but. In fact two buts: we still have a lot of costly clinical work ahead of us to get through the FDA, and we can only guess at the eventual size of the penile erection market. Don't," he said and raised his hand. "I know what you're going to say: 'it's the erectile dysfunction market.' I'll promise to stick to those words — *after* we have raised our first ten million dollars. Until then, 'penile erection' or even some cruder term will do just fine."

"But that's just hype." Renu wrinkled her nose. "First art and now hype."

"Come now." Gestler had smiled through much of his earlier discourse, but now he turned serious. "'Hype'? — perhaps. Although in our case there is much less of it than usual. But Renu, enthusiastic hype is the sort of PR even the purest scientists engage in. Just think when you brag to your colleagues about the hot experiment you've just completed — every one a 'breakthrough.' There seem to be so many breakthroughs that there is nothing left to break through." Gestler's voice had started to rise. "Or the way you people practice grantsmanship: promising to cure cancer or whatnot when all you're proposing is some basic research that's still light years away from the first rat, let alone a human patient. Isn't that 'hype'?"

"In a way," she conceded. "But you still haven't explained how you arrived at the four dollar share price. How can you defend that? You told me we'd start with ten million outstanding shares. That's a forty million dollar evaluation for a company that hasn't even. . . ." Her voice failed as her eyes swept around her modest office.

"Your arithmetic is impeccable," he said. "And if I can't convince them with four dollars, we'll offer to part with stock at three fifty."

"Which is still awfully high," Renu countered. "Thirty-five million."

"All right. Let's go through it." He pulled up a chair in front of Renu's desk and sat down. "It's essential that you understand this, because stock value is the most important tool at our disposal —

and especially *yours*," he jabbed a finger across the desk, "for attracting the key personnel we haven't yet got. Without them, we have nothing. Well . . ." he hedged, "not exactly nothing, because SURYA already has quite a bit, but not enough to carry it all off."

Gestler reached for a pad of paper and took out his pen. "Of the ten million shares, we'll sell 25 percent — not more, I hope — to outside investors . . . *sophisticated* investors," he emphasized. "Individuals, or perhaps funds, that are prepared to put up at least one hundred grand at a throw. That's too rich for the proverbial old ladies in tennis shoes, although I wouldn't hesitate to recommend this particular investment to my grandmother, if she were still alive and had a use for a potential windfall, because I myself will buy some shares at the four dollar offering price. So will Alfredo Zaffanori, which ought to convince the outside world how serious we are." He shook his head impatiently. "But we're spending too much time on the investors — the future four dollar per share owners — important as they may be. You and I need to talk about the distribution of the other 75 percent of the company. First, a 60 percent ownership, equally divided, will reside with the three founding institutional owners — Ben-Gurion, Hadassah, and Brandeis — and this will be 'founder's stock,' specifically common stock with a par value of one cent. So you see, right at the outset, as soon as the investors have purchased their shares for four dollars, each university, with its two million shares, has made a paper profit of nearly eight million dollars. Not bad, is it? Although, of course, at this stage it will hardly keep them in paper clips, let alone allow them to construct new buildings. I know you'll wonder how we can rationalize a one cent stock for the founders compared to a four dollar cost to the initial investors. Just bear with me."

As he spoke, Gestler had been scribbling numbers on the paper. Now he circled the words *founder's stock*. "They are entitled to that 60 percent in return for what they are putting into the pot: the patents, your NONO-2, the clinical results — all of that accomplished and funded through their own efforts during the riskiest time of the venture. Surely, that has a great deal of value, especially given that now, when the investors enter, the risk of failure is greatly reduced. Remember, investment is all about risks and rewards. The justification for the huge price differential is that *they*," he circled the words *outside investors*, "will get *preferred* stock. Having gone to business school, you know what that means: in case of dissolution of the company, they have first call on the remaining assets." He snickered to himself. "As they and everyone else know, if the venture goes belly up, there will be precious few assets on which they could call. But, of course, that's part of the sport. This isn't General Motors, Coca-Cola, or IBM. It's a speculation, pure and simple, in which the investors gamble not only that the company will not go bankrupt but that it will succeed beyond or even slightly below their wildest dreams." Again he chuckled. "Still, giving them preferred stock — which, of course, will eventually be converted into common stock if and when the company goes public — gives their stock a separate legal status and, to that extent, extra value. You always pay for that. And now," he drew three exclamation marks on the paper, "let's get to the as yet unassigned 15 percent of the shares, which is really why I went into such detail. This is your, and, of course, also my, ammunition. These 1.5 million shares — an unusually high percentage — are reserved for stock options. We can't afford to pay high salaries to employees, and we have even less to pay consultants and board members. So . . ." he leaned back expansively, "instead, we offer them stock options, which will permit them to buy over the course of ten years SURYA common stock at forty cents per share. Not bad, eh?"

Renu did a quick calculation. In their preliminary discussions Martin had promised an initial stock option of seventy-five thousand shares. If she could buy the shares at forty cents, when investors were paying four dollars, her profit of three dollars and sixty cents per share would give her an instant gain of two hundred seventy thousand dollars!

"Forty cents," she exclaimed. "How will you explain that to the four dollar investors?"

He waved a hand in the air. "I won't have to. You are dealing with very sophisticated people — especially here in the Bay Area — who know all about options. It's quite normal in such start-ups for the option stock — which, after all, consists of common and as yet nonmarketable shares since they aren't yet registered with the SEC — to have only 10 percent of the value of the preferred stock. Remember, at this stage preferred stock has a higher legal standing and, besides, at this point all profits — including yours — are pure paper."

Renu started to redden, as if Martin had read her mind about cashing in her option windfall.

"People can only start thinking of real money, Renu," he added gently, "when the company goes public, which the outside investors dearly would like to see happen — and the sooner, the better. And if stock options will cause the management and employees to work harder toward that common goal, then why not share some of the goodies? There's plenty to go around." He rose from his chair. "Capitalism at work. We know it sells in Peoria. We now have to see how well it'll work in academia. It's the only currency you've got for the job ahead of you. It may be highly inflated, but it still looks like gold — at least judging by its glitter."

So here I am, almost seven months pregnant, sitting in economy class, on my way to Boston to get myself the best scientific advisory board stock options can buy.

I'm beginning to think and talk like Martin. So what's wrong with that? I like his mixture of irony, hard-nosed realism, and infectious enthusiasm. I like him.

Not so long ago, he admitted that he's testing me the way he was tested twenty-five years ago. A newly minted MBA from Stanford, he became the first management associate at Zaffanori Laboratories. Right from the start, Zaffanori made it clear that Martin was the heir to the throne, so long as he did the job Zaffanori had hired him to do — a real trial by ordeal for a kid just out of grad school! So if I perform well . . . ?

I think I'm up to it. For one thing, right from the beginning, Martin divided the labor. "Before we can tap investors," he announced one day, "we need a larger board of directors, a scientific advisory board, and a medical advisory board." Martin would work on building the board of directors, while SURYA's Princess of Wales, as the only scientist in the room, would carry the responsibility for the SAB and MAB.

When I told that to Jephtah, he just looked at my bulging stomach. "You better name your committee chairmen in a hurry "

"Chairpersons," I corrected him, but he didn't smile.

The secret to assembling these boards is networking: you find a few suitable candidates with professional oomph and they help you find the rest. I decided that I would start with Professor Frankenthaler and that I would meet with him personally. I hadn't been back to Brandeis since my short stopover in 1981 nor had I seen him during the last couple of years. I wasn't doing research — at least not what the Prof considered research — so our contacts were more of the Christmas letter type, although he had sent us a lovely silver menorah as a wedding present. He's always been a superb networker — invariably in the middle of the net — and while he's never been involved with industry, I felt comfortable about speaking to him. And wouldn't he make a first-class chairman of the SAB, considering his knowledge and experience of the NO field?

Martin just shook his head. "It's your responsibility," he said, "but I'll tell you why I don't think it's a good idea. First, we need a chairman who's not only known among scientists — we need somebody with glamour. To be very blunt, a Nobelist. I know they aren't a dime a dozen, but I'm sure you can catch one by dangling enough stock in front of him. Of course, he should be in some relevant scientific field. Too bad, nobody has won a Nobel Prize for NO — yet."

I couldn't resist saying, "Somebody will." He just gave me a long look — so long that I became embarrassed and quickly asked for his other objections to the Prof.

"He's your former professor and not just any professor. Not even just your postdoc mentor," he said. "You and he really started the whole project when he sent you to Israel. I have met enough scientists in my life to know how complicated personal identification with an important project can become. Do you really want such a father figure chairing the SAB? Even just sitting on it?"

Martin was very gentlemanly about it. He said, "Don't answer my question, just think about it." Then he told me about his own activities in putting together an initial board of directors, which settled it for me. Right from the beginning, the three universities had agreed that Martin was the ideal chairman — at least at this stage: he was already a commuter between Israel and California, dedicated to Jewish causes, highly experienced in fund-raising and biomedical industry, and even willing to invest some of his own money. What more could one hope for? He, in turn, felt that the principal stockholders — the three universities — ought to be represented. Ben-Gurion immediately chose Menachem Dvir — again an obvious choice. He had executive as well as fund-raising responsibilities at the university, and he'd been involved, at least peripherally, with the project since its inception.

The Hadassah proxy was also straightforward. It was clear that with SURYA's present focus on erectile dysfunction, a board member with an MD, preferably a urologist, would be desirable. Martin, who believed in small, working boards, felt that with Yehuda Davidson he'd be filling two positions at one go. But Brandeis? Martin barely knew the Prof, so he contacted Brandeis's financial vice president with whom he'd been dealing for some time. "Forget about professors," was his advice, "we'll be happy just to be kept informed — and, of course, to cash the checks." According to Martin, this made sense, since Brandeis's interests and equity stake were identical to those of the other two institutions, who were already represented. But Martin was diplomatic: he called Frankenthaler to feel him out on whether he'd be insulted.

To his surprise, the Prof openly admitted his lack of business acumen or even interest and proposed an alternative Martin considered brilliant: Melanie Laidlaw, the executive director of the REPCON Foundation. In her, the SURYA board would get a woman, a scientist with broad knowledge of reproductive biology, and a representative of the foundation that had initially supported some of the NO research. Had she accepted? I asked, intrigued by the proposal.

"I haven't been able to make an appointment yet," Martin said. He'd never met her personally and felt he'd have to have a face-to-face meeting in New York.

So after all that, still pregnant, I'm on my way to Boston. Martin agreed that it would be politic, perhaps even fruitful, if I asked the Prof for his advice about the SAB. I could ask him about leads to some Nobelists, because he's certainly been known to cultivate them. And I was curious, I had to admit, to hear what he would say — both about the SAB and about the size of my stomach.

I liked the way he greeted me: no fuss, straight to the point. "You certainly have grown," he said, looking at my stomach. "So you're taking on one more job?" I wasn't sure whether he meant mother-hood, my additional executive function, or what. But I'm pretty sure that he's now dropped any thoughts of convincing me to look once more for an academic position on the bottom rung of the tenure ladder. It didn't take the Prof long to get intrigued with my search. He was very sporting about it all, after emphasizing that industry was simply not his cup of tea (although I hadn't really asked him to consider the position). He'd never even accepted any consultancy, and he was not about to start now. "What do I think of a Nobel laureate?" he mused. "Yes, they can be useful," he laughed, a bit disingenuously I thought, but then recovered very quickly, in fact with a brainstorm.

"I.C.," he said.

I looked blank, thinking he'd said "I see."

"Isidore Cantor," he clarified, "the man who shared the Prize in medicine for his cancer work. Everyone calls him 'I.C.'"

I started to ask him for other names, but he acted as if he hadn't heard. "Think about it: you don't want a specialist as chair, you want a generalist with panache. Cancer is certainly relevant when you deal with nitric oxide — people worry all the time about the potential carcinogenicity of nitroso compounds. Having a cancer Nobelist heading your SAB would show you cared. Besides, you know that NO is starting to play a role also in tumor suppression. That ought to interest I.C. I know him pretty well. I'll call to see whether he'll meet you."

I liked the Prof's suggestion. He'd immediately understood what we wanted to accomplish in putting together our SAB. Its function wasn't PR for the investment community, although Martin warned

---

me not to underestimate that when the IPO frenzy would start in a few years. (Less than two years ago, as a pure and poor academician, I would never have guessed that these three letters were business lingo for Initial Public Offering; now one can wake me up at three in the morning and I would mouth these magic words with gusto.) If NONO-2 for erectile dysfunction therapy really takes off, we can't remain a one-product company, unless we are willing to be bought out by a pharmaceutical giant and lose our identity. This may be our fate — as it is the fate of the vast majority of biotech ventures, at least of those that survive — but it isn't part of our current strategy. Ours is quite simple: first bring NONO-2 to the market; second, start working on the next generation of products; and, third, explore some of the other therapeutic possibilities in which NO releasers or blockers could play a role. We could become the nitric oxide powerhouse of the pharmaceutical industry! The SAB would play a key role in keeping us abreast of the newest science — the as-yet unpublished work — and help us bring in bright new research talent. Network, network, network.

"What about Max Weiss?" he suddenly said. "He might be suitable." "The Princeton biochemist?" I asked. "For chair?" I didn't want to admit that I wanted nothing but a Nobelist. "A superb biochemist." The Prof held up his right thumb and index finger in a circle, as if he were describing the taste of some spectacular dessert. "And you need biochemistry on your SAB. If you can't have me, why not Weiss?" I felt we were suddenly getting unto tricky territory. "But isn't he retired?" I asked. "Wouldn't we start with a rather geriatric SAB?"

The Prof looked pained. "Why not say mature, experienced, deliberative . . . ?"

"Of course," I agreed quickly, but he didn't let go.

"Cantor is probably my age, maybe early sixties. Weiss may be pushing seventy, but he's still active in the lab. Rumors have it that he's onto something very hot." I was getting nervous that I was being painted into a corner.

"An excellent suggestion," I said, "but we need to focus first on finding a chair and then clear all other candidates with him."

"Or her," he said.

"Or her," I concurred. But I didn't mean it. Martin had challenged me with catching a Nobelist and I intended to go fishing, starting in Lake Michigan, which, to my knowledge, contained only males. I don't even know where to find a Nobel pond with female fish.

14

"Dr. Krishnan. Do you enjoy anagrams?" Professor Cantor asked. He had just pointed Renu to a wing chair that she accepted, grateful for the armrests and the straight firm back.

I can take them or leave them — mostly leave them — she thought while wagging her head noncommittally. She was here as petitioner, and Cantor had been unexpectedly gracious in agreeing to receive her in his Chicago apartment. The view of Lake Michigan — the kind of view Nobel money can buy — was itself almost worth the trip. "Why do you ask?"

"Take *Pithecanthropus erectus* — "

"I'm afraid paleontology is not my forte." Renu wanted to forestall any questions on a topic she knew little about and cared for even less. She had all of four hours between planes on her way from Boston to San Francisco; she was in no mood for Paleolithic chitchat.

"I'm not talking about hominids," Cantor chuckled good-naturedly. "What would you come up with if someone asked you for an anagrammatic equivalent?"

"I'd first have to write it down to be sure I didn't misspell it," Renu admitted.

"I like your answer, Dr. Krishnan: honest and to the point. You know who asked me that question?" Cantor didn't wait for an answer. "Your Professor Frankenthaler. His answer? 'Pursue the person, catch it,'" he said. "Clever, isn't it?" He leaned forward as if wishing to get her into better focus. "And you've never heard him say that during all the time you spent with him at Brandeis?"

"Never," she said firmly, yet startled to note how appropriately descriptive those words were to her present purpose.

"I'm impressed. I would have bragged to everyone in sight if I'd thought of that anagram."

"Maybe he didn't think of it. Someone just may have told it to him. The Prof doesn't take credit for ideas that aren't his."

Cantor's eyes narrowed. "I see," he said, sounding like his initials. "Perhaps that's why I pay attention to him. Is that why I took him seriously when he called yesterday about you? Even though he volunteered precious little about your mysterious mission? But your timing was lucky — I'd say spectacularly so. This is my chamber music weekend in Chicago, and my colleagues won't be here for another couple of hours."

As if on miscue, a singularly tall, glamorous Amazon type entered from the hall, one hand around the neck of a cello, the other carrying a bow. "I'm so sorry, Leonardo darling," she exclaimed. "I thought you were alone."

"Come here, come here," he waved her toward his guest. "This is Dr. Renu Krishnan, Felix Frankenthaler's former star postdoc, who has come on some covert mission. You my dear, of all persons, know how seriously I take star postdocs. And this is Paula Curry," he pointed to the cello-bearing giantess. "Felix Frankenthaler — you remember him Paula, when he came to our concert in January? That marvelously tough one; starting with the Hindemith No. 5, and then the last Bartók quartet — "

"Stop, Leonardo," she planted the cello like a shield and turned to Renu. "Leonardo is the violist in our quartet, so some Hindemith is almost obligatory. But don't let me interrupt you."

"Do you want to join us, Paula? Do you mind?" He glanced at Renu, who saw all of her careful plans disrupted.

"Not unless it's about music," Paula Curry said.

"I'm afraid it isn't music," Renu said quickly. "Just science."

"In that case, I'd rather look at the score in our music room." She addressed Renu. "We're starting with the Shostakovich No. 14 in F major. We haven't played that before."

"And where, precisely, are you in the corporate food chain?"

"I beg your pardon?" Renu asked.

"You know," Cantor motioned dismissively. "Where in the chain of command are you?"

"We don't think that way at SURYA," she replied curtly. "No one is feeding on anybody else." Renu did not consider it wise to volunteer that at present the entire corporate staff amounted to seven persons.

"So what is this? A corporate kibbutz?"

Renu burst out laughing. It broke the ice. "Since we did our original clinical studies in Israel, that may be apt. Still, not everyone gets paid the same."

"I thought so."

"Professor Cantor, aren't you a bit harsh? Is there no food chain in academia? How do you operate in your lab?" By eating grad students for breakfast, I'm willing to bet, and postdocs for lunch.

Cantor gave her long look, and for a moment she feared she had spoken that last part aloud. "You're right. Let's talk about what you really came for. Why should I join your scientific advisory board? Your SAB as I'm sure you call it."

Renu flushed. Was it his Midwestern intonation or had he actually called it SOB? If so, then she might as well catch an earlier flight.

But Cantor continued. " . . . I, who, like your own professor, has never before been involved with any company venture? Or am I wrong about Felix? Is he joining your SAB?"

Renu flinched. She made a mental note never again to use those initials. She ignored the last question. "Actually, we didn't just want you to join. I came to ask whether you'd head our scientific advisory board. And then, of course, to vet other prospective members."

"And why should I?"

"We do interesting science. NO is one of the most fascinating molecules in contemporary biology."

"Maybe," Cantor conceded. "But I'm not working in the field. I'm in cancer."

"I would be surprised if NO weren't also involved in some stage of tumorigenesis. Or in fighting it."

"That's the sort of pious hope people have all the time with lots of molecules. Surely you're not offering that as an incentive."

"What about getting exposed to interesting science that is *not* in your field?"

"But that can be said of innumerable things."

"Innumerable?" Renu had started to become uncharacteristically combative. She was now sure that Cantor would turn her down, but that was no reason to accept pompous, irrelevant arguments. She might depart beaten, but it would be unbowed.

"But there are two other reasons that should interest you. As a man and as a scientist."

"Name them."

Renu was taken aback by the brusqueness his discourse had assumed, so different from the polite, almost genteel manner in which he had welcomed her. Was he testing her? All right, then, she said to herself. I believe I can pass this one, too.

"Prostatic cancer and impotence," she replied, as bluntly as he had asked. "As you probably know, the first frequently leads to the second. Consider for instance total prostatectomies — "

"My prostate is still in reasonable shape," he said stiffly. "Anything else?"

Despite herself, Renu was flustered by the turn the conversation had taken. "Well . . ." she muttered, "there's functional impotence in men with diabetes mellitus, in cardiovascular — "

Cantor stopped her again. "I mean, are there reasons, other than scientific or medical ones, why I should consider joining — "

"Heading. Not just joining." If he can interrupt, so can I, thought Renu. "And there is always money."

"Aha."

Renu wasn't sure whether this was meant derisively or not. "We don't pay much for attendance at the board meetings — we are too small a company, with too little cash. But we offer a generous stock option to all members, and twice that amount to the chair." She proceeded to outline quickly the profit potential of a thirty-thousand-share stock option at forty cents per share, being careful to point out that an IPO — the first time when such option would actually start to have a marketable value — might well occur at fifteen dollars rather than the present four dollar price per share. "That's well over four hundred thousand dollars, and the stock could rise far beyond that if our nitric oxide releaser is as effective as the Israeli clinical studies indicate."

"I don't really need more money," Cantor said, "not unless I want to buy Paula a Guarneri for her birthday. In case you don't know," he added, "one of the Guarneris also made cellos." He shrugged. "I live comfortably, I have an income that allows me to do the things I want to do. I have no dependents — "

"But that's not the only reason to make money," she interrupted. "Even if you decide not to buy the Guarneri for — " Again, Renu became flustered. She wanted to say "Mrs. Cantor," but somehow the cello player seemed to play a different role in this home.

Cantor saved the situation without realizing it. The Guarneri had already been dropped. "Name one more reason," he said.

"Would you and your colleagues value the Nobel Prize as much if it paid one dollar rather than one million?" The moment the words were spoken, Renu wished they had remained unspoken. But she had been too irritated by his piety about money.

"When I won my Nobel, it paid eight hundred thousand, not one million," he said primly. Renu had not yet learned about a Nobel laureate's sensitivity when it came to the cash value of the Prize. "Besides, I shared it."

"I'm sorry I said that. And I certainly didn't mean *your* Nobel Prize."

"Go on. You were giving me another reason for wanting money."

"To give it away."

Cantor looked astonished. "Does that motivate you?"

"As a matter of fact it does. And don't forget, giving it away doesn't only make you feel good, it also offers you power."

"And is power important to you?"

"It's starting to be."

———

"I appreciate your willingness to receive me in your office," said Martin Gestler. In spite of his professed disregard for outward appearance, today he wore a well-pressed blue suit, black shoes still glistening from the shine-stand at the airport, and a white, lightly starched shirt with a smartly knotted, blue-and-gray striped necktie — the most conservative one in his limited wardrobe.

Melanie Laidlaw inclined her head. "I always take Felix Frankenthaler's recommendations to heart. I may not *follow* them, but I do pay attention. Felix told me you wanted to discuss my joining your company's board of directors. I appreciate the thought, but I ought to inform you right at the outset that I'm not serving on *any* board, other than REPCON's, and that in an ex-officio capacity."

"Excellent," said Martin. "That takes care of any possible conflicts of interest."

"Not so fast, Mr. Gestler!" Laidlaw was amused but also slightly irritated. "First and foremost, I am not on any other boards for reasons of time commitments. I'm the executive director of REPCON — "

"But there are other foundation directors and university presidents who serve on corporate boards," he interjected. "Both parties find such exposure mutually beneficial."

"Sure," she said, not wanting to add that until now she had not been invited, "but I'm also the mother of a very young son."

Gestler was not ready to concede a single point. The moment he had entered the REPCON offices and shaken hands with Melanie Laidlaw he had decided that she was the right candidate. Only rarely did his first impressions require revision. "But lots of people have children." He smiled disarmingly. "We won't have more than six meetings a year. If necessary, we might even hold one or two here in Manhattan. Surely, the domestic front can be manned by the father on those few occasions."

"There is no father."

"I see," he said, uncharacteristically abashed.

Laidlaw helped him extricate himself. "Tell me more about what you're planning. Remember, I had something to do with the early developments of the nitric oxide work. We funded Renu Krishnan's stay in Jerusalem. By the way, what's she doing now? I gather from Felix that she has joined your venture."

Gestler felt a rush of relief. Her questions had opened several avenues, and he decided to pursue them all. He started with Renu, emphasizing the prominent role he was envisaging for a young woman scientist, who was about to give birth to her first child. His instincts, as usual, were right: this was precisely what Melanie Laidlaw liked to hear. He finished by telling her about Renu's current efforts in recruiting a medical advisory board.

"Why do you need two such boards?"

"Good point," he said, seeing another opener for explaining their corporate plans. "The SAB plays a longer term role: we've got to prepare ourselves for the next phase of our development: what research and development to push *after* we're successful with NONO-2. They'll recommend or critique research for the next generation products as well as for other medical applications of nitric oxide biology."

Laidlaw nodded. "So why the MAB? I presume that's what you call your medical advisory board"

"We do. The reason is quite simple. Our highest priority is to complete as quickly as possible the Phase III clinical trials in this country on about two thousand diverse subjects in maybe fifty different centers."

Laidlaw looked astonished. "That many?"

"It'll probably take that many to get FDA approval, and we could lose a lot of time if we went to them with a smaller number and then were told to come back with more. As you can imagine, such a clinical trial is expensive, to the tune of millions. That's why the REPCONs of this world are not sufficient in the development of a new drug, why venture capital investments are required. We want to spend as little as possible on in-house MDs — by far the most expensive kind of personnel. Dr. Krishnan will supervise a group consisting mostly of nurse practitioners and a biostatistician, who will assemble the clinical data as they come in. But we need some independent medical audit — and perhaps even more important, a buffer with the outside clinicians. They are mostly urologists — a tough group of men — who would look down on a mostly female in-house staff at SURYA with not even the letters MD after their names. That is the function that the MAB will fulfill."

"Which in turn will consist mostly of male urologists?" Laidlaw's tone was derisive, but Gestler had expected that.

"I hope you are wrong. Dr. Krishnan has the responsibility for the MAB, and you may assume that she will try to achieve some gender balance. Maybe not 50 percent. . . ."

"Like your SAB?" She laughed. "But go on. I didn't mean to interrupt."

He breathed a sigh of relief. "Just as with the SAB and, of course, our board of directors," Martin gestured toward Laidlaw as if she were already on board, "most of the MAB's compensation will come through stock options. That will conserve a lot of cash."

Laidlaw's eyebrows rose perceptibly. "I guess it's time for you to tell me about the stock option."

Well, well, Gestler thought. I bet she takes the bait. But when he finished painting the most optimistic scenario, with only a minor caveat here and there — "of course, we can't predict short-term fluctuations in the stock, but for the long term . . ." he looked skyward to some imaginary god of options.

But Laidlaw didn't even nibble.

"I see," she said. "Now tell me something about the people who have already joined your company."

Gestler, acutely aware of the size of SURYA's current staff, stalled. "Let me tell you about some of the SAB members — at least the ones who have so far committed themselves. As chairman, we already have an acceptance from Isidore Cantor — you know," he pretended indifference, "the man who won the Nobel Prize for his tumorigenesis theory."

"Who else?" she asked deadpan.

"Max Weiss, an emeritus professor of biochemistry at Princeton. But still very active in research," he hastened to add. "And Michael Marletta, a rather young full professor at the University of Michigan. According to Dr. Krishnan, who worked with him while he was at MIT, he's just about *the* authority on the biosynthesis of nitric oxide. A very complex field, I understand, but you'd better discuss that with Dr. Krishnan. Now let me see," he pretended deep thought, "who else has already accepted?" He knew that he'd reached the bottom of a rather small, though valuable barrel, but why volunteer that?

"Quite impressive. But who are the current members of your board of directors? My colleagues, if I decide to join."

"Ah yes," he exclaimed enthusiastically. "Our first meeting will be held next month, by which time I trust we'll be able to welcome you there. I might as well start with the chair," he smiled disarmingly. "That's me. We already have on board Dr. Alfredo Zaffanori, the founder of ZALA and before that president of Syntex. He is a biochemist by training and the founder of several other intriguing ventures, such as — "

"Who else?"

"Dr. Yehuda Davidson — "

"From Hadassah? A first-class man. REPCON funded his early clinical studies. Congratulations. Anyone else?"

"We have a lawyer on our board, Mort Heartstone, who, incidentally, has a very human rather than stony heart — about as big as his stomach, which is substantial. He's also our corporate counsel. Some people say you should never have your legal counsel on the board, because you never know which hat he is wearing. But we accept that risk, because he also serves as the board secretary and in the end saves us quite a bit of money through free legal advice, even when he doesn't know he's providing it." He grinned conspiratorially.

"You're certainly careful with your money, Mr. Gestler. Maybe we should have you on our board here at REPCON. But is that your total membership? I'd say it's rather small, isn't it?"

"Our current corporate by-laws allow for an eight-person board, which is fairly standard for companies our size. We're keeping two spots open for some of the major outside investors with whom we are currently negotiating. And you, of course, if you accept."

"I'd like to think it over. Can you give me a week?"

———

She was leading him to the door when she suddenly stopped. "You said eight persons, including the two investor vacancies and me. But that makes only seven."

For a moment, Martin Gestler, who was not known for making arithmetical mistakes, looked blank. But then he clapped his forehead. "You're right," he exclaimed. "How could I forget Menachem Dvir? He represents — "

Laidlaw's abrupt change of expression startled him. "Anything wrong?"

"No," she said. "Nothing at all."

15

"This is a historic occasion: the first full board of directors' meeting of SURYA, Incorporated." Martin Gestler, tieless, with shirt sleeves rolled halfway up to the elbows, pronounced the words in a proud voice. "Of course, we're still in borrowed quarters." His gesture indicated thanks to Alfredo Zaffanori on his left, the proprietor of the great expanse of smoked glass around which they were seated; Zaffanori nodded benignly, with a trace of diffidence to show that he did not wish to be considered in the role of host here. "But within a couple of years," Martin continued, "I expect us to be sitting in our own building, in our own boardroom, like this one. . . ." He stopped, somewhat theatrically, to run his finger along the cold, slick glass surface of the long, oval table.

"Before we begin," he added, "I'd like to extend a special welcome to our long-distance traveler from Amsterdam, who seems to be immune to jet lag." He leaned forward to bow toward Baron Magnus Van Zwanenberg on his right, an imposing man of military bearing, his flax colored hair brushed back without a part, the nose narrowly aristocratic, cheeks incongruously rosy.

The Baron's smile seemed distant. "We international bankers learn how to cope with time deficits, which is probably why we always fly first class."

Martin Gestler looked pained. He hated to hear broadcast his concession to the Baron's condition for joining the board: flying in steerage simply wouldn't do. Martin had gone along, because the

Baron's presence, aside from giving confidence to a group of European investors, was indeed a coup. The name of a titled Amsterdam banker, who also happens to be on the boards of Royal Dutch Shell, of Philips Electronics N.V., and of the Boymans–van Beuningen Museum in Rotterdam — to name only some of his current affiliations — will add real style to the annual proxy statements.

Martin looked quickly at the other two intercontinental travelers. Yehuda Davidson had noted this capitulation to a banker's — or perhaps a Baron's — travel standards. Martin was sure he'd hear about it later; he could tell from the sudden tightening of Davidson's jaw and the quick scribble on the yellow legal pad that had been placed before each director.

And Menachem Dvir, who sat next to Davidson? One glance convinced Martin that Dvir hadn't heard a word. Dvir had been studying Melanie Laidlaw across the table, who, in turn, was focusing on the Baron. She *had* heard but seemed amused. Better change the subject and do so quickly, thought Gestler.

"Mort," he addressed the corporate counsel at the opposite end of the glass oval, "you should start. Perhaps some corporate boilerplate?"

———

After confirming that all of the directors had received the corporate bylaws, Heartstone asked whether there were any questions. There were none, which — based on long exposure to corporate boards — Heartstone took to mean that most had not bothered to read them and probably would not do so in the future. He didn't mind. It would expedite matters when the time came for him to use the bylaws as irrefutable precedent for some legalistic maneuver. His gaze swept around the glass table to focus on his colleague's legs — one reason why he liked glass tables in board rooms. Only his wife knew about his psychometric reading of under-the-table postures of directors' legs. His own legs, he knew, were totally uninformative, gravity simply overruling any psychological influences: his stomach was so monumental that he had to sit some distance from the table, legs planted immovably on the ground like columns supporting a weighty frieze. But the rest?

Martin Gestler was slouching, his legs spread-eagled, totally relaxed. Zaffanori's legs were crossed, the knife-sharp crease of his trousers undisturbed; Heartstone was sure that he'd hitched his trousers, most likely at the knee, before sitting down. By contrast, the Baron's legs, bent but close together, the feet poised on their soles, one slightly in front of the other, showed that he was ready to pounce. Dvir, like Gestler, sat relaxed, legs apart, but not quite so sprawled as the CEO. Davidson's he couldn't see, and he'd kept Laidlaw's for last, because female director's legs are still sufficiently rare to be relished. But at this point, his inspection was interrupted by Gestler's voice.

"Let's elect the officers quickly. I want to go through the committee assignments." In this instance, the election of officers was pure rubber-stamping, and short stamping at that, given the size of the present management: Gestler as president and chief executive officer; Renu Krishnan as vice president and chief scientific officer; and Roger Quistsal, a new addition, as treasurer, chief financial officer, and vice president for administration. Combining titles and responsibilities saved money. The rest of the staff required no board approval.

"Now to decide the board committees. I'll ask Mort to go over the tentative assignments he and I came up with — subject, of course," he switched from his slouch to a more vertically formal position, "to your concurrence. We don't believe in drafting people — only in enthusiastic volunteering."

"All right." Heartstone moved as close to the table as his stomach permitted. He examined the list in front of him. "First, the audit committee. For that, we need two outside directors, preferably knowledgeable in financial matters. We suggest the Baron —"

"Call me Magnus."

"Thank you, Magnus. We propose you and Alfredo Zaffanori. Agreed?" Seeing their nods, he proceeded. "For the compensation committee, we propose Professor Davidson — "

"Call me Yehuda."

"Yehuda then, and Martin. Is that okay?"

Not hearing any objection, he turned toward Melanie. "The third committee, though not requiring much time, is extremely important at this early stage: the stock option committee. We need two outsiders, so we propose you, Dr. Laidlaw. . . ."

He waited for the expected "Call me Melanie," but none came. "And Menachem," he concluded, somewhat lamely. "Any objections?"

Menachem looked directly at Melanie. For the first time, their eyes met and locked. "Why not?" Dvir said after an awkward pause.

Martin Gestler took over again. "With that taken care of, let's turn to the agenda all of you should have received ahead of time. Item number one, the financial report: this will be given by Roger," he motioned with his head toward the young man, who had been sitting against the rear wall next to Renu Krishnan, his chair balanced on two legs. When he heard his name, Roger Quistsal rocked abruptly forward, his expression both confident and eager.

"But today, I'll use the chairman's prerogative and start before turning the floor over to you, Roger, if you don't mind."

Quistsal shrugged, returning to his balancing act.

"I do so because I first want to report the great news that our ten-million-dollar financing went smashingly well at four dollars per share."

"Maybe you should have asked for five dollars," laughed Dvir.

"Don't be greedy," Martin said quickly, seeing the Baron, who, after all, had been nominated as director by the four dollar purchasers, frown. "Those investors who paid hard cash should feel they got a good bargain. I know you're thinking of Ben-Gurion University, but the real payoff will come later when we go public."

"*If*," the Baron interjected.

"*When*," Martin responded firmly. "I'm sure you'll join me in my optimism when you hear about our clinical plans from Dr. Krishnan."

Renu started to smile, because she appreciated Martin's gesture in referring to her by title and last name. But the pain, moving slowly from left to right across her midsection stopped her. It was the second one she had felt during the meeting. She had been having sporadic contractions — Braxton-Hicks was the technical term, the books had informed her — for almost two months. But two so close together? Was it the effort of sitting stiffly in the back of the room, her heavy belly resting on her knees, or was it the beginning of labor pains, overdue by nearly one week now? Fortunately, Jephtah was working in the same building and could drive her to the Stanford Hospital within minutes.

She raised her hand. "Martin," she said hesitantly, "I hope it's not a major imposition if I ask whether I could speak before Roger. I feel somewhat squeamish." She gave a slight pat to her stomach.

"Of course not," Martin said quickly. "As you have all noted, Dr. Krishnan is expecting, so we shouldn't keep her here too long. Go ahead Renu."

Renu had started with an outline of the studies that needed to be done in preparation for the FDA submission, including the seemingly pointless repetition of some results that had already been accumulated in Israel, as well as the endless crossing of toxicological t's and the dotting of seemingly superfluous in vitro i's, given the advanced stage of clinical knowledge of the active NONO-2 ingredient. She sympathized with Yehuda Davidson, who more than once rolled his eyes in disgust at the American regulatory bureaucracy and their disregard of some of the Jerusalem data. But since her year in ZALA's regulatory affairs department, Renu had become expert in FDA matters and her response to Davidson's questions were unequivocal.

"We would save nothing by arguing with the examiners. It would just take more time; in the end they may simply become irritated and retaliate. Remember, we have the disadvantage of being the pioneers in a new therapy, which makes it necessary for us to answer every possible question — however remote. The FDA examiners learned a bitter lesson from the thalidomide disaster. They get no brownie points for expediting a new drug application but could get their heads chopped off if something goes wrong."

She proceeded with a report on the initial staffing of the clinical department — the three nurse practitioners and the biostatistician who were now on board — and moved on to the medical advisory board. "The MAB will play an absolutely crucial function for us, especially since currently we have no full-time MD. Aside from wishing to save money," she looked at Martin, because she had learned that paying public tribute to his thrifty nature would earn her credit when she really needed extra funds, "the reason we do this is because we already have a wealth of clinical data from Israel and Professor Davidson — "

"'Yehuda,' Renu," Davidson interrupted her. "You might as well call me 'Yehuda,' now that I am working for you."

Renu was startled. She'd heard the 'call me Magnus, call me Yehuda,' exchanges, but they all had applied to men who were playing on the same turf. Was it a remainder of her Indian caste consciousness that had made her so sensitive? "I'll try," she said with a shy smile. "Yehuda had agreed to send one of his younger clinical associates, Dr. Shalit, to Palo Alto for two months to help us construct the clinical protocols for the fifty odd centers."

"So whom have you identified for your MAB?" Laidlaw asked. "Who will be the chair?"

Renu looked out of the corner of her eye at Davidson, who was the only person, other than Martin Gestler, to be privy to her coup. Noland had only accepted a few days ago. "Dr. M. L. Noland," she said and waited.

"I'll be damned," exclaimed Laidlaw. "Noland from Stanford?" Seeing Renu's proud nod, she continued. "REPCON funded some of M.L.'s research when she was still at Yale. Maybe I'll look her up while I'm out here."

"A woman?" asked the Baron.

Zaffanori, who had been doodling, looked up. "From what department?"

"OB-GYN, isn't it?" answered Laidlaw.

"Actually, here at Stanford, just to be different, they call it 'Gynecology and Obstetrics,'" added Renu. "She's head of the department: I understand, the first woman to hold that position in the school's history."

"But why an obstetrician? Or gynecologist?" The Baron sounded irked. "This company is dealing with *penile* erection — "

"Just a moment, Magnus." Laidlaw had never formally been made the offer "call me Magnus," she had simply appropriated it as a form of directorial unisex privilege. "Penile erection is not unconnected with gynecology. Not if you think where the erect penis ends up most of the time."

Renu was startled. The Baron's rosy cheeks had turned perceptibly darker. If Renu had looked at his feet, she'd have noticed that now only his toes were touching the floor. But Laidlaw seemed oblivious of the effect her comment had caused. "Or for that matter obstetrics," she said smugly. "Most of the time, erections lead to ejaculations and more often than intended, also to pregnancy and — " She finished the unspoken sentence with a QED motion of her hands. "Furthermore, penile erection may well be relegated soon to a secondary role in human reproduction, considering how much of current research is focusing on assisted reproductive technologies, like in vitro fertilization — "

"Or ICSI," Menachem interjected in a low voice.

"Or ICSI," she echoed as she looked at him for a moment before lowering her eyes.

Renu Krishnan, of course, had no inkling of the significance of the last exchange. "Precisely," she exclaimed anyway, grateful to have had the Baron's objections silenced by someone else. "And the Stanford department seems to have particularly good relations with the urologists, who, after all, are the constituency with whom we at SURYA have to deal. Dr. Noland even has a joint program in andrology — "

"What specialty is that?" asked the Baron.

"It ought to be the mirror image of gynecology, but few medical schools teach it and even fewer men know of its existence." Melanie Laidlaw had leaned over to catch the Baron's eye, thus precluding any eye contact with Menachem.

"Still," Renu continued, "there are some interesting joint projects in andrology at Stanford, primarily dealing with endocrinological aspects. Here at ZALA," she pointed to Zaffanori, "we, or I should say, *they* are working on testosterone patches for men, now that they have solved the problem of estradiol skin patches for women. So you see, Baron, if there were andrologists around, they'd be the ones to prescribe them to men. But to return to Dr. Noland: we thought it diplomatic to have a woman head our

MAB, which in any event is likely to be dominated by men — a chair who at the same time has no real vested interest in who'll get first crack at testing our device in the States."

"Congratulations, Renu." Laidlaw beamed at her. "Getting M.L. to head your board was a first-class idea. Now be sure," she wagged an admonishing finger, "that you get some women onto your SAB. From what I understand of its function, its aim is to look way beyond andrological applications of nitric oxide biology. No reason to stick just to men, is there?"

Renu was about to reply when a sharp pain stopped her. So sharp that she gripped her stomach with both hands. Martin Gestler, who had been quietly listening to the exchange, immediately noticed. "Renu," he said quickly. "Why don't you take a rest. In your present state — "

"Thanks," she said quickly and left the room.

─────────

During the coffee break, Dvir motioned to Laidlaw to join him on the adjacent balcony, the only nearby spot that offered any modicum of privacy. Neither one spoke as they leaned, side by side, on the balcony railing looking down on a well-kept lawn, in the center of which stood a concrete column carrying two giant L's mounted on ball bearings — a stainless-steel kinetic sculpture by George Rickey. The two L's moved slowly in the light breeze, each in its own cylindrical path, seemingly ready to crash into each other but, of course, never doing so. The simplicity of the construction coupled with the complexity of the separate motions of each giant letter L were the secret behind its magic.

Finally, Melanie broke the silence. She pointed to the moving Rickey sculpture: "Try to catch them with your eyes when they are in a mirror image relation: one L facing right, the other to the left. . . . There they are!" she exclaimed. "Did you see it?" For the first time, she turned to face him directly.

"The letter L," he said in a low voice, without meeting her glance, "is probably the best letter in the English alphabet: liberty, light, laughter, leisure — "

"Don't forget love and libido," she laughed.

"I wasn't finished yet. Also luck and lust; lips and legs — "

"Yes," she murmured. "And liaison, logic, and loss."

He looked at her. "You're right. It's not a perfect letter. There's also lie, larceny — "

"Don't, Menachem," she pleaded. "What about leniency?"

He nodded. "*Lama lo.* Two more L's, but they don't count: they're in Hebrew." He touched her lightly on her arm. "Tell me, Melanie, I need to know something: did you realize I'd be on this board when they asked you to join?"

"Not at the outset."

"But then you found out?" he asked more urgently.

"Yes, but that was before I had accepted."

"And yet you agreed?"

"Well?" she said. "You see I'm here."

———

"Jephtah, I know this isn't the best time or place for talking business, but something just came up at home. I've got to fly back to Israel tonight."

Dvir had his arm over Jephtah Cohn's shoulder as the two men paced up and down the corridor outside the obstetrics ward of the Stanford Medical Center.

"Relax, Jephtah. Millions of men go through this experience every year. There is nothing you can do right now while your wife is in labor, except wait."

"Sure," Jephtah grumbled, "but how do I know everything is okay?"

"I'm sure it is," Dvir squeezed his shoulder. "In the meantime, listen to what I have to say. Let's go out to the courtyard to talk."

The two men sat on a bench, Jephtah hunched over, head supported by his hands. His eyes were focused on the ground.

"As you know, I'm here for the SURYA board meeting, which just finished an hour ago. I'm in a peculiar position. As the company's counsel put it, we're all here as directors representing the interests of *all* stockholders. Yet he knows, and the rest of us know, that this is part fiction: most of us look out for the interests of our constituency — in my case, for Ben-Gurion University's. Of course, to the extent that Ben-Gurion's benefits coincide with those of the rest of the stockholders, I represent all of them equally."

The younger man looked up briefly, but his eyes seemed not to focus. "Is that so?" he asked.

"Well, just look." Dvir's tone had turned defensive. "Yehuda Davidson is here on behalf of Hadassah; a Dutch baron is on the board because a group of important European investors wanted him there; Alfredo Zaffanori, your nominal boss at ZALA, ostensibly sits there because he's a major investor, but I'm sure he also is considering ZALA's possible interest in SURYA. As you know much better than I, ZALA has a major stake in new approaches to drug delivery and ours, via the urethra, certainly qualifies. If we are successful, other companies might well make an offer for SURYA that we stockholders — especially the universities — might find irresistible. This way, ZALA might have the advantage by bidding first. Not that his presence is not also of overall advantage to us. I've only just met him, and I already see that he is impressive. He has a fabulous reputation in the investment community — certainly an advantage when we go public."

"Renu likes Dr. Laidlaw," Jephtah said distantly.

This time, Dvir's gaze dropped to the ground. "Yes," he said, "she's the exception. In more ways than one."

"Do you know her?" Jephtah remembered the conversation he and Renu once had about Dvir and Laidlaw.

Dvir shrugged, his eyes still on the ground.

"Who is *Mr.* Laidlaw?"

"Now why do you ask that?" Dvir had turned to face his questioner.

"Renu told me she has a young child, which has not prevented her from continuing full-time work. It's an issue we've been debating lately."

"Ah, yes." Dvir straightened up. "That's what I wanted to discuss with you. I told you I'm on the SURYA board to represent Ben-Gurion University. Everyone knows that — it's even stated in black-and-white in the proxy statement going to all stockholders. But Ben-Gurion is different from all the other stockholders. We also have a stake in SURYA's sole supplier of MUSA units for the clinical trials. And perhaps most importantly — and I take full credit for that — I persuaded our Beersheba mayor to put up some cash to set up the pilot plant for the production of NONO-2 in our budding industrial park. Your work, Jephtah, you should be proud of it. Your MUSA design started it all."

"Not quite," said Jephtah, though clearly pleased. "There's Renu's work on the NONOates and then — "

"Precisely!" interrupted Dvir, "your work and Renu's. That's what I wanted to talk about. If SURYA is successful here in the States — and I, for one, see no reason to question that — then we stand to gain beyond any stock appreciation or royalty income out of our shared patents with Hadassah and Brandeis. We — and I mean not just Ben-Gurion but Beersheba and the whole Negev — will also benefit from this kind of industrial development: high-tech, low-volume, high-value export items. After all, that's why we went to the incremental expense of constructing everything with FDA standards in mind."

"So?"

"So if those facilities are to grow beyond the present pilot-plant stage to turn into a real manufacturing facility, someone highly qualified should run it and at the same time be able to think up ancillary products that could be produced there. You'd be the right man to do all that: you have the technical background, you have always been interested in practical applications of your work, you certainly acquired some useful background here and so did your wife — "

"Yes. But that was before we found out about Renu's pregnancy." Jephtah looked up at the second floor windows of the building facing them as if he suddenly remembered why they were there. "I ought to go up and check."

"One moment." Dvir placed his hand on Jephtah's arm. "I know about Renu's position at SURYA. Martin told me about it at a board of governors meeting in Beersheba before he even talked to Renu, before he knew she was pregnant. Have you discussed how she'll combine raising a baby with a rather demanding job in management? Especially of a start-up company, where all kinds of unanticipated problems might arise?"

"You're telling me!" Jephtah sounded angry. "It was our first real fight."

"And?"

"And nothing. Renu feels that she has a right to professional advancement just as I do, that she has to bring the child into the world but the subsequent raising is a joint enterprise and that together we can do it. Especially since Martin offered extra money for a nanny." Jephtah's tone had turned bitter. "She said there are plenty of working professional women who are also mothers. 'Look at Melanie Laidlaw,' she said. 'She manages.'" He turned to Dvir. "By the way, what does Dr. Laidlaw's husband do?"

"There isn't any."

"There isn't? So who's the father?"

Dvir dodged the question. "Renu would not want to combine motherhood and work in Beersheba? I guess not," he answered the question himself. "Martin is offering her quite some opportunity. I think he's grooming her for his job."

Jephtah had resumed his earlier position, hands cupping his cheeks, eyes staring at the ground. "I know," he growled, and straightened. "I asked myself: who's the more ambitious in the family? It's a question I'd never considered before. Now I know the answer. We better go."

He was about to leave when he stopped. "What would you've done if you had been in my place?"

"I don't know," replied Dvir. "I've never been in your situation."

"I forgot," said Jephtah. "You have no children. By the way, how's your wife?"

"Not well. That's why I'm returning tonight."

Palo Alto, December 1, 1983
My dearest Ashok,

　　As you can see from the enclosed pictures, you are now an uncle. Naomi was nearly a week overdue (no wonder she weighed almost 3900 grams!) and then decided to make her appearance on the very day, November 21, of our first full board of directors meeting. You will undoubtedly note that she is a Scorpio.

So far, she's been a joy and no trouble, day or night, provided she is fed on time. We will see what happens next week, when she goes on a bottle. Jephtah is very unhappy about this. He firmly believes that a baby should be breast-fed for months. I am not against that in principle, but with the initiation of our clinical studies I have enormous obligations. I have to admit that I enjoy making decisions and establishing deadlines — for others and for myself. As I said, Jephtah disapproves entirely, but then he is a man who just works in the lab, while I now carry some major responsibilities for others and, of course, for SURYA.

You may wonder how I have solved combining motherhood and executive status. Martin Gestler, our CEO is very careful with money, but he is generous when generosity is needed. I got a handsome raise to enable me to hire an au pair — a pleasant English nanny-type of 22, with a driver's license, a complexion that most women would envy, bad teeth like many Brits, and amazingly red hair. She's had two years of college and plans to stay in California for a while, which I take to mean until she finds a husband. For the time being, Naomi and she share a room, but we'll have to move into something bigger within the next couple of months. Between Jephtah's salary as a full-time scientist at ZALA's new ETS venture and my vice presidential remuneration (are you not proud of your sister?), we'll cope with the rather substantial mortgage that will be facing us. You have no idea what real estate costs are like in the Palo Alto area, but I have no intention to commute. I'm sure that I'll have to drop by the office some evenings, and being just a few minutes away will help.

I will write separately to Mummy.
With love, Renu

16

I don't think I've cried once in the past three years. I'm not counting the tears of joy in the delivery room, just after the umbilical cord had been cut and my freshly wiped Naomi — skin still crinkled, black hair still matted, body still folded in a fetal position — was placed at my breast. Her eyes were open, saying "What now?" to me and then to Jephtah when they brought him in a few minutes later. My tough sabra didn't have the stomach to be present at the delivery.

There may have been other tears of pleasure, a light sprinkle here or there, but none of pain or sorrow — at least not that I recall — and most certainly none like last night's monsoon. Crying is supposed to be some sort of flushing of the psyche's toilet and, if it is, last night's volume of tears should have solved the entire problem. Initially, I blamed it all on that four-day trip to the Midwest, first to Michael Marletta's lab in Ann Arbor, then to the SAB meeting in Cantor's pad in Chicago.

Pad? What makes me use that slightly derogatory term for his beautifully furnished lakefront condo on the fifteenth floor with its "269° view of Lake Michigan," as Max Weiss called it with a touch of envy and an excess of angular precision? Is it that I still haven't figured out the precise nature of his relationship to Paula Curry? When I first met her, I'd thought she lived there, or at the very least slept there. "Leonardo darling," can hardly be the usual address for a fellow chamber ensemble player. But now, two years later, I'm not so sure. She certainly wasn't there the third time I visited, when the SAB met in Chicago around the most highly polished antique table I'd ever taken notes on.

"I've asked a good deli around the corner to bring some assorted sandwiches, a pasta salad, and fresh fruit," announced Cantor after they'd settled around his dining table.

"Georgian?" asked Max Weiss, indicating the shiny mahogany surface of the circular dining table resting on a pillar-and-claw base.

"No, later: Regency," Cantor replied, "circa 1815. The sideboard over there is Queen Anne, just before the early Georgian period. I didn't know you were interested in English antiques, Max."

"My new wife is, so I'm starting to learn."

"Ah yes, your wife. I understand she has one of those MacArthur 'genius' awards. What's it like to live with a genius?"

"So far, great. About the only disadvantage I see is that I'll never get a MacArthur. I don't think they'd give another one to a spouse."

"I know how you must feel, Max," Cantor eyed him craftily. "They don't seem to give them to Nobel recipients either. They must think we're now completely satisfied."

"And are you?" asked Celestine Price, who had listened to their exchange with increasing annoyance.

"You should know," Cantor said somewhat brittlely. "You're living with one." He turned away to address the rest. "The deli promised delivery by twelve. There will be wine, of course . . . quite passable vintages, if I may say so, from California, naturally, in honor of our corporate sponsor and of Renu, who's flown all the way to Chicago to simplify life for us busy academics." He inclined his head in Renu's direction, ignoring Celestine Price, who had come in from Los Angeles. "Although we should abstain from alcohol until we have completed at least some of our business. In the meantime, there are plenty of non-alcoholic drinks over there," he motioned in the general direction of the kitchen, "soft drinks, juices, mineral water. . . ." His eyes cruised around the table, past his four colleagues, to rest, with undisguised disapproval, on the plastic mineral water bottle by Celestine Price's side. At least, he observed, she'd had the courtesy to place it on her notepad, but the fact didn't mollify him sufficiently, especially since she found it necessary to take a sip or two every few minutes. Cantor was old-fashioned enough to object to the current vogue among younger women, notably the "organic" members of that class, who ostentatiously carry their water bottles with them whether they are jogging or going to the opera — like wearing Nikes with a formal dress. In his home, it offended his sense of esthetics and propriety, implying as it did the unavailability of anything but "ordinary" H_2O from his kitchen faucet. He'd never forgotten his falling out of sync during a quartet performance when he'd noticed a young female listener taking a swig while he fiddled rapturously. But Celestine Price of all people!

His irritation was fueled by the realization that he had only himself to blame. Chairing the SAB was hardly onerous — this was only the third meeting they'd held in two years, and he'd even persuaded Renu Krishnan to schedule this one in Chicago. "Marletta is practically next door, in Ann Arbor," he'd said at the conclusion of their last meeting in Palo Alto. "And Weiss can fly here in a couple of hours from Newark. Let's meet in my apartment in Chicago. It's properly off-campus — after all we shouldn't conduct non-university business on hallowed academic turf," he'd added with a conspiratorial wink that seemed out of character, "and we can all be back in our homes the same evening. That is, everyone but you, Renu. But think of the money SURYA saves by our not flying to the West Coast."

Yet Cantor had started to feel the occasional twinge of guilt. Two months ago, he had learned that SURYA was about to embark on a second round of financing through a private placement of stock, projected at eight dollars per share. Cantor couldn't help but realize that in such an event, the paper profit in his thirty-thousand-share stock option would approach two hundred thirty thousand dollars — or, as Renu had emphasized suavely, "get closer to a Guarneri." Cantor had to admit that the time had passed when he might allow himself occasional trivializing, or even deprecating, commentary about his industrial connection — he, the academic purist, who had always looked down his nose at colleagues tainted (in his view) by industrial consultantships. The direct amount of work he'd done for SURYA was insignificant and certainly of no detriment to his academic duties, but the value of his paper equity had now become significant, indeed weighty. No outsider would look at a quarter million dollars — paper profit or real — as trivial. And what outsider — say his dean or some of his "tainted" colleagues, who once had been the subjects of his implied disdain for pandering to industry — would truly believe that he'd received such a sum for attending three one-day meetings in two years, one of them in his own home, without some other more precious or sinister commitment? Cantor had started to realize — but not with unmitigated pride — that his chief value to SURYA had so far consisted largely of his Nobel, which the company was happy to use to glamorize its annual reports.

Celestine Price's mineral water bottle had produced a sense of malaise, quite beyond its visual impact. It reminded him to take his duties as SAB chair more seriously in the future. When Renu had telephoned him that she wanted to invite another member to join their SAB, a very promising young assistant professor of organic chemistry at Caltech who had just published an exciting paper on a novel class of NO-releasers, he had consented without further inquiry. Renu had mentioned a class of organic compounds, polyzeniumpolyolates, she'd called them, which had meant nothing to him even though he had once prided himself on his knowledge of organic chemistry. But a Nobelist does not easily admit ignorance; besides, Renu's arguments made sense: it was only prudent to diversify beyond SURYA's current emphasis on NONOates when the opportunity presented itself. "At this stage, all attracting new talent takes is a fifteen-thousand-share stock option," Renu had explained, "at eighty cents," she underlined, "twice what it cost the original board members. But still a handsome incentive, especially for a young, untenured professor who's never before been approached by industry." Cantor didn't bother to inquire after the name of the Caltech polyzeniumpolyolate hotshot nor about the candidate's gender. "Sure," he said, "why not give it a try?"

———

Renu flew down to Pasadena for the day. Not only did she want to meet Price face to face but she also wanted to get a firsthand impression of her Caltech research group and perhaps pick up some NO-releasing scuttlebutt. The size of Price's group, six graduate students plus one postdoc as well as three undergraduate seniors, was impressive, especially considering that Caltech seniors were easily as productive as the average second-year graduate student elsewhere.

On the day Renu flew down to Pasadena to make the offer, the two young women — only five years apart in age — had hit it off splendidly. By the time they broke for lunch at the Athenaeum — Caltech's unexpectedly genteel faculty club — Renu had made her the formal offer and Celly had accepted.

"I hope you don't mind being the only other woman on the SAB," said Renu. "It's not for the sake of feminism, but because — "

"Don't apologize," interjected Celestine. "My mother used to tell me when I was in high school that feminism is good for everyone — especially for men. I humored her then, but now I know she had a point. Especially about it being good for the other half of mankind. Still, I wouldn't want to be invited solely because I have ovaries. I hope it's primarily because of our current triazenium-triolate research."

"That helped. We need a good organic chemist on board — "

"Fine. I'm one. And in another two years, I'll see whether my Caltech colleagues agree," she grinned while tapping the wood surface of the table. "I hope they do, because for that vote, my ovaries — active as they are — won't be sufficient."

"I hope you don't mind my asking. Do you have any children?" she laughed self-deprecatingly. "Ever since I had a child, I'm always looking for other professional women who are in the same boat."

"Of course, I don't mind." Celestine waved any objection away. "You know how it is," she said in a reflective tone, "Some women are born mothers, some grow into it, and others have motherhood thrust upon them. I belong to the third group. I wasn't even married. But when I found out I was pregnant, I decided to have the baby and tie the knot at the same time."

"And are you a good mother?" Renu laughed again, this time frankly embarrassed. "I'm sorry. I don't mean to be rude. I just worry about it all the time. Do you know what I mean? Do you think it's possible to be a good mother and get tenure at the same time?"

Celestine thought for a minute before answering. "I *hope* I'm a good mother — I mean I hope my child thinks I am — but, no, I don't think I am a good mother generically speaking. My son is lucky in that he has a first-class father. There's also good child care available around Caltech, and fortunately we don't live far from my lab. A ten-minute bike ride for me. My husband does the commuting."

"What does he do?" asked Renu.

Celestine looked up surprised. "You don't know who he is? I thought you had done some background checking, but in a way I'm glad you didn't. His name is Jeremiah Stafford. I kept my maiden name when we got married."

"Stafford? *The* Stafford? The man who shared the Nobel Prize with Cantor?"

Celestine nodded.

"Does Cantor know you?" Renu asked.

"He sure does. You mean you didn't tell him about me? Wait till I tell my aunt!"

"Your aunt?"

"Her name is Paula Curry."

Until now, the SAB has met so infrequently that I felt the time was overdue for me to bring them up to date on the progress of our clinical work. SURYA is about to move into high gear and so will our SAB. "It's time to bring in some working scientists," Martin told me, and so I planned my trip to include a stop at Michael's lab. What Marletta doesn't know about current NO research is hardly worth considering. I thought that it would be more diplomatic if I briefed him separately and then let him be the one to present the SAB with what I have in mind. I also decided to tell him about my forthcoming elevation to the SURYA presidency, which I have so far only shared with my husband. Jephtah's response seemed rather ambivalent — at least so I thought then. It's surprising how little insight I have these days into his problems. Or maybe the problems are just perceptions, but perceptions turn into problems when they aren't discussed.

Martin Gestler had informed me that he'd decided to announce to the board that he was ready to relinquish one of his three titles, that of president. There were only two obvious inside candidates, and he was dead-set against an outside search. Not counting the Beersheba personnel, we now have over forty full-time employees reporting to the two vice presidents, Roger Quistsal and me. Martin runs such a tight ship that Roger, who is handling finances and accounting, human resources, and general administration, heads a very lean staff. I, on the other hand, have responsibility for the clinical support staff and, of course, regulatory affairs, which deals with the FDA on an ongoing basis, in addition to quality control, an increasingly sophisticated metabolic-analytical department, and — finally — the beginnings of a small research group consisting of eight scientists, half of them Ph.Ds. It was my responsibility for this last group, coupled with my ex-officio membership on our SAB, that took me to Ann Arbor. It would have been an interesting trip under any circumstances — the work itself, meeting my old undergraduate mentor — but it was odd how much more exciting it became when I undertook it as the presumptive successor to the presidency of SURYA.

Martin Gestler has proved to be a marvelous mentor. Right at the outset, he told me not to let people address me in my corporate life by my first name without expecting me to do the same with them. He liked informality, he stressed, but one-way streets in address promptly change the power dynamics. "Renu, remember you're now in top management — even if the top is not very high and the management very small." So now I call Dr. Zaffanori "Alfredo," and every time I do so it becomes easier. The same is now true of the SAB, where I've started to "eye-see" Cantor although I'm conscious of the fact that much of the time I try to use sentences that simply avoid any direct reference to his name. "You" has become the compromise, which is so easy in English. God only knows how I'd have handled this in French or German. Is my diffidence caused by I.C.'s Nobel aura, which he certainly does not try to dispel, or is it simply the age difference, which in academic circles seems of such greater consequence?

Whatever the reason, I'm much more at ease with Marletta,
whom I've "Michaeled" ever since I was a senior at Wellesley. Of
course, he's only fourteen years older than me, and women have
always been comfortable in the Marletta lab, at least when he was
still at MIT. I wonder whether that's still the case at Michigan?

"Michael, you haven't changed."

Renu's pleasure was undisguised as Marletta guided her into
his office after the obligatory tour of his labs in the U-M pharmacy
building. "You're still surrounded by adoring women. Only the
names have changed: Amy, Regina, Kristin, Melissa. . . . And, as
usual, none of your lab assistants has a last name."

"I'm sure they do," he said, his grin mirroring Renu's. "But all
I care about is that they're smart and hardworking — "

"Like many women," she interrupted. "But, let me get down to
business. SURYA business." She pushed her chair closer to his
desk. "As you'll hear tomorrow in Chicago when I make a formal
progress report to the SAB, we're pretty much on schedule. We
just raised plenty of new money to complete the clinical work and
all the other stuff needed to apply for regulatory approval."

"When do you expect to go to the FDA?"

She eyed him cautiously. "This is highly confidential. We expect to do so within twelve months. If there are no hitches, about
six months from now we'll go public. There's no point in going over
all that today; you'll hear about it tomorrow. I've come for something else. Now that we've raised over twenty million dollars, less
than half of which is needed to complete the FDA package, I've
convinced our board that our own in-house research has to be ex-
panded — and that we have to do it now. There is so much going
on in nitric oxide biology that we've got to get into some other
clinical applications, quite separate from the penis. It's a great
organ, but there are others to consider."

Marletta shook his head in wonder. "Renu, you *have* changed."

She laughed. "I guess I'm not that prim little Wellesley girl any
more, am I? But what about you? When I worked with you at MIT,
you were an assistant professor who was in the process of not getting tenure, and now look at you: a dual appointment in pharmacy

and the medical school, an endowed chair — you're a full professor squared!"

"That's only a quantitative change," he dismissed her compliment. "But you? You're another person. Self-assured, rising very fast in a totally different world from where you started: first India, now the States; first academia, now industry. Me. . . ." He made a noise like leaking steam. "I started in academia and I'm still there."

Renu looked at him curiously. "You were going to say something else. What was it?"

"Well. . . ." he hesitated. "You also have a child, you're still married to the same husband. . . ."

"Now what makes you think of that?" she prodded.

"It isn't easy combining a highly demanding professional life with being a spouse and a parent. Look at me: not only did I fail to get tenure at MIT, I lost matrimonial tenure as well. I'm on my second marriage now — a first-class one, I might add. Still, you seem to have managed everything the first time around."

"So it seems," she said slowly.

————

"I'll be happy to do that," Marletta had said after Renu asked him to propose additional members for the SAB. They would have to be active in some of the areas of nitric oxide biology she had enumerated: cancer, parasitology, cardiology, pulmonary hypertension . . . the list went on. "It's the least I can do to earn my keep," he'd said. "I'm starting to feel guilty about my ever-increasing stock option. I know it's only paper money, but if you're really going to go public that soon . . . ?"

The following day, however, Marletta found he had to find a place in line: Cantor's guilt had precedent.

"It's time to use the P word," the chairman said, "although I'm perfectly willing to admit that scientists — at least academic ones, like me — abhor it. But since I'm supposed to chair the scientific advisory board of a profit-seeking organization . . ." he looked slyly at Renu.

"'Profit-seeking' has a critical ring," she interjected, "which I'm sure you don't mean. But if you do, let me remind you that there's nothing wrong in a business aiming for a well-earned profit. So why not admit openly our interest in profit, rather than hide behind 'the P word,' precious as it may sound?"

Cantor frowned. "I meant priorities, not profit."

"And I'd assumed," Max Weiss broke in, "that you were referring to the penis."

Cantor ignored him. Renu's criticism had irked him. "I'll admit that even academics succumb to the lure of profit. If it isn't money, it's fame. But priorities? Who likes those?"

"Actually, I do," broke in Marletta, who had rather enjoyed the brief tussle while admiring Renu's spunk. "I'd like to say something about our future priorities."

"Before you do, Michael," interjected Renu, "let me finish with the capital P for profit. I'd like to bring all of you briefly up to date on the potential for profit by SURYA and," she allowed her gaze to sweep around her board colleagues, "by all of us."

Renu repeated the information she had divulged to Marletta in Ann Arbor about the new SURYA financing, the increased paper profit in their stock options, and the projected dates for an IPO and the FDA submission. "You may well wonder why it should take another twelve months before we can go to the FDA. They will be assembling a special advisory committee of outside specialists — not that they will find it easy to find well-known urologists whom we haven't already enlisted in our clinical trials," she chuckled. "But," her index finger rose skyward, "the stakes are high. We'll be the first on the market with such a new approach to erectile dysfunction, and the FDA will rely on their advisory board to raise all possible scenarios that might cause problems."

"Such as?" asked Max Weiss, the fingers of his right hand drumming impatiently on Cantor's Regency mahogany. "I'd think that men with an erectile predicament would tolerate all kinds of problems."

Renu couldn't restrain herself. "'Erectile predicament.' What a marvelously delicate term. Do you think we should we use it in our marketing?"

"Help yourself," he said gruffly, "but first answer my question."

"Sorry," she said. "You're probably right with respect to the men who fall into a range of categories: sufferers of Parkinson's or multiple sclerosis, or surgery-induced nerve damage to the penis. Remember, every man who undergoes a prostatectomy risks penile nerve damage; there are up to three hundred thousand new cases of prostatic cancer every year in the States alone. Then there are men with diabetes mellitus, and finally men with various vascular diseases: atherosclerosis, hypertension . . . you name it. But we already knew about this patient population from the Israeli studies. That, incidentally, is the reason why our American work didn't cost as much as originally estimated: we just had to extend the Israeli data. But the FDA is going to throw a much wider net — and who'd blame them?"

"How much wider?" asked Max.

"Some examples are erectile problems caused by antihypertensive and cardiac prescription drugs, hormonal imbalance, renal dialysis, pelvic surgery — the list goes on and on. And they'll also be concerned about potential *misuse*. I'm sure there will be all kinds of jocks who'll think it would be great to have an hour-long erection on demand. I could tell them something about *that*." Renu stopped when she saw Max Weiss's expression.

She clapped her hand over her mouth and turned beet-red. "I'm sorry," she said. "I'm referring to some of the stories I'd heard back in Israel." How could she tell Max and the others about Jephtah's experiment? "It can be painful," was all she could say before continuing, in a more professional tone. "We have to learn about the relationship of dosage and the incidence and severity of such discomfort. It was reported by around 20 to 40 percent of the patients during our Phase III clinical studies. Unlike Gertrude Stein's rose, an erection is not necessarily an erection."

"Do you want to elaborate on that?" asked Max.

"Do you want me to?" countered Renu.

"If I didn't, I wouldn't have asked."

I must be pressing some wrong button, thought Renu. "All right. First, how do you . . . sorry," she caught herself, "not *you* Max, but any person, quantify an erection?" She proceeded to explain their rating system, Jephtah's "buckle meter," even the "stuffable" quality of an erection of score 3.

"I see," Max said primly.

"But there's more," Renu was a little surprised to find she was enjoying herself. "Some of our subjects have told us that they found themselves with a perfectly good erection without even the slightest trace of sexual desire. One of the subjects, a novelist, expressed his feeling in very elegant prose: 'Every tumescent centimeter proved to be a disappointment.'"

"I'll have to write that one down," Weiss exclaimed, picking up his pencil. "It's for my wife," he added to no one in particular.

"Let me continue," said Renu. "That potential separation of erectile function from erotic sensation is related to one of our time-consuming ongoing studies. This is not the extension of the Phase III clinical trials to the U.S. in terms of number of patients and different centers nor the double-blind, placebo-controlled protocols nor even the different organic causes of erectile dysfunction but rather what we call the Quality of Life studies. We enrolled 612 subjects from our Phase III clinical trials for eighteen months of follow-up *with their spouses* to study the quality of their sexual relations. How satisfied were they — the men *and* the women? Of course, the dice are somewhat loaded in favor of the MUSA, because we did not enroll anyone in our Phase III protocols who had not suffered from erectile dysfunction for at least three years. And three years of impaired sexual relation does make people less choosy, wouldn't you think?"

The resulting silence had started to assume awkward proportions when Celestine Price intervened. "What else is taking so much time?"

"Women and unborn babies would be a catchy but not inappropriate response. It's lucky we have a woman, Dr. Noland, chairing our medical advisory board."

"I suppose it's time to repeat Max's question," said Celestine. "'Would you elaborate on that?'"

"Already back in Jerusalem, the Hadassah IRB — the institutional review board — asked about the possible effect of nonmetabolized material transmitted to the women by the men during ejaculation. We had some volunteers masturbate at different time intervals following transurethral administration of NONO-2, and it was my job to analyze the collected semen for its NONO content. But we need bigger numbers for the FDA: wider-ranging age groups and semen volumes. That's when Dr. Noland came up with another question: what about the time of the woman's menstrual cycle?"

"I don't get that," remarked Celestine.

"Think about the changes in viscosity of cervical secretions and of other factors at ovulation compared to early on or late in the cycle. And then the possible mutagenic and teratogenic effects of residual NONO metabolites during the first few days after fertilization if a woman were to become pregnant by a man with a NONO-induced erection. We felt it wise to do some relevant toxicology. Finally, to return once more to the man, we observed a few cases, mostly with the highest dosages, where some men had a perceptible drop in blood pressure. With some cardiac patients, this could be serious. Much of this will come out in the wash when we break the code at the end of an extended maintenance study."

"I'm impressed," said Cantor. "Lab scientists just aren't aware how time-consuming such clinical trials can be."

"And how expensive," added Renu. "But, precisely because of the long time requirements, we ought to think early on what the next products might be. Celly," she looked across the table at her colleague, "why don't you explain why we should take your work on polyzeniumpolyolates so seriously?"

Celestine Price looked around the table, a tinge of arrogance in her eyes. "You all know organic chemistry, of course, or else you wouldn't have reached such eminence in your respective fields. Still, I'd bet that none of you has heard of polyzeniumpolyolates, because even 98.6 percent of all *proper* organic chemists," she grinned outrageously, "would be hard put to come up with a correct definition or their chemical formulas."

"Formulae," Cantor mumbled under his breath.

"I beg your pardon? I didn't catch what you said?"

Cantor looked embarrassed. "Ignore it. It's the Latin that was drilled into me back in high school."

"I had Latin," said Celestine. "Through Ovid."

"You did? Then you might understand. I said 'formulae.'"

"Oh," laughed Celestine. "I used to say formulae until one of my grad students — a woman, needless to say — told me that it sounded too affected; like 'hippopotami' and 'octopi.' So now it's 'formulas,' although I still go ballistic when I read something about 'the media *is*.' I also draw the line at saying 'the data *is*.' Does that explain it?" she looked guilelessly at Cantor.

"Go on with your chemistry, Celestine. I shouldn't have interrupted." Cantor's capitulation was there for all to see — even if no one else at the table understood just why he seemed to be signaling a surrender or why Price should look quite so triumphant.

"Okay. Back then to the polyzeniumpolyolates. As I said, don't feel guilty about not knowing what they are. Renu, who belongs to the remaining 1.4 percent who do know, could have simplified life for you if she had admitted that her NONO-1 and NONO-2 are formally called 'diazeniumdiolates.' As you know," Price now focused exclusively on her three male colleagues, "in her NONO-ates, two NO molecules are attached to a nucleophile — an organic chemical tail that can be modified in innumerable ways. That, of course, is why your SURYA patent on NONOates is so broad. It's the possible range in chemical variations of the tail that makes it so. Although Renu's diazeniumdiolates," she had purposely switched back to formal, chemical terminology, "are stable as solid salts, in solution they release two molar equivalents of NO, which is what makes her compounds so attractive in the clinic. On paper, this sounds trivial, although *you* should just try to make such compounds in the lab! You'll find how much ingenuity is required."

"Get to the point, Celly," Renu's tone was friendly. "You're promoting me, but I want you to promote *your* work."

"Okay," Celestine said, her tempo picking up. "We decided to see whether we could raise the ante by stringing more NO molecules together. First, we managed to work out a synthesis for the hitherto unknown class of triazeniumtriolates — "

"In other words, NONONOates," Marletta interrupted triumphantly. "You organic chemists! Why don't you speak English."

"You enzymologists," Celestine had waited for such a comment. "What if we managed to combine six NO molecules, which, incidentally, we have just accomplished? Would you like "NONONONONONOates" better than hexazeniumhexolates?"

"Ah, those women chemists," Marletta made a mock bow across the table, "they're always sharper than we. Seriously, though, that's quite a trick. But can you control the release of the NO molecules to produce longer-acting drugs?"

"Precisely the question," interrupted Renu. "And that's why we wanted to get Celly into our camp."

"You might as well admit, Renu, that SURYA's *dia*zenium patent does not cover our *tria*zenium analogs." Celestine's precision was emphatic. "When I called this to the attention of the Caltech patent counsel, we ended up with a broad claim for *poly*zenium types."

"True," conceded Renu. "That's why we negotiated for an exclusive license with Caltech and threw in some stock warrants as sweetener."

"If you can't beat them, co-opt them," remarked Cantor. "At least, that's what I told Renu when she mentioned Celestine's work."

"You knew it was me?" Celestine refused to look at Cantor.

"In point of fact, no. Renu talked about the exciting work, not the person behind it."

"And how had you thought she could 'co-opt' me?"

"I probably didn't use that word. More likely I said 'bribe.' Of course, I was referring to the stock option. Isn't that why we're all here?"

"This may be true of you," Celestine said coolly, without making it plain whether she meant the singular or plural. "I found the stock option attractive and . . . quite deserved. After all, I'm bringing something very concrete to the table: a brand-new class of proprietary compounds of potential interest to SURYA. What really interested me, though, was to see whether any of our products might make it into the clinic. I'm not a purist when it comes to having interactions with industry. Unlike some academics." For the first time, she focused on Cantor. "So you see, I needed no bribe."

Renu was starting to worry. Even without the inscrutable tension between Price and Cantor, the conversation had moved onto a slippery plane from which she wanted to step off as quickly as possible. "Stock options are standard currency in start-up companies. They are called 'incentives.' In business school, they've even coined a verb: we're all being 'incentivized.'"

"Good God!" exclaimed Weiss. "I refuse to accept that word. I'd rather be bribed than incentivized. How ghastly!"

Renu interpreted the resulting laughter as a return of civility. "I've just used another P word: prospects, which is closely related to I.C.'s 'priorities.' Michael," she turned to Marletta who had been scribbling on his notepad, "you wanted to talk about priorities. Would it be okay if Michael spoke now?" Renu had addressed the last words at Cantor, to demonstrate that she was not trying to usurp the chairman's function.

"Right." Marletta straightened up, at the same time pushing his chair away from the table. He wanted a wider perspective of his audience. "Not so long ago, Renu had reminded me of some of the hot — or at least warm — areas of NO biology. She thought it might be a good idea for SURYA to turn its attention there. The easiest way of doing that would be to 'co-opt,'" he threw a quick glance at Cantor, "some additional experts who, like Celestine here, have something concrete to offer. So let me throw out some names, starting with I.C.'s area: cancer."

As she listened, Renu began to relax. Michael isn't just smart, she thought, he's also suave. Before even mentioning new names, he'd already buttered up two of his colleagues.

"Take Hibbs at Utah. You, I.C., probably know all about his work: that activated macrophages inhibit tumor cell growth through production of NO."

That again was smoothly done, reflected Renu. He didn't *ask* I.C. whether he knew of Hibbs's work; he *acted* as if I.C. knew. Michael never faced him with the question. Celly would have tested him and so probably would have I.

"We ought to think of target-specific NO-releasers that could deliver the NO right to the tumor. For instance, via a monoclonal antibody? Or maybe manipulate the nucleophile portion of Celestine's NONONO . . . NO — I'll stop there," he winked at Price, "that some intracellular enzyme might then cleave to yield unbound NO. I don't know if any of you know Hibbs personally — "

"Never mind," said Renu, "I'm writing down all of the names. We can determine later who approaches whom and in what order."

Marletta nodded. "Hibbs is an intellect, but he's saddled with clinical duties. Renu, why not add Carl Nathan from Cornell to your list? He's not only a macrophage biologist working with knockout mice to see what NO can kill specifically, but he also knows a hell of a lot about parasitology."

"Good!" exclaimed Renu, who had been scrawling away furiously. "Parasitology is hardly a field that the big drug companies spend much effort on, because it's mostly the poor part of the world — the other three-fourths of the population — that is affected. But I haven't lost all of my Indian social consciousness: why not add someone who might point us in that direction?"

To the group's general assent, Marletta added, "Let me put another idea on the table. Parasites have many species-specific metabolic pathways. Suppose Celestine's organic chemists design a . . . polyzeniumpolyolate that would release NO from its chemical tether only *after* being cleaved by an enzyme *peculiar to that parasite*." Marletta tapped the table for emphasis. "Under such circumstances, only the parasite ought to be killed because NO doesn't diffuse very far beyond its site of release."

"Marvelous, Michael," Renu exclaimed, and turned to Price. "Celly, now that we've raised some real cash, I'm about to set up an in-house organic synthetic program. If anything hot comes out of your ideas, we'll do them at SURYA and patent them there — not at Caltech. Of course, if we publish — "

"*When*, not *if!* If my ideas are good enough to be worked on, then they're good enough to be published."

Renu threw up her hands. "If, when . . . whatever. Your name, Celly, will be on such a paper. That, you know, was part of our understanding."

Celestine nodded absentmindedly. "I know a little about parasites from my grad school work on insect hormones. I wonder, though, if there's anyone at Caltech working in the field. I'll have to do some checking. . . ."

"I can point you to someone," said Marletta. "As a matter of fact, if SURYA were to enter that field, it would be a good idea to appoint a bona fide parasitologist to our SAB. For instance, Dyann Wirth. She's now a professor of tropical medicine at Harvard, but she got her Ph.D. at MIT. She might be a good candidate, because she's also a molecular biologist. . . ." He stroked his chin pensively. "Tell me, I.C. You — "

Weiss, who had been doodling for minutes, suddenly tuned in. "You're right," he said musingly, "Think of ICUs. One group of patients that always ends up in intensive care units are patients with toxic shock. That, as everyone knows, is associated with a precipitous drop in blood pressure, which, in turn, is caused by the mammoth production of NO. Now," he shook his pencil at his listeners, "suppose our organic chemistry colleagues were to focus on NO-*inhibitors*, rather than on more efficient or longer-lasting NO delivery. An inhibitor might represent a life-saving drug in the treatment of shock."

———

For Renu Krishnan, this SAB meeting had finally justified the existence of a scientific advisory board, not for the investor PR window dressing Martin Gestler had envisaged and also exploited but for brainstorming potential new avenues of research — research that might actually lead to clinically useful products and eventual profits. Which again raised the other P word: priorities. Weiss's suggestion was eminently reasonable, but it did entail a new program for the organic synthesis group she was about to establish. It probably would make more sense to give a higher priority to SURYA's current emphasis on NO-releasers. It was a topic worth discussing with Celestine.

"Celly," she said during their afternoon coffee break. "Let's have dinner tonight. I'd like to talk about specific enzymatic cleavage features one could incorporate into NO-releasers. This might really be worthwhile for SURYA."

"I'd love to, Renu, but I've got to catch a six o'clock flight to L.A. I promised Jerry that I'd be home in time to kiss my son goodnight. He's accustomed to seeing both his parents tuck him into bed. As it is, I may be too late."

Renu felt a twinge of guilt. Naomi was almost the same age as Celestine's boy.

"Let me see whether I can change my reservation to a flight tonight. We could talk some in the cab on the way to O'Hare."

The taxi did not lend itself to much chemical speculation. Instead, the two women reviewed the various proposals that had been placed on the table. They still chuckled about the tale Michael Marletta had told when he'd introduced the question of NO-releasers for the treatment of pulmonary hypertension in infants and adults. According to him, the standard gas given patients on respirators is now mixed with nitric oxide. What, he asked, if a time-releasing NO compound of the type they'd been discussing all afternoon were substituted? He ended by regaling them with the story of Warren Zapol at Mass General, the first clinician to have actually used nitric oxide gas for pulmonary hypertension. Apparently Zapol had managed to persuade the higher-ups at that Harvard-affiliated hospital to let him try NO, arguing that federal OSHA standards (based on the amounts short-order cooks breathe in all the time) already permitted a certain level of NO exposure. Zapol's "what's okay in a diner ought to be okay at MGH," had carried the day, Marletta concluded. The rest of the audience — all of whom had had some experience with Harvard's firmly held belief that it was in no way the equivalent of a diner — roared.

I should have realized that it's a mistake to surprise your spouse with unannounced schedule changes, be they departures or arrivals. But especially arrivals. I thought I'd surprise Jephtah, but when I pulled into our driveway, I encountered a dark house. It was only 9:15 in the evening. As I opened the front door and was about to switch on the light, I thought that I'd heard some sounds. I stopped and listened.

"Ah, aah, aaah, aaaah . . . ah, aah . . ." it went rhythmically. At first, I was amused, perhaps even slightly titillated, and then irritated. Is our au pair fornicating with a boyfriend while we're paying her to look after Naomi? But then, like an icy shock, a second possibility hit me.

In some respects, I'm still too Indian for brutal confrontations. Quietly, I closed the front door and drove to the nearest pay phone at our neighborhood gas station. I dialed our home number and waited. The voice answering, even the breathing pattern, would tell me much. But when the ringing stopped, the voice greeting me was my own on the answering machine of our bedroom phone. "This is Renu," I said after hearing the beep. "It's about half past nine and I'm calling from a gas station, because I'm low on gas. We finished early in Chicago so I caught an earlier plane. I'll be home in five minutes."

When I drove up the second time, the upstairs lights were on. As I stood by the door, my key already in the lock, I'd decided on two alternative actions, depending on whom I'd find. My mouth was dry as I turned the key, but all the time I was praying nonsensically that it wouldn't be our au pair — good child care was hard to find. But when I thought of who else it could be, my heart started falling down a bottomless pit. As I loudly shut the door, I saw first the bare feet, then the jeans, and finally the T-shirt at the top of the stairs. I turned off the light in the entrance hall as Jephtah came running down. I didn't want to see his face, nor the look in his eyes. "Hello darling," I called out or maybe I just croaked, considering that I'd stopped salivating minutes ago. Quickly — so I wouldn't have to say anything — I kissed him, with lots of tongue. But I could have skipped the taste test. Jephtah couldn't have had enough time to shower; he'd probably just thrown some cold water on his face and tried to comb his hair. I could smell their coupled odors.

"Come," I dragged him into the dark living room. "I missed you so much," I murmured as I started to rip off my clothes. "Fuck me," I whispered furiously. I never use that word while making love. "Quick," I panted, pulling at his jeans. "Right here, on the carpet." I pulled him down on me and reached for his flaccid prick. "Fuck me," I said louder. "Now!"

"I can't," he whispered. "Wait for a little while."

"Now!" I hissed.

"I can't," he repeated. I couldn't make out his face, but I didn't have to. The tone of his voice made me feel sorry — for both of us, but especially for me, the president-presumptive of a company dedicated to penile erection.

That's when the monsoon started.

17

Palo Alto, December 15, 1985
Dearest Ashok,

Happy Hanukkah! I suggested to Jephtah that the time
had come to expose Naomi to some of the joys of Judaism.
What easier way than surprising a two-year-old with a gift
each day for eight days? It also helped her get over the loss
of Pandora, our nanny. This was a sudden decision, I admit,
but I hope I was not brutal about it. I just realized that
Naomi is approaching a very verbal period, and I want very
much for her to be bilingual. We are going to have a fifty-
three-year-old Nicaraguan woman, already a grandmother,
come in during the day. *Estupendous!* as a Paraguayan
acquaintance of mine would say. Aren't you impressed?
I am quite certain that Pandora understood why we had to
let her go — a blow softened with a handsome severance
package.

I missed you very much during the past couple of weeks,
more than you can imagine. Isn't it strange that just when I
have decided that running a small company and seeing it
grow is what I really want to do — in other words, indulge
in another form of motherhood — I yearn for the presence
and counsel of an older brother? I'd be curious to know what
you think of me now. Or perhaps, since Mummy's death, I
feel I should be looking after you.

Your sister has changed a lot. I think I'm getting tougher,
in a very un-Indian way. It is probably the scar tissue one
acquires while knocking around in a mostly male world,
and I am not sure I like it.

I am so busy now at SURYA (we're in the process of
becoming a "public" company) that it is not realistic trying to

organize a trip home to Madras, especially with my increasing commitments to domestic "quality time" (a very American term, probably coined by guilty working mothers). But how about your coming from India's Silicon Valley for a visit to the Bangalore of California? Isn't it time for your sister to advise you about potential brides, perhaps even construct an advert for the *Indian Express?* If I do, it won't list a horoscope or green card. I would focus my search on a modern Indian woman who would be comfortable calling you *mehra prem* and expect to be treated like an equal.

All my love for a prosperous and happy 1986!

Renu

As all Indians know, even the most violent monsoon ultimately exhausts itself. In the end, Jephtah and I did fall asleep in each others' arms in our own bed (after I'd ripped off the sheets and pillow covers and replaced them), exhausted, though not from the connubial carnal contact that was finally consummated after hours of emotional catharsis on both sides. It wasn't great sex, far from it. I am one of those lucky women for whom sex almost always leads to an orgasm. Not this time, though. Yet there was an element of primordial, wifely satisfaction — of matrimonial reaffirmation — when I felt my husband come inside me. I have no intention of letting my marriage collapse, especially since I now realize that some of the blame is mine.

My Jephtah, like so many sabra males, is not a complicated husband. With such men, marital unhappiness is usually about sex. So why did I not notice his feelings earlier? "All you talk about is Michael this and Michael that," he blurted out. "How smart he is, how many women work in his lab, how. . . ." His bubble of jealousy, filled with the biblical double standard of male-defined infidelity, slowly deflated. "And that 'stopover' in Ann Arbor: how do I know you didn't . . . ?" Jephtah was not usually one to end sentences in midair, but this time they all lacked closure.

"Don't tell me you fucked Pandora because you thought I was fucking Michael," I yelled at him. "I, your wife, who has never been touched by another man since meeting you!" I think it was those

words — "never touched by another man" — the almost Orthodox severity of them, that made him embrace me and start to cry. Tears are a great equalizer.

"You never ask these days what I'm doing," he murmured through my hair.

"How could I?" I said, but the defensiveness in my voice told me he was right. "You're working for another company," I hedged. "Perhaps not the direct competition, but still. . . ."

"That doesn't seem to bother you. Hardly a day passes when you don't brag about what you people are doing at SURYA."

"Brag? That isn't fair," I countered, but I knew he was right about that as well.

"All right," he yielded slightly. "Maybe that's too strong. But you do talk about your work with me."

"Of course," I exclaimed, "why shouldn't wife and husband confide in each other?"

"Precisely," he said. I could tell from Jephtah's tone that he was starting to feel better, now that he'd won an argument. "So why don't you ever ask me about my work?"

I didn't ask him then, of course. It would have been forced, like mouthing "I love you" on demand. But another day, long after this fight had faded into a bad memory — more scar tissue — without thinking too much about it, I did. What happened then almost made the fight worthwhile.

"What are you reading, *mehra prem?*" Renu asked.

Jephtah looked up, holding out the journal.

"*Fertility and Sterility,*" he answered as she hefted the bound library volume while balancing on the arm rest of his easy chair. "What are you doing with that? And 1958? This is ancient history."

Jephtah riffled through the pages to the beginning of an article. "And what do you think of that?"

"'Comparative Study of Cervical and Nasal Smears in Women?' I don't get it," she said flatly. "Why are you interested in that?"

"Because of this." He picked up a second journal by his side: *Archives of Otolaryngology.*

"I can't believe this," Renu exclaimed. "Aren't you always complaining that you have too many journals to read? This can't have anything to do with what you're working on."

"Not with what I'm working on *right now*," he concurred, "but it may have something to do with what I *will* do. Sit down," he pointed to the chair facing him, "and listen to your husband for a change."

Renu felt her hackles rise; she was about to rise to the bait, but at the last second decided to pass. Let him get this out of his system, she thought.

Jephtah seemed oblivious to her response. "Our entire group at the ETS division of ZALA is working on electrotransport approaches to drug delivery through the skin. This is public information. It's also obvious that knowledge of changes in electrolyte concentrations and in pH of body fluids and tissues is absolutely essential for our work, since we're dealing with *charged* molecules. So I started reading about the nasal mucosa and what do I find?" He pointed to the *Archives of Otolaryngology.* "Already forty years ago, a man named Fabricant — and I hope he didn't fabricate the data — reported major variations in the pH of nasal secretions, depending on sleep or wakefulness, on infection, even on *emotion.* That led me to the second article." He leaned forward. "What I'm telling you now falls under the category of matrimonial confidence. Remember when we talked about that?"

"Go on," she said stiffly.

"Almost exactly forty years ago, Papanicolaou — he of the Pap smear — described fern crystallization in cervical mucus smears. Originally, it was thought that the exact form of the arborization was dependent on a mixture of electrolytes with some proteins and carbohydrates, but then Abou-Shabanah — one of the authors of this *Fertility and Sterility* article," he lifted the second volume from his lap, "showed that ferning is primarily dependent on the concentration of electrolytes. Which is where things start to get interesting."

Renu loved seeing her husband's face alight with enthusiasm, especially when it was related to his work. She had not seen him that way for a long time — or was it really that she had not asked since the day he'd announced that work on the urethra had become too constricting? "So tell me," she nudged him.

"These people here," he stabbed the open page in his lap, "Davis and the same Abou-Shabanah, show pictures of a series of smears — each time taken from the cervix and the nose — obtained at different periods of a woman's monthly cycle. It's been known for some time that the ferning pattern from cervical smears is reproducibly different during the early phase of the cycle — the estrogenic phase — from that of the later period, when the concentration of progesterone is much higher. So look at these pairs." He handed her the open journal. "The respective pictures taken at the same time of the woman's cycle from either the cervix or the nose are almost indistinguishable."

Jephtah waited for Renu to examine the evidence. "Remarkable," she exclaimed. "But how come — "

"You see," he interrupted her, "salt metabolism is greatly dependent on hormonal effects, so why shouldn't electrolyte concentrations in the nasal mucus mirror the menstrual cycle — or the hormonal changes in pregnancy?"

"Still," Renu said thoughtfully. "Who'd think that changes down there," she pointed to her lap, "could be detected simply by blowing one's nose?"

They both laughed, and then Jephtah continued. "Of course, it isn't just a question of blowing your nose. In fact, the nose is not the most convenient organ when it comes to reproducibility of results. You can have colds, infections. . . . But, still, I asked the same question. Why the nose? So I continued reading. Do you know that Hippocrates commented on the relationship of nasal and genital function? I'm not talking about the sexual role of odors — perfumes, pheromones. That's a very different matter. I'm referring to things like reports of the occurrence of nasal congestion during menstruation. Have you ever noticed that?"

Renu snuffled twice before replying. "I'll have to check that," she said half-seriously.

"But here is the most remarkable part. The tissue covering a portion of the turbinate bones in the nose and even the septum is anatomically similar to the erectile tissue of the penis!"

"Jephtah!" She reached over to take the journal from his hand, but he pushed her away playfully.

"Not yet. There is more: this nasal erectile tissue only develops fully at puberty and atrophies with old age! And now I quote: 'engorgement of this tissue occurs at the onset of each menstruation.' Just think of that, President Krishnan: turgescence of a woman's nose may have an anatomical relation to tumescence of a man's penis." He leaned over and kissed her on the nose. "Does that turn you on?"

"It could," she pushed him away laughingly. "But not now. I want to hear more: like, what all this has to do with your work."

"Wait," he grinned back, "there is one more detour you must hear. Late last century, a German physician named Wilhelm Fliess was so convinced of the functional connection between a woman's nose and her sexual organs that he considered nasal surgery an answer to problems in the vagina. For a while, he even convinced Sigmund Freud of the correctness of his ideas — so much so that Freud let him remove surgically the turbinate bone of the nose in one of his patients in an attempt to cure her hysteria."

"And?"

"She nearly died from hemorrhaging and blood poisoning. A crazy story."

Jephtah returned to his seat, still shaking his head. "But in spite of Fliess and Freud, the pH and electrolyte changes started me thinking. Women can determine their fertile period by daily examination of their cervical mucus, whether it's thin and watery and can be stretched for a couple of inches around the period of ovulation or is thick and sticky during. . . . All right," he said, seeing Renu's upturned nose, "*some* women do so. Others, like my modern wife, stay on the Pill. But if a woman could accurately determine the specific stage of her menstrual cycle — pre-ovulatory, ovulatory, and post-ovulatory — and do so conveniently at home, wouldn't that be useful?"

"Sure," Renu replied. "But can't we already do that with home pregnancy tests — "

"I'm talking about women who are not pregnant," countered

Jephtah. "Who don't want to get pregnant or maybe the converse: who want to know when they would most likely become pregnant."

"Aren't people working now on do-it-yourself urine tests that would enable women to measure the different levels of estrogens and of progesterone and LH — "

Jephtah stopped her. "I'm not talking of urine tests. I'm thinking of the electric conductivity changes that might be associated with the different phases of the cycle. I have an idea. . . ." He stopped. "I have a couple of things up my sleeve that I'd like to try. I'll tell you about them if they work out."

Renu's look had turned sober. "Isn't it ironic? For the last half dozen years, all my work has focused on the penis and now my husband is heading for the vagina."

"The cervix," he corrected her. "Not the vagina."

It was an odd conversation. Can a woman's nose really mirror her sexuality? Odd, but in the end quite sobering. I had the distinct feeling that I was present at the beginning of a story — and who knew where this one would lead? Yet it was good to talk with Jephtah about his work.

I wonder how Celly handles all this with her husband — the youngest American ever to have won a Nobel Prize in Medicine. My talks with Celly have started to cross over from shoptalk to woman-to-woman confessional. I hadn't realized how much I had missed that kind of contact with another woman. I'm sure Celly feels the same way. Otherwise, would she have agreed so readily to our semi-monthly meetings? Ostensibly, we're coming together so frequently because of the polyzenium project, but we're taking very long lunches and we don't talk much organic chemistry.

Tomorrow I'm going to ask her about her husband. She hardly mentions him.

"What's it like to be married to a Nobel Prize winner?"

Celestine laughed. "It depends. In bed, you wouldn't know the difference. Not even the day after the prize ceremony. Did you know I was there, in Stockholm, with my Aunt Paula? She managed to get us invited at the very last moment so we could watch our respective men being anointed."

"Paula Curry?" Renu had wanted to talk about Celestine's husband, but she was not going to miss this opportunity to find out more about Cantor's mysterious companion. "What is her relationship to I.C.? Are they living together?"

"It depends." Again she laughed. "I seem to be repeating myself. Some people would say yes, others no. My aunt obviously spends time in his Chicago pied-à-terre, as he calls his rather sumptuous condo, and I'm quite sure she has slept there on more than one occasion. But does she actually sleep with Cantor? I don't know — and somehow, I've never felt comfortable asking her directly. She does maintain her own apartment, a place that you ought to see sometime. My aunt is an interior decorator with quite superior taste. Officially, she and I.C. have a professional relationship, Curry and Cantor Antiques."

"You're kidding," exclaimed Renu. "Our I.C. a shopkeeper?"

"Hardly," Celestine chuckled. "But he's very knowledgeable about antiques. As you saw, he has some first-class pieces. But you should see his campus home — full of Viennese fin de siècle stuff."

"You've been to his home?"

"Yes." Celestine's reply was terse. "Remember, I got my Ph.D. on the same campus."

"Sure," Renu persisted, "but in chemistry. Cantor is in cell biology."

"I was there once with Jerry." Celestine's answer was almost curt.

Renu took the hint. "Sorry," she said. "I hadn't meant to pry. But where does I.C.'s money come from? I presume he didn't just start collecting antiques when he got his Prize."

"The money came from his former wife. Some of the Nobel money, however, has gone into the joint business with Paula. They only deal with private clients out of her home. He puts up most of the capital, and Paula looks for the goods at auctions or estate sales. But enough about them." Celestine seemed uncomfortably eager to shift the subject.

"You are right. I asked about something else: what's it like to live with a Nobel Prize winner?"

"Ah yes," Celestine resumed her jocular manner. "Most top researchers are like women of breeding age. Some crave to become pregnant and don't stop at anything until they succeed, others just get pregnant accidentally, and the third group never makes it. My Jerry's Nobel very much resembles my motherhood — it happened accidentally. Cantor, on the other hand, clearly falls into the first class. I'm sure he'd love to get pregnant again." She laughed out loud. "Max Weiss, I suspect, will remain barren. Though he's done some damn good work."

"What about you?"

"I already told you: I'm an accidental mother, who — "

Renu cut her off. "I'm not talking about motherhood."

"Oh that," Celestine's snort was brief but audible. "Look. I may never reach Nobel standards in my research, but that's okay. I can't stomach all that pretense. I want to reach the top even if some committee in Stockholm never notices. That's what bugs me about Cantor, what bugged me about him way back in grad school when Jerry — who worshipped him — first told me about him. Cantor always pretended not to lust, but lust he did . . . mightily." She reached for her water bottle to take a swig. "Yes, I do fantasize about the Nobel Prize. I have ever since I saw Jerry get his. I'm really very ambitious, Renu. You probably have no idea how ambitious." Her gaze moved away, past Renu, to a leafless tree outside the window. "Or perhaps it shows," she added. "Think of our SAB meeting. I wasn't well-mannered with I.C. But then, John Maddox, the editor of *Nature*, once wrote that science is intrinsically bad-mannered."

"Come now, Celly. That's overstating it."

"No, it isn't. Each of us wants to be there first. We push pretty hard to get there, and if someone should beat us we break our backs trying to prove him wrong. In my case, especially if it's a *him*. Of course in science, having others trying to prove us wrong is what keeps us honest. But in the process, we do lust — blood-lust, I think it's called."

"Oh come now, Celly. Are you suggesting that people do science because it's some kind of competition? A contact sport for nerds?"

"It's an unpleasant proposition to defend," sighed Celestine, "but how about this? The evolutionary argument has been made that humans have a mixed allegiance to two contradictory codes of conduct: friendly cooperation within their community, but competition and warfare outside it. We approve of amity, but enmity between states is a necessary condition for human evolution. Maybe that's what made William James ask whether one could find a moral equivalent for war. It seems to me that you'll only have to read 'competition' for 'war' to find yourself in the scientific world, which at the same time pays homage to cooperation. What I'm saying is sad in a way but probably true."

Renu broke the silence. "Are you competing with your husband?"

"Maybe at one time, when I first met Jerry. He was already a postdoc with I.C., while I was still working for my Ph.D. with a young woman professor in another department. But that all changed in Stockholm. I told you, Jerry's Nobel is like my son Valentine: they were thrust upon us. Except that now I relish my Valentine, whereas Jerry has completely put the Nobel behind him."

"Why? And when?" Renu could not hide her amazement.

"The why is too complicated, but the when occurred still in Stockholm. He announced it quite publicly. That was probably the moment when I decided that I might manage living with a Nobel laureate — if he moved to wherever I'd get my first academic job. It was quite a moment. . . ." Her look and voice had turned pensive. "Cantor made some very elegant remarks at the Nobel dinner. I'll have to give him credit. Instead of the usual verbiage about just being a spokesman for his group, he quoted T. S. Eliot. But then Jerry's turn came, and to my utter surprise he surpassed Cantor by also citing Eliot but in a very different way. I've never forgotten the words."

"Let's hear them."

"'The Nobel is a ticket to one's funeral. No one has ever done anything after he got it.'"

Celestine laughed out loud as she saw Renu's dumbstruck expression. "That's just the look I had on my face. After all, it sounded like an insult to everybody in the Stockholm City Hall. But Jerry carried it off superbly. He started with the Eliot quote to make the point that, at his age, it would be best for him not to act like a professional Nobelist, resting on his laurels or pontificating with them invisibly around his head, but to start a new life, untouched by the huge shadow thrown by a Nobel award. He was right, of course. He decided to use part of the money to go into medicine, which meant returning to school to get an MD. That's why he could move with me when I got my Caltech job. He only just graduated from the UCLA medical school. So you see, we don't compete. What about you, Renu? Do you compete with your husband?"

Renu pushed her hand through her thick black hair before answering. "In Jephtah's eyes, probably yes."

"And yours?"

"I didn't think so — certainly not consciously. But now? I'm not so sure. I do enjoy exercising the authority that goes with my present job, but, until recently, I had not thought how that looked through my husband's eyes."

"Come now," said Celestine. "Him working in industry and then seeing his wife become president of the company?"

"But we don't work in the same company!"

"So? What's *his* title in *his* company?"

"But he doesn't want to become president of ZALA. He wants to do novel science and then see it used."

Celestine eyed her for a long time before speaking. "Are you so sure?"

"No," Renu said quietly.

Celestine reached across the table to pat her hand. "Enough of husbands. Let's talk about us women. I've never asked before, but why didn't you consider an academic career?"

"But I did." Renu's reply was instantaneous. "In contrast to what you told me about your own training, about getting your Ph.D.

with a woman professor, I had no women role models. My supervisor in grad school at Stanford was a man. Even my undergraduate research was done with a man, Michael Marletta. And then came my postdoc with Prof Frankenthaler. They all were very supportive and assumed all along that I'd stay in the academic pipeline, but," Renu's tone turned critical, "no one talked about the extreme leakiness of that pipe, especially for women. I know there are exceptions. You're a remarkable one: a tenure-track job in one of the top universities without even a prior postdoc. Now don't take this as a criticism." She leaned forward. "But, in the process, you seem to have accepted all of the male values. Right now, how much leeway do you give your graduate students? Aren't they expected to work on what you tell them to work on? And won't you be tempted to keep the best students just a bit longer, precisely because they are so productive and because that productivity will help *you* get tenure? And when you do pass that hurdle and get lots of grants, will you be tempted to have an army of two or three dozen pairs of hands like some of the big shots in organic chemistry?" Renu realized her voice was getting loud. She straightened and tried to calm down. "Even if none of that should apply to you, just think what you said a moment ago about competition."

"And you're so different?" Celestine said coolly. "In your position as president of a high-tech company? In testosterone-soaked Silicon Valley?"

"No and yes," Renu acknowledged. "I'll concede that I seem to have acquired *some* male characteristics, but I still think that in industry I'll have more scope to mold them to fit my own criteria. You, Celly — most certainly before tenure, but even afterward — need to follow a very rigid behavioral standard. I have more leeway, because I operate within a much narrower circle: *my* company. And as president, and maybe one day also as CEO, I can set the tune myself — most of it, anyway. But I'm different from you in that I didn't set out with industry as my ultimate goal. I was almost seduced into it by Martin Gestler — and by my own interest in the second stage of R and D: how to bring basic research discoveries into practical reality. And there is one fundamental difference between the two of us." Renu pointed at Celestine's cheek and then her own. "The color of our skin."

"Come now," protested Celestine.

"You're like Prof Frankenthaler." Renu's voice had assumed a scornful tone. "You're both unwilling to concede the existence of racial prejudice, because you two don't happen to be tainted by it. When I first raised the issue with the Prof — when he asked whether I was ready to look for an academic job — he pointed out that one-fourth of all members of the National Academy of Sciences are foreign born. I asked him how many of them were dark skinned *and* women. I know, this sort of discrimination is illegal and some of it not even conscious, but I didn't even have a green card — I was still on a J-visa. How many universities would have gone to the trouble of helping me change my visa status? It was Zaffanori at ZALA who did that — perhaps because he himself came to the States as a graduate student from Paraguay." Again, she pointed to Celestine. "I'm like you with your motherhood, or your husband with his Nobel Prize: we didn't choose where we ended up."

"At least you made it," Celestine said quietly.

"Have I really?"

18

"Can I see my son?" Menachem seemed to be addressing the huge silvery L swaying slowly in the breeze.

Melanie hesitated as the second L swung up. For a moment, the two giant letters remained frozen, back to back, mirror images, before the wind nudged them into their separate orbits. "When?" she finally whispered.

"I don't know yet," he replied in the same low tone. "I have to fly back to Israel tonight. Something came up suddenly."

She turned around. "Let me know when you're ready."

"I will," he said, touching her lightly on the arm. It was their first physical contact in seven years and it made her shiver. "And thanks for agreeing."

———

Menachem was standing by the tenth-floor window, looking down at the headlights of the passing cars refracted by the pouring rain.

"I was sorry to hear of your wife's death," Melanie said.

Melanie had proposed that they meet first in her office; it seemed appropriately neutral for a conversation too private for a public space yet not personal enough for home. Now that they were there, the two of them alone, the room unnaturally quiet, Menachem at the window monolithically still, she wondered if she had made a mistake.

"Menachem," she continued in a soft voice, "I know what it's like to lose a spouse. Remember, I'm a widow."

"It's totally different," he said, his back toward her, his eyes still focused on the rush-hour traffic below. "Did *you* feel guilty when your husband died?"

"Of course not." Her voice had risen. "Why should I — "

"You see," he turned around. "You cannot know what it's like to feel guilty for a quarter of a century."

"But Menachem, it was an accident." Melanie had never forgotten the story of biblical retribution Menachem had told her: how his second wife was paralyzed in a car accident. "And so long ago. That's not why she died now."

"My brain should agree, but my heart does not. The blood clot that killed her might never have happened. . . ."

"Menachem! My rabbi says '*might*' is the word that keeps us human."

He looked at her, a wry smile briefly flashing over his face. "I *was* touched by your conversion. You did that for me, didn't you?"

"In part," she nodded. "That, and my own guilt. . . ."

Menachem finally sat down. "For the rest of this evening, let's not mention that word — neither of us. I came to talk about today and the days after that. Agreed?"

She nodded. "What brought you to New York?"

"Why ask? What's the difference?"

Melanie looked down at her hands, folded together as if she were praying. "You're right. I was just stalling."

"Actually, the question isn't irrelevant. What brought me here this time will bring me to New York regularly — at least for the next couple of years. Do you remember our bombing of the Iraqi reactor at Osirak?" He didn't wait for an answer. "Ever since that time our government asked me to join our UN delegation as an advisor on nuclear matters. You know what a drubbing Israel has been getting these past few years. . . ."

"I know," she said.

"Until now, I had to decline. Shulhamit's health was deteriorating too fast. But now?" He held up a pair of empty hands. Then clenched them. "Let's talk about my son."

His tone made Melanie wary. "All right," she said slowly. "He *is* your offspring."

"'Offspring'? What a cold word! Like 'issue' or even 'progeny.'" Menachem frowned. "It sounds so biologic — even legalistic. Why not simply 'son'? Or Adam."

"Adam then." It sounded like a concession. "But there is nothing limiting about 'offspring.' You're right, it's a biological description and I'd meant it as such. 'Son' carries a lot more baggage — "

"Melanie! I hope we won't indulge in wordplay, but 'baggage' means 'burden.' Why apply this to Adam?"

"I'm not," she said firmly. "I simply meant that the word 'son' carries with it all sort of connotations," she pronounced the word carefully. "Social connotations. A relationship far beyond the simple question of paternity — "

"Or maternity," he interjected.

"Or maternity," she agreed. "But let's stick to the point. So far, you have not had any social relationship with Adam — "

"Melanie, how could I?" His voice nearly broke. "He doesn't even know that I exist. Or does he?"

She shook her head.

"Let's not indulge in legalistic haggling, in arguing about the meaning of a simple three-letter word. I'm sure the dictionary spends preciously little space on that definition. I have not come to demand custody," he said matter-of-factly. "I've simply come to ask for your advice on how to meet my son for the first time — a meeting to which you agreed." Again he cracked his knuckles, this time so loudly that Melanie flinched. "Let me be blunt: I'm scared. I'm almost sixty-four years old and about to see for the first time in my life my son — the only one I'll ever have." He attempted a smile, but it came out so crooked that tears formed in Melanie's eyes.

"Menachem," she said with an effort. "I do feel for you. I also can never have another child. Don't think I haven't thought about this first meeting between you and Adam. I've thought about it every day since he was born. Before that. I don't know how to make it easy. Or simple. But that's the only plan I have in mind. If you two must meet, then just . . . meet. Why don't you just come home with me tonight, as if you were a friend — "

"As *if?*"

"*As* a friend," she said quickly. "The four of us will have dinner — "

"Four?"

"I have an au pair living at home. We always eat together."

"I see," he said, relieved. "I thought there was. . . ." He didn't finish the sentence.

"There is," she said. "But not tonight."

———

"That wasn't so difficult," said Melanie. "He liked you, Menachem. You saw that, didn't you? And he didn't even know who you were."

"Maybe that's why he liked me. I wonder what he would think if he knew I was his father?" Menachem mused. "What a tall boy, he is. Not yet five and already so mature."

"Good genes. All around," she reached across the table to pat his hand. "He's already started to read." She smiled with pride. "You'll see more of him. We can take it one step at a time." She rose from the table. "It's getting late." Dvir stood abruptly, rattling china. "But before you go," she said, "I want to leave you with one question. What role do you plan to play now? I presume you are not willing to emigrate to the States. Or are you?"

"No. That I am not." He rose. "You're right. It's late. A lot has happened this evening. I can wait until next week." He reached for the door then turned. "There is one other question. Years ago, when you told me how you got pregnant, you wrote of 'stealing my sperm.' I never forgot that phrase."

"Those weren't my words," Melanie exclaimed, withdrawing. "I was quoting someone else."

"I don't care whose words they were," he said flatly. "I'm not thinking of moral or legal compensation, real or sham, for theft of my seed. I'm just raising an issue of my own for an eventual two-person Kirchberg Conference on the Rights and Obligations of Fatherhood. Or don't you think I'm entitled to that? And now good night."

———

"Is this going to become our regular meeting place?" Menachem asked as he entered Melanie's office the following week. "What will your secretary think? Or do you often stay after hours?"

"Why should my secretary care? I see lots of men. . . ."

"I suppose you do," he mumbled.

"Indeed. And they all come here to talk about money." She shrugged. "And interesting science. Is that why you're here?"

"What, money?" He laughed. "You know me better than that. Science, maybe. Some people would say ICSI is damned interesting science . . . with complicated implications . . . maybe too complicated." He shook his head as if to clear his mind. "That's for later. You asked that I come to talk to you about fatherhood."

"I didn't mean a philosophical discussion. I meant it specifically: what role do you envisage for yourself?"

"I'm not sure what should come first, ICSI or roles. Chronologically, I'd say ICSI, but don't worry," he raised a calming hand, "I'll follow your agenda. Let me start with a bit of history. *My* history." He leaned back, his legs stretched out in front of him. To Melanie, he seemed curiously relaxed.

"When I wrote you last, back in . . ." he furrowed his brow, "1979 I guess it had to be, because Adam was not yet born, I congratulated you on your pregnancy. I'd simply assumed you had married or had met — "

"I know that," she waved him on, wanting to move the conversation past the cause of her pregnancy, "but why did you never write me again?"

"Why?" he asked wryly. "That's the history we need to cover. When I heard from *you* the last time, it was nearly two years later, through that letter Felix Frankenthaler brought me personally — the one from which I learned how I had become the father of a son. It was a long letter, a complicated letter . . . even a beautiful letter. But put yourself in my position." Menachem suddenly leaned forward, his eyes boring into Melanie's. "How would you have felt — a supposedly infertile person — if you were suddenly faced with your fertility, however artificial the means that brought it about. I was surprised, shocked, touched, moved . . . you name the emotions — I had them. But I was also angry. Angry that you had not confided in me, *before* the fact, that is, rather than two years later, but even angrier about the position you had placed me in." He stopped.

Melanie's hand moved slowly across her forehead, as if she wanted to shield her eyes. She said nothing.

"You asked whether I would want to acknowledge my fatherhood in case something happened to you — a sort of insurance policy for which you were not prepared to pay any premium. How could you even *imagine* I might say no? But how was I supposed to acknowledge my paternity while you were alive — you who are seventeen years younger than I? I was angry because you had presented me with an impossible problem: I had to choose whether to destroy my wife's confidence in me after I had already destroyed her body or to keep quiet and never know the only child I shall ever have. So what was left to me?" His voice sounded exhausted. "I kept quiet and never wrote to you."

Melanie reached over and touched his sleeve. "I'm sorry, Menachem. So sorry."

"Don't," he said. "I wasn't asking for sympathy. It was an explanation — a base on which to build. When Gestler first approached me about the SURYA board and then told me that you had also accepted, I took it as a sign of providence, unbeliever though I am. It meant that we'd meet again — in neutral territory and in public."

He turned to her. "And now?"

Melanie realized that her turn was approaching. "And now that you are a widower," she said hesitatingly, "what do you plan to do?"

"What do *we* plan to do?" he corrected her gently. "Do you remember how you ended your long letter to me? With the Ethiopian version of the Queen of Sheba story: how the queen sent her only son, Menelek, to Solomon for further education. I couldn't help but go to the Church of the Holy Sepulcher in Jerusalem to look at that cartoon-like Ethiopian representation of the legend you said was hanging there. I had tears in my eyes when I saw the picture in which Menelek asks his mother, 'Tell me about my father,' not knowing that he was King Solomon. By the way, Melanie, how old was Menelek when the Queen of Sheba told him?"

"I don't remember any more. Perhaps fourteen."

"And do you plan to wait that long with Adam? Hasn't he asked yet about his father?"

Of course he's asked. I had prepared myself for that moment. When it came, I thought I was ready. I couldn't tell Adam the whole truth — not at thirty-six months — but I didn't want to burden either one of us with lies. When the day arrived, I took paper and pencil and drew a circle. "This is an egg." Below it I wrote MAMA in big, capital letters. "And these are egg, lots of them." I must have drawn twenty or more surrounding the egg. "But only one is needed." I adorned one with an extra-vigorous tail and a pointed head.

One day, I thought, I will tell him about the acrosome and how it penetrates the zona pellucida, just as I'd told his father by the canal in Little Venice.

"That one is the papa sperm," I said, writing PAPA in somewhat smaller letters, "and when it enters the mama egg, after some time Adam is born." I drew a small figure and labeled it ADAM.

"Adam," he said proudly. Then: "How much time?"

"Nine months," I replied, thinking that would end the first lesson. But I was wrong.

"Who picks him?" Adam asked, pointing a stubby finger at PAPA.

"I did," I said, and got up.

I still remember how pleased I was with the first lesson. I had not lied; I had not even told a half-truth. But the next time proved much tougher. "Where is my Papa?" he asked two or three months later. I went back to my drawing skills. This time, under MAMA, I drew the figure of a woman, whereas under the single sperm, whose tail and head I now colored with crayons, I drew a male figure.

"Usually," I said, "the papa sperm comes from a man." I added a hat and cane. "But sometimes," I drew a big X across the male figure, reducing him to insignificance, "the sperm just comes from a bank." I pointed to the multitude of anonymous sperm surrounding the egg.

"A bank?" He screwed up his face, trying to reconcile sperm with what little he knew about finance.

I took great care to describe the function of that institution, much more than the circumstances merited, but it served its purpose: I had drawn Adam's attention away from sperm to money. From that day on, I realized that I had set out on spinning a maternal Scheherazade tale in which a sperm bank would be the central focus. It worked, because in the process I always told the truth except for the actual collection of the sperm, which so far had not interested Adam. I told him about Justin, how he could have been the source of the PAPA sperm if he hadn't died, and that so far I hadn't found a suitable replacement.

Around his next birthday he asked, "Why didn't you wait, Mama?" So I drew more pictures, grateful to be moving to the safer terrain of female reproduction. One day, I realized that my son was probably the youngest person in Manhattan to know about the menopause. And why not? Isn't that appropriate for the son of the head of the REPCON Foundation?

Of course, I didn't have any illusion that I was telling an Arabian Nights version of reproduction, with my son the surrogate King of Samarkand. Shelly Frankenthaler's intervention helped. Since she and Felix were the only persons privy to my secret, I turned to them more and more often. Before Adam's birth I had been much closer to Felix, but now I shared more with Shelly.

"A son needs a man around the house," she announced one day out of the blue. "What are you going to do about it?"

It isn't that my social radar, looking for potential father signals, was turned off, but it was moving sluggishly, with hardly a blip on the screen. Between my work and motherhood, there wasn't much left to share. So I turned on my radar's sensitivity, at the same time following Shelly's answer to what she'd do in my place. "Other than look for a husband? I'd hurry up and get a male au pair."

Orlando has been with us for three years now; I hope he'll stay for another. . . . I don't know how many more years. I still remember Shelly's flippant response when I asked where to look for a male au pair. "Just think of all the poets who are waiters or cab drivers. I bet they could write more and better poetry as a mother's helper."

The best luck I ever had was finding Roland Whybrow, "Orlando" to us. The dedication page of his first chapbook showed how true to the mark Shelly's advice was: "To Adam, who started it all." He's about to publish a second chapbook, and judging from the hints he's been dropping, someone from the Laidlaw household will appear on that first page as well.

I was rather pleased that Menachem liked him. I won't forget his expression when I first told him that we'd be four for dinner. But of course Orlando can't be the long-term solution. As Adam grows up, more men should be around him — including a true father figure. Last year there was a blip on my radar that I thought looked promising, and to my surprise he still does. But he doesn't know about Menachem and Menachem doesn't know about him.

"In the abstract sense, he has asked about you," replied Melanie.

"'Abstract!'" Menachem's tone bordered on the caustic. "What's abstract? I acknowledge that there is abstract fertilization — say in a petri dish — but fatherhood is a *relationship*."

"Menachem," she pleaded. "All I mean is he was very little when he first asked. The question of a two-year-old."

"And?"

"I explained a little at a time. I told him that I wanted a child — which is true," she added quickly. "That my husband had died and that I had not found a replacement. Which is also true. The only untruth I've told him so far is that I went to a sperm bank."

"Okay," he said, partially placated. "And now?"

"Let's be gentle. All of us. Come as often as you can. As a friend — of the family. Let Adam get to know you and you him. Can you be satisfied with that?"

"For the moment, yes."

19

The initials IPO invariably mark a crucial point in a public company's life, a sort of corporate bar mitzvah. But just as a bar mitzvah does not actually make the boy a man, so a company's Initial Public Offering only admits a start-up to the field where the big boys play: the stock market. What happens next has little to do with the company's initial promise: everything depends on continuing performance, on the stock market's perception of that performance, and, indeed, on the overall economic climate. If the economic outlook is bleak, even the most stellar corporate achievements are overshadowed by Wall Street's bearish mood.

In the spring of 1986, SURYA's board of directors concluded that the time for the IPO had arrived — a unilateral decision lacking any operational meaning absent the participation of some other key parties. In a corporate IPO, these outside parties consist of an underwriter — an investment banker or a brokerage firm — and the SEC, the all-powerful Securities and Exchange Commission in Washington. Underwriters are matchmakers; like most matchmakers, they are not unbiased. Once they have agreed to play that role and finish haggling about the size of their fee, their sole function is to make the client appear as attractive as possible. Like other matchmakers, underwriters rarely undress their client in public.

Displaying the most attractive features while veiling the rest is part of the game. The rules of that game are established and enforced by the SEC, which, like the FDA, is feared as well as held accountable by the industry it regulates.

On the face of it, SURYA looked like a marvelous IPO candidate: the company balance sheet showed no debts and seventeen million dollars in the bank, assets included a virtually complete FDA package for an exciting drug, potential markets were seemingly enormous, and, best of all, the company's image was sexy in the truest sense of the word. Martin Gestler — a veteran of underwriter wheeling and dealing, IPOs, secondary offerings, and other vagaries of the stock market — had taken on the primary responsibility for greasing the rails for what he hoped would be an express to and through the regulatory stops of the SEC.

"Renu," he announced one day, "you'll have to watch the shop while I'm concentrating on the IPO. What we need now is a pair of underwriters: one impeccably staid, the other a go-go operator from the West Coast. Somebody like Robertson Stephens, Hambrecht & Quist, or Montgomery Securities."

"Which would you pick if you had your druthers?" Renu — whose MBA was, after all, from Santa Clara, a blue-collar school catering to part-time students — was curious what the Stanford-trained Martin would choose.

"For the staid one? Any from the first tier would do," he waved a dismissive hand. "Goldman Sachs, First Boston, Morgan Stanley. You wouldn't be able to tell them apart in a lineup. The second group is trickier. Montgomery is full of aggressive sales types: pushy, athletic, you see them with open shirt collars. Among the go-go class, I'd rate Robertson Stephens the classiest: they all wear striped ties and would never be caught in designer blue jeans. I'd probably go for them, because I want a classy IPO." He winked conspiratorially. "The problem is not how to convince any one of them to take us on but to discover which pair would be willing to work together. I hope penile erection will sway them. How often can underwriters do business in so sexual an arena without looking tacky?"

Gestler was dead right. His display of exciting science, reasonably conservative financials, and one-upmanship carried the day.

"When last did you put your name on an ithyphallic red herring?" he deadpanned during his meeting with the senior management of Goldman, Sachs and Robertson, Stephens — SURYA's ultimate choice.

The managers looked puzzled.

"'Ithyphallic'?" One of the investment bankers said at last. "Spell it." Gestler did so. A long pause ensued, at the end of which one of the junior managers present made his way to the large dictionary stand in the corner. He straightened abruptly, then returned to whisper in his superior's ear. "Of course," the senior manager observed, "we can't use that word."

"Maybe, *they* can't," Martin reported to Renu, "but just wait and see how I plan to use it."

Renu looked it up too. "And where will you display that nugget of erudition?" she asked.

"Wait and see."

———

As usual, the actual preparation of the "red herring" — the preliminary prospectus required for SEC approval — was a joint enterprise involving the intramural talents and experience of the lawyer Mort Heartstone and the entrepreneur Martin Gestler and the extramural vetting by the underwriters. How much of such vetting is simply fancy rubber-stamping depends on the seriousness of the underwriters. In SURYA's case, the Goldman and Robertson firms proved to be serious, at times even annoying — at least as far as Renu was concerned.

Renu's role — unlike that of the minions in Heartstone's legal firm and in the underwriters' offices — was very much tutorial; she was both a teacher and a student. As SURYA's chief scientist, she was responsible for producing a generally intelligible introductory section dealing with the basic biology of penile erection, with special attention to the role of nitric oxide. That and the subsequent description of the MUSA system and the NONO-2 active ingredient were supposed to impart a serious, intellectual aura to the text of what was, crassly speaking, a promotional sales document — albeit one dotted with legal caveats. Thus Renu was treated with some deference by the underwriters cadre. Nevertheless, they kept asking so many questions that Renu became impatient. Had they truly managed to avoid all exposure to science since high school? And why, she wondered, did they seem to consist only of a variety of vice presidents — plain, "executive," "senior," or "assistant" — and secretaries, but nothing in between?

But in addition to providing scientific expertise, Renu was also the recipient of valuable information, primarily from Mort Heartstone, SURYA's master of the legal caveat. Initially, after Heartstone tutored her on his reasons for inserting so many faintly damning statements into the prospectus, Renu felt insulted, then irritated, and finally overwhelmed.

He titled Renu's description of the MUSA system, "Dependence on the Company's Transurethral System for Erection." He killed the scientist's proud, upbeat starting sentence, replacing it with what Renu considered sickening pessimism: *The Company currently relies upon a single therapeutic approach to treat erectile dysfunction, its transurethral MUSA® system for erection. No assurance can be given that the Company's therapeutic approach or its proposed pharmacological formulations involving nitric oxide releasers will be shown to be safe and effective or ultimately approved by regulatory agencies.*

As if this were not enough, Heartstone added a sledgehammer summary: *As a result of the Company's single therapeutic approach and its current focus on NONO-2, the failure to obtain eventual FDA approval of its New Drug Application (NDA) for MUSA® on a timely basis, if at all, or to successfully commercialize such product would have an adverse effect on the Company and could threaten the Company's ability as a viable entity.*

Reading the draft in Heartstone's library, the walls lined with elegantly bound tomes, so different from the ratty mixture in SURYA's budding scientific library, Renu couldn't contain herself. "Mort," she exclaimed, "after reading this, who'll want to buy a single share of our stock?"

"Read on," the lawyer admonished her. "Then we'll talk."

Renu started to read out loud, her tone expressing her mounting distaste. "'Since the Company's product involves transurethral delivery, a new therapeutic approach, regulatory approvals may be obtained more slowly than for products encompassing more conventional delivery systems.'" She let out an impatient sigh. "'The Company completed pivotal clinical trials . . .'" Renu stopped to glance at Heartstone. "The first complimentary word: 'pivotal.' Thanks, Mort."

"You better continue," he warned her, "before going overboard with gratitude."

"' . . . and is about to submit its NDA to the FDA while pursuing further clinical trials.' Nothing wrong with that," she said.

"Mm-hmm," he grunted.

"'There is no assurance that these clinical trials will be completed successfully within any specified time period, if at all.'" Renu nearly yelled the last three words. "Mort, for heaven's sake be sensible! Given all of the clinical work we have completed — on time, I must remind you — how can you say — "

"Relax, Renu. We'll both save a lot of time if we discuss this when you're through reading."

"Okay." She took a deep breath. "'Furthermore, the FDA may suspend clinical trials at any time if it is believed that the subjects participating in such trials are being exposed to unacceptable health risks.' Christ," she muttered, "what else is there?"

"Try the section on manufacture."

Renu flipped through the pages. "I see you changed the title," she said. "'Limited Manufacturing Experience.'" She shook her head in exasperation. "And inserted a new sentence before my stuff. 'The Company has no experience manufacturing its product in volumes necessary to achieve significant commercial sales at commercially reasonable cost.'" She looked up, eyes narrowed. "Thank God, my husband isn't running that facility. I can imagine what he would say. But just wait till Menachem Dvir reads this," she warned him. "Let me see what you did to my section on patents."

"You won't like it," he said mildly.

"'While the Company's success will depend, in large measure, on the strength of its current and future patent position, the latter, like that of other pharmaceutical companies, is highly uncertain. Patent claims may be denied or significantly narrowed; furthermore, there can be no assurance that the Company's products will not infringe on patent or proprietary rights of others. In any event, the Company believes there will continue to be significant and expensive litigation in the pharmaceutical industry regarding patent and other intellectual property rights.'"

Renu put down the draft which was already bound and printed — one aspect of the prospectus preparation she had admired with undisguised envy. "It's extraordinary that your financial printers can bring out such documents overnight, while we poor scientists have to wait months to get a journal article printed."

"Wait till you see the bill," laughed Heartstone.

Renu looked at the cover page, the left margin framed by a block of boilerplate printed in startlingly bright red: "Information contained herein is subject to completion or amendment. A registration statement relating to these securities has been filed with the Securities and Exchange Commission. These securities may not be sold nor may offers to buy be accepted prior to the time the registration statement becomes effective."

"While it may not make you feel any better, look what I've had to add to some of the other people's sections." Heartstone's paternal timbre was meant to calm her. "'Since the Company intends to market and sell the MUSA product through its own direct sales force in the United States but has no experience in the sale, marketing, and distribution of pharmaceutical products, there can be no assurance that the Company's sales and marketing efforts will be successful.'" He closed the document. "It's full of that."

"Why indulge in such terrible overkill, Mort? What will the underwriters say?"

"They will love it," he grinned, "and then add a few more ifs, whens, and buts. Maybe you will appreciate it more if I let you in on a little secret: at the next board meeting, you will be elected to the board."

While Martin Gestler had privately alerted Renu to that promotion, her cheeks still reddened. It was the first pleasure she had experienced all morning in the lawyer's office.

"With the exception of Martin, all of the directors are outsiders. It's time more management enters the board. You not only deserve it Renu, but it's desirable that the chief scientist of a high-tech company is actually a director. Or for that matter, to have more than one woman on the board. But one of the privileges of a director," Mort chuckled, "is that you will automatically become a defendant in any stockholder's suit. If SURYA's stock does poorly — or perhaps even exceptionally well — I guarantee that we shall be sued." Renu's dismay caused him to raise two reassuring palms. "With very few exceptions, these are nuisance suits filed by shyster firms. All they do is fill the pockets of the shysters . . . and, of course, those of the shining legal knights asked to come to the rescue. Like my firm," he grinned disarmingly, but then turned serious. "Renu, it is none of my business, but have you ever been on the Pill?"

Renu looked nonplused. "My answer to most men — other than my husband — would be that it's none of their business. But in your case, I suspect a legal motive. Am I right?"

"Absolutely."

"In that case, the answer is yes. As a matter of fact, I am on the Pill."

"Good," he said, heaving himself out of his chair. "Have you read the package insert?"

"Not recently. I probably read it when I first got a prescription. Why?"

Heartstone lumbered to the bookshelves, running his finger along the leather spines. "I used to be corporate counsel to one of the pioneers in the oral contraceptive field." He removed a volume, entitled *Syntex Corporation Registrations*. A slip, apparently serving as bookmark, stuck out on top. Still standing upright, the heavy volume resting against his bulging stomach, Heartstone started to read from the loose page. "Occasional side effects include nausea, vomiting, disturbance of hearing and vision, anemia, asthma, mental confusion, sweating, thirst, diarrhea, allergies, occasional gastrointestinal bleeding. . . ." He looked at Renu. "If you read all that in a package insert, would you take such a drug?"

She hesitated. "I'm not sure."

"Of course, you aren't. Who would be, reading this in isolation? What I read to you," he paused, "were the reported side effects of aspirin. Now," he said, satisfied, "look at this." He opened the bound volume. "The 1978 text, which I prepared and which is still unchanged, of the side effects of the Pill. Three pages long, single-spaced, small print — the stuff you don't recall reading, if, in fact, you ever looked at it. Suffice it to say that this list covers the gamut from cancer and stroke to bleeding of the gums and reduced earwax. The lesson is simple and sad: list every conceivable side effect, however unimportant or infrequent, or you will be accused of not having warned the consumer. In the most litigious society in the world, the potential benefits of serious warnings are totally diluted by all the detritus. Now let me return to the red herring."

He shoved the slender prospectus toward Renu. "It would be naive to assume that this document is only so named because of the red print of the warning legend on the first page." Heartstone ran his finger along the margin. "You probably know the dictionary meaning of the term: 'something that distracts attention from the real issue.'" He shook his head so vigorously that the wattles under his chin quivered back and forth, "the dictionary definition very much applies."

"Rather discouraging, isn't it?"

"Not totally so. Think of this as truth in advertising. The people who read these prospectuses are the sort you will be meeting on the road show: pension and mutual fund managers, security ana-lysts, portfolio or money managers, some stockbrokers. The people who show up are sophisticated and have read dozens upon dozens of these stock offerings; they know what to ignore and what is just legalese, but in the end they're all professional gamblers. While they know the inherent risks of the game, they usually think that the lousy odds do not really apply to them because they're more clever than the rest. Of course, with SURYA's stock, I think their odds are actually very good."

"How would anyone conclude *that* in view of what you've writ-ten here?" she asked sarcastically.

"That, my dear, will depend on Martin, on the CFO — although the financials are pretty straightforward — and on you. On what you will tell them on the road show."

"On me?" she exclaimed. "What am I supposed to say? That we have a gloomy, cynical lawyer as corporate counsel?"

Heartstone laughed so hard, he had to embrace his bouncing belly. "No, it's your tone, your facial expression, your mysterious 'no comment' when a critical question is asked, your coy response, 'now what do *you* really think?' and the like. Martin is very good at this; he will certainly prepare you ahead of time after Goldman, Sachs and Robertson, Stephens have presented you with a list of people and places you will visit. And there is one more thing: usually, companies are represented by the CEO, the CFO — in SURYA's case, Roger Quistsal's successor, because I understand that he is leaving next month — and the chief technical officer, usually the VP in charge of research. But Martin and I concluded that, in this instance, we will emphasize the science, and do it glamorously. So we thought we should include the chairs of the scientific and medical advisory boards, respectively. It will be your job to convince them to participate — especially Cantor, because Martin, who seems to have fallen in love with the word — "

"I know it only too well," interjected Renu.

"Martin thinks that a truly ithyphallic presentation should be ennobled by a Nobelist." He raised his eyebrows in mock dismay. "I'm never convinced that the luminosity of a Nobel Prize penetrates very far beyond its immediate murky terrain, but anyway," he gestured toward Renu, "that's your department."

––––––

"Road show?" Cantor's disdain rang over the phone. "What's next? A traveling circus? When you first visited me in Chicago, you never mentioned that entertaining financial types during breakfasts at ungodly times or at mega-caloric lunches was one of the functions of the SAB chair. I really can't be bothered. Besides, I'm on a diet. If some serious security analyst wants to call me, you can give him my office number. I'll answer questions by phone."

"Private phone calls are precisely what I don't want Cantor — or any other naive scientist — to take," growled Martin Gestler after hearing Renu's report. "During this preregistration phase we have to be very careful and stick close to what's written in the red herring. Don't forget, the red warning label vanishes only after

SEC approval — only then does the herring turn into a black-and-white prospectus. Until that day, I don't want any improvisations. Everything should be said in front of witnesses. Convince him Renu. Remind him of his stock option."

A successful road show almost guarantees a successful IPO, and that, in turn, converts a stock option into real currency. Money persuades in direct proportion to its perceived value, and Cantor's thirty-thousand-share option at forty cents per share now stood a real chance of appreciating to a cool half million *if* the seventeen dollar IPO offering price — so far only whispered in SURYA's boardroom — indeed materialized. Renu whispered the whisper to Cantor, accompanied by diplomatic commentary, the combined effect of which made his subsequent acceptance appear graciously reluctant rather than coarsely greedy.

"I.C.," she said in a louder tone after having led him sotto voce through the simple arithmetic, "our first set of meetings will all be in New York and Boston. Dr. Noland, the chair of our MAB, will come with us from San Francisco. It really would be helpful if the chair of the SAB were also there. Even the first couple of days would be very helpful. You do offer panache, you know."

"You mean me? Or the Nobel Prize?"

Renu wondered about the facial expression on the other end of the telephone line — arrogant? lupine? amused? "The Nobel Prize doesn't hurt," she replied diplomatically. "It would be beneficial if you commented on the potential of tumor-targeted NO-releasers in the cancer field. Remember what Michael Marletta mentioned in your apartment?"

"So why not ask Michael?"

Renu started to get impatient. "Our audience does not consist of scientists. They don't know who Michael is. Your name — "

"Okay," he said. "Two days. New York and Boston. But no more."

A pre-IPO road show may very well be a traveling circus, but fund and pension managers, even though they play with other people's money, come to be persuaded, not amused. In the final analysis, their jobs depend on making money for others. The road show started on an auspicious note at an altitude of over thirty thousand feet. The delegation heading for New York consisted of Martin Gestler, Renu Krishnan, Dr. M. L. Noland of Stanford's GYN/OB department, the new chief financial officer David Warbler, and one indispensable member of all road shows: a young hod carrier, responsible for the slides, the overhead transparencies, the handouts and, most important, for collecting the business cards at all stops. That was one way of determining whether the competition had managed to sneak in.

Under ordinary circumstances, Martin Gestler would have had them fly economy class, but this time they were accompanied by three representatives from the San Francisco offices of their underwriters. Although only assistant vice presidents — and after all, with a projected forty million dollar IPO, SURYA was comparatively small fry — they would not have been caught dead flying anything but first class. Gestler, who was well aware of the importance of status during this sensitive period, had signed off on first class tickets for all but the audiovisual aide-de-camp. The latter flew steerage on another flight, because having him sit in back on the same airplane would have been boorish.

Renu's seat was in the last row of the first class compartment, David Warbler's next to hers. A short, athletic Yalie with a high forehead bordering on intellectual baldness, Warbler boasted a c.v. that featured an MBA from Stanford and four years of investment banking experience on the East Coast; he had recently been brought in by Martin Gestler whose hunter's nose for savvy financial types had quivered at their very first interview. Three years younger than Renu, Warbler was not only smart — in fact, aggressively so — but also the possessor of a highly honed sense of humor. Spending five hours together, undisturbed by phone calls and other interruptions, seemed to both of them a good way of becoming better acquainted. Warbler knew plenty about IPOs and road shows but very little about NO — all in all a situation unlikely to stress their social compatibility.

Warbler had just returned from the forward toilet after the plane had reached cruising altitude. "Do you know who is sitting in the first row on the other side?" he whispered to Renu. "Mother Teresa."

"You must be kidding!" Renu whispered back. "How do you know?"

"Listen, ever since she won the Nobel Prize, her picture has been all over the place. I'm going to try something," he said. "Let's see if she will bless our red herring."

Before Renu even had a chance to respond, Warbler had reached into his briefcase for a copy and headed for the front of the plane. Renu saw her short colleague disappear behind the backrest of the empty aisle seat, only to return a few minutes later with an expression mirroring the beatitude of a pilgrim from Lourdes, or possibly St. Bernadette herself. He could barely contain himself.

"Listen! She did it! She blessed it! Look!" He pointed to Mother Teresa's scribbled signature across the red print of the red herring's cover page. "I asked her to date it! We'll have to put this into a safe. Renu, quick," he whispered, "give me your copy."

With the skill of an origami virtuoso, he folded her proffered prospectus into a passable facsimile of a hat, extracted two twenty dollar bills from his billfold and dropped them in. "I'm starting a collection for Mother Teresa's Calcutta mission."

Renu covered her mouth to hide the onset of incipient hysteria. "Quick," he urged her, "I need a couple more bills to hide the text." Only then did Renu notice that Andrew Jackson's expression on the bill staring at her from the depth of the SURYA hat seemed startled.

During the next few minutes, Renu felt tears of repressed laughter running down her cheeks as she saw Warbler moving slowly up the aisle, bills of all denominations dropping freely into the hat.

"Do you know how much I collected?" he asked breathlessly upon his return. "More than five hundred dollars! Mother Teresa not only blessed me again, but she wanted to keep the hat. I nearly gave it to her when I remembered some of the pictures: the colored representation of the cross section of a penis and the enlargement of a MUSA. Thank God, they weren't on this page." He spread out the crumpled sheet. "But she blessed this one as well!"

"David, are you religious?"

He grinned. "Only superstitious. How can we possibly lose after two blessings from a virtual saint?"

———

It was difficult to tell whether Mother Teresa, the glamour of penile erection, or the elegance of the scientific presentations was responsible for the success of SURYA's IPO. The breakfast and lunch audiences were so intrigued by the science that only the odd question here or there dealt with financial matters. Any other company's CFO would have felt depressed for days, but David Warbler just sat there, an exalted expression on his face, convinced that he had already made his contribution. Even I. C. Cantor earned his keep, using his legendary pedagogic skills to captivate an audience at the earliest lecture he had ever delivered: a 7:00 A.M. breakfast! He waxed lyrical about the potential of tumor-specific NO-releasers — so much so that Renu decided to initiate an exploratory synthetic program, making a note to brainstorm the topic with Celestine Price.

The presence of M. L. Noland turned out to be surprisingly relevant. The audience, virtually all male, could not contain themselves, asking questions that at times departed considerably from penile erection, though never left entirely the area of the groin. Many of the questions dealt with recent newspaper articles on the putative deterioration of male sperm in various parts of the world, including alarming reports of a 50 percent drop in sperm concentration. Using her best gynecological bedside manner and andrological benchside experience, Noland calmed the men.

"Relax — at least the New Yorkers among you. Recent studies have shown that average sperm counts are higher in New York than anywhere else and have not dropped at all during the past couple of decades. In contrast to Los Angeles," she added, bringing down the house. Still, she qualified her solace by calling for more extensive, carefully controlled epidemiological studies.

Deftly, she returned the discussion back to SURYA and its IPO, pointing out that the company's MUSA system was aimed primarily at sexual intercourse, rather than reproduction.

"There is plenty of research going on with respect to infertility, in women as well as men. Take, for instance, ICSI." Noland had met the preceding day with Melanie Laidlaw, and they had talked about the genetic implications of widespread use of intracytoplasmic sperm injection. Laidlaw's detailed knowledge of the subject had caused Noland to prick up her ears. University professors always pay attention to the interests of potential dispensers of research funds.

But the acronym ICSI had triggered an auditory reflex in Martin Gestler. It reminded him to throw out to the audience a comment about the ithyphallic quality of the company's R and D results — a remark that he had planned ahead of time but that fell totally flat, with one exception. One of the analysts, in his subsequent report to his clients, warned that an apparent side effect of the MUSA was an itchy phallus. After the questions started to come back to SURYA, Gestler never said the word ithyphallic again, in public or private.

———

The SURYA management team and underwriters, without Cantor or Noland, continued on a European extension of their road show, with obligatory stops in London, Zurich, Geneva, and Paris. The day before their departure for Europe, a new revision of the red herring arrived from Heartstone's office in San Francisco, which contained the last changes requested by the SEC. Ten copies of a signature page, bearing the original signatures of all directors, was required. Baron Van Zwanenberg and Professor Davidson were getting theirs by Federal Express and Renu was asked to collect signatures from Melanie Laidlaw. David Warbler was assigned the job of locating Menachem Dvir at Israel's UN Mission.

Renu arrived at the REPCON offices at a quarter to five. "Dr. Laidlaw already left for home," the receptionist announced. Renu decided to walk to Laidlaw's East Side apartment, some eleven blocks away. Having sat all day in meetings, she wanted to clear her head and get some exercise on this pleasant June afternoon.

But when Renu reached her destination, the male voice on the intercom informed her that Dr. Laidlaw had not yet arrived. She was expected any time.

"May I come up and wait for her?" Renu asked. "I have some urgent papers for her to sign. It will only take a minute."

A young man opened the apartment door. "I am Roland," he said. "I run the house," he explained with a disarming smile, "and take care of Adam. Please come in."

"Mama!" a voice called out, followed by footsteps and the appearance of a young boy. "Oh," he said, "I thought you were — "

"Adam," Roland bent down, "this is a friend of your mother's. Say hello to Dr. Krishnan."

"Hello," Adam echoed. "Pleased to meet you."

"Adam," a male voice rang out from the living room. "Where are you? We haven't finished our game."

"Come," Adam said, taking Renu by the hand, "you can watch me play checkers with Menachem until Mama comes."

20

I was taken aback, coming home to find Renu Krishnan kibitzing with Adam and Menachem over their checkers game. When I noticed Renu's discomfort my surprise turned into embarrassment. She was about to embark on a hasty retreat when Menachem made a remark that changed everything. I still don't know whether it was deliberate.

Waving the papers she had brought for me to sign, Renu mentioned that Warbler, the new CFO, had been looking for Menachem to secure another set of signatures. "Tell Warbler he can catch me tomorrow at the Israeli Mission," he told her. "Tuesdays and Thursdays are my regular weekdays with Adam."

I could tell from Renu's expression that whatever conjectures she may have had before were now reduced to a virtual certainty. That's when I bit the bullet. "Renu," I said, "could you have lunch with me tomorrow? Here, in my place?"

Has it really been two years since Menachem first laid eyes on his son? My world as single mother did not collapse on that day, but it certainly was never the same again. Since announcing that he was coming to spend time with Adam, Menachem has raised no questions, insisted on no conditions, caused no complications, committed not a single indiscretion. . . . Yet I know that the day is approaching when we must stop treading water while floating slowly out to sea. So far, Menachem has not once questioned my authority as the sole parent of Adam Laidlaw. He has never raised the specter of Adam Dvir. Yet my singular position is being undermined; I have no doubt about that. The "regular" Tuesdays and Thursdays are one example. Menachem simply decided on those days; he comes here while I am at REPCON. I remember saying to myself there was nothing wrong with that, but now, after five months of these afternoon stag parties, I feel a twinge whenever Adam reminds me — and a six-year-old finds so many ways to remind one — how much he looks forward to them. What will follow as he grows up, when — as Shelly said — the need for a man around the house grows exponentially?

I am really worried about this. There are only two people I can talk to about it. I would confide in Shelly Frankenthaler, but her advice is always the same: "Get married." Felix is the only other with whom I've been tempted to speak. He also is judgmental, but at least one can argue with him. He is willing to consider options. Of course, if I tell Felix that Menachem, now a widower (a datum he is aware of), is also a frequent visitor to Adam's sanctum, that he is about to teach him to play chess, that he has enrolled him in a kid's judo class ("boys, and especially Jewish boys, need to learn how to defend themselves," Menachem said with only a half-smile), that they shop for sneakers together, he'd cease talking about options. I can see his eyes, usually so warm, turn adamant. I can hear him say categorically, "what options are you talking about? Menachem is the father, period. Biologically and in every other sense. So act accordingly!"

It's not the first time I've imagined this conversation with Felix. It's been going on for several months, but the time has come to talk to a real person. Why not Renu? I suddenly asked myself. She knows, or at least now suspects, the part still hidden from Felix. So why not start with someone who knows the end rather than the beginning of the story?

Melanie led her guest directly to a table set for two in the dining alcove. "It's nice of you to come, Renu."

"Thanks," said Renu, eyeing the covered casserole and fruit bowl. "And thank you for serving something simple. The road show is beginning to show," she patted her stomach, "and we're not even half finished." She shrugged and settled herself to eat — and talk. Having assumed that Melanie had invited her here to discuss SURYA, Renu launched herself on a discussion of the matters that had consumed her every waking moment for the past several weeks. "The chaperones — our underwriters — are the ones who arrange all the occasions, invite all the people, checked us out in rehearsals, and will see to it that all the offered shares actually find buyers on the day the SEC lets us sell our stock. So far so good. And they did give us some good advice: they said that there is nothing wrong with some intellectual arrogance, provided it is tempered with openness and an occasional dash of humility, and, most important, that we should avoid talking down to the customers. The purpose of these private meetings, they remind us over and over again, is for us to confirm what the customers already believe."

"You better eat," Melanie interrupted. "Otherwise, this lunch will be like your road show lunches."

"Not really," laughed Renu. "There, I'm not the only one speaking. But let me finish making one point about something that has started to bother me: the multiple and potentially competing functions of the underwriters. I understand what they are doing for us, even though they are collecting a very healthy fee — something like 7 percent of the total proceeds, which we hope to be at least forty million dollars. But they are also touting our stock to investors — "

"'Touting' sounds a bit strong. Anyway, everyone involved knows about that."

"At this stage, yes. These are sophisticated investors. Many of them, however, have a very short horizon. They hope that the initial stock offer is oversubscribed, that the unfilled demand will drive up the stock in the open market, and to unload it within a few days — to make a quick profit and look good to their clients. Those are not the investors SURYA wants. While we do hope that there will be an active market for our shares, we're looking for long-term stockholders."

"You sound like an old-timer, Renu. I thought this was your first experience with an IPO?"

"It is, but the competing role of underwriters, who are also stockbrokers, together with their impact on the general stock market is something I got in biz school. There it was theory; I'll be curious to see how it works out in practice. In school, where I first heard the automobile analogy, the professor asked bluntly, 'when you go car shopping, do you look at *Consumer Reports* and take the car to an independent mechanic or do you take the salesman's word for it?' The record suggests that investors off the street, who purchase shares from brokerage firms acting also as underwriters shortly *after* the IPO more often than not get screwed. My biz school instructor's words, not mine," she added quickly. "And now I shall eat," she said, and took the first forkful.

For a long moment, neither woman spoke. "Renu," Melanie said, her eyes focused on her food. "Let me ask you a question. I never met your husband, although I remember hearing about him when your grant application landed on my desk. When was that . . . eight years ago? How time flies! What's it like being married to an Israeli? And you, an Indian to boot."

Renu wagged her head, without realizing that she did it in classic Indian fashion. "Pretty much ex-Indian, I'd say. Next year I'll be an American citizen with an American-born daughter eligible to become president. Of the country, I mean, not just SURYA."

"I understand," Melanie sounded impatient. "But to return to my question. . . ."

"About an Israeli husband? I've never had another one, so I

have no basis for comparison. Nor have I ever tried a placebo." Her laugh died away when she noted Melanie's frown. "We've had our problems," she said slowly, "but I'd be inclined to ascribe them to the fact that we're both ambitious working parents with a two-and-a-half-year-old daughter. Still, Jewish husbands take their families seriously."

"Have you considered moving back to Israel?"

"Are you asking that as one of the SURYA board members?"

"Of course not," Melanie said quickly. "I just wondered whether you had ever considered living there."

"At one time I did. But not now — not with the opportunity I have at SURYA."

"And your husband?"

"Yes," Renu let out a brief sigh. "He probably would have preferred to move back."

"How are you handling the question of religion?"

"When Naomi is old enough, we'll take her to Reform synagogue."

"Did you know I converted?"

The question caught Renu unprepared. "You?" she gasped. "To Judaism? Why?"

"I wanted my son to be born a Jew."

"I see," Renu murmured.

Melanie started playing with the half-full glass in front of her, swirling it to see how high she could bring the water without spilling. "You can guess why, can't you?" She set down the glass.

"Why are you telling me this?" Renu's voice was low, almost timid.

"Whenever people have asked about Adam's father, I have stalled. When they pressed me — and you'd be surprised how many people, especially women, do that — I told them a half-truth. Note that I said 'half-truth,' not 'half-lie' — to me a crucial distinction."

Renu looked at her quietly.

"Don't you want to know what that was?" For the first time, Melanie's tone had turned mocking.

"I didn't think it was my place to ask."

"Thank you for saying that. What I tell people is that I planned to be a single mother and got pregnant by artificial insemination."

"And what did you tell your son?"

"The same. But I can't continue doing that much longer. Pretty soon, I'll have to tell him the other half."

"That you had not really planned to be a single mother?"

"Not at all!" She sounded almost angry. "That would be a half-lie. But whenever I said 'artificial insemination' I implied that I went to a sperm bank. I need to tell Adam who his biological father is. Only two people knew that and I didn't feel comfortable discussing the matter with them. They have already prejudged the case. Now that you are the third, would you mind very much if I asked you for advice?"

I probably expected too much from Renu. She may be a dozen years younger than I, but she seems remarkably conventional when it comes to marriage and parenthood. She's probably more Indian than she realizes — or is it her marriage to an Israeli? Or maybe she just didn't feel comfortable speaking openly with me. Still, our talk was useful — like a third opinion before surgery. As the opinions pile up, there seems no purpose in shopping around for more.

Everyone seems to agree that I must move from single motherhood to some form of joint parenthood. But how? Renu didn't want to commit herself, but I bet she also wonders why I'm not considering marriage. And why am I not? Talking with Renu — or rather, having talked to her — has started me on the process of evaluating seriously the number of options open to me. Options! The word arose in every one of my hypothetical mind-talks with Felix. So what are they?

Number one: the status quo. At least I am making progress, because I have now concluded that this is not anymore feasible.

Number two, Shelly's exhortation: "Get married!" A forty-five-year-old widow with a six-year-old son does not sound like too marketable a commodity, but that's only an excuse. When I look at myself in the mirror, I like what I see. I've kept in shape. I'm interesting company: I know more about reproductive biology than most people, for instance, I go to the opera, I read . . . but? But what? If it were

*not for Adam, for that incipient guilt about depriving him of some
essential male influence, would I be so anxious to find a mate? The
need for a bed companion has burned out. There may be an ember
smoldering here or there, but it will take a powerful bellows to revive
the fire that burned so bright seven years ago with Menachem. My
radar seems to pick up potential fathers and social companions, but
bellows simply do not register. The "radar man" is such an example.
I have finally sent him packing because a surrogate father figure
for Adam is not anymore a viable option now that Menachem has
convinced Ben-Gurion University to set up a fund-raising office in
Manhattan. That and his UN advisory function will keep him here
for at least two years he said. And two years of regular Tuesdays
and Thursdays and occasional weekends simply means that Adam
would also start treading water. No wonder I keep avoiding being
caught alone with Shelly Frankenthaler. Option two is out.*

*That leaves Number three: Menachem. I don't know whether he
is waiting for me to raise the issue or what? What I can see is that
the patient must decide about the surgery. I must talk with Menachem — about Adam, about us. I must find out what has happened
to him emotionally during the past eight years. It's a topic neither
one of us has broached.*

"Renu, look at this." Jephtah held up the device, about the size
and shape of a ball-point pen. "Would you be willing to insert this
probe into your vagina until you touch the cervix?"

"*Mehra prem,*" she exclaimed with a mixture of amusement and
surprise, "father of my daughter, you can't be serious. I travel
twenty thousand miles, come home expecting tender kisses and
endearments, and instead you want to know if I'll stick this tube
up my. . . ." She looked at him more closely. "But you are serious,
aren't you?"

"It's not a big deal. It's like inserting a tampon, but only for a
few seconds until — "

"Until nothing," she stopped him. "I withdraw the Indian
endearment as totally inappropriate to the occasion. Put down
this . . . gadget . . . or doodad . . . or whatever you want to call it
and explain yourself. Or, as an American wife would ask, 'honey,

what the hell have you been doing while I was on the road bringing home the bacon?'"

Renu's resolute good humor cooled Jephtah's growing irritation, though not totally. "Okay, okay," he placed the tube on the table. "Since you're finally showing some interest in what your husband has been doing all these weeks . . . or has it been months?"

"Jephtah. What's bugging you?"

"All we've been talking about, I don't know for how long, has been IPO, IPO, and IPO — "

"But that's not fair — "

"And red herring, road show, Goldman, Stephens and Robertson, Sachs . . ."

Renu covered her mouth, not wanting to fuel his anger with derision. "It's Goldman, Sachs and Robertson, Stephens," she murmured.

He glared at her. "I don't give a damn what they're called. Do you really want to know what I've been doing or are you just pretending?"

The earlier wound had not healed; the balm of my spontaneous interest in his research had not been rubbed deeply or frequently enough, especially since we had decided to go all-out for an IPO. I should have explained how crucial the timing was: the Dow-Jones had risen some 30 percent in the last six months, more than four hundred points, and the number of IPOs had doubled compared to last year. Our underwriters had started to prod us mercilessly, reminding us that such windows of opportunity do not stay open indefinitely. And they slam shut with little warning.

I found my involvement in this corporate rite of passage very heady stuff, I admit — but if I think about it, Jephtah was hardly permitted to partake of any of it. Confidentiality and discretion were drummed daily into our conscience, Mort Heartstone making the point that even pillow talk would be condemned by the SEC. I could have made life easier by focusing more attention on Jephtah, especially since my travel schedule has left him with all of the child care.

So I held my tongue. "I'm sorry," I said. "Tell me about your work." He calmed down — he really wants nothing more than a chance to talk about his work — and started to remind me of his nasal and cervical smear reading of some six months ago. "You mean you actually followed up on this?" I asked, astonished. Instead of answering my question with a simple yes or no he lifted the gizmo from the table and announced that I was privileged to gaze on the very first "Wizard of Ov."

Looking at my husband, I felt as if I was looking eight years back in time, at the man who had shown me the first MUSA device. In a flash, I realized that this was for real, that if I merely humored Jephtah I'd be skating on dangerously thin ice. I pointed at his ball-point tampon and asked, "This will tell me when I'm ovulating?"

"I'm not absolutely sure yet," he hedged, but his eyes seemed convinced. "If I'm right, it will do more than that: it will give you several days notice before you ovulate."

For once, I was astute enough not to interrupt, even though he started with some pretty elementary aspects of female reproduction. It's true that many women know very little about their own cycle — when they ovulate, that they're only fertile for about twenty-four hours per month — or other useful facts, such as that a sperm's viability extends beyond three or four days. So I just nodded when Jephtah told me that for such a device to be useful for birth control, it would be essential to predict the time of ovulation by about four days.

But then I suddenly sat up. Jephtah was telling me something that I hadn't known, that I had in fact refused to believe: in a study from New Zealand, John France claimed that intercourse three days prior to ovulation favored male offspring whereas coitus at ovulation shifted the gender ratio toward females. "Now," he concluded triumphantly, "if my Wizard of Ov could predict the time of ovulation by about four days, we would actually have the means of — "

"Producing only boys?" I interrupted. "How terrible!" I meant it, because I could just imagine what would happen back in India, where sons are valuable and daughters a burden, but he just waved my objection away.

"I said shift the sex ratio, not alter it totally."

"All right," I conceded, not wanting to start him boiling again, *"but what's this all about?" I pointed to the tube in his hand. "What are you measuring?"*

This time I paid close attention to his lecture. I have to grant that my admiration was touched by just the slightest tinge of jealousy. Now that I'm busily climbing the very last rungs of the executive ladder, I can't help but ask myself when did I last come up with some new science of my own? Now I "facilitate" other people's ideas. I "prioritize" them. Of course, I'm good at it, because I understand what the research people are trying to do, but it isn't the same as what Jephtah has just been describing.

It's lucky that his lab back at Ben-Gurion was staffed by an interdisciplinary group from mechanical and electrical engineering, because even though he was on the biomechanical side, the electric types were all around him. That's why he fit so readily into ZALA's new electrotransport project. But once there, my Jephtah was not satisfied to stick to the skin — the therapeutic terrain mapped out for the ETS unit at ZALA. During his cruising of the nose and the cervix, he came up with the idea that there may be consistent and reproducible electrical changes associated with redox reactions taking place in the cervical mucus at different times of the woman's monthly cycle. I was amazed by the terms my domestic bioengineer was now bandying about. "My Wizard of Ov easily reaches the posterior fornix — the transition region of the cervix at the top of the vagina — and thus should measure changes of oxidation-reduction reactions occurring in the glycoproteins of the cervical mucus — which may be one possible source for this phenomenon. If these changes are reproducible, it should be possible to monitor the maturation of the dominant follicle. . . ."

My head was swimming. This was my husband speaking? "But that's all speculation," I said weakly "It's all 'if'. . . ."

And how had he come up with the name 'Wizard of Ov'? I wanted to know. It almost beat MUSA in terms of originality. "Oh that?" he made an airy gesture. "One of Djerassi's women students, Julie Switzer, suggested it. 'Feel free to use it,' she said, 'if you like it.'"

"Djerassi?" I exclaimed, "you mean Carl Djerassi? What does Djerassi have to do with this?"

Once Jephtah had gotten the idea that redox changes in the cer-

vical mucus might constitute the basis of a new ovulation monitor, he had gone over to M. L. Noland in the Stanford hospital and asked her for advice. I hate to admit to a second twinge of jealousy when I learned that my spouse had consulted with the chair of SURYA's medical advisory board, but, of course, we don't own M.L. Besides, she's working with us on the penis, whereas Jephtah was delving into the cervix. "She sent me to Djerassi in the Stanford chemistry department, who's now teaching a human biology course called Feminist Perspectives on Birth Control. It's true that he was involved in the very early work on the Pill, but now he seems to be interested in much softer areas: fertility awareness, women's autonomy in reproductive issues . . . even new approaches to ovulation prediction that he calls 'jet-age rhythm method.'"

I just gaped. Is that what this Stanford chemistry professor can afford to do now, just because he's got tenure for life? "It turns out that students in his class — a group of women seniors — do some actual research: surveys, interviews . . . at times even more than that. Together with Noland, he persuaded four women in his current class to try the Wizard — to insert it for a few seconds every day to measure bioelectric activity. Here's what they found, plotting electric current versus day of cycle."

He sketched a figure showing two peaks and two troughs, the line then trailing off to the right. "Starting with the first day of a new cycle, bioelectric activity drops to a minimum around day six, and then starts rising to a peak around day nine, the highest reading of the cycle. The values then fall to another minimum around day fourteen, rise to a short second maximum the following day — not as high as the first peak — and then drop to an absolute low at day sixteen. So what you see here," he drew a big circle around that portion of his figure, "is an asymmetric M-shaped curve produced by every one of the four women. Our working hypothesis is that the eight-day interval between the first peak at day six and the minimum around ovulation is associated with the maturation of that month's dominant follicle."

"Wow," I said. I meant it.

Jephtah laughed, looking satisfied. "That was also Alfredo Zaf-

*fanori's response. He encouraged me to pursue the idea, even though
it has nothing to do with the mission of ZALA."*

It was good to see Jephtah in such a mood. But then he asked me
once more.

"So now," he said, "I repeat my question: are you willing to
become the fifth guinea pig?" I knew right away that this time
Jephtah, who'd had me insert the first MUSA into his urethra, was
not fooling.

"Only if you do it," I replied.

21

Palo Alto, September 26, 1986
Dearest Ashok,

I want to brag to you. As of five days ago, your sister is a
millionaire twice over. In theory, at least. I shall get to that
in a moment, but for now let me revel in being what we used
to call a millionairess. I have a small idea now (a theoretical
idea) how it felt to be one of those women in the Trollope or
Henry James novels our Anglophile Papaji force-fed us so
many years ago. But those fictitious women all married or
inherited their wealth, whereas your sister earned it all
by herself!

You are probably dying to know what happened. All right.
You remember about my stock options? Five days ago, our
shares started trading on the open market at $17 per share.
Today they're at $21! As of September 26, 1986, my options
are worth a cool $2.5 million.

Okay, so I am only a paper millionaire. It is good for my
ego, but not very relevant to the real facts of life such as the
type of automobile I drive (still an 8-year-old Volvo) or the
size of our mortgage or, in fact, of the house itself. Like all
the other optionees and original stockholders, I am prohibited

from selling a single share for 180 days, but even afterward (when the stock may be much lower or, knock on wood, even higher), as the president of SURYA and the newest member of its board of directors, I cannot sell much stock without raising serious problems with which I will not bore you.

Jephtah barely blinked five days ago when SURYA went public. To my knowledge, he has not so much as opened the business pages of the *San Francisco Chronicle*, our local paper. He is totally enmeshed in a new project that initially seemed weird to me but that is becoming less so with every passing day. For the time being, for reasons of confidentiality — and of delicacy — I cannot tell you more about it. I find it odd that it is science rather than money that currently drives the male in our family, whereas the reverse seems to apply to the female of the house (though no housewife she!).

Ashok, my dear, I have changed! At times, I wonder whether it's all for the better.

Much love,

Renu

P.S. You have never responded to my offer to handle an *Indian Express* advert on your behalf. Is that an expression of independence (understandable, I would concede) or of indifference (puzzling, I would admit) to the topic of matrimony? In either event, *write!*

Martin Gestler looked around the boardroom table — not the elegant glass oval at ZALA but the walnut rectangle in what was SURYA's all-purpose conference room. Although proud of the company's achievement, Gestler was far from smug: experience had taught him to expect a rough ride. Mort Heartstone had urged him to open this first post-IPO board meeting with some down-to-earth counsel that only two of the directors — Alfredo Zaffanori and the Baron — could have dispensed with.

"Remember, Martin," Heartstone had advised, "we have four individuals on our board who've never been directors. They're about to find their names identified with large stock ownerships in the next proxy statement — a public document that will soon go out to all stockholders. In the case of Renu, we're talking about two-and-a-half million dollars; for the outside directors, well over five hundred thousand apiece. I'm not thinking about Alfredo and you — you people own much more, and you know the ropes and have diversified portfolios. I bet for those four, their SURYA options now constitute the overwhelming portion of their total equity. Somebody has got to keep their feet firmly on the ground before they. . . ." He threw up his hands. "God knows what they might be tempted to do."

———

"Friends." It was an oddly formal start for Gestler. "Our stock has done spectacularly well. Our offering at seventeen dollars was oversubscribed. Selling a little over two-and-a-half million shares netted us forty million dollars after the underwriters' commission, in spite of that awful omen in London witnessed by Renu. Now that everything has gone swimmingly, the grisly secret can be disclosed. During our European road show, Goldman, Sachs had arranged for a luncheon presentation at the Cordwainers Company on Fleet Street, one of those Dickensian livery halls still surviving in London. I presume you all know what a cordwainer is?" he asked, disingenuousness splashed all over his face.

"Come on," growled Mort. "Your Anglophilic slip is showing."

Martin's mood could not be spoiled. "All right, in deference to Mort I'll skip the cordwainers and continue. We were seated on the dais. Just as I was ready to open the proceedings, a black cat somehow got in and slowly slunk in my direction. She — I say 'she' because at that point I was convinced it was a witch — hunkered down right in front, staring at me. No one said a word. Nobody moved. It was just me and the cat — until my colleague here," he gestured toward Renu, "saved the situation, by stepping forward, picking up the cat, and stroking the witch in her lap while I talked. So she never crossed in front of me."

As soon as the laughter had died down, Mort Heartstone spoke. "Now that all the important news about the IPO has been divulged, let me continue with the trivia." He sounded uncharacteristically irritable. "And if any one of you is superstitious, yes, the cat could still hex us. As Martin pointed out — perhaps a bit too glibly — the offering succeeded, the underwriters seem happy, and the stock has risen almost one point every day. Yesterday, SURYA closed at twenty-one dollars. If you consider that great news, think again."

Martin had shifted into his characteristic slouch, every once in a while stroking his chin. He knew that part of the lawyer's irritation was fueled by the fact that he was the only director specifically excluded from the option plan. Given his ongoing (and sizable) legal fees, the stock option committee had felt it wisest not to dip further into the option pool for Heartstone's benefit. Those one-and-a-half million option shares were originally set aside to (in boardroom lingo) "incentivize" outside directors, advisory board members, and consultants — none of whom received any direct compensation — and to offset the comparatively austere salaries of the key management team. That was why Renu had been granted two options, now totaling one hundred twenty-five thousand shares and Gestler his three hundred thousand shares. Considering what options had been assigned to some of the other employees during the past three years, mostly to those in research and development, only about one-fifth of the initial one-and-a-half million pool was still available for distribution. It was important to husband that rapidly depleting incentive tool, which, in any event, had by now become less exciting. With SURYA stock now openly traded, any option would have to be at market value. With a highly volatile stock, such an option might still be attractive, but for the next couple of years, most of the upswing had clearly been cannibalized. None knew that better than Mort Heartstone. Martin could sympathize with the man's silent resentment. He decided to help.

"Let me interrupt Mort for a moment," he said, straightening up. "First a word about percent stock ownership, which, of course has been diluted in the light of the most recent offering. Compared to the initial ten million shares, 60 percent of which were owned by our three university stockholders, we now have well over fifteen million outstanding shares, which means that each university has a 13 percent slice. Nothing to complain about, because at today's stock price of twenty-one dollars, the paper value of SURYA Corporation is now a staggering three hundred twenty-one million dollars."

"'The operative word is 'paper,'" muttered Heartstone.

Martin wagged his head. "Yes and no. For the purposes of what you're going to say later, Mort, I'd have to agree. But not totally so for the three academic owners, if I may wear my Ben-Gurion hat for a moment."

"All right, wear it," said the lawyer.

"At twenty-one dollars, each two-million-share slice is worth forty-two million dollars — all profit for the respective universities, whose cost basis was one cent. Of course, they can't unload it now. Like all of us here," Martin's gaze quickly swept around the table, "they're legally restricted from peddling a single share for 180 days. Even afterward, selling such a quantity would depress the market tremendously. Besides, I would strongly urge Ben-Gurion to hang on to these shares, because over the long run — "

"How long is 'long?'" Yehuda Davidson chimed in.

Gestler looked at him. "It depends who's asking: Yehuda, the private individual, or Professor Davidson, Hadassah's representative on this board. For you, Yehuda, probably five to ten years maximum."

"Now wait a minute," Mort snapped. "Since you certainly can't make that statement outside this room, you'd better not make it at all."

Gestler looked chastened. "Mort is right: no investment advice from me, and most certainly not during this sensitive post-offering period. So all I will say is that the life expectancy, and hence investment perspective, of an institution can be considerably longer than that of an individual. But to return to my original point: while Ben-Gurion can't, and therefore won't, unload its stock, it certainly could borrow against it — putting it up as collateral for a bank loan — "

"Which they can use toward the construction of a sorely needed medical school building," said Menachem.

"For example," agreed Martin.

"I'd better resume," broke in Heartstone, "before anyone else starts thinking of bank collateral. I agree that if Ben-Gurion used

10 percent of its present stock value as a collateral for a four-million-dollar building — "

"Hold it," interrupted Menachem. "What kind of a medical school building will four million dollars buy — even in Beer-sheba?"

"That's precisely my point," trumpeted Heartstone. "Using 10 percent of your stock equity for a loan is reasonably conservative — I emphasize the word *reasonably* — because in the present go-go stock market climate, shares can fall as fast as they are rising — or even quicker. Wealthy institutions might be prepared to gamble by taking out a bigger loan, because they could always bail out if SURYA drops below the danger point. Ben-Gurion University, however, isn't wealthy. It would have to run to the Israeli government for a bail out. And I can well conjecture what they would say. Now," he shook a warning finger at his listeners, "imagine if one of *you* considered that. After 180 days, many a bank will accept your options as collateral, but remember, in contrast to Ben-Gurion you don't even own the stock yet: you'd have to buy it if your collateral was called. Admittedly, it won't cost you all that much. For Renu to exercise her entire option, for instance," he eyed her sharply, "she'd only have to put up seventy thousand dollars — a real bargain if SURYA stock remains where it is — although I wonder whether she has that sum in her household checkbook. But suppose the stock dropped and dropped — "

"Mort, don't be such a pessimist," remonstrated Renu.

"That's exactly what you are paying me for," he shot back. "I don't know how rich all of you are, absent your stock options, but if I were you, I'd be extraordinarily cautious about using those options as collateral."

"Because?"

"Because, Yehuda," Mort turned to his questioner, "none of you here is truly liquid, even after the 180-day period has passed."

"Are you saying that my option is still unreal paper?"

"'Real it is not, not unreal either.'" For the first time that morning Mort Heartstone permitted himself a chuckle. "From an old Japanese poem."

Heartstone cracked a half-smile, seeming to have recovered

some of his good humor. "But Yehuda's question brings me to my second point. All of us here are *insiders*. Don't ever forget that. Not even at night, in the privacy of your marital beds," he chuckled for the second time.

"And what is your definition of *insider?*" asked Melanie.

"When in doubt, assume you're one!" He laughed outright. "At least then you're safe."

"Safe from what?" she persisted.

"The SEC, stockholders' suits — nasty things like that." He turned grim again. "All of us are assumed to be privy to confidential information, not available to the shareholder out on the street. Even if you have forgotten some information or perhaps not even known it, your position as a director or officer presupposes that you had access to it. You're considered an insider unless proven otherwise, and such proof is very difficult to get and very costly. Only I and the plaintiff's attorney are likely to benefit from a suit, which may be why I'm not burdened by an option. Not that I would have minded such a burden," he added sotto voce. "Therefore, before any one of you plans to exercise any stock option or trade in the open market, see me first. There will be black-out periods — some long, others short — when there will be no trading whatsoever by any of you. And don't ever dream that you can get away with any selling or buying on the Q.T., because every trade of yours has to be reported to the SEC before the end of the month, thus becoming instantaneously public information. If a director or officer sells, even if for perfectly sensible reasons of equity diversification, the word on Wall Street is that insiders are dumping the stock. Nobody feels sympathy for a millionaire — not even a paper millionaire."

"What black-out periods?" Davidson demanded.

Heartstone's doomsday tone mellowed as he perceived the growing concern of his audience. "Now, for instance. Within the next five weeks the FDA will convene a special advisory committee to comment on our application for the MUSA system. This would be an absolute no-no period, no pun intended."

"We're bound to clear it with flying colors," remarked Renu.

"Don't say that, Renu," he barked. "Not even jokingly, although

I imagine you really believe it. If you say it here, you'll be tempted to say it elsewhere. You don't know who later may claim having heard you, having taken you seriously, and having bought stock on the basis of that insider's opinion. Don't look so chastened," he added in a calmer voice, "just remember what I'm saying. SURYA has just passed through its IPO. The stock is selling at an outrageous price — "

"Should you say that?" Renu's voice was timid.

For a moment, Heartstone looked nonplussed. "You're dead right — I shouldn't. Certainly not as a director. But since I can claim a client-attorney privilege, which I'm now exercising, I can tell you that our stock is selling at an extremely high market value for a company with no sales. Sales cannot start until we get FDA approval — a point that cannot be guaranteed, as I tried to make ferociously clear in our prospectus. So we're very vulnerable. And precisely because our stock has appreciated so quickly — primarily because the demand at the IPO was greater than the supply — it's bound to drop. The question is only when, because no stock can just keep rising." He looked at Melanie. "If our stock drops, say by ten points, to eleven dollars per share — still a handsome price for a company without sales — you will have lost three hundred thousand dollars. And you, Renu?" He turned to face her. "An even one-and-a-quarter million dollars. So here's my advice to all of you: assume that your option is still just a piece of paper. Ignore day-to-day or even month-to-month fluctuations of stock quotations. If we all work hard, if the FDA favors us, and if our patent position does not get challenged, we'll all be rich one of these days."

"And if the FDA comes up with some unexpected question?"

Mort Heartstone gave Melanie a long look. "If that happens next month and our stock drops precipitously, expect to be sued. All of you."

"And not you?" asked Renu.

"I'm in the same boat. That's why we'll need outside counsel. So knock on wood. All of you," he barked a mock command while pounding the table. "Anything else I should tell them?" he asked Martin after everyone had dutifully used their knuckles.

"D and O?" Martin mouthed.

"Ah yes, directors' and officers' liability coverage. How could I forget? The long and short is we have none."

"We have none?" Until now, Baron Van Zwanenberg's silence had been complete, his detachment almost Zen-like — or perhaps he had only been bored. "How come?" As he spoke, his face revealed a dawning uncertainty, almost self-doubt. He knew "how come." What he meant was "how come I never asked before?"

Heartstone ignored the Baron. His intended audience was the four novices, who needed tough guidance but also reassurance. "We have none because we can't afford it. D and O for a company like ours would be prohibitively costly, if we could get it at all. Corporations with no earnings and a highly volatile stock are not attractive risks for insurance carriers. Any money we can spend on insurance premiums is much better spent on liability insurance for MUSA — in clinical studies and later, when we are on the market. For that we do carry insurance, though we could never have enough. But as far as we directors are concerned, we're better off being self-insured."

"Mort, you can't be serious," exclaimed Melanie. "*I* should carry my own insurance?"

"Relax. I meant that SURYA would be footing any legal bills and be responsible for any defense strategy, unless one of you committed some personal mayhem — of which I consider you, at least, incapable."

"Okay," she said, visibly relieved. "But just to be safe, I want your legal definition of 'mayhem.' Later," she offered. "Not now."

"There is another advantage to being self-insured, aside from saving some outrageous premium at Lloyd's. The most likely suits are frivolous stockholders' class-action suits with very little or no merit, instituted solely at the instigation of specialty firms — some people, me included, call them legal extortionists or worse — looking for deep-pocket victims. Insurance companies are generally willing to settle, which makes them more-favored prey, while SURYA, being uninsured, looks less inviting. That's the end of my lecture. Let's hope that it's all academic, having knocked hard on wood." He knocked once more for emphasis. "Unless, of course," he looked around mischievously, "Martin's black cat has jinxed us after all."

———

In the end, the black cat's power was stronger than the wooden knocks. On Thursday, October 30, 1986, following a week during which SURYA stock had been battered, dropping — in spite of a general bull market — from its all-time high of twenty-one dollars to twelve dollars per share, a summons server appeared at the SURYA offices, asking to see either Mr. Gestler or Dr. Krishnan. It was Renu's misfortune that Martin Gestler was then in Jerusalem.

22

The inventor's daily morning insertion of the Wizard of Ov into his wife had affected their conjugal life in more ways than one.

"If you want me to become your guinea pig," Renu had pointed out, "then I can't be on the Pill."

"Naturally," Jephtah said.

"And return to our '*candom*' days?"

"Only for a short while," he said. "Once we've established your profile, we'll do *candoms* on the fertile days, naked sex the rest of the month."

"And if that doesn't work?"

"We'll be parents again."

———

"That should prove something." Renu reached over Jephtah's head to mark another point on the graph. "If the last three days haven't affected my readings, then neither stress nor trauma seems to interfere." She tousled Jephtah's hair, pushing him away gently. "Not this morning, *mehra prem*. I've got to get ready. Today is D day."

The Wizard of Ov had changed more than their method of birth control; it had also affected the timing and rhythm of what Renu liked to call their "carnal congress." The morning bed warmth, the spreading of her thighs, the disappearance of the Wizard past

Renu's abundant, black pubic hair: on many an occasion, the ten-second insertion of the Wizard was followed by a much longer, more active, and much more pleasurable insertion. Making love in the morning, Jephtah told her solemnly, also made sense in terms of a man's hormonal rhythm: testosterone levels are highest in the morning, so why not be hormonally leveraged?

But today, Renu's thoughts were far from sex. They were focused on a more contentious aspect of penile erection: the legal summons served on her three days before. A special board meeting via conference call was scheduled at 8:00 A.M. to accommodate Davidson and Gestler in Jerusalem — where it was already early evening — as well as the Baron in Amsterdam. Laidlaw and Dvir were standing by in their respective New York offices.

———

"I sure didn't know what I was letting myself into when I joined this board." Melanie Laidlaw's grumble came through clearly over the speaker phone in Palo Alto around which Renu, Zaffanori, and Heartstone were hunched.

"Don't even think about it," replied the lawyer. "You *are* in it. We're all in it. I've spent the last two days going through the legal papers. Yesterday Renu and I argued for hours without much success," he sighed audibly. "Renu has her own view of the matter — quite understandable, I hasten to add. I look at the situation more conservatively, perhaps because I've been bitten before."

"Come on, Mort." Gestler's impatience was unmistakable. "Let's skip the preambles. Fact number one: we're being sued by Black, Black & Hood from San Clemente, probably the most ruthless class-action shysters in California. Excuse my language, Mort."

"Be my guest."

"Number two: I gather that Will Hood, himself, and two other John Doe stockholders — cumulatively holding fewer than five hundred shares — claim to have been defrauded because in our press release announcing our FDA filing we stated that we had carried out adequate safety and efficacy studies of the MUSA in men with erectile dysfunction *as well as having examined its effect on women.* I'm quoting here from your fax. Is that correct?"

215

"Correct," said Heartstone. "But — "

"I'm not finished." Gestler's tone was angry, although it was not clear whether his anger was addressed at his Palo Alto listeners, who had gotten SURYA into this fix during his absence, or the firm of Black, Black & Hood. "They claim that our stock started sliding as a result of newspaper reports that the FDA advisory committee was dissatisfied with our data. Furthermore, they assert that when a *Wall Street Journal* reporter called SURYA Renu reiterated that we had carried out adequate studies in women. Two days later, when the FDA confirmed that our New Drug Application would not be approved until more clinical studies with women were performed, our stock hit ten dollars. The suit claims that the stockholders had bought the stock at over twenty bucks on the basis of our implied warranty — "

"We warranted nothing." Heartstone's voice was sharp and unequivocal.

"Let me finish, Mort. I'm reading your own fax, not opining. To continue: . . . that NONO-2 had no deleterious effect on women, and that when we did not correct that statement when the *Journal* reporter called we misled stockholders, some of whom have now suffered a 50 percent loss. Is that a correct summary?"

"And they seek restitution for all stockholders that purchased stock during that time plus twelve million dollars punitive damages," Heartstone said calmly. "Most of which will end up in their own pockets if the suit ever comes to trial, which of course it won't."

"Which is where Mort and I disagree." Renu could no longer restrain herself.

"This is Magnus Van Zwanenberg speaking." His powerful voice caused the Palo Alto listeners to jerk back from the speakerphone. "May I ask Mort to summarize for us the strategy he recommends and his views of the most likely outcome?"

"Easy," said Heartstone. "But first one correction: Martin seems to imply that Renu should have responded differently to the *Wall Street Journal* reporter. Renu did exactly what was required of her: she first checked with me for legal advice. I told her not to confirm any rumors, just to stick to the facts. At that stage we had not yet heard from the FDA. Furthermore, the FDA action was by no means as negative as the press reported. I will ask Renu to comment on that in a minute. She thinks, and Dr. Noland concurs, that we can take care of all FDA objections within the next three months — certainly no later than the beginning of March. I suspect that we'll get clearance by then and that our stock will start to recover. Now that we have the formal response from the FDA, we can publicly announce how we will handle it. In fact, Renu, why don't you tell the board about that now. I will then respond to Magnus's question."

Renu leaned over the speakerphone. "If it weren't for this bloody suit, I would have categorized the FDA action as pretty favorable. They questioned none of our results with our male patients nor the incidence of observed side effects: minor priapism, occasional distressful erections, very few hypotensive episodes in cardiac patients except on the very highest NONO-2 doses. . . . But precisely because we had looked out for those side effects and because of the FDA's extreme caution they wanted to know what would happen to severely hypotensive female coital partners of MUSA users."

"But I thought you had resolved all this by analyzing the masturbation semen samples of MUSA subjects for their NONO content," Melanie interrupted.

"We thought so, but the FDA wants more. They wanted to know how many of the women were severely hypotensive. Quite frankly, we don't know."

"And why not?"

Melanie's tone raised Renu's hackles. "Because we didn't think it was an issue. The amount of NO-equivalent in the average semen sample of these patients — given that most of them are middle-aged men or older and their average time to ejaculation is many minutes long — was so low that we weren't worried. But the FDA indulged in its usual overkill: what if we had some young diabetic who might have a much larger semen volume? What if he suffered from premature ejaculation so there was little time for NONO to metabolize? What if the woman was severely hypotensive? What if they had frequent intercourse? What if this and what if that?" Renu's voice had grown increasingly sarcastic. "We couldn't have picked this up in our tests, because the chance of finding such a weird combination in a sample of two thousand is minimal. But rather than argue and delay matters further, we proposed a compromise."

"Who is we?"

Mort quickly raised a finger to his lip to stop Renu. "The protocol was constructed by Renu, who has done all the early work on semen samples in Jerusalem, and by Dr. Noland, the head of our MAB. All of which will be part of our legal response. Now go ahead, Renu."

"Okay," she said. Mort's intervention had given her valuable breathing space. Calmer now, she continued. "The following compromise was immediately accepted by the FDA because they aren't out to get us. They just want to protect their butts. Noland and I calculated the very top level of nitric oxide and asked a cardiologist at Stanford to apply such quantities to a few hypotensive patients intravaginally. There is plenty of work being done on nitric oxide releasers in cardiology right now. Remember, old drugs used in angina pectoris, like nitroglycerine, or newer ones, like molsidomine, all work by releasing nitric oxide. The only thing people haven't done yet is to administer the agents intravaginally, as in sexual intercourse." Renu chuckled. "Molsidomine produces NO via a metabolite, a sydnonimine, known as SIN-1. If it weren't all so damn serious, we could have offered the flippant response that 'original sin' has already shown what can happen with erections. Come to think of it, that's what I should have told the *Wall Street Journal* reporter. In any event, the experiment is straightforward and can be done right here at Stanford. I'm fairly optimistic that we can get the data to the FDA by the end of January, but, just to be safe, let's call it the beginning of March."

"I'm glad to hear that matters are under control on the clinical side," barked the Baron. "Now the legal one. Mort, can you hear me?"

Heartstone retrieved the speakerphone. "Magnus, you of all directors know that the legal mills grind slowly. It is my intention to make them slower still. Of course, we have to file a response. But we can also file all kinds of motions to delay matters for many months. Because, you see, at this stage, there is only one danger."

"Which is?"

"Discovery."

"Discovery?" At least two, perhaps more directorial voices had produced a warbly echo. "What is there to discover?" demanded Melanie.

"I am referring to 'unlimited discovery' which is the only weapon in frivolous class-action suits that can draw real blood at the start. Will Hood is evidently taking on this case himself: he always pushes for essentially unlimited discovery. You see, he doesn't want to waste much time. If the court accedes to his demand, he's betting that we'll settle promptly, rather than submit. And if we were insured, he'd probably be right."

"But what does 'unlimited discovery' mean?" Melanie asked impatiently.

"Asking for all records in our files that could possibly be relevant to their case. In other words, a fishing expedition, trawling right through everything we have: clinical data, research results, internal memoranda . . . the list goes on and on. And guess who pays to assemble all that stuff? In a recent case, a local company in Silicon Valley spent two years and nearly one million dollars just collecting some seven hundred fifty thousand pages for the plaintiffs to examine. Of course the plaintiff doesn't really want to read any of it — not in a suit like this. They're simply counting on our being willing to settle rather than go to all that trouble — and expense. Of course, there's always the chance that here or there a damning statement can be extracted — often out of context — that will lead the defendant and its insurance company to settle promptly."

"I know all that," grunted the Baron. "What settlement terms do you think they would offer?"

"They'll pay lip service to restitution of stockholder's losses, but what they're after is money in *their* pockets. They know we have forty million dollars in the bank — a very important reason why they pounced when their computer sniffed our drop in stock price. Their settlement offer is bound to start with at least half of the twelve million they're suing us for. As soon as they find out that we're not covered by insurance, they'll shift to asking for part of any settlement to be paid in stock or perhaps ten-year warrants, which, not unlike your stock options, would mean that for ten years they'd be able to buy our stock at a predetermined fixed price, which, they hope, will be much lower than what SURYA will eventually trade at. In any event, all this is premature until the court rules on their discovery motion. Rest assured that we'll do our utmost to delay and fight that attempt."

Renu could not hold back any longer. "I really must interrupt. Mort and I have argued about this for hours, but now that everyone has read the faxed material and heard us, let me present my opinion. I don't think that we should even *dream* of settling with these extortionists. Not until we've given them a real fight."

"Renu, be reasonable." Alfredo Zaffanori had been sitting next to her, observing her slow boil. He patted her on the arm. "Of course, I agree that they are extortionists — *espectacular* extortionists. Most of their suits have nothing to do with protecting stockholders from real fraud. But fighting these characters all the way through depositions, court hearings, jury trial, appeals . . . this will not only cost millions but will waste valuable managerial time and talent. You have more important aims to accomplish than to teach them a lesson. A lesson, I assure you, they have no desire to learn."

"Mort already told me that." Alfredo's calm tone had had its desired effect on Renu. "Basically, he convinced me, but I still don't like it a bit. But I'm not talking about a protracted *defense* battle. I propose that we go on the *attack*. Immediately. Instead of delaying motions, I propose we file expediting motions."

None but Zaffanori could see Mort Heartstone's vigorous head shakes. "Better explain yourself," said Alfredo. "Remember, I wasn't present yesterday."

Renu grabbed the speakerphone, while addressing Zaffanori directly. "I would argue that we proceed immediately with a suit for damages resulting from intentional interference with our business, or whatever the legal term would be. Mort explained to me how these shysters operate. They don't care about a company's fundamentals: they just have computer programs that track the market, looking for victims, and when they find a likely target they move in for the kill. Now suppose we claim that they are deliberately — maliciously — out to interfere with our business, which in our case could well be corporate infanticide since we are a new company with only one potential product. Their suit would complicate our getting the product on the market for reasons that Alfredo already outlined. Suppose we immediately press for unlimited discovery of *their* files? I bet their files are much larger than ours: they've been in operation for decades. There must be an enormous amount of dirt in those files — they must be swimming in it. By suing right away and asking for expedited treatment from the court, we'd compel them to pull back from forcing unlimited discovery on us, because they'd run the risk of exposing themselves. I believe time is of the essence, so that both suits operate essentially on parallel tracks."

Heartstone realized that he had to let his client have her say, but to him it didn't make sense. "Renu," he started in the calmest voice he could muster, "I sympathize with your feelings. In fact, I share them. But they'll just claim attorney-client immunity for these files, and I doubt that you'll find a court willing to deny such a motion."

"Ask for it anyway," she persisted. "And when you get turned down, focus on more specific discovery: what about their stock market dealings, correspondence with brokers, their share holdings in other companies they sued and the extent to which they benefited, their efforts to find John Doe stockholders to use for class-action suits? None of those things should be covered by attorney privilege."

"You know, Mort," it was Gestler's voice from Jerusalem. "There is something appealing about Renu's suggestion. At the very least, they'd get a dose of what they're usually dishing out."

"Of course it's appealing," Renu exclaimed. "We can always drop our suit if it looks counterproductive. At least let's show them that they are dealing with men and not mice!"

"You mean with an angry woman," observed Heartstone.

"Still better than being a chicken."

"Now, now." For the first time, Zaffanori's voice rose. "There's nothing gained by bringing in mice or chickens — "

"Or angry women," Renu said.

"Least of all. Let me propose a compromise. Let's ask Renu and Mort to meet by themselves — *calmly* — and work out a plan of attack, what it would involve in management time, what an outside legal firm would charge for the first run to push for unlimited discovery through their files, and whether we have, in fact, even a theoretical case. Then let them come back to us. Let's give them one week. This is a motion. Any seconds?"

"I second it." It was Menachem's first intervention.

"All in favor?" asked Gestler, who'd remembered that, as chairman, he ought to be asking such questions.

"Yes," the speaker warbled.

"Any nays?"

"I think Renu and I should probably abstain," observed Heartstone.

"Agreed. Anyone against?" Gestler waited a brief moment. "The ayes have it. It's dinner time in Jerusalem. Let's adjourn until next week."

———

Mort Heartstone had not reached the pinnacle of corporate legal practice by antagonizing his clients. He felt that the most diplomatic route was to let Krishnan speak first. He understood and sympathized with a defendant's outrage at spurious lawsuits, the desire to fight come what may, the wish to extract revenge. A lawyer with a short-term perspective might simply accede and collect his fees. But Heartstone considered himself part of the defendant's corporate family, not just its advisor or spokesman. In this instance, it seemed to him that displaying conservative prudence in estimating the cost of a countersuit, yet yielding on some minimal initial steps, would be the best strategy. And even he could enjoy the faint taste of blood in the water; the files of Black, Black & Hood would make no small trophy for his personal collection: the head of Wilfred Hood himself, stuffed and glass-eyed on his office wall, would hardly be much better. But when he and Renu Krishnan met that afternoon, she surprised him.

"Mort," she said the moment she had sunk into one corner of his leather sofa, "I hadn't meant to lose my temper this morning. You know it wasn't you I was mad at — "

"Don't give it another thought," he waved her disclaimer away. "I've already forgotten about it. Let's talk about this countersuit you'd like to launch."

"Actually, let's not — at least, not yet. I don't know much about such matters, but of course I see your legal bills: $350 per hour. Stop," she laughed, seeing his impending response. "Every penny of it is deserved. But at that rate, I'm sure we're talking in six figure aliquots. So before you estimate how close we'd get to seven figures, I'd like to begin with a bargain."

"You don't have to bargain with me."

"Not with you, Mort. Just a bargain — at least by comparison with what initiating legal proceedings would cost us. What do you think the hourly rate would be for a private detective?"

"What for?" He looked startled.

"One thing at a time. Surely, private investigators would be much cheaper?"

"Cheaper, surely. But worth it? And, in the long run, how much cheaper? I'd have to check. But why are you looking for one?"

"Just a hunch — an outside chance. When I asked you yesterday who Black, Black & Hood were, you said two brothers and their brother-in-law, Wilfred Hood."

"So?"

"And you thought they were in their middle or late sixties?"

"Yes, yes. But get to the point."

"All right," she leaned even further back, "here's a woman's wild guess. In fact two guesses."

We pay Mort $350 an hour. It never occurred to me to wonder if he was worth it; now I know. He could have laughed at my idea, or humored "an angry woman"; he could have just coasted along until I forgot about the idea. But here we are, barely into the New Year, and he really has produced. Of course, so did the private detective. And M.L. In some respects, her contribution was the trickiest, but that only entered when my hunch turned out to be more than a *hunch. In retrospect, it sounds very simple: what are the chances that one out of three white males — two in their late sixties, and the third already past seventy — might have prostate problems? I'd guess pretty high. What about prostatic cancer? Less so, but still. . . . At latest count, there may be three hundred thousand new cases diagnosed every year, which would approach 2 percent of the male population over sixty. And most diagnoses must be made among the more affluent population — the men who have annual physicals, like rich lawyers — so that should raise the odds in my favor. All I wanted to know was whether Randy Black, Herman Black, or Wilfred Hood had had a prostatectomy during the past four years. That didn't require high-tech surveillance, phone tapping, or whatever private detectives do. In the end, it was a San Diego journalist — gossip columnist really — who produced the goods for our private investigator; the operation was performed in La Jolla — where all three live — and not at Johns Hopkins or the Mayo Clinic, which would have been much, much more difficult to trace. I wish it had been Will Hood, but for our purposes Herman Black will do almost as nicely. Having hit pay dirt when the statistical chances were small, the odds from that point turned in our favor: the vast majority of prostatectomy patients suffer from erectile dysfunction because penile nerve damage is almost unavoidable. There were no fewer than three urologists in the San Diego area who participated in our Phase III clinical studies, with one of them running our Southern California long-term maintenance study, which is still going on. Could M.L. in her capacity as chair of our medical advisory board find out whether Herman Black was one of the clinical subjects? The codes had all been broken prior to our FDA submission, so the question of medical ethics was at worst tenuous. Anyway, the answer came in yesterday: Herman Black had been a MUSA patient for well over a year, although his present status was unknown.*

I can hardly wait for tomorrow.

"We'll file a countersuit, and push it for all it's worth. I can hardly wait to get my hands on some of their files."

Mort," Renu called out in mock horror, "we can't afford to have a senior partner at $350 per hour read these files. You've got to pick your cheapest paralegals for the first run."

"Nothing doing," he beamed. "I'll do it for nothing. Well, not nothing. . . ."

"What about my second hunch? Do you think it's worth following up on that?"

"Absolutely. The Black brothers must have a genetic streak of vindictiveness, with Hood bearing at least double that load. They might well have displayed it intramurally. It may be more difficult to trace some of their ex-employees and legal associates, but still, it's worth a try."

23

"This sounds serious," Renu's laughter erupted over the telephone.

"It is," Jephtah replied. "When was the last time either one of us did any cooking on a weekday? Tonight, the master of the house is taking over. I already told Maria del Carmen that she could take off as soon as I arrive. Just make sure you don't bring home any work."

"What about you and your journals?"

"No journals tonight. A family meal, prepared by your loving husband. And then a serious talk."

"It's a deal." But why tonight? she wondered. And did Jephtah mean *serious* serious or just serious?

———

"Thank you, master of the house, for feeding your wife and daughter. Even if you do need a bit more practice, *mehra prem*. I know al dente vegetables are now the vogue in California, but couldn't you have cooked the cauliflower just a bit more?"

"Complaints, complaints," Jephtah muttered good-naturedly. "And what about the dessert? Was that too cold?"

Renu reached across the table to pinch his cheek. "For ice

cream, it was just right. And now, let's take turns reading to Naomi."

"*Winnie the Pooh* again?"

"Until she gets tired of it."

"Okay," he said. "But then, let's talk — seriously."

I never would have guessed what Jephtah had in mind. The topic wasn't just serious, or even serious serious — Papaji's expression, whenever he called me into his study — but it was serious raised to the third power. I wonder whether Jephtah had rehearsed his strategy or whether it just flowed out of a father's heart as we put Naomi to bed. "Three more months and she'll be three," he mused. "And you're already past thirty-five." I was about to remind him that this made him nearly thirty-eight when he took me by surprise. "If we want another child, we shouldn't wait much longer. Once a brother is four years younger. . . ." He never finished the sentence. "Brother?" I finally asked when I realized that he was not going to continue. "You seem to have planned it all." "Okay, okay," he said, "'child,' then. What about another child?" I didn't know what to say. He reminded me how much had happened at SURYA during the past eight months: our FDA approval had gone through, the MUSA had been launched commercially, our stock had recovered — lifted first by the FDA's action and then by the general buoyancy of the stock market — so why wait? "It won't get any easier for you at work," he argued, "and you're not getting any younger." This time I did reply, with a crack about his impending male climacteric, but he just laughed. "Climacteric, shlimacteric . . . whatever male clock is ticking ticks much slower. Seriously, though," he continued, and I had to admit he had a point: one shouldn't just have one child. But the timing?

"What about that damn suit of ours?" I reminded him. Those economic terrorists down in San Clemente had started to stall once we had served Wilfred Hood, Esq. with a summons. In some respects, their stonewalling showed that our countersuit strategy was being noticed, but on the other hand, eight months had passed without a single motion or countermotion even having been acted upon by the court in San Francisco. "Forget about the suit," Jephtah said.

"If you're asked to testify while you're pregnant, you'll only get sympathy. Who's prepared to harass an eight-months' pregnant woman?"

"Eight months?" I hooted. But he just looked at me, a little forlorn, a little wistful: Jephtah, out of words. "All right," I said, "lama lo?" I hadn't used my Hebrew for many months. "But what about this boychik business?" I continued. Jephtah nearly cracked up. But then matters became more serious.

"So you agree that having two children is better than one?"

"Not always," hedged Renu. "But I agree in the case of Cohn and Krishnan, Incorporated."

"In that case, you also agree that it's better to have a boy *and* a girl?"

"Again, not always. But with us, I'd say that if I could choose, this time I'd go for a boy."

"In that case, let's have a boy."

"I said 'if I could choose.'"

"But we can." Jephtah reached into his jacket pocket to produce his Wizard cervical sensor. "You are one of the most regular cases."

"You're not sleeping with a *case!*" Renu exclaimed. "I'm your wife, who happens to be blessed with a regular cycle."

"Renu," he said beseechingly. "I know that. But even with a less regular cycle my Wizard of Ov can accurately predict the time of ovulation by at least four days. And you do remember — "

"Darling, you can't be serious. You really want us to try having intercourse four days before ovulation in order to guarantee a boy?"

"Well . . . not guarantee. But it will certainly increase the odds."

"But to do that, we must have intercourse only once during the month at precisely the right time."

"Not quite: only once during the first half of the cycle — "

"And you are prepared to stick to that?"

"If it takes that to produce a boy? We can always make up for lost time once you get pregnant. Between you and my Wizard, I bet we'll accomplish that in a couple of months."

Renu shook her head in wonder. "You're something, *mehra prem*. And I'm not just saying this in light of your proffered sexual discipline. Do I detect the whiff of a prospective father who's already picked a name for a son not yet conceived?"

"Don't you like 'Joshua'?"

"It's not bad, but you're not going to pull another Naomi on me."

"You don't like 'Naomi'?" he challenged her.

"I love the name, and I love my daughter. But how do I know what we might have come up with if we'd thought longer about it? There are dozens of interesting names for boys: Vikram, Arun, Nirad, Madhav, Akbar, Ravi." With each name, she poked him slightly in the chest. "For instance, Ravi Cohn-Krishnan: an Indian name that even sounds Jewish."

"Maybe we better think about it." He sounded dubious, not knowing whether she was serious about the avalanche of exotic names she had produced.

"No wonder you cooked tonight," she laughed. "You really did soften me up. And this *was* a serious conversation."

He hesitated. "There is one more thing. Do you remember what you once said about your stock option?"

"No."

"That you considered it 'our' stock option."

"Oh that," she said. "Yes, I do remember. What about it?"

"I've been thinking. All together, we have now accumulated 260 cycles with the Wizard — enough to show that the principle works. Not unlike the first studies in Jerusalem with the MUSA."

"And how does that relate to my stock option?"

"I have talked to Alfredo. He asked how serious I was about it — whether I wanted to continue the work. When I said yes, he asked if I'd be willing to stake my professional life for the next five or ten years on this project."

"You never told me this."

Jephtah looked sheepish. "I wanted to think through all of the ramifications of his last question. In the end, I realized that this may be SURYA all over again. Like you, I'm being asked to decide whether to pursue an initial research observation to its final, general application. This brings me to the option question. I think that it will take two million dollars and two to three years to get to the stage SURYA reached two years ago."

"Two million dollars?" she scoffed. "To get to an IPO? What sort of stuff has my husband been smoking? Do you know how many millions we had to raise to get to that point? And it's been six years since we started the clinical work in Israel. Be realistic."

"I talked it over with Alfredo. The additional clinical work has no animal toxicology requirements or questions of side effects. We are not administering a drug like your NONO-2. My Wizard of Ov is just a novel diagnostic device. FDA clearance ought to be easier."

"You hope," she said derisively. "It always takes longer than you expect."

"I'm sure it does," he answered excitedly. "That's precisely why I've come up with an in-between solution. Alfredo bought the idea. Martin Gestler bought the idea — "

"You talked to Martin as well as Alfredo? And you haven't breathed a word to me?"

"Renu, darling, all this is only a few days old. There was a reason to raise it first with them. I addressed them as potential outside investors, not as executives of ZALA or SURYA. If their answer had been 'no' it would all have been moot. Here was my question: 'Would they be willing to commit seven hundred fifty thousand dollars each if I was ready to put half a million dollars of my own into the kitty, for which I'd retain 50 percent of the initial equity, with them getting 20 percent each?'"

"That doesn't add up to 100 percent."

"The rest would go to ZALA, for having offered facilities and money for the first stage of the work. Alfredo and Martin considered that fair: after all, I came up with the idea."

"The idea? Yes. But the money?"

"Yesterday, SURYA stock closed at nineteen, which means that your stock option is now worth about $2.3 million. You said that the option is really 'our' option, so I was wondering. . . ."

"But I can't sell some twenty-five thousand plus shares! I'm an officer and director. Word of a sale of that size would hit the Street immediately. If people found out I was unloading stock just as our first product was entering the market, they'd think I didn't believe in the product. After what I have said in so many public announcements — before reporters, security analysts. . . . I certainly don't need another suit." Renu stopped. She realized that her response was too colored by her irritation at not having been consulted first. But these were all arguments Mort Heartstone and, indeed, Martin Gestler had drummed into her again and again, as the stock had resumed its gradual climb and the stockholder suit had dulled from an acute pain to a mere ache in the balance sheet.

"Is that what Martin had in mind?" she asked. "He must be aware that except for our salaries and savings, my stock option is our only equity. He knows what I'm getting paid at SURYA. Does he think we have half a million in the bank?"

Jephtah's discomfort was so evident that Renu took pity on him. "I don't mean to sound so negative, because your device seems promising — "

" 'Seems'? It works, pure and simple. All I need now is to accumulate bigger numbers: more women in different age groups — from teenagers to women approaching menopause, heavy smokers, consumers of various drugs or nutritional supplements, members of different ethnic groups. . . . You know the kind of questions the FDA will ask. And, of course, I need to confirm the Wizard-derived ovulation times with independent measurements. None of this requires new technology — only time and money. I have a consultant down in Silicon Valley who has designed a computerized Wizard of Ov model, whereby the daily plotting you and I have performed won't be necessary."

"I'd miss that, *mehra prem.*"

Jephtah looked pleased, though a bit distracted. "The stored data can be downloaded to one's own computer or at the physician's office, where data can be accumulated over several months — maybe even a year. Think of the implications! This is way beyond birth control — "

"And way beyond two years or two million dollars. I know I'm acting like a wet blanket."

"No, I know you're right. For that portion of the work, we'll have to raise more money. But we'll do that later, after we demonstrate the veterinary possibilities, which may turn into a cash cow. That's where I would like to spend the first million dollars."

Renu wagged her head, Jephtah couldn't tell whether it was in amazement or irritation. "What sort of cash cow are you talking about?"

"I'd like to concentrate on dairy farmers, because in a dairy, fertility awareness goes right to the financial bottom line: cows must be pregnant to produce milk. Furthermore, you have them all together daily, during milking, so you don't have to chase cows all over the range."

"And you expect farmers to walk around every morning with a giant Wizard and stick it up . . ." Renu wrinkled her nose. "Be realistic. Not even Krishna, when he was a cowherd, would have been willing to do that."

He shrugged. "I couldn't care less about the problems of Indian deities. What I have in mind, and what we'll spend some of our first money on, is a permanent vaginal insert, maybe a cervical ring, which I'm calling the Tele-Ov. The farmer can 'read' the data by means of standard telemetry. He'll be able to determine the time of ovulation so that the cow can be inseminated at precisely the right time. He'll know whether a cow is pregnant; he should even be able to predict imminent calf birth. Think of the money he'll save. And to top it all, as far as I can tell, we don't even need FDA approval. Compare that with what you had to do with the MUSA!"

"I've long learned not to take you for granted, but, *mehra prem*, where did you pick all this up? Next thing, you'll tell me that you were a cowherd in a kibbutz."

Jephtah grinned proudly. "I get around. But what about the option? I know what you're saying, and I'm not suggesting you sell a single share. All I'm asking is whether you'd put up some of your option as a collateral for my taking out a half-million-dollar loan."

"Hmm."

"What does that mean? 'Yes?' or 'I'll think about it?'"

She sighed. "Somewhere in between. In principle, the answer is 'yes,' because I consider it *our* option. But I must get legal advice. If Mort says 'yes,' then it's 'yes.'"

———

Mort Heartstone, the master of caveats, said "Yes, but. . . ." There were no legal barriers, especially since at the moment they were in a period without trading restrictions. But given the high volatility of SURYA's stock, a bank would surely require as collateral at least twice the number of shares corresponding to the face value of the loan; to be really prudent, Renu should count in her own mind on "locking up" at least seventy-five thousand shares. "Are you willing to do that?" he asked.

"For my husband, yes."

"In that case, head for the bank." Renu was about to hang up when she heard Mort's unconscious verbal Morse code — two short clearings of the throat, followed by a pause and then a deep bark-like cough — indicating something delicate still needed to be said.

"I appreciate the fact that you're not considering selling five hundred thousand dollars worth of stock, because legally nothing would prevent you from doing so."

"It wouldn't look very good if I actually sold that much stock, would it?"

"Granted," he said, "and appreciated. However, you ought to know that one of your fellow directors — not an officer — has cashed in all of his options, meaning that he's exercised his option and then sold all of the stock on the same day, specifically on October 3."

"Wow. Who was that?"

Mort hesitated. "I might as well tell you, since it'll be public knowledge soon enough. It was Menachem."

"I'd never have guessed. Do you know why he chose this particular time?"

"He needed the money. For what, I don't know."

"He could have borrowed it — as I'm doing — and used the option as collateral."

"Not quite. He sold it at twenty-two dollars, our all-time high, clearing over six hundred thousand dollars. If he borrowed the money, he'd have gotten only half. As I told you, banks are cautious these days. The Dow just topped 2700, so I'd say he acted wisely. Neither the market nor SURYA can go up indefinitely."

"I suppose not. Well . . . anything else?"

"One more thing, Renu. This is confidential, because it will not be published. But I thought you should know: there is one other person — not a legal insider — who informed me that he was considering exercising his entire stock option. I had to tell him that, legally, there was nothing in the way. It's the chair of your SAB."

"Cantor?" Renu sounded shocked. "Did he say why?"

"I had no business asking him. Besides, he only said he was considering it. Have there been any problems on the SAB? Is he thinking of resigning?"

"I have no idea," stammered Renu. "I'll have to see if I can find out."

———

"Tonight will be a special night." Jephtah's voice on the phone sounded jubilant. "And not because it's the start of the Sabbath. Today, October 16, 1987, is the official birthday of OV, Inc. Our two million dollar infusion from Alfredo, Martin — and you — has cleared the bank. I've quit ZALA officially. And . . ." he stopped for a dramatic moment, "I just signed a one-year lease for office space on Palo Alto Square. That address brought SURYA good luck, and I'm superstitious."

"*Mehra prem.* Congratulations. I can hardly wait to hear all the news tonight."

"Not at home! Your husband is taking you out for dinner to the fanciest restaurant on the Peninsula. Just the two of us: Dr. Renu Krishnan, president of SURYA, and Dr. Jephtah Cohn, the new CEO of OV, Incorporated."

———

On the same evening, some two thousand miles east of Palo Alto, on the shores of Lake Michigan, Paula Curry unwrapped a fastidiously packaged container, the label — Lyon & Healey — discreetly displayed on one side. "Leonardo darling," she exclaimed. "I don't believe it!"

With great caution, she closed the case before embracing

Cantor. After a long kiss, her arms still around him, she murmured in his ear. "It's the real thing, isn't it? How did you find it? And how could you . . . ?"

"Hush, my dear. You ask too many questions. Just enjoy it." Cantor saw no reason to volunteer at this point that two days before he had exercised his entire SURYA stock option, all thirty thousand shares. At a share price of $23, he had netted $678,000.

―――――

Monday, October 19, 1987, will be long known on the New York Stock Exchange simply as "Black Monday" — the day of the biggest one-day decline in stock market history. The October 20 *New York Times* bannered the news in a 108-point headline: "STOCKS PLUNGE 508 POINTS, A DROP OF 22.6%," with the ominous subtitle: "DOES 1987 EQUAL 1929?" While the thirty blue-chip companies making up the Dow-Jones Index lost nearly 23 percent of their combined valuation that Monday, smaller companies, trading over-the-counter, took a much bigger hit. SURYA's stock closed at $10.50, a 54 percent drop in less than six hours.

When Renu and Jephtah clinked champagne glasses on Friday evening, the fifty thousand share collateral requested by the bank had been worth $1.15 million — a very comfortable safety margin for a $500,000 loan. The following Monday, their collateral's value had fallen to $525,000 — within a hairbreadth of triggering a call from their banker.

24

"Tomorrow is one of my regular afternoons with Adam. I'd like to stay for dinner. Is that okay with you?"

"Of course," replied Melanie.

"Afterward, I'd like to have an important talk with you."

"Important? That sounds serious." Her attempt at flippancy fell flat.

"It is serious," said Menachem.

"I feel somewhat embarrassed speaking about SURYA stock," Menachem started.

"Oh, that," Melanie sounded relieved. She had been sure he had wanted to talk about Adam. "You can't blame the company for the horrendous drop: $10.50." She shuddered daintily. "It's only paper. I know that sounds cavalier. For the last two weeks, the newspapers have been full of Black Monday and its consequences, but I'm taking the long view. I've had a very reassuring confab with the head of REPCON's investment committee. He thinks this correction was long overdue and that we're on a path to a slow but long-term recovery. Still, seeing one's stock option decline in one day from over six hundred thousand dollars by about half is a blow, but as I said, it's only paper."

"For me, it *was* paper. I've liquidated my entire option."

"You have?" Melanie looked at him with surprise. Is that what he wanted to discuss? "That's too bad. I wish I had told you earlier about my conversation with our banker. You should've held on to the stock. The fundamentals of SURYA are first-class. Just think of the last report we directors got: the MUSA system has been on the market for barely three months, and they can't produce enough to fill the demand."

"I know all about that," muttered Menachem.

"Well . . . tough luck, Menachem. Although even three hundred thousand dollars is nothing to sneeze at. We may have assumed some legal liability as directors — that suit is still pending, after all — but we can't complain about our initial stock options, even at today's price. What did it close at? Eleven dollars and a fraction, I believe."

Menachem nodded absentmindedly. "I haven't paid much attention to the stock market. SURYA shares were the only ones I've ever owned. But you don't have to feel sorry for me: I sold mine at the beginning of October."

Melanie gave a low whistle. "Congratulations," she said, her tone a mixture of admiration and envy. "*You* certainly needed no banker's advice. Or do you need some now to help you diversify?"

"Not anymore. I have spent it all. That's what I wanted to

discuss with you. Come," he pointed to the front door. "Let me show you."

Melanie headed for the coat tree in the foyer, but Menachem stopped her. "You won't need a coat. We're just going up a couple of floors in the elevator."

———

"What is this?" Melanie exclaimed as she looked at the empty living room. "You aren't . . . ?"

"Moving in?" Menachem completed the sentence. "Most of the SURYA option was spent on this condo. The leftover will go toward furnishing it. That's one of the reasons why I brought you up here. Would you help me with that?"

"Well . . . yes," she faltered. "But isn't it mostly a matter of taste?"

"That and convenience. For instance, I'd very much like to furnish Adam's room together with you."

"Adam's room?" Melanie stared at him. "And the other reason?"

"Come to his room. It's time to talk about Adam and me. Seriously."

They entered a large, airy room, recently painted, with a futon and a floor lamp in one corner. A small suitcase sat next to it.

"Have you been sleeping here?" Melanie asked startled.

"Only last night. I wanted to get a feel for the place. Tomorrow I'm going back to my old place until this apartment is habitable. Can you manage?" Menachem pointed to the futon. Grunting a little, they sat awkwardly side-by-side.

"It's been nearly two years," he continued. "Yet I've never pressed you or Adam. Ostensibly, I came as a friend of the family."

"And you became that," Melanie said eagerly. "It's one reason why I have stopped. . . ." she uttered a short, embarrassed laugh. "I was going to say 'dating,' but that sounds so . . . dated." She grimaced.

Menachem grinned crookedly. "It's such an American word. So . . . baroque . . . for adults in this day and age. Though, in my opinion, the real reason for the no-dating is this: we are both burned out emotionally, aren't we? I think Adam has made us into friends of sorts — polite, sociable, but it's all on the surface. We've never spoken about deep personal issues — "

"I thought you didn't wish to."

Menachem had been playing with a tassel of the futon pillow. He looked up. "Perhaps I didn't. But I do now. When we first met in New York, you asked whether I could live in the States, and I said no. It's different now. Mostly because of Adam, but also because my widower's guilt is receding. Besides, the job with our UN Mission appeals to me. Even some of the fund-raising for Ben-Gurion can be done more efficiently from New York." He resumed his fingering of the tassel, running each small string between thumb and index finger as if he were toying with prayer beads.

Melanie reached over to cover his hand. "Adam has brought us so far. Where do you want to go now?"

"I want to become his father."

Melanie withdrew her hand. Clasping her arms around her knees, she looked down into her lap. "You *are* his father — "

"Yes," he said sharply. "*You* knew that all along, and then, much later, I. The time is long overdue for Adam to be privy to that fact. That's why I decided to move here, into this building. I don't think we can live together, Melanie. I'm too burned out. But this way he can live with both of us without a particular schedule. Two floors apart is close and yet not together. I will certainly share all financial burdens — it's high time I do so. Private school in Manhattan must be terribly expensive. And we should change his name."

"What?" Melanie exclaimed. "Change Adam's name?"

"Not Adam's. Adam Laidlaw's. My name is Dvir and I'm his father."

"Don't be so . . . Levantine . . . biblical . . . patriarchal." Melanie's pique caused her to raise her voice with each word. "You're confusing responsibility with entitlement." Her voice rang harshly off the bare walls.

Menachem shook his head. "Patriarchy is not necessarily immoral or unconventional."

"Of course not," she interrupted. "On the contrary, it's all too conventional."

"Melanie. I'm trying hard to be fair, and so should you. At the outset, you had no difficulty claiming that you were solely entitled to parenthood. You did not acknowledge the name or even the existence of Dvir. Naturally, Laidlaw was the only feasible name. But you have now openly conceded that I am Adam's father: Felix Frankenthaler knows it, and so does his wife; I bet Renu Krishnan has guessed.

"Now I ask you: what did it mean for you to become a Jew? Because of *your* conversion, Adam was born a Jew. I am very glad of that. And we Jews have always recognized maternal rights, perhaps more than most peoples. But Jews also recognize paternal rights. In the old days, Adam would have been called Adam Ben Menachem."

"Surely you aren't suggesting that?"

"I'm not. Nor am I suggesting that we continue with Adam Laidlaw. What's wrong with Adam Dvir-Laidlaw?"

"Why not Laidlaw-Dvir?" The words shot out before Melanie realized what she had done: conceded the principle of a changed name.

"I think I could make a very good argument in favor of Dvir-Laidlaw — and not just on alphabetical grounds — but I'll accept Adam Laidlaw-Dvir."

For a long moment both were silent: exhausted by the brief eruption, surprised by its sudden resolution.

"When shall we tell him?" she asked softly.

"Now. Tonight."

"But Menachem, he's asleep!"

"So? We'll wake him up. It's time he goes to sleep knowing who his father is."

I'm beginning to wonder whether I shouldn't have stayed in the lab rather than yield to the temptations of industry. How would I have reacted to Black Monday as an associate professor with tenure — or even as an assistant professor still bucking for tenure — rather than as the distinctly untenured president of SURYA? Probably, it would been nothing more to me than a headline for one day. Whereas now? It's almost laughable. I really did say the words

Martin had warned us about: "what's a million more or less?"
Jephtah and I don't live like millionaires, we don't behave like mil-
lionaires, we don't even think that we're millionaires. And yet, we
did borrow half a million, and for a week or so I expected any
moment for the phone to ring with a request from the bank to pro-
duce more stock collateral or else! Our stock did teeter close to $10,
but it never crossed that magic line. Now it's starting to creep up
again. Yesterday it was $12.25, but all we need is another day like
October 19! The toughest part was that, with Martin still in Jeru-
salem, it fell solely on me to reassure everyone that SURYA won't go
belly-up. We still have nearly thirty million dollars, but with our
negative cash flow for the next couple of years, we'll have to watch
our pocketbook — even though demand for our MUSA is growing
handsomely. In fact that's exactly why I worry: we need more sales
reps, we need to expand our manufacturing facilities, we need to do
more promotion, we need lots of expensive post-marketing clinical
follow-up. The list goes on and on.

And then there's the lawsuit! Black, Black & Hood's strategy at
this point seems to be to stall; it's costing us plenty — which, of
course, is part of their ploy. It's still not clear whether discovery will
be granted to one, both, or neither party. Mort has come up with a
daring move: he's petitioning the court in a sealed motion to sub-
poena, without advance warning, copies of all the computer disks at
Black, Black & Hood pertaining to stock dealings, claiming that
there is a real risk of the computer records being sanitized. He vol-
unteered to do the same at SURYA and to keep all copied disks
sealed until the court acted one way or another on the question of
discovery. That should light a fast-burning fuse in San Clemente.

And now this cryptic letter from I.C. He mentioned neither the
stock market nor what he'd done with his options, he just asked
whether we could hold a special SAB meeting in Chicago. He was
emphatic that we should all count on staying overnight in Chi-
cago. I don't know what it's about, and I don't know if I'm annoyed
at the mystery or if there's some lingering envy of his good luck in
unloading all his stock before Black Monday. It's almost as if he
and Menachem had a premonition about the stock market.

And why did he give me such a hard time when I told him that we couldn't hold the meeting on November 20 but only after the 21st? "Why?" he kept pushing. How could I tell him that my sex life is now controlled by a metallic sensor that makes no exceptions. According to the Wizard of Ov, Jephtah Cohn — if he intends to father a boy (and he does!) — is scheduled to lie with his wife on that day and no other.

Everyone commented about the upbeat atmosphere of this SAB affair. There were good reasons for it. Of the three candidates proposed by Marletta, two — Carl Nathan from Cornell and Dyann Wirth from the Harvard School of Public Health — had accepted, and they fit in nicely. They had introduced a new perspective from the fields of parasitology and tropical diseases — latent interests of Renu's that had gradually acquired more importance in her mind and even in those of her SAB colleagues. Whether it would make commercial sense for SURYA to pursue leads in those directions was still open to question. The immediate challenge before the company was to strengthen its position in the penile erection field, before any competitors could take the technological lead — and the market — away from them.

Now that SURYA had laid the groundwork with the FDA, it was clear to them — and consequently had to be even clearer to the competition — that the next NDA submissions would be processed more quickly, especially if they were based on the principle of transurethral drug delivery. Celestine Price's new series of NO-releasers sailed through the patent office without interference. Extensive in vitro pharmacokinetic studies demonstrated quite clearly that her tetrazenium series — consisting of four NO molecules strung together and tethered chemically to a tail with just the right fat-solubility — were prime candidates for the Mark 2 generation of MUSAs. Everyone agreed that this would have to become the highest-priority development target. With that decision out of the way, the discussion focused on other possible applications of these NONONONOates.

Within the first hour, Renu dismissed any concern about Cantor's possible resignation. Even the stock market collapse of some four weeks ago only elicited a little gallows humor from Weiss, and Cantor had let it pass without comment. The lunch was light because Cantor had invited everyone for a *serious* dinner, but it was also indecently luxurious: blini with caviar, smoked trout with horseradish, cassis sorbet. "It's all on the Cantor household — to express our gratitude to SURYA," he had remarked somewhat cryptically.

Paula Curry, who had never before appeared at an SAB meeting, acted as hostess. "I usually steer clear of scientific meetings, but this is different." She was addressing Michael Marletta, who had been standing by the window, a plate in his hand, chatting with Celestine. Paula put her arm around her niece's shoulder. "At least your meetings provide a reason for my favorite niece to grace us with her presence. We hardly ever see her otherwise, and we never see Jerry." A short warning cough from Celestine caused her to change the subject. "What have you two been chatting about?"

"Just sociological chitchat," said Marletta. He gestured with his fork toward Celestine. "Now that Professor Price has received tenure," he said with mock formality, "she has started to express quite openly her critical views of our foibles."

Paula arched her eyebrows. "Tell me more. As you will learn this evening, I have become quite interested in the foibles of you all."

Celestine disengaged herself from her aunt's embrace. "I wasn't so much talking about foibles as making an observation. Look at this group." She motioned with her head around the large room. "All of them — no, all of *us* — are passionately engaged in publishing. It isn't just disseminating scientific information; it's also pushing our names. But look how differently we do it. Max Weiss and Michael always put their names last. They can afford to do that. Everyone knows they're the senior author, irrespective of the number of co-authors."

"Is that true of . . ." Paula was about to say *Leonardo*, but then she caught herself, "I.C.?"

"No. I.C. uses alphabetical precedence. A luxury only the As, Bs or Cs can really afford." Celestine's sarcasm was unmistakable. "But what about me? Quite frankly, until I was sure I'd get tenure,

I always made sure my name came first. I didn't think I could risk generosity."

"Now, now," admonished Marletta.

"Now nothing," Celestine countered. "What we were talking about, before you came," she turned to Paula, "was the subtlety of how to apportion credit among all the authors. These days, four or more authors is par for the course in any competitive field of chemistry or biology. Having settled who is last, the question now is who comes first."

"Really?" said Paula. "I'd think you'd pick the person who has done most of the work."

"You think that's easy? That's exactly what we've been discussing. Recently, John Scott from Portland published a real first in *Science*. He had five co-workers, all women — a real harem — but what made it a first was that the first two names listed in the article were marked with an asterisk. Can you guess what the footnote said? 'These authors contributed equally to this manuscript.'"

"Brilliant," exclaimed Paula.

"You see?" laughed Marletta.

"Brilliant?" Celestine snorted. "Suppose the first asterisked name had been Smith and the second Price. I would have gone to Scott to point out that in any citation that article would be referred to either as 'Smith et al.' or 'Scott et al.' To me, 'et al.' does not mean 'equal.'"

"So what would you have had Scott do?"

"Ah," grinned Celestine. "As a first try, I'd have separated the names Smith and Price by an equal sign rather than a comma. But since no editor would allow that, I'd have told him to do it alphabetically."

"You mean I.C.'s system? Why should Smith agree to that when your name starts with a P?"

"Fair enough. That was also Michael's point. So I asked why not toss a coin? And you know what the fair-minded Professor Marletta said?" Celestine poked him lightly with her index finger. "Why don't you tell Paula."

"In my lab, I decide such issues, not the drop of a coin."

"How would you have handled it, Celly?" asked Paula.

"A coin. And that, in my opinion, is one of the differences between a male and a female professor."

"If it is," said Marletta, "it's the only one. Come back in five years and show me in what other respects you behave differently from me."

———

The invitation to dinner had been mailed to each member of the SAB. The hand-addressed envelope, the announcement, the RSVP card, and its smaller envelope were of a quality normally reserved for wedding invitations. The guests arrived in street clothes but were nevertheless well-dressed. Marletta and Nathan, who usually made a point of attending SAB meetings in open shirts or sweaters, wore ties. Even Celestine had left her water bottle behind; she looked quite dashing in a dark green pantsuit with high heels. Renu decided to come in a yellow sari.

"My goodness," whispered Celestine, as a tuxedo-clad waiter took their coats. "What's the occasion?"

The waiter led them into the empty living room.

"We must be first," remarked Renu, silently congratulating herself on having decided to pack the sari. At that moment, Paula Curry and I.C. appeared, each resplendent in formal attire.

"Greetings," Cantor exclaimed. "As usual, the youngest are also the most punctual. I know you are wondering about the occasion. Rather than explain it piecemeal, let's wait for the rest. In the meantime," he waved to the waiter hovering in the background, "help yourself to drinks and hors d'oeuvres. We won't be eating for another hour."

Renu had never seen Cantor in such a jovial humor. Smiling, sociable, moving from one guest to the other with Paula by his side, Renu realized that Cantor was a man of masks. This evening, he had either taken one off or put on a new one.

———

Cantor tapped a silver spoon against his glass. "Friends," he beamed, "we are about to pass around some champagne for a toast." He paused until the waiter had filled everyone's glass. "Paula and I thank you for coming — all six of you." He raised his glass. "And now a toast: to the new Mrs. Cantor!" While the guests gasped, I.C. clinked glasses with Paula and then kissed her on the cheek. "Before you drink," he said quickly, "let's touch glasses all around."

"And when did this happen?" Cantor asked rhetorically. "Two days ago, in total privacy. We were going to announce it last evening, but I wanted all of you here. Since one of you could not make it yesterday," Cantor's gaze brushed by Renu without even the briefest of censorious stops, "we postponed the announcement until tonight. And why only the six of you? It isn't solely because the dining room table barely accommodates ten — at least in the style in which we plan to dine tonight — or that the music room seems crowded when filled with many more. There is a reason that is directly connected with SURYA, and I want to pay tribute to that reason in your exclusive presence. This weekend, we shall have a real shivaree down on the campus, and since neither my students nor my colleagues know as yet anything about this nuptial knot, I ask that you keep it quiet until then."

Paula, who towered over Cantor, bent down to whisper in his ear. He nodded briefly. "Replenish your glasses, if you wish, and then find a chair in the music room. We have planned a short musical interlude for you before starting dinner." He motioned to the open French doors behind him. "Paula and I will join you in a moment."

The seats in the music room were arranged in a slight curve, facing two upholstered Hepplewhite chairs, each with a music stand. Shortly after the guests had sat down, Cantor entered, viola under his arm.

"The only piece we'll play — all of four minutes long — is one that most of you are probably unacquainted with: a duet for viola and cello by Paul Hindemith, himself a violist. This instrumental combination is rare but, if I may be so bold as to say, so is the alliance of Curry and Cantor. The reason for playing this piece for you is threefold. First, Paula and I met when she joined our amateur quartet as a pinch-hitting cellist. What a terrible phrase," he grimaced, "but what a superb consequence. Also, duets are the most intimate of musical collaborations — and intimacy is certainly what we celebrate tonight. But this piece is also a joint gesture of appreciation from the two of us, via you, to SURYA. And now, Paula Curry, the new Mrs. Cantor." He bowed formally, while pointing with his bow toward Paula who had been waiting behind the guests.

Renu looked sideways at Celestine. She had come to admire Celly's innate toughness in professional matters but often had wondered about the source of that extra touch of acerbity she displayed so often when interacting with Cantor. None of that was now evident. Was it Cantor's open affection for Paula, expressed in rather formal, even shy gestures, that had affected her or the fact that the pairing of Cantor and her aunt was now official?

Paula in her black formal silk gown, the absence of jewelry emphasizing her slightly daring décolletage, planted the pin of her cello in the carpet before clasping the instrument between her thighs. She closed her eyes, bending her head slightly until her left temple almost touched one of the pegs. Renu could not help but sense an erotic quality in the way Paula ran her hand along the shiny golden varnish of the cello's rib before resting it on the top of the soundboard. Only then did Paula open her eyes to look at Cantor with a slight nod. They played.

———

"Paula, do you want to tell them about your instrument?" Cantor's voice sounded eager, almost boyish after the applause had died down.

"Of course," she said, rising from her seat until she towered over her audience. "This," she raised the cello by its neck, "is a Guarneri — "

Renu's gasp of surprise was sufficiently audible that Paula stopped. "It really is," she reassured Renu. "If you were a cello player, you could tell from its responsiveness, the evenness and quality of its tone, that you're dealing with a Cremonese instrument. Among the Guarneris, Giuseppe Giovanni Battista, also known as 'filius Andreae,' made the best cellos — almost in a class with Stradivari's — and this is one of them. Just look at its boldness, the balance of its sound holes. . . ." She smiled at Cantor. "My wedding present." She stopped. "I know I must sound silly to you scientists, but. . . ." She turned toward Cantor and lifted the handkerchief out of his breast pocket.

It was a curiously touching sight. The blond Amazon dabbing at her eyes, clutching the cello with her other hand, while her new husband, easily three inches shorter, patted her on the shoulder. "Friends, you've now seen the reason why I wanted you to be the first to celebrate with us. A cello first introduced us. *This* cello, which we'll call the SURYA cello, will hold us together."

Renu felt almost guilty, thinking of her feelings when she had first heard of Cantor's exercise of his stock option. She rose, walked over to the couple and planted a kiss on Cantor's cheek.

"I'm glad you agreed to become the chair of our SAB," she whispered.

"That was quite an evening," said Renu in the taxi. "I note you — the youngest of us all — had the place of honor, to the right of I.C."

"That's not why he picked me," replied Celly, her face periodically illuminated by the headlights of oncoming cars. "He would like to bury a hatchet I inherited when I paired up with Jerry. I can't blame him for wanting to do that. And after tonight, I'd like to help. Marrying Paula has made him a member of the family — as well as more human." She leaned forward to catch Renu's eyes. "Don't you feel that way about him?"

Renu nodded. "I liked the way he talked to me about his feelings toward SURYA. He admitted that if it hadn't been for his friendship with my former Prof and my dangling the stock option in front of him he would never have accepted. He was quite honest about his former disdain of industry, although he claims that he now looks at it through different glasses, having learned what it takes to bring a research discovery to fruition."

"I gather he cashed in his option for the Guarneri. That must have softened his views about industry. Yet," Celly mused, "I like how he used the money. I wonder what I'll do with it if I should —"

"Wait for a while," interrupted Renu. "We're going to become quite a company. Unless you need the money now."

"Need? We lead a fairly simple life: work, work, and work, and taking care of Valentine. Remember, Jerry shared the Nobel Prize with Cantor. We've invested his half very conservatively: we don't touch the capital; we just use the income. Maybe I'll use the SURYA option for a trust for my son. Or blow it on some way-out research ideas no one else will fund."

"I know it's none of my business," said Renu, "but what's the hatchet Cantor wants to bury?"

Celly sighed. "I'm afraid it's a rather ignoble Nobel story. Jerry worshipped I.C., who, in turn, considered Jerry his best student. But there were problems with the Cantor-Stafford experiment — the one for which they got the Nobel. Initially, I.C.'s biggest competitor, Kurt Krauss from Harvard, could not repeat it. Eventually he did, but by that time, I.C. had started to mistrust Jerry." She shook her head. "The story is more complicated than that, but this is not the place or time to rehash it. I.C. and I actually talked about it this evening — the first time I ever heard him do so. He asked me about Jerry — whether he regretted leaving a research career to go into medicine. I told him no, that deep down Jerry was not an extremely competitive person."

"Unlike you?"

Celestine gave Renu a curious look. "That's just what he asked me. 'Are you infected with Nobel lust?' were his precise words. When I admitted being infected, he really opened up. 'Pioneering, exciting, productive science is truly noble,' he said, 'but it is only rarely performed in a climate devoid of Nobel lust.' I.C.'s point was that noble science without Nobel lust is almost an oxymoron. Rather reassuring, isn't it?" Her brief laugh sounded skeptical. "But he didn't stop there. 'Lust is never ennobling,' he said, 'so where does that leave us academics? None of us is as pure as we pretend to be — but why should that surprise anyone? The world around us is not black and white; it's only shades of gray. The best we can strive for is to be light gray rather than dirty gray.'"

They sat in silence a minute while the cab rumbled on through the city.

"You look pensive, Renu."

"Yes. I'm starting to wonder about my own grayness."

25

Most lawyers tend to procrastinate; at hourly billings in the two to four hundred dollar range, elapsed time is gold in their pockets. For a defense attorney, stalling may even be good strategy: witnesses move or die, passions cool, memories dim, court calendars jam. . . . A plaintiff's legal counsel, though equally aware of the monetary benefits of elapsed time, is often strategically aggressive, adrenaline overcoming acquisitiveness. But the dynamics and personalities in the case of *SURYA v. Black, Black & Hood* were more complicated.

Renu's gut response — *sue the bastards* — though initially spawned by grievous outrage had turned into more than simple emotional catharsis. The success of her hunch about the statistical chances of prostate problems in aging males had converted Mort Heartstone — himself no blooming youth — into a potential prosecutor, a rare emotional or professional role for a consummate corporate counsel: calm, judicious, composed. His antipathy for Black, Black & Hood had turned visceral. He had served as defense counsel in many spurious class action suits initiated by that San Clemente firm; he considered the kind of frivolous litigation practiced so frequently by his opponents fodder for attorney-bashers who drew no distinction between the Heartstones and the Hoods of the legal profession. Now, though, it was personal: as a director of SURYA, Heartstone had become a defendant in the suit filed by Black, Black & Hood, and thus a client — albeit a highly vocal and informed one — of the outside law firm retained by SURYA. As SURYA's chief counsel in the countersuit, however, Mort's firm was responsible for devising and executing the plaintiff's legal strategy and tactics. His emotional involvement was such that, at times, he almost forgot to keep track of his hours.

In this case, Wilfred Hood, the most senior and most aggressive of the Black, Black & Hood partners, was following a familiar pattern. Assuming the mantel of a legal Robin Hood, he claimed for his firm the role of protector of small investors and pensioners from the fraudulent practices of corporate executives, insider investors, accountants, and stockbrokers. While fraud and malpractice does occur among those business circles, whose affluence generally buys them little sympathy from media, public, or even juries, scant attention is paid to the pernicious and self-enhancing roles some of the legal firms are known to play. Hood's claim that he and his associates were solely concerned with the interests of the small investor, even if their actions resulted in gutting the corporations involved, might have carried more validity were it not for the facts that few of his suits ever went to trial, that, of those that did, hardly any were won by the plaintiff, and that the overwhelming number were settled out of court with often half of the settlement ending up in the pockets of his firm.

His strategy was simple: Never sue anyone with shallow pockets, focus on defendants covered by insurance, go on giant fishing expeditions with enormous nets of unlimited discovery, then wait while the defendant's pocketbook bleeds. Carrying out the maximum number of such suits while expending the least amount of actual time had proved to be worth millions of dollars. While de jure, the firm's partners served solely as legal counsel, de facto, they were frequently the real plaintiff hiding behind a few small stockholders they had solicited.

Black, Black & Hood made a mistake in underestimating SURYA's countersuit: by not taking this corporate stripling seriously as a legal opponent — in spite of the risk of becoming the victims of a fishing expedition in their own teeming pond — they allowed themselves to become de jure both defendant and defendant's counsel. Will Hood and his two brothers-in-law, the consummate predatory plaintiffs, were too avaricious to hire outside counsel in their own defense. By stalling on SURYA's demands for access to their files, while proceeding with their own request for unlimited discovery in their class action suit, they meant to wear SURYA down. Clearly, the direct out-of-pocket legal expenses at this ping-pong stage of motions and counter-motions was much higher on the SURYA side, and SURYA could ill afford to waste its precious cash on legal maneuvers. But Will Hood and brothers-in-law underestimated Mort Heartstone's flair for gambling — a submerged talent only rarely displayed in his corporate legal career.

––––

The Black, Black & Hood strategy had worked for fifteen months at a cost to SURYA of over three hundred thousand dollars. "Mort," Renu had groaned, "how much longer is that going to go on? I'm beginning to see why insurance companies settle and move on to more productive pastures — "

"Like raising premiums," he interjected. "In the final analysis, it's not their money. But you're right, the time has come. . . ." He eyed her speculatively.

"To do what?"

"To gamble. We couldn't have done it earlier, because we had to demonstrate that our opponents are simply stalling. Fifteen months ought to do it. Here is my plan." Heartstone usually sat when he spoke, but this morning his excitement caused him to roam across the carpet. The sight of his usually stationary bulk in motion made Renu straighten in her chair. In contrast to most of his colleagues, Mort's office was not cluttered with files stacked on the floor — the usual ploy of a lawyer disguising inherent messiness as a visual cue for presumed overwork. There was plenty of space for his moving bulk.

"I already told you about the gambit we are about to try: to ask to have all potentially relevant computer files copied and sealed. By volunteering to subject ourselves to the same treatment, we are likely to preempt most of their obvious objections, although you can never tell with Will Hood. Part of my strategy is to petition Judge Patel. Our suit is before the U.S. District Court for the Northern District of California, and she sits in San Francisco."

"She? A woman and an Indian?"

"Marilyn Hall Patel. Not an Indian." He stopped in front of Renu. "But married to one. And while neither one of these facts should make much difference, the fact that SURYA's president and chief scientist is a woman and an Indian won't hurt, especially since the judge is a mother of two herself and a former board member of the National Organization for Women to boot." He eyed her pensively. "When did you say you expect your baby?"

"September." She looked at her stomach. "It's starting to show, isn't it?"

"Far be it from me to talk about stomachs, but . . ." he uttered an impish laugh, "your bulging stomach ought to help all around. I'm thinking of the depositions." He settled in a chair in front of her before continuing. "If we're to make any use of your prostatectomy lead, we've got to hear from Herman Black in person. In an accompanying motion to Judge Patel, I am going to ask that she order the initiation of depositions and interrogatories."

"What's the difference?"

"One is oral, before a court reporter; the other written answers to written questions. I'm going for both. Again, to preempt their stalling I shall volunteer for us to be questioned first. They'll hardly object to that. But then, since our respective suits were filed so close together and because we have continually emphasized their interconnection, I'll request that we alternate each week: they get us for a week and then we get them. And once that process is under way, and since you are their most important target, I'll use your pregnancy to undercut any attempts of theirs to procrastinate. That's where the perspective of a woman judge with children of her own is bound to come in handy."

If someone had told me in October 1981, when Jephtah and I first arrived at ZALA, that just a few years later I'd become president of a corporate start-up, I'd have laughed. But if they'd predicted that less than seven years later I'd also be involved in a multi-million-dollar lawsuit and actually enjoying it, I'd have judged them daft. Yet here I am, back from San Clemente after my first deposition, and I can hardly wait for our turn next week.

The conference room of Black, Black & Hood seemed to come right out of the movies or a TV sitcom: the smoothly polished mahogany table, long enough to accommodate at least two dozen persons the size of Mort; the brown leather-upholstered chairs, again ample enough for our Mort; one long wall lined with shelves full of leather-bound U.S. Supreme Court and California Supreme Court

Records, the opposite wall featuring a giant credenza with a huge model of a sailboat encased in Plexiglas, two heavily framed English maritime scenes hanging on either side. I began to wonder whether affluent law firms ordered the complete set from a central stage supplier. And were the legal tomes real or just fake spines to impress clients and victims?

I'd never seen Mort in such a marvelous mood, but why not? Everything worked out as he'd hoped. Even though we were the defendants, Mort had offered that we'd fly down to San Clemente for the first set of depositions. He was hoping that Randy and Herman Black might also be present, even though the actual questions were being posed by Will Hood.

Mort made them focus on me as the principal culprit as well as the most available top executive of SURYA. Fortunately, our CEO had been abroad when the FDA fracas had developed; following Mort's strict orders, Martin now stayed outside Hood's reach in Jerusalem. Mort wanted to position me as the ivory-tower scientist who had been propelled into top management without knowledge of the vagaries of the stock market and the manipulating power of financial analysts and journalists. Fidgeting with my hair, displaying my six-month-big belly, and speaking in the softest, most faltering voice I could muster, I was supposed to be easy prey for Wilfred Hood, Esquire.

When the three partners and their stooges marched in, I would have put Hood on the bottom of the pile — a Dickensian caricature of an indentured clerk in Southern Californian garb. His nondescript height and size didn't register until much later, because I couldn't take my eyes off his head. How could a man in his middle sixties have such preposterously curly red hair unless he wore a wig? And aviator glasses? And a tinselly silk suit — clearly expensive, I noted, as he shook my hand but of such poor taste! If it weren't so outlandish I would have concluded that this had to be an act to distract his victims. It was his voice — high, almost shrill, but aggressively domineering — that showed who was a clerk and who the boss.

In addition to all the stammering and hair-pulling, Mort had coached me to focus on the science as much as possible, to head toward seemingly harmless scientific tangents and their societal bene-

fits whenever I could but not to enter the territory of prostatectomies and associated erectile dysfunction. The idea was to give Hood every opportunity to express opinions that we could use against him the following week in Palo Alto, when our respective roles of defendant and plaintiff were reversed. It was an elegant trap, but from the way he conducted himself that day I had the feeling Hood would have blundered into something much simpler: the man just couldn't conceive of himself as a defendant.

On the stand, under Hood's no-doubt formidable questioning, I conceded — and why shouldn't I? — that I had indeed expressed open confidence in the adequacy of our clinical data to a Wall Street Journal *reporter, that at that stage I had known nothing of the FDA's subsequent demand for more data, and that I certainly had not anticipated the stock market's precipitous response. After all, neither I nor any other insider had sold or bought a single share during those weeks. That's when Hood expressed his first opinion. He couldn't care less whether we had benefited; the stockholders whom he was protecting had suffered losses during that phase of the stock market's reaction, which had clearly been exacerbated by my unwarranted optimism. When I protested that we were able to persuade the FDA of the validity of my optimism within weeks of the Advisory Committee's initial deferral, he informed me that this was irrelevant to the case at hand. When I complained of the difficulty of providing answers in advance to every possible worst-case scenario considered by FDA committees, "That's your problem," he growled, "not mine." Wasn't he aware of the medical advance the introduction of the MUSA system would represent? "Irrelevant to our case," he countered.*

"May I ask one more question?" I said it in the most timid tone I could muster: there was one more question I had to get in, and although I had smuggled in all the rest as the naive protestations of the woman scientist, I couldn't afford for him to catch on now that he was the one being interrogated. I probably shouldn't have worried; he was convinced he had me on the run. Interpreting his grunt as acquiescence, I inquired whether he realized what the loss of twelve million dollars in claimed damages plus all the legal expenses and managerial time consumed and the consequent time delay in bringing MUSA to the market — if at all — would repre-

sent for the company. "Couldn't care less," he announced, almost proudly.

At which point, Herman Black, who until then had quietly observed the scene without saying a word, felt moved to intervene. "Instead of blowing your horn about what you can do with your MUSA," he added, "SURYA ought to have spent more time finding out what it can't do for people. Or the problems it might cause."

I looked at Black (the antithesis of Hood: tall, muscular, virile — almost handsome) and then Hood, not knowing whom to address. "Still," I asked them, pretending that it was part of the same question, "do you know the clinical profile of the men for whom the MUSA system could make an enormous difference in their lives?"

"I don't give a shit — strike that," Hood barked, turning to the court reporter. "I'm here to defend the damaged stockholders, not men who can't get it up. Strike that," he repeated, "and now let's get back to my queries."

After he had questioned me for the umpteenth time about minutiae of my public responses to the FDA-raised issues and all the work we should have done in advance but hadn't, I felt Mort's gentle kick under the table. It was his signal for me to become once more the ingenuous scientist. "May I ask you a question?" I said. "What was I supposed to do? Hang up on the reporter? Pretend that our data were less complete?"

"That's your problem — or really your counsel's problem," he motioned with his head toward Mort without actually looking at him. "You should have referred them to your prospectus." He pointed to the heavily marked-up copy in front of him.

"But by then, that wasn't up-to-date," I protested, but he cut me off.

"I'm here on behalf of the stockholders who are entitled to know all the relevant facts so that they can make up their minds whether to hold on to their stock or sell it."

"Okay, okay," I said and proceeded with the story Mort and I had rehearsed.

"From our published document," I pointed to the prospectus, "you know that nitric oxide is responsible for penile erection in men as well as for many other biological consequences, which can also be the source of possible side effects," I gestured toward Herman Black *to let him know that I hadn't forgotten him, "as well as of other potentially important applications. We're actually working on some of them in order to expand SURYA's therapeutic offerings, because we don't want to remain a one-product company."*

"What's that got to do with our case?" he asked suspiciously.

"Wouldn't new research activities of SURYA, leading to possible new products, be relevant?"

"So?" he asked.

"Nitric oxide regulates sexual behavior in mammals."

"We know that," he interrupted me gruffly. "That's what this is supposed to be all about." He lifted our prospectus, only to let it flop dismissively on the table.

"Excuse me sir," I murmured, "but I'm not referring to tumescent penises or stock values. I'm referring to nitric oxide involved in brain function."

"So?" he asked.

"Aha," I trumpeted, forgetting that I was not supposed to gloat. "In male mice, absence of neuronally generated nitric oxide causes aggressive behavior, including the rodent equivalent of rape: mounting non-estrous females. Don't you think that work on neuronal nitric oxide levels in higher mammals, and especially man, might be interesting?"

"I suppose so," he grumbled, "but what has that got to do with —"

When cool, sophisticated Herman Black interrupted his red-haired terrier of a brother-in-law with "Let her finish, Will," I knew that someone was nibbling at my bait.

"Subsequent work has shown that neurons in the hypothalamus also produce such nitric oxide, which in female mice controls the release of hypothalamic releasing hormones." I raised my hand to stop them from asking me what I was talking about. "One of them is called LHRH — the luteinizing hormone–releasing hormone — which induces ovulation and, at least in mice, also facilitates female sexual behavior." I could hardly wait to tell Jephtah that I'd managed to smuggle this nugget of NO esoterica into my testimony, simultaneously trespassing on his Wizard of Ov territory. Who knows? If his OV company is successful, maybe one day he will sit

here sparring with the San Clemente legal Mafia. By now, I had begun looking at such spurious class action suits as a badge of honor for a start-up. "And to top that, even more recent studies have shown that this effect of nitric oxide is not limited to mammals but also affects the sexual behavior of newts."

"Nudes?" asked Herman Black, seeming to recover, for a moment, his prosecutorial edge. "What kind of nudes?"

"N E W T S," I spelled it for him. "Nitric oxide controls courtship behavior in male newts but not female newts — behavior that is very complicated. I gather you don't know much about newts?" I asked innocently.

"Not about your nudes," he said with a wolfish grin, which I ignored.

"First, the male approaches the female and sniffs her head. Then he starts fanning his tail, eventually lashing her about the head. Having gotten her attention, he displays the tip of his tail and deposits his spermatophore, whereupon the female picks it up with her cloaca." I didn't know whether I could keep a straight face, but my avalanche of newt minutiae propelled me to a question that some people could have considered offensive. "I'm sure I don't have to define 'cloaca' for you, do I?"

"Go on," prodded Will Hood.

Even the court reporter, who until now had only displayed a deadpan expression and fierce concentration while focusing on her keyboard, looked up. I was almost tempted to ask her whether she had recorded Hood's last two words, but I didn't. "And why am I telling you all this? Since nitric oxide, generated in different tissues, can have such an extraordinary range of effects on sexual behavior, at SURYA we're now investigating the extent, if any, to which these observations might apply to humans. Furthermore, if nitric oxide — NO to the chemist — does that, then our NO-releasers, SURYA's proprietary NO-releasers, ought to do the same. Right?"

"I guess so," murmured Black, who until now hadn't looked to me like the murmuring type.

"Shouldn't I have told all that to the Wall Street Journal *reporter?" I asked quickly. "Can you imagine the commercial potential if one of our NO-releasers could be used to modify sexual*

behavior in men or in women or maybe even both? Isn't that all
information that stockholders should have at their disposal to make
an informed decision whether to buy, hold, or sell our stock?"

Black looked at Hood, and Hood stared back at Black, with nei-
ther uttering a word. "And if I had done so, wouldn't you have ac-
cused me of grossly hyping our stock?"

"Great! Really great!" Mort's ebullience bubbled over the moment
we entered our rental car. "It's all on the record. Not that it will
have much relevance to our case if it ever comes to trial, but you
can rest assured that I will include that section of the deposition
in my brief to Judge Patel. I bet she's never read anything like it
in a brief. 'Courtship in newts'!" He chuckled in a low, rich tone.
"Newts!"

"Do you think the court reporter knew how to spell 'cloaca'?"

"I'll give the transcript to you for proofreading. By the way," he
asked sheepishly, "what's a 'spermatophore'?"

Renu grinned. "Does that mean you do know what a 'cloaca' is?
Or are you too vain to ask for *two* definitions?"

"The latter."

"You're a marvelous combination, Mort: honest as well as vain.
A spermatophore is a sort of capsule in lower animals containing
the male's sperm which he secretes so that the female can pick
it up for eventual fertilization. Remember, newts don't indulge in
carnal relations. And the cloaca? In female newts, it's the equivalent of the human anus, urethra, and vagina — all in one. Rather
economical, I'd say."

"Maybe you should have included that in your testimony. Still
— I just loved the way you threw out the bait and then played the
line for all it was worth." He stopped chuckling. "But we've also
established a useful precedent: we can focus on the real science
and hence on societal benefits, rather than just on supposed stock
manipulations. We'll be back next week, but then *I'll* be asking
the questions."

Will Hood was asked only perfunctory questions, because the real
quarry was Herman Black. Since Mort was doing the questioning,

I was free to study the men across the table. I'm not sure whether Hood had noticed the change in my manner. I was sitting upright, I'd stopped playing with my hair, which was now in a tight chignon, and I was looking at them the way a cobra eyes a small dog. I was still pregnant, but there wasn't much I could do about that — nor did it change my mood.

Hood may not have noticed, but Black did. Every once in a while his watchful eyes wandered in my direction. Once he was sure I'd noticed he slowly inspected me, his tongue briefly moistening his lips. There was something irritatingly provoking about him — amazingly so for a man in his middle sixties.

Mort handled Black quite brilliantly. He started out by repeating the same questions I had asked of Hood, about the societal benefits of our work, the impossibility of having answers in advance to all possible FDA questions, and the gray area between irresponsible public disclosure and corporate confidentiality. Black's answers were the expected ones, though less rude than Hood's. But then Mort closed in: how much did he know about the MUSA system, its utility, its potential problems?

"Nothing beyond what is in your prospectus."

"Nothing? You are under oath, you know. Two more questions," he drawled. "Do you happen to know a local urologist, Dr. Timothy Spivack? And could you tell us why Cindy Findon left your employ?"

Herman Black had powerful hands. I had wondered what they felt like when I first noticed them, the nails carefully manicured, calmly resting on the table surface. Suddenly they closed into a boxer's tight fists. "What's that got to do with this case?" he snapped.

"It's their turn," announced Mort over the phone, "and this time I told them they'd have to question you on our turf. But yesterday Herman Black, rather than Will Hood, called to ask for postponement. Not formally through the court but as professional courtesy."

Renu guffawed. "Professional courtesy? I trust you told him where to get off."

"Actually I didn't. He asked for three weeks and I gave them to him."

"You did? What about using my pregnancy as grounds for turning them down? I'm starting on my eighth month."

"Don't worry. I bet there won't be another deposition. It wasn't so much the mention of Dr. Spivack as that of Cindy Findon that has him spooked. I bet he doesn't want me to pursue that line. He needs the three weeks to find out how much I know, and when he finds that out the case will be settled."

"You never told me anything about Findon other than that she was Herman Black's secretary and she quit suddenly. What happened?"

He hesitated. "I don't want to go into how we really got the goods on Black. The following three facts ought to be enough, but keep them to yourself. Number one: Mrs. Herman Black is seventy-one years old, four years older than her husband. Number two: Cindy Findon is in her middle thirties and quite attractive, at least judging from her photos. Number three: according to your clinical protocols, all of the MUSA subjects during the experimental phase were supposed to show up with their female partners. You know better than I why you people have always focused on dealing with the couples rather than just the men."

"I know all that," she said impatiently. "What's the point?"

"The woman accompanying Herman Black to the initial sessions in Dr. Spivack's office was not seventy-one years old but rather roughly half that age."

26

Melanie was following the mesmerizing movement of George Rickey's double L in the light breeze. She turned to Renu, who was leaning against the railing, her hands supporting her bulging stomach.

"You look very well, Renu," she smiled, "but so. . . ." She waved her hands in ever-expanding circles.

"Gravid? That's how I feel. It's any day now."

"You seem to be timing your impending deliveries to the board meeting schedules. Or is it the other way around?"

"Who knows?" she laughed. "So far, we have only two data points, and I don't think I'll provide any more. Besides, had we planned this meeting, the SURYA boardroom wouldn't be commandeered by decorators. It's nice to visit ZALA again, though it no longer feels the same."

"I'll take this sort of unplanned meeting any time," chuckled Melanie. "You must be pleased with the good news. And, of course, Mort: I've never seen him in such an exuberant mood. He's prancing around as if he'd lost a hundred pounds."

Renu turned back to the moving sculpture below them. "A dancing L — a dancing lawyer. And 'lapsed litigation.' What do you think of the terms of the settlement?"

"Getting those characters in San Clemente to pay our legal expenses was a tremendous coup. What do you estimate them to be?"

"Almost $850,000," said Renu, "not counting our time and aggravation."

"I liked that Mort held out for some additional cash payment, even if it only came out to $65,000 more. To him, it seemed a matter of pride to have actually collected additional restitution — apparently a first for that firm. What an odd amount, though — $65,000 — and rather paltry."

"In spite of my paper wealth, I hardly consider $65K a paltry sum."

Melanie seized her by the shoulders for a congratulatory shake. "You're right. It was boorish of me to call it 'paltry.' I'm happy the board voted to hand it all over to you as a bonus. You deserve it, Renu. If it hadn't been for you, I doubt very much we'd be here celebrating today. But tell me, is that business about courtship in male newts really true? I thought I was up-to-date on reproductive biology, but that one has escaped me."

"Cross my heart," exclaimed Renu. "Zerani and Gobbetti from Italy published it in *Nature*. They ended their article, 'NO is probably an internal cerebral stimulus, suggesting that its involvement in reproductive behavior could be conserved throughout vertebrate evolution,' another reason why we are now taking a serious look at neuronally generated NO. Just imagine what would happen to SURYA if we could find out how to deliver NO at the right time to the right spot in the brain!"

"They're calling us back in." Melanie jerked her head in the direction of the boardroom. "Speaking of mating, do you know the sex of your baby?"

Renu shook her head vigorously. "I refused to find out. I had an amnio and the usual sonograms, but I told them I didn't want to know. I can wait. It's only a few more days."

"And your husband? Isn't he curious?"

"A mild understatement! He is counting on a boy."

Melanie nodded with a mock frown. "Typical man. Or should I say Israeli?"

"'Man' will do."

The two women headed inside. At the door, Melanie put one arm around Renu's waist. "I'm staying in San Francisco for a few days. Adam has never been out West and I convinced his school to let him come out to celebrate his ninth birthday. Call me at the Fairmount Hotel if you should deliver before I return to New York. You know I like to hear good news."

———

"Renu darling, I feel terrible. And so happy." Jephtah sat by Renu's hospital bed while she nursed the baby. He had arranged to be back from Wisconsin by the expected date, but in the end he had been late by eleven hours.

"Ravi was getting too big for his britches, as well as for his mother, and he's ravenous for her milk." Renu gazed down at the baby by her breast. "Just look at him. He's studying you while suckling me. I'm sure he'll turn into the sort of man who can do two things at the same time. Like his father." She reached over for Jephtah's hand. "Tell me quickly what happened in Madison and then go home to Naomi. I'm sure she's getting jealous. Then come back with her."

"My news can wait. Especially since it's good news. Let's talk about him." He reached over to stroke his son's matted black hair. "You see, I told you: the combination of sexual discipline plus my Wizard guarantees a male baby."

"Discipline, maybe. But your Wizard? We'll have to repeat it at least six or eight times to make it statistically meaningful. Can you imagine arguing about another half-dozen boy's names? You aren't even dreaming of that, are you?"

Jephtah patted his wife's hand absentmindedly. "Still," he mused. "It worked. Of course, it will have to be tried on a big scale. Not with one couple six or eight times but with eight couples once each. And then a few hundred. Let's talk about it once you're home."

_____

"Dr. Laidlaw's room, please," she addressed the Fairmount Hotel operator. It was 9:30 in the morning and Renu, with her son asleep in his acrylic box by her bedside, was content and wide awake. Why not tell Melanie the good news, she'd thought.

She had been ready to form the words, "It's a boy," when the young male voice answering the phone threw her off. "Who is this?" she demanded.

"Adam," he said.

"Oh, excuse me, Adam," she exclaimed. "I didn't recognize your voice. This is Renu Krishnan. You may not remember me, but we met once before in New York. Is your mother in? No, wait," she said quickly, "let me first congratulate you on your birthday. Happy birthday, Adam."

"That was yesterday," he said matter-of-factly.

"Still, better late than never. Did you do anything special?"

"Yes," he said, "we went to the opera."

"Oh my! You _are_ grown up. It's a beautiful building, isn't it?"

"Not really."

Renu was taken aback. Was she asking the wrong questions? "You didn't like it?"

"It was okay. It's got a very small stage. Not like the Met. I've been to the Met with my mom."

Renu was no opera fan, but she had been to the ballet at the San Francisco Opera. A small stage? "But the stage isn't small," she remonstrated.

"Are you kidding? It isn't much longer than our living room."

"Adam, where did you go to the opera?" Renu was drawn into

the conversation in a way that had made her forget the purpose of her call.

"The Pocket Opera. Actually it's neat." For the first time, his voice sounded engaged. "The orchestra was just a few strings. And one man, named Donald Pippin. He was neat. He played the piano and conducted at the same time. Every once in a while he stopped the singers to explain what was going on."

"And what did you see?"

"Handel. My mom said it was Mr. Pippin's specialty."

"I didn't mean the composer. What Handel opera did you hear?"

"Some story about Alexander the Great and some Amazon. I forget her name."

"And did you like it?"

"It was okay. But they loved it. We got home pretty late."

"They?"

"My mom and my father."

"Oh," Renu said, taken aback. She had not realized that Menachem had also stayed behind after the board meeting. "May I talk to your mother?"

"They told me not to wake them this morning. I think they're still asleep next door."

Last night, Jephtah and I had one of our serious *serious talks — one of those summing-up talks that couples should have more frequently. Life had been so hectic lately that neither one of us had done any reflecting. Maybe it's because we've been suffering from chronic sleep deficiency for the past seven months. Ravi is certainly no Naomi. He is still keeping both of us awake. Jephtah is very decent about it at night, but during the day he's now working harder than I.*

He husbands OV's two million dollars as if he'll never get another dime. He's the CEO, the president, the chief negotiator, the chief manipulator, and the chief operator — in the technical and every other sense. God knows what else he'd do if he got more sleep.

SURYA is clearly making it, and I'm becoming quite an expert at delegating. David Warbler, of course, has turned out to be this mother's godsend — especially now that he's been promoted to executive vice president, which means that I can spend more time on science. Only recently have I realized how much I've really missed it.

This time, it was I who announced that it was time for a serious serious talk. Ravi is now on a bottle, and I asked Maria del Carmen to sit while I took Jephtah to San Francisco for a night at the Fairmount. What made me pick the Fairmount? I think it must have been that phone call last fall, when I finally got through to Melanie.

After sleeping for eleven hours, Jephtah and I had breakfast in bed. That's when we both agreed that our lives had become crazy. Yes, we were workaholics and enjoyed that addiction. But we have two children, and there has to be something more to life than just being chained to a treadmill. With my latest stock option, I was now a paper millionaire four times over, but you wouldn't know it from the way we live: our house is too small, our two cars don't even get washed, we're not taking any vacations. . . .

Step number one, I announced: we'll buy a new house. Step number two: we'll get some sleep-in help, which will help us get more sleep — a middle-aged or older woman, I emphasized. Step number three: we're going to take real vacations — a minimum of two weeks in the summer and at least one week in the winter. "Step number four," my husband added, "you'll sell another half million dollars worth of stock in addition to what you'll sell to buy the new house and new cars."

"Volvos," I said quickly, "safe family cars."

"One Volvo," he countered, "and one — " That's when I pressed my hand over his mouth.

"Enough about cars. What's this extra half million for?"

"To put it into Radha," he grinned. When Jephtah saw my blank look, he hooted triumphantly. "Israeli one-upmanship! Have you truly forgotten about your Krishna, fosterling of cowherds and lover of gopis?" My sabra didn't have to remind me that gopis were Indian cowgirls, but I had completely forgotten that Radha was Krishna's favorite gopi.

But who was Jephtah's Radha? His trip to Wisconsin, which had made him miss Ravi's arrival by some hours, had been to arrange the first large-scale trial of his Tele-Ov vaginal sensors in cows. Now, barely half a year later, one of the largest dairies in Wiscon-

sin wanted to start a joint venture with OV, Inc., to develop a com-
mercial version and market the product. He sold them on the name
Radha, claiming it was in homage to his Indian wife. I don't know
whether he meant it seriously, but they bought it — so Radha it is.
My financial wizard is so sure of the bovine version of his Wizard
that instead of raising more capital from the outside and diluting
his equity — "our" equity, he corrected me — he wants us to "di-
versify" from SURYA into Radha and OV.

"Lama lo?" I said. It's amazing how easy major decisions become
after eleven hours of sleep followed by breakfast in bed with your
husband.

"Mort," Renu said as she settled herself in a chair facing Heartstone's desk, "don't turn on your time clock. I'm here for some personal advice."

He raised both hands, palms facing her. "You see? No clocks."
He nodded approvingly. "You look well, Renu," he said. "I wish I
could shrink a stomach as efficiently as you did."

"We have different talents," she replied brusquely. "Let me tell
you why I came. I have vested stock options worth over four million
dollars and I would like to sell about half."

Heartstone gave a low whistle. "That much?"

"Before we talk about amounts, let me first ask about the timing. Am I correct that there are no legal impediments? I certainly
know of no business reasons: things are going swimmingly for
SURYA; unless there's another Black Monday, our stock should
keep rising."

"True," he conceded. "But no time is a good time for a president
to sell shares of his company."

"Her company." Renu had come in a somewhat touchy mood,
and none of their conversation had made her feel less so.

"I beg your pardon." He inclined his head as far as his double
chin allowed. *"Her* company."

"But if I followed your advice, my paper profits would always
remain paper. I did earn those options, you know. Many of them in
lieu of salary."

Heartstone raised a calming hand. "I didn't say you couldn't sell shares. Nor did I say that you should not. All I did was anticipate public perception. If you intend to sell, then now is not worse than any other time. In fact, now may be a reasonable time to do so. Furthermore, people forget with time — especially if the stock doesn't decline soon thereafter. But if it does, look out!"

"Okay," she said, relieved. "Now, why do I want to sell that much?"

Again he raised a moderating hand. "It's none of my business. I only suggest that if you intend to divest, pick the minimum necessary."

Renu had calmed down. Still, she felt it necessary to defend her decision. "I don't mind telling you. It's not a secret: we need a bigger house, and we might as well also get a better one. We have two small children and, with both of us working long hours, we need live-in help. I want a study and Jephtah needs one at home. That alone will take up six rooms, ignoring even a guest room."

He kept nodding. "And real estate in this area is very expensive. But people do carry mortgages — even wealthy people. They're precisely the ones who can use the tax deductions."

"We have no intention of paying all cash. But both of us are fiscally conservative. The house will be our single largest equity. We want to put down at least 50 percent."

In his corner of the sofa, Heartstone started to fidget, at least as much as his bulk permitted. "I repeat: it's none of my business, but unless you're buying a huge place and do so in Atherton," he motioned with his thumb as if that wealthiest of all South Bay suburbs started behind his sofa, "you don't need to sell two million dollars worth of stock options. I grant you that over one-third will go for taxes, but — "

"We need another half million for diversification. So far, all our equity is in SURYA options and part of those are pledged as a collateral for Jephtah's investment in his own company."

"Ah yes. OV, Inc. I heard about it. Alfredo and Martin both seem rather bullish about your husband's venture. Let me know when they go for an IPO. I am a great believer in Zaffanori's business judgment. If he and Martin invested, I'd be willing to put some of my own dough in it." He looked at her speculatively. "No one can argue against diversification, yet you won't earn any brownie points for it when it comes to the accusation that you're dumping your own company's stock." He shrugged. "You can't satisfy everyone. I hope you picked a good financial advisor."

"I've already got an advisor." She rose. "Thanks for listening. And don't worry, you'll be one of the first to hear about OV's IPO."

Ravi's first birthday! I don't think that I'll ever forget this day. Odd: I remember very little of Naomi's. But that one was just a day celebrating the completion of the first year of my daughter's life. Today? I'm sure it was a watershed. And I say that sitting in the dark in the living room with a blanket wrapped around me.

It was a good birthday. We made it a family affair — just the four of us. We're lucky with Naomi. She'll soon be six years old, and Ravi is bringing out maternal instincts in her. She helped bake the cake, she made a big production out of helping Ravi blow out the single candle, she even told him a story until he fell asleep. Thank God, he's finally sleeping through the night. And now they're all asleep: Ravi, Naomi, and Jephtah.

But I'm wide awake. For the past few days I seem to have suffered from some form of malaise, vague discontent, even grumpiness. But tonight, as I watched Jephtah playing happily with the children, I suddenly had an epiphany. I'm thirty-eight years old, I have seemingly acquired everything a modern professional woman desires: position, power, money — even a family — yet I've started to feel discontented. And here is my husband, just a couple of years older, who now seems to be at his most contented. What's the difference? Suddenly it hit me: the order in which I had listed what other women might envy: position, power, money. . . . Family, I listed last.

There is no doubt that I enjoyed getting to the point where I am now. Or rather, the point I reached a year or two ago. More money I don't need. Position? The only one higher is Martin, and he's made it plain that in another year he'll hand the CEO post over to me. Come to think of it, he's an interesting example: he had served as CEO of ZALA for years and then, not yet fifty, had chucked it for a more diverse Jerusalem–Palo Alto commute. So strike out position. Power? I grant that power is tempting, particularly to a modern professional woman. But except for control over my own destiny (really synonymous with economic self-sufficiency), I don't lust for it. What I enjoyed so much with SURYA was the creation of a new entity based on research to which I had contributed heavily. But that baby is now growing so fast that it will soon reach adolescence. Just as when real children turn into teenagers, one's nurturing role moves into a supervisory and supporting function — one that leaves me vaguely dissatisfied now.

I've never spoken to Jephtah about these feelings. In our professional life, until fairly recently there was an unacknowledged competition in which I seemed to be ahead. How many men — especially profil-97 Israelis — are likely to accept that? But now, with the creation of OV, things have changed. Isn't it ironic that when I was leading it was in the field of penile erection, whereas my husband's sudden flowering is based on the female's ovulatory cycle. Even more impressive is the fact that he is a virtual autodidact: a biomechanical engineer, with some electrical engineering background in Beersheba, shifts in California into studies of electrotransport across the skin from where he jumps to electrical changes in the cervix and implanted sensors in a cow's vagina. But he's not stopping with the Tele-Ov: that's only his temporary cash cow to finance studies of the Wizard in humans.

The eventual use of the Wizard of Ov by women is an issue we've been debating, and even though we aren't of one mind, I am impressed. My Jephtah is not just a technocrat. While he does want to prove that changing the time of fertilization can influence sex — in my opinion, dangerous knowledge in countries like India — that is not his primary objective with the Wizard. Nor is it birth control, because he doesn't think that the Wizard will make a measurable difference in birth rates. Demographically speaking, I agree, though as a woman I still want all options open to me, whether they are demographically efficient (what a terrible phrase!) or just personally convenient.

But we do agree that, if that M-shaped pattern of alternating electrical troughs and peaks during the first half of the menstrual cycle is replicated in enough women, his Wizard will have an impact on women way beyond birth control: on personal fertility awareness, indeed on female empowerment throughout a woman's reproductive lifetime. My Jephtah is not a feminist — far from it — yet he may make a major technical contribution to feminist goals.

When I said that to him, he asked, with an expression suggesting that he'd just tasted some bitter fruit, what I really meant by feminism. Instead of giving him the usual dictionary definition about "organized activity on behalf of women's rights and interests," I simply said "power relations." Offering a woman advance knowledge whether and when she'll ovulate is presenting her with the most fundamental power. What she does with that information is her business: her personal exercise of power. Which brings me back to where I started: Renu Krishnan and power.

Exercising executive power in the conventional sense has started to bore me. I've been handing portions of that power to David Warbler, first unconsciously and lately more deliberately. His appetite for it is growing at about the rate that mine is diminishing. The power that I have retained so far is responsibility for all R and D activities of SURYA. But what I realized tonight is that even that should end — that the time has come for a rebirth. If I succeed, then I'll have acquired all the power I now crave.

27

Woodside, California, December 23, 1989

Dearest Ashok,

This is my first Hanukkah-cum-Christmas letter from our new home. We moved over Thanksgiving. It's still a bit of a mess, because both Jephtah and I have been extraordinarily busy at work. But we have now taken off for a week and are truly getting settled, which means that all books are actually unpacked and shelved and most boxes and packing material have been carted off. The garage houses one new Volvo station wagon, one two-year-old sports car (self-restraint prevents me from disclosing the make, but you can guess who in the family is driving which car), and a lot of junk in the remaining space.

The garage is attached to a rather generously proportioned house in Woodside — an affluent, "horsey" town with lots of riding trails, some fifteen minutes' drive from SURYA's labs on the Stanford Industrial Park and about thirty minutes from the San Francisco Airport — an important consideration, given Jephtah's current hectic travel. He has not yet learned to delegate as efficiently as his wife, although he claims that OV, Inc., and its subsidiary with the charming name of Radha (you remember who she was?) can't afford all the executive talent that we now have at SURYA. So my Jephtah thinks he must do most of it by himself — and is thriving in the process.

We have two acres (which is modest to average in this neighborhood), including a small corral and stable, which the previous owners built for their quarter horse. It is now inhabited by the pony we gave to Naomi in eight installments for Hanukkah. (It was Jephtah's idea to cut up a large photograph into eight segments — one for each day — with the actual pony only materializing when Naomi got the eighth slice showing the tail). I expect the novelty to wear off, although right now she spends most of the time outdoors with the pony, while Ravi, the super-active toddler, demands almost continuous attention indoors. Thank God for our Maria del Carmen, a wonderful motherly type, who has simplified life for me enormously. We even have a guest room permanently reserved for my brother if he can ever be inveigled to visit his California relatives.

So much for domestic news. And now, in business news: Last week, President Renu Krishnan of SURYA Corporation tendered her resignation! If you think you're surprised, you should have been at our last board of directors meeting. To my consternation and even mild annoyance, some of my colleagues assumed that I was being tempted by an outside offer or negotiating for bigger compensation. But when I explained my reasons (more extensively than I am telling you now), my colleagues all went along, especially since I made it plain that I was only resigning from the presidency, not the company or even the board of directors, unless they wanted me not to stand for reelection at the next shareholder's meeting. That's when Martin Gestler quickly made a motion of confidence, which Melanie Laidlaw seconded. I was touched that Martin took the initiative, since he could well have been miffed that I had not warned him ahead of time. But how could I? I had been agonizing about that decision for several months after many discussions with Jephtah, who understood my position right from the beginning, and finally with one off-site academic friend in Pasadena. Get to the point, Renu, I can hear you muttering, so here is my summation.

I feel good about the decision, for a great many reasons. SURYA is doing fabulously well with our MUSA product for erectile dysfunction. Our annual sales have passed the first $100 million mark and are climbing rapidly. The Beersheba plant has expanded again and is operating on three shifts. Our European distribution network is nearly complete, and now we're looking at Asia. Our current annual R and D budget amounts to $14 million and is carefully focused along three lines: expansion of clinical applications of NONO-2 beyond the area of penile erection; development of a second generation of nitric oxide releasers, based on some quite outstanding ideas of an academic consultant of ours; and rather promising progress on the development of an NO-inhibitor for coping with the sudden, dramatic drop in blood pressure in septic shock — a real killer. If our initial results pan out, we'll have the kind of miracle drug that the stock market just loves.

So if things are so great, why bail out now? Jephtah and I have more than enough money (and are likely to earn considerably more if Jephtah's company pans out). When you take money out of the picture, all that's left is executive power, and when it comes to that topic, I could write you a long and somewhat carping letter, which I'll skip. As we say in the local vernacular, executive power does not "turn me on" — not to the extent that science does. Which brings me back to all the questions I started with years ago.

Academics have a tendency to pooh-pooh research in industry, but in the biomedical field — given adequate resources — one can be much more efficient in industry than in academe, so long as one is interested in practical goals, *which I am.* In my opinion, the real efficiency is not offered by the giants, but by companies of SURYA's size and stage of development. I want to grasp the opportunity before we become too large, too cumbersome, and consequently too inflexible. The biology of NO really turns me on. So having tasted power, and having made money, I now wish to return to my roots as a scientist. I want to once more start with a basic scientific observation and to carry it all the way to final application in man — a process that is impossible in a university. Provided I can make the case that SURYA might ultimately derive meaningful commercial benefits, I won't have to scrounge for money by writing interminable grant applications, I won't have to indulge in academic politics, and most important (and it took me some time to realize this last), I am now in a position to base a research program on a serious examination of societal needs. I admit that you often can't do that in industry, but I think that I can do so here at SURYA. I hope you will be happy with my plans, because they will show you that I have not completely forgotten my Indian roots.

To me, some of the most dramatic potential applications of nitric oxide are in parasitology and tropical diseases. A lot of exciting research has been performed in this area by academic researchers, but hardly anything has been initiated by the big drug firms. They're not interested in the comparatively unprofitable market represented by the poor of the Third World. But here's a partial list of diseases caused by parasites that are highly vulnerable to nitric oxide: schistosomiasis, leishmaniasis, toxoplasmosis, trypanosomiasis. . . . The list goes on, and I am not just citing these four as proof that I can spell complex words that my computer hotshot brother may not even know how to pronounce, although I could have used simpler names such as Chagas Disease, which is the South American form of trypanosomiasis. Rather, I am listing them because hundreds of millions of people suffer from these diseases in South America, Africa, and Asia — a very significant portion of whom are in India. Take malaria — the biggest killer of them all. More people die from this disease than any other, but the eyes of most executives of large pharmaceutical companies would just glaze over if you suggested that a significant amount of their research budget be directed to those therapeutic targets. So what makes me think that I could convince SURYA to let me work in that field? The fact is that I *have* convinced them.

I have become rather good at dramatizing the effects that NO can generate. Recently, during some legal testimony, I wanted to illustrate the action of NO on sexual behavior. And what did I pick? Courtship behavior in male newts! And don't think that people did not pay attention.

In the case of malaria, I based my presentation on a moving rather than an amusing example: cerebral malaria, the deadliest form and one of the biggest killers of African and Asian children. Researchers at Duke have shown recently that NO produced in the brain exerts a protective action: healthy children have the highest NO levels and sick ones the lowest. You will probably ask the same question every other layman asks: if NO is a natural defense mechanism, why don't we give the kids nitric oxide? The answer is that we don't yet know how to do that. In the body, the half-life of the gas generated in the brain is on the order of seconds, which from the body's standpoint is an advantage: its short life guarantees that the NO is only delivered to the target — the parasites — and not to other cells of the host which would otherwise also be damaged.

Ashok, I don't want to be carried away and present you with a scientific lecture on the fiendishly clever biochemical mechanism whereby this extremely simple molecule, NO, exerts its protective action. All I want to tell you is that one of the biggest problems, then, is to find a way of getting the right amount of NO to the target. And that's where we at SURYA are becoming experts. Your sister's NONOates, especially NONO-2, are good tools for this, but we are now also starting to look at some compounds called sydnonimines — SIN for short. Isn't it strange that NO and SIN mean one thing in ordinary life and something very different in chemistry?

So I managed to convince my board to commit up to 10% of our R and D budget for NO research in the field of parasitic diseases under my direction. Even with heart-rending material like cerebral malaria, it wasn't easy. I had to have an economic justification. The multinationals in the drug field are interested in drugs with sales in the hundreds of millions or even the billion dollar range. While the number of potential patients in the Third World may reach these numbers, the dollar figures are much smaller. Whatever money will be spent on purchasing such drugs will come mostly from impoverished governments or from aid agencies and the like. In terms of potential sales, we may be talking tens of millions or maybe a few hundred million dollars — peanuts to the drug Goliaths but manna to Davids like us. As long as SURYA remains in the David class, one can make an economic argument that neglected therapeutic areas of high societal value are still sufficiently large to be interesting to us. I asked them to give me five years, so wish me five years of luck.

All my love,
Renu

"I envy you." Celestine Price's admiration showed in her tone as well as in her eyes. "We academics would trade — what *would* we trade for five years of research support? And without having to write grant applications!"

"Your souls?" teased Renu.

"Too cheap. I think I'd offer the last five years of my life. Seriously, though: I envy you. You got just about to the top of the ladder, and then? Instead of settling on the last rung and looking down at the world below you, you do this!"

"Envy? Why?"

"Because I interpret your move differently from your colleagues at SURYA. You are now behaving like an academic — at least the sort of academic I am — yet you're doing it in industry. You had a pretty meteoric career, and your SURYA colleagues valued you. Rather than lose you, they've agree to a deal where you don't even have to trade your soul or the last five years of your life."

"Come now, Celly. You make it sound as if I hadn't made a persuasive case. It's true, I didn't have to write a grant proposal, but the case I made is pretty much the one you make in your applications: a justification for your research. In this instance, I had to make an economic case, but I also showed that the fallout from the research I proposed — and remember, it's all in the general area of SURYA's interest — may impinge on a lot of other immunological or neurochemical problems. That won't hurt the company's prospects."

"Granted," said Celestine, who had not intended to irritate her friend. "Let me say what I really meant: you have shown that you can operate in a man's world and reach the top without compromising."

Renu shook her head. "I'm not so sure about that."

"I am," Celestine said firmly. "At least from my perspective. You also made a lot of money with your options — or have you forgotten that? Remember, I get the annual proxy statements, so I know how many shares you got. I even know how many you sold recently."

Renu reddened, but Celestine did not stop. "That's no criticism. It's just a statement of fact, colored by just the faintest tinge of jealousy. Not that I can complain about my stock options, which in the final analysis I owe to you. But all that's beside the point. What I envy is something else." She thought for a minute. "I guess what I'm jealous of is your courage — and the time you've bought yourself. Having done all that, you chuck it all and return to science — and focus totally on *research*. My God, Renu, I can't do that at Caltech. I've got to teach, I serve on lots of committees, I've got — "

"Stop," laughed Renu, now completely mollified. "I know you have a tough life."

"No, you won't interrupt me." Celestine grinned back. "I've got to hustle all the time for money, and even when I get it, it's not for five years at a stretch!"

"Okay," said Renu. "Go on. What else do you envy?"

"That you see the end point in your research and actually try to reach it."

Renu frowned. "Don't you do the same?"

"Most of us get our money from the NIH. We've got to justify the biomedical relevance of our research, and most of us are pretty good at doing so. All of us *claim* to want to cure cancer or Alzheimer's or whatever, and some even *believe* it. But none of us in the university is actually in a position to carry it all the way to practical application. Of course, that's not the function of a university. But you seem to have picked the right niche: a growing company, large enough to afford to gamble more than a million dollars annually on your project yet small enough to make them appreciate what you might achieve. There is something I wanted to ask you. Remember the dinner at I.C.'s place, when he and Paula announced they'd gotten married?"

"How could I've forgotten that?"

"Remember the discussion about Nobel lust? What I.C. said about it? And when you asked me whether I was infected by it?"

"You said 'yes.'"

"What about you? Now that you're moving back to the lab? Do you lust?"

Renu started to play with her hair. "Nobody has asked me that."

"Well, I'm asking."

"I suppose I do," Renu said. "I think Cantor was right: noble science usually goes with lusting for recognition; one of those gray aspects of science he spoke about. Why are you looking at me that way? Are you disappointed?"

"Disappointed?" Celestine shook her head. "On the contrary. I'm relieved. Welcome to the tribe."

Carl Djerassi

is a professor of chemistry at Stanford University.

IIis books include the novels *Menachem's Seed* (Georgia, 1997),

Marx, Deceased (Georgia, 1996), *The Bourbaki Gambit* (Georgia, 1994),

and *Cantor's Dilemma*; the autobiography *The Pill, Pygmy Chimps,*

and Degas' Horse; a play, *ICSI*; and essay,

short story, and poetry collections.

Djerassi has been awarded the National Medal of Science in 1973

(for the synthesis of the first steroid oral contraceptive),

the National Medal of Technology in 1991

(for novel approaches to insect control), and the 1992 Priestley Medal,

the highest of the American Chemical Society awards.

He is also the founder of the Djerassi Resident Artists Program,

an artists' colony near San Francisco that supports

working artists in various disciplines.

Meet Carl Djerassi on the World Wide Web

http://www.djerassi.com